Aütland

THE CHRONOLOGICAL AÜTLAND

D.E.X.

Býleistr

Aütland

DAY OF THE SANGUINE

Aütland

Rabon Vincent Jr.

A Býleistr Book
Edited by Douglas A. Long
Continuity Editing by Cheryl L. Vincent
Dust Jacket Art by Aleksandar Milisavljevic
Hard Cover Edition – ISBN: 978-0-578-41793-6
1 2 3 4 5 6 7 8 9 10
Second Edition. First Printing – August 2019

Dedicated to the natural spirit of nurturing and protection inherent in all peoples around the world and, in particular, those true environmentalists and Protectors among the First Nations People of the Americas, not least of whom are the Cherokee and Choctaw, my ancestors.

"Before the writing, there was the telling. Before the telling, there was the living. Those who lived the story also told the story as their young ones wrote the story. When the living Tellers lived only in the writing, the Scribes became the Tellers. So is the living, so is the telling and so is the writing."

The children looked in eager anticipation at their teacher, the aged Teller, who turned toward them and said, "I am Torrid-Waters, the eight hundred and twelfth Teller of Tribe Sanguine. What Telling will you hear of me?"

The oldest of the children spoke up before the others and said, "I will hear of the time when cold winds once blew and the soft, white rain still fell upon the ground and cloaked the tops of all the high mountains. I will hear of the time before Tribe Sanguine, before the first Teller."

"Erdon always gets to choose the telling," said Mara, "I don't want to hear about the cold winds, frigid streams and the creatures with thick hair to endure the chill."

Torrid-Waters smiled and said, "Erdon, have you not grown weary of my tellings of the old world? Let your sister choose the telling this evening. Mara, what telling will you hear of me?"

Mara's eyes grew wide as she said, "I want to hear the telling of Day and Eryl and the Shimmering Bow."

Erdon frowned in disappointment as Mara settled herself and waited for the Teller to begin. The Scribe found the proper place in the codex so that he might follow along with the words. Torrid-Waters closed her eyes and began the telling.

Wan

The Army of the Crimson Dæmon pursued the rebel pair through the flames along Perdition's Way. The quad suspensor fields of the Sling Skate were straining hard to maintain a safe height for the rebel vehicle at the all-out speed at which Dabrill Kinselo was piloting it. Over-powered for its diminutive mass, the SS was fast, agile and shaped like a tailless version of the aquatic creature for which the craft was named.

At its present speed, the tremendous aerodynamic down-force pressed the sleek shape of the craft deep into the Savannah grass. Like the striking plate on a pack of brimstone light sticks, the undercarriage of the SS ignited the dry stems, which burst into the flames now trailing the craft. Smoke billowed from the trail of fire like a rooster's tail behind the SS, blocking Eryl's view as she glanced behind them trying to see if their pursuers were gaining.

If we can just make it into the passages of the Great Spirit Mountains, Eryl thought. The couple were racing along an ancient, overgrown route known as Perdition's Way. Looking toward the horizon, she hoped to catch a glimpse of the vast, gray mountain range, knowing that the peaks were yet beyond the horizon and still beyond her gaze.

Eryl looked at Day, who was concentrating on keeping the SS headed straight for those as yet unseen mountains. Dabrill's ruddy, clay-colored skin was taught, encapsulating the muscular, masculine body of a true warrior. His hands held a tense grip on the steering rack as he tilted it from side-to-side to maneuver past the random bone shrubs growing throughout the thinning edges of the Savannah.

The couple had been in flat-out flight from the Gru for two dawns now and they had been eluding the soldiers for several syphi, since just after the Battle of Huila. As she continued to stare at him, Eryl thought about how much she loved Day and she regretted that she had not yet told him her secret. She took no comfort in the fact that there seemed to be no appropriate time to discuss the news in the few dawns since she had learned the unexpected truth.

Embarrassed by her previous silence, Eryl stopped looking at Day. She again stared toward the horizon in the direction of the Great Spirit Mountains. The tops of the ancient peaks were just becoming visible on the horizon. The distance teased, almost taunted her. The glaring sun beat down on the flat land lying just beyond the grass and bone shrubs of the Savannah. The intensity of the apex sun caused heat dæmons to materialize. Eryl thought that they seemed to pirouette upon the tops of the mountains, mocking her as they performed their imaginary war dance.

In contrast to the tauntings of the heat dæmons, Eryl found herself considering the old tales of bitter cold, wind-wisped mountain tops cloaked in powdery white. *Myths*, she thought. Still, she looked in anticipation of the refuge afforded by those mountains as if they were mythologic beacons to their present plight. She considered that the white mountain tops must have been a metaphor created by the Society of the Ancients. A metaphor of a similar sanctuary now gone, erased by the many passing millennia.

As Day concentrated on piloting the SS, he thought that the distance seemed alive, even imagining that it labored against them, begrudging every relinquished furlong as the peaks of the mountains hung forever on the unattainable horizon. The grass was becoming thinner and the bone shrubs more plentiful as their craft gained speed heading toward the edge of the wide, flat, dead zone between the grassland and the Great Spirit Mountains.

The SS was racing toward the narrowest part of the continent-dividing wasteland known as the Lava Flats, yet it was still a daunting eight hundred and twenty furlongs across. *No one has ever crossed the Lava Flats on foot*, Day thought, recalling the words of the ancient, mythological tale of *The Camel and the Müul.*

"We're approaching the Lava Flats; hang on!" Day shouted. A moment later, the SS leaped from the edge of the grassland and onto the smooth, glassy surface of the Black Mare. The shiny plain of cooled lava served as a natural boundary between the Savannah and the foothills of the Great Spirit Mountains. No longer impeded by the resistance of the grass, the sleek craft bounded forward, pressing both occupants deep into their seats.

Dabrill glanced at the image on the rear-view screen. The multiple vehicles that were trailing the SS soon emerged from the natural smokescreen generated by the burning grass. They sprang onto the Lava Flats behind the SS like a pack of stone wolves pursuing its prey. As impressive as the Sling Skate was, it was unable to match the velocity of the stripped-to-the-bone military vehicles pursuing them. The couple were losing ground to the army sleds.

Day knew that the Destroyer class sleds were equipped with eight suspensor fields, a fact that made them capable of hauling armored compartments and a twelve-troop squad of soldiers. These D-class sleds, unencumbered by the weight of the armored compartment, could exceed a furlong per moment with just a pilot and sonic cannoneer.

He taxed his concentration further, as he calculated how swift the distance to the relative safety of the mountains ahead was diminishing versus how rapid their pursuers were closing the gap. *It's going to be close*, he thought.

"We need to slow them down!" Day shouted.

Acknowledging the urgency in his voice, Eryl lifted the acoustic rifle from between her feet on the floor of the craft and flicked the toggle switch to disengage the acoustic side-shielding of the SS. She then began firing out the right side of the vehicle and into the surface of the Lava Flats. The concentrated sonic blasts created large divots in the surface of the lava erupting geyser-like clouds of razor shards into the air. Flipping the weapon to the opposite side, she leveled it behind Day's head and fired several more bursts, which produced the same result. Satisfied with the effect, Eryl replaced the weapon and re-engaged the side-shields.

Wicked, Day thought as he saw the cloud of razor shards form a fence-like barrier behind them on his rear-view screen. The first of the pursuing army sleds emerged from the shard-cloud and veered off course, its pilot and cannoneer hemorrhaging from dozens of lethal wounds. A second sled then emerged, broadsiding the first and producing a violent electrical explosion of sparks and synthetic lightning.

Cursing, the remaining pilots of the Destroyer sleds stopped just short of the shard-cloud and allowed it to settle before continuing their pursuit. Day watched the rear-view screen and saw the shard-cloud fall many furlongs behind before the army sleds began to emerge from the lingering dust haze.

Eryl could now see that the Great Spirit Mountains were indeed growing closer on the horizon. The heat dæmons continued to writhe in their spiteful dance. They refracted the light as they rose from the flats and blurred her view of the mountains in the distance. Even so, the approaching mountains gave her a new sanguinity. *We're going to make it,* she thought.

In the periphery of his vision, Day noticed movement to either side and ahead of them and focused his view on a disheartening sight. Day's keen eyes had spotted the mottled ashen hue of the vehicles, though their shapes were obscured through the blur of the heat dæmons and against the darkness of the mountain foothills. He knew that they were Gru Army suspensor sleds, identical to those pursuing them. The Gru military leader directing the troops, General Sul, had anticipated their heading and his pincer-like move had all but trapped his quarry.

"Harness up!" Day shouted. He knew they had one chance, and it was a long shot.

Day did not slow the SS or attempt to negotiate a possible escape via any obtuse angle through the small gaps in the oncoming sleds. He headed straight for the vehicles that were approaching on a direct path between the SS and the foothills.

This is going to hurt, Eryl thought as she snapped her harness into place and braced against the looming impact.

The cannoneers on the army sleds began firing low-angled sonic bursts toward the oncoming craft, hitting its forward acoustic shielding, which formed wave distortions and limited Day's field of vision. Unlike the sleek, low-slung form of the SS, the tactical engineers who designed the D-class sleds insisted that they have the high angle of attack for just such close quarters combat. Even when the sleds were laden with the added weight of the armored compartment, the designed operational elevation of the suspensors placed the undercarriage of the sleds neck high to the typical soldier.

The pilot of the oncoming sled did not waiver. He knew that death in a fiery crash would be more desirable than any death that General Sul would invoke for the soldier who allowed these fugitives to escape. The pilot closed his eyes and awaited the looming electrified death.

In the moment before what would have been certain death, Day shoved the suspensor actuator lever forward, disengaging the magnetic fields. The aerodynamic force slapped the SS hard against the glass surface of the Lava Flats; causing Day to blink out of and back into consciousness.

The skid created another cloud of particles, similar to Eryl's impromptu acoustic rifle generated shard-cloud but more focused, its effect limited to the sleds and occupants in the near path of the SS as it performed the slide.

After sliding under the sled, Day yanked the lever rearward, restoring the suspensor fields and elevating the SS to its former cruising height. In addition to shedding a lot of speed in the maneuver, and unnoticed by Day, the impact disrupted the starboard cancellation shield. The shielding breach allowed a crack cannoneer aboard one of the nearby sleds to snap off an accurate blast from an acoustic canon.

The blast disrupted the right-aft suspensor field, causing the front of the SS to lurch obliquely upwards. The same aft corner grazed the glassy surface creating another shower of metallic sparks and shards. The reverberation from the impact spun the front of the craft circuitously downward, oscillating the SS into another skid. Day struggled to keep from piking the craft, flipping it end over end. After a long, noisy, bounce-laden skid, the battered craft came to a stop with the Gru sleds fast approaching.

Day looked at Eryl and her at him. They took one another's hand and leaned in touching foreheads, fearful of what was about to happen. The army would return Eryl to the awful Gru, Silas Mis, to whom the courts had betrothed her to serve as concubine. After a farcical trial, the High Court would order the execution of Day for numerous offenses against society in this time of war.

Day could accept many of the charges against him but he was unwilling to attempt to obtain the mercy of his accusers by repenting of what was perhaps his greatest crime against society. There was no repenting from love, no matter how earnest society might object to his kind of love. The love of a Hü for a Rubicund, regardless of the rank of either, that is, whether Lehu, Chu, Loru or Gru, was illegal. Their present society had long since deemed Rubicund-Hü relations as an abomination, amoral and repugnant; a crime punishable by death to the Hü involved.

Four of the Gru soldiers dismounted their sleds and walked toward the SS. Eryl stared at the crimson skin and yellow, dual-pupiled eyes of the approaching soldiers and felt a wave of repulsion and nausea overtake her. She could not remember a time when she ever thought of a Gru as attractive. Now, after the things she had witnessed over the last few months, Eryl looked on most of their caste with complete and utter contempt.

Day looked at Eryl's glimmering bronze skin and stared into her teary, amethyst-colored irises. Her similar tinted hair was flowing in a gentle breeze that emanated from across the Lava Flats. The warm air from the glass sea moved toward the foothills of the Great Spirit Mountains, fueling the orographic lift of the mountain thermals and creating the ever-present fog and cloud cover of the enigmatic range.

Regardless of what might happen to him, Day could not bear the thought of this being the last time he saw her. He pressed his forehead against hers then gave her lips a gentle kiss, hoping it would not be their last moment together. The Gru soldiers then ripped the couple apart and led them away toward separate sleds for transport to General Sul.

"I am with child!" Eryl yelled, trying to raise her voice over the flood of the low-pitched humming from the suspensor fields of dozens of army sleds. Though this was again no appropriate time for the news, Eryl could not risk the possibility of the love of her life never knowing the truth.

Day did not hear her.

TU

Twenty-Five First Moons Prior

"So, you're saying you believe in this place called Outland?" Farlay Singh asked, somewhat dismissive. Far was a tall, masculine Chu with an athletic build and easy-going manner. Of dark brown complexion, like other Chu, Far's skin was without blemish and had a rich, silken quality to it that many, regardless of race, found both appealing and assuasive. With looks, social graces and intelligence going for him, Farlay was well-liked by all who knew him.

"I believe it is pronounced Aütland and yes I do," Day answered in an assertive, annoyed voice. He was more than a little irritated by his friend's trivializing tone, which he took as condescending. As a Lehu, Dabrill Kinselo felt like he had been talked down to all his life. The very name that all of society used for his race, Lehu, was derogatory. Everyone understood it to be just a shortened form of the less polite designation of Lesser Hü.

As Farlay continued piloting the commuter class craft toward their job site, Day looked out his side of the craft over the wide expanse of bloodfruit shrubs. The dim light of the setting full second moon, Sis, was starting to fade as the first light of dawn was just beginning to illuminate the plantation.

The earliest beams of the sunlight caused a glittering effect on the shiny golden outer skin of the fruit. Teams of harvesters, most of them Lehu, were donning their waders and making their way into the shrubbery at the edge of the marshy plantation to start the morning's harvest.

Day thought about how difficult was the life of the typical harvester. They, like the majority of Lehu, had no mechanism by which they might advance their status in society. He hated the caste system of the world; Lesser Hü, Common Hü, Lower Rubicund, Greater Rubicund. *What gives any individual the right to decide that he was lesser than any other based on the color of his skin? Ludicrous!* he thought.

Day understood that much of his feelings came from his being a member of the lowest of the castes. Yet, his attitude stemmed from more than that. Day was what many referred to as a colored or painted Hü. While most Lehu had a light sandy complexion and the majority of Chu had brown skin, Day's skin was a distinct, clay-like reddish color. This abnormality of pigmentation was thought to be a vestigial genetic marker, the implication being that Day belonged to some more primitive race of Hü; a race extinct several millennia before even the Rubicund refugees arrived.

Being an orphan from a young age, Day had no knowledge of his ancestry. This made conversations difficult, even uncomfortable to the point of embarrassment whenever anyone asked Dabrill about the color of his skin. He went out of his way to avoid talking about his indeterminate ancestry with anyone and considered it to be a subject of particular soreness in conversation with Hü of the ordinary skin tones.

Despite the origin of Day's rare complexion, it afforded him a somewhat better standing among the Rubicund when dealing with them; but among Hü, even the Lehu, he was an outcast. Perhaps this was the ultimate reason that Day hated the caste system. Perhaps it was why he needed to believe in places like Aütland, an entire land of outcasts, or so it was rumored.

The low hum of the harvest and farm craft used to haul the picked fruit to the processing plant where Day and Far worked was dying down as those craft parked at the edges of the marshland. The waning of the low-pitch hum of a hundred HF craft gave way to the insect-like buzzing of the suspensor harvesting baskets, which the workers pushed ahead of them into the wetland farm.

The short-crest receiver in Farlay's C-class vehicle droned to life. All vehicles constructed over the last twenty anni were equipped with similar short-crest receivers, by government mandate, used by the Public Information Agency to broadcast news and general announcements at various intervals from dawn to dusk.

The adjustment of most such receivers was limited to the ability of reducing the sound level, a little. The broadcast could not be turned off. The force-fed "news" of the PIA annoyed Day to the point of disgust as it did most Hü. Many among the lower castes misappropriated the acronym, calling the agency the Propagandists and Informers Association.

On this dawn, the voice of the broadcaster was feminine, quite nasal and with an air of obnoxiousness that made Day want to regurgitate his morning meal. For a moment, Day considered overstepping personal bounds and turning the sound level down on the broadcast without asking Far's permission. Adjusting the short-crest receiver without the vehicle owner's permission would be a complete breach of etiquette.

As Dabrill had decided to plead with his friend to turn down the volume of the insufferable, intrusive sound of the propagandist, he heard the adenoidal voice say something interesting.

"And in other news, a young Lehu was apprehended attempting to obtain access to restricted areas of Capital City. This marks the fifth such attempt at accessing restricted areas this annum. Citizens will remember that, on three previous occasions this annum, individual Lehu have attempted to enter the Council chamber of the Eastern Steppes. On all three of those attempts, the Lehu were killed by security forces,

"Prior to those criminal acts, a Chu gained momentary access to a secure military area of Capital City and was then killed by agents of the Loru Security Services as he tried to steal sensitive government information,

"Government sources have informed the Public Information Agency that the investigations of these incidents revealed no connection between them and that each of the individuals appear to have acted alone and of their own accord. To quote one government source, 'They were just common thieves',

"In other news, it is registration time again. All Hü are required..."

Now less interested and unable to withstand another moment of her abrasive voice, Day reached for the sound control potentiometer and turned it to the minimum. As an afterthought, he positioned his leg so as to block most of the sound from the speaker on his side of the vehicle, then lean back in his seat, closed his eyes and smiled because he had all but rid himself of the obnoxious voice of the brain-invading PIA announcer.

Day's smile soon faded as he thought about what might happen to the Lehu who had been apprehended in Capital City. He'd heard stories about a secret detention center where political prisoners were tortured, ultimately to death. *Just rumors*, Day thought, sighing in some small relief at his tenuous dismissal of such a heinous place as a government run torture center.

"Don't sulk, Day," Far said, though he was not offended by Day's breach of etiquette in turning down the volume of the PIA. Rather, it was his friend's silence that had got the better of him, "I'm just a natural skeptic on such things as secret, mysterious places like Aütland."

"Do you ever think about the analog of the bloodfruit with the Rubicund?" Day asked, having moved on from their previous dialog.

"What?" a puzzled Far asked.

"The skin of the bloodfruit is golden, similar to the color of the skin of the Loru. It is thick and protects the meat of the fruit from pests. Like the color of the Gru, the meat of the fruit is a deep, blood-red color, hence its name," Day mused.

"What are you getting at?"

"I'm just thinking about how the Loru provide protection for the Gru, much like the golden, thick skin of the bloodfruit protects the soft, bloody meat inside," Day answered.

"Protection for the Gru? From what?" Far asked.

"Pests," Day said, letting out a slight chuckle.

"Day, you're a good friend, but sometimes you are just plain weird," Far said as he pulled the craft into the parking area of the processing plant.

Far eased the field power lever forward, de-energizing the suspensors and allowing the small, commuter class vehicle to settle to the ground. The two climbed out and began walking into the sprawling processing plant to begin the new dawn's work. Keeping pace alongside his friend, Day noticed that their shadows were cast ahead of their path in equal, indistinguishable silhouettes. *Shadows cast do not define as shadowy castes*, he thought.

***

Jaylon Leeks stormed out of the analytical lab carrying a small vial of bloodfruit juice. Jaylon was a Loru of short stature, equipped with a somewhat shorter temper and a rather ill disposition. As her short strides carried her down the office corridors, she looked at the vial of the scarlet-colored liquid in her golden hand, increased her pace and deepened the frown upon her golden face. *I will not take the blame for this*, she thought.

Jaylon soon found herself turning the handle of the office door with the frosted glass labeled *F. Singh, Chief Chemist*. Jaylon did not realize that an involuntary, disgusted sigh escaped her lips this and every time that she read that door. She believed, not in secret, that the chief chemist position should have been hers two anni ago. Jaylon Leeks had a deep resentment and ill disposition not because of any legitimate mistreatment. Rather, her demeanor reigned sour within her because she was stepped over for a Common Hü.

"The hydrogen potential values are low again," she said, bursting into Far's office and waving the vial in his face.

"Come in Jayles," Far said.

Jaylon huffed at the sound of Far saying her nickname. It had been cute when the subordinate Far had started calling her that several anni ago. Now it was a reminder that she was *his* subordinate.

"Don't *Jayles* me, this is serious," she said, "if the acidity gets any worse, they'll shut the plant down and we'll have an investigation."

"I realize that, Jayles. This is just the natural consequence of the plantation governors pushing the limits of their harvests to get higher yields," Far answered.

"We have reached *our* limits," Jaylon replied, "the blends of early and late fruit are as optimized as they're apt to get."

"How are the rinds?" Far asked.

"The rinds are fine," she answered. Visibly calmer, she placed the vial in her lab coat pocket.

"We'll see if we can improve the efficiency of the pith sugar extractors and feed the extra yield back to the juice blends," Far offered.

"It won't be enough; and even if it is, it won't help if the hydrogen potential drops further," Jaylon responded, then turned and left Far's office. Her determined, confident stride accentuating her arrogance.

As he watched Jaylon leave, Farlay knew she was right but he also knew something she did not. In fact, few knew the true cause of the decline in sugar and rise in acidity of the bloodfruit crop: the plantations were victims of blight. Far detected the blight in three out of the seven plantations he tested. Although he was unsure of the method of the transmission of the disease between shrubs, he was beginning to have his suspicions. His question about the rinds was in furtherance of his investigation.

Inspired by Jaylan's abrasiveness, Farlay realized that he needed more information, some very specific information. He also knew who best could help him with this particular data collection. There was just one catch; he would have to bring Dabrill Kinselo up to speed on the entire situation. Day was always so inquisitive. *Sack!* Farlay thought, as he reached for the intra-plant intercom transceiver.

***

Like most any other dawn, Day was watching over the incoming fruit for stems and leaves. Though the harvesters were paid by the actual fruit count and size since the advent of the high-intensity photonic sorters, there always seemed to be a fair number of such otiose items in the harvest. The HIP sorting machines were advanced but there was still no substitute for a pair of keen eyes.

As the supervising inspector of the incoming fruit, Day took his job serious. The position was menial and involved a fair amount of manual labor for a modern, automated facility. He made the job more manual than it needed to be by often walking the lines among the six inspectors of his shift to make sure undesirable materials did not get past them and into the peeling machines. He knew that the leaves and stems contained mild toxins that could cause an entire batch to be rejected should enough of them make their way into the peelers and, from there, into the juicers.

"Dabrill Kinselo, please come to the office of the Chief Chemist," Farlay's baritone voice reverberated over the plant's intercom system.

What now? Day thought. He motioned for the inspection trainee with whom he had been working to take over and made his way out past the conveyors and toward the stairs. It was rare for Farlay to call Day to a conference during work shifts without assigning him some unusual task. It was with some mild trepidation that, a few degrees later, Day was pressing the latch bar to the door of Far's office.

"Close the door and take a seat Day," Far said as Day entered.

"Sounds serious," Day replied, as he sat in one of the comfortable chairs Far had picked for his office for the purpose of relaxing his visitors.

"What do you know about the chemistry of the bloodfruit?"

"What?" Day asked, more than a little surprised by his friend's question.

"I mean, what do you know about the relationship between the dietary requirements of the Greater Rubicund and the chemistry of the bloodfruit?" Far asked, clarifying his query.

"Well, I'm not a chemist or bio-techie," he answered, "but I know that there is a chemical nutrient in the juice of the bloodfruit that is a nutritional requirement of the Gru."

"That's correct," Far said, "there are some rather complicated biochemistries involved but the simplified version is that there are several genes in the Gru sequencing that are tied to the chemical chrysanthemin, or chryst as most Gru refer to it."

"So, that's why they call the juice chryst-blood," Day interrupted, "I thought it was a jab at an ancient Hü religious group."

"It may well have been intended as a slur," Far continued, "but that is neither here nor there. The main reason that I called you in here has to do with the way the chryst works. The ability of the Gru biochemistry to absorb and utilize necessary quantities of the chemical hinges on the juice being maintained in a narrow window of acidity."

"Okay, so now I understand why Jayles keeps popping in to get samples of the incoming fruit; she's always mumbling about 'blends' when she's down there. That still doesn't explain why you called me here," Day said, his impatience evident.

"We are having difficulty maintaining the hydrogen potential within the window," Far said with a simple urgency in his tone. He then gave Day a stern look and continued, "What I tell you next is to be held in utmost secrecy."

"Of course," Day said, now more interested.

"There is a fast spreading blight among the bloodfruit plantations. It is an unusual phage in that it has a single symptom: it reduces the hydrogen potential of the fruit outside the necessary range for the Gru."

"Can't your lab magicians raise the hydrogen potential with their chemical wizardry?" asked Day, his interest further piqued.

"As I said, there are some complex biochemical interactions involved. More than a few scientists have tried, over many anni, to balance the hydrogen potential in other fruit and plants that contain chryst. Nothing seems to work, other than the natural equilibrium of the hydrogen potential of the bloodfruit."

"Sack!" Day exclaimed, "What do you think *I* can do about this?"

"First, let me ask you something," Far said, "have you noticed anything unusual about the stems or leaves of the shrubs that you have been inspecting?"

"Nothing."

"No dehydration *of* or unusual blisters *on* the leaves?"

"No."

"Any signs of brittle or dry stems?" Far continued to press.

"Nothing like that," Day answered, becoming impatient again.

"Thank you," Far said, "it all seems quite puzzling. We see the same lack of abnormalities in all other parts of the fruit. It effects the seeds, the meat and the juice of the meat, which are the same parts of the fruit that contain significant quantities of the necessary chryst. It's almost as if the hydrogen potential is targeted by the phage. But that makes no sense either."

"Why is that?" Day asked.

"The phage is destroyed when the hydrogen potential drops. The disease eradicates itself when it re-sequences the fruit to produce the increased acidity."

"Is it depressed?" joked Day.

"This is quite serious," Far scolded.

"I know, but I still don't understand how I can help you."

The chemist sat back in his chair, rested his elbows on the arms of the chair, pressed the tips of his fingers together and perched his chin upon them. A moment later, Far spun his seat around, got up and started browsing the shelf of codices behind him. Another few moments and he'd found the volume for which he was searching. Farlay then retook his seat and started turning through the leaves until he found the object of his search. At last, he placed the open codex in front of Day.

"I also don't understand why you still use these old relics," Day chided, smiling.

"Just read," Farlay said, then pushing the volume a little closer to Day, he added, "Besides, most of these codices were lithographed less than thirty-five anni prior".

"In other words, still before *my* lifetime," Day quipped, as he broadened his smile and leaned forward just enough to read the title of the section to which the codex was opened. His smile vanished as he glanced up to look at Far who was nodding and pointing back to the codex with both index fingers of his otherwise interlocked hands.

Far rested his elbows on his desk and perched his chin upon his interlaced fingers, waiting, like a patient professor, as Day read the chapter, leaf after leaf. As he read, Day found himself sinking into the words in the text, his countenance becoming ever more distressed. Once he finished reading, Day slammed the codex closed and pushed the volume back across the desk toward Far as if it had burned him.

"You can't be serious," Day said, breaking the long silence of the office, "A biological weapon? Who? How?"

"That is what you are going to help me determine," Far answered.

***

100,000 Furlongs Away, in the Bloodfruit Plantations of the Eastern Steppes

Müur Lesle emptied the last canister of solution into the channel of the dark marsh water and smiled, having completed the task for which he'd been hired. He slinked back to his bi-field suspensor craft parked at the edge of the plantation with his idle thoughts of the many ways in which he would use his ill-got reward. Upon returning to the small suspensor craft, Müur donned his helmet as he saw the lights and heard the siren of a patrol vehicle bearing down on him.

Jumping astride his B-class, Müur touched the power on and twisted the throttle to full an instant before a shot from a night patrol officer's acoustic pistol slammed into the spot he and his craft had vacated. Müur looked back to see that he was leaving the night patrol craft and its occupants far behind. He grinned beneath his helmet and returned his gaze forward just in time to see the club as it smashed his visor, removing him from the B-class. Müur landed hard and unconscious upon the ground. His craft coasted to a stop almost a furlong away, its throttle no longer torqued by his grip.

The short but stout Loru who caused Müur's rapid dismount stood over his unconscious body as the night patrol arrived. Two Gru patrol guards climbed out of their vehicle and recognized the gleaming golden insignia of the Loru as that of a district sheriff. The passenger in the patrol vehicle who had fired the errant shot from her acoustic pistol holstered her weapon. The sheriff began talking into his headset intercom as the guards approached.

"Yes, the situation is under control," the sheriff said, "it appears that a Lehu was tampering with the bloodfruit crops and was killed in a shootout with the evening patrol while attempting to escape."

The two Gru guards looked at the suspect lying on the path and saw that he was beginning to rouse, moaning in pain. They then looked at one another with quizzical expressions as if each were asking the other the obvious questions: *Killed? Shootout?* The passenger guard glanced at her holstered weapon, reassuring herself that the pistol was on its lowest setting and not capable of delivering a fatal shot.

"Yeah, I'm sure he's dead," the sheriff said. He then pulled an acoustic pistol from his waistband, leveled it at Müur and fired a lethal sonic blast into his chest.

"Hey, what the sack?" the feminine Gru guard yelled, "You can't just execute bloodfruit thieves around here."

"Yes, that's right sir," the sheriff said, continuing the calm conversation, "it appears the subject managed to kill both guards before succumbing to his injuries."

The sheriff then raised the weapon and shot both surprised guards to death, "They'll probably get posthumous heroism citations when news of what the subject was doing gets out. Yes, I'll clean things up here, sir."

With the deed done and his conversation ended, the Loru sheriff walked to his vehicle, which he had earlier parked on the berm of the path and picked up his transceiver to call in the incident to the sheriff's district headquarters. He was careful to relay his version of events much as he'd just invented them.

After placing the transceiver in its cradle, the sheriff produced a half full canister much the same as the one Lesle had just emptied into the marsh. He tossed the canister near the now lifeless body of Müur and planted the acoustic pistol in his hand. The sheriff then placed each of the guards' own acoustic pistols in their hands. Completing his masterpiece, the sheriff leaned back against his patrol vehicle admiring his contrived crime scene and waiting for the sheriff's deputies to arrive.

Trė

Excerpt from *My Aunt was a Renegade – My Dad was a Müul* by Lea Syz

Erol Syz has been described as tenacious, stubborn, resolute and dogged. His determination in accomplishing any task was often compared to tales of the obduracy of the mythical animal, the Müul. To those close-minded individuals among the Hü who perceived Erol's obstinacy to be the architype of his race, the personality of his twin sister would be the glaring exception proving the paradigm. However, the dad I knew was so much more than that stereotypical view of him; and the same is true for his sister, the Renegade Eryl Syz.

Eryl achieved results with equal success to that of her brother; she was just somewhat less precise and calculating in her approach. Though most historians describe the typical Lehu rebel as unwelcoming of restraint or even free of spirit, records show that no member of the Resistance embodied that character more than the Loru, Eryl Syz.

Confidence was ingrained in every fiber of Eryl's being. Her gregarious nature was considered inviting and comforting to many of the lower castes. Juxtaposed to this, her extreme aversion to authority was considered threatening to the Gru. She questioned the dogma of the caste system at every opportunity and butted heads with establishment thinking whenever she deemed it convenient to do so.

By any standard, Eryl was beautiful. Most who saw her in person say image graphs do no justice to her golden Loru skin, which was smooth and without blemish. Her large almond-shaped, symmetrical eyes enclosing lavender irises were complimented by her silken hair, which glistened in any light. Her tall frame was unique in its unification of the athletic and feminine forms. Erol was handsome, in a rugged way, but his sister caught every eye that fell upon her.

As an individual, either Erol or Eryl was a formidable adversary. Together, the determined and rebellious twins were an almost unstoppable force whenever or wherever they joined to pursue a singular goal. It is little wonder that the Gru aggressors feared the twins so soon; even within a couple of months of the first annum of the rebellion.

***

"I will never be a concubine to that gruesome Gru," Eryl spat the words out as if each syllable were a condensed droplet of lethal venom.

"Be reasonable, dearest sister," Erol pleaded, "It is well known that Silas is not interested in his Loru concubines in any physical sense. He is too much of a bigot and is gathering a large harem for one reason: it adds to his popularity in the Council."

"Oh, my dear brother, you are so naïve," Eryl said, reprimanding her sibling, "*How* do you think it gains him popularity in the Council?"

"Because it makes him look more masculine among his peers," Erol answered.

"He loans his concubines out to members of the Council and Grus in high leadership positions as coitus favors," Eryl said.

"That...that...What?" he asked without wanting an answer. Erol was beginning to understand how such a relative unknown Gru had become so powerful in the Council in so short a career.

"There are rumors that he even has some secret masculine Loru among his harem just for members of the Council that are so inclined," Eryl added.

"What? That can't be...true," Erol said, stammering a little at the thought of what his sister was telling him.

"You are right about one thing, dear brother," Eryl conceded, "Silas Mis is a bigot. I feel he has the imminent goal of increasing the divide among the castes in furtherance of some more heinous end. And he is just aggressive, ambitious, clever, and monstrous enough to succeed."

"I don't understand what you think we can do about this," Erol argued, "On the next first moon you will be twenty-one anni of age. You were betrothed to a prominent Gru as payment of debt by our father. I don't know how we could manage to buy your freedom."

"I don't intend to buy my freedom, I intend to take it," Eryl proclaimed.

"You are not talking of the rebellion," Erol whispered, though no one could hear his words.

"Would that be so bad?" she asked.

"The rebellion is a mere rumor, a fairy tale and to even repeat such gossip is sedition," he warned.

"Is it sedition to talk of equality?" Eryl asked.

"Yes, it is, and you know it," Erol answered, "besides, the majority of these myths arise from the Eastern Steppes."

"Well, I don't think I will need to go quite that far," Eryl said as she pulled a modest travel case from under her bedstead.

"You intend to run?"

"I intend to hide," Eryl corrected, "then I intend to see if rumors of the rebellion are true; running may come later."

"Where will you go?" Erol asked.

"It is better that I do not tell you," Eryl said, "you could be questioned and it is best if you don't know anything to tell them."

"I'll do anything I can to help you, dearest sister," Erol promised, "Never think that it is my wish that you become a concubine in the harem of any."

"I know," Eryl said. Then she kissed her brother's cheek and touched her forehead to his in the deeper display of emotion more common to the Loru. "Farewell, dearest brother of our mother's womb," she said, then turned and left the apartment with a confidence and forward permanence in her stride that impressed upon Erol that she wasn't going to waver or even look back. For the first time in his life, he considered that he might never again see the sister of his mother's womb.

***

Day was becoming impatient again. Farlay Singh had him working undercover as a harvester in the bloodfruit plantations in hopes of discovering how the fields were being infected with the phage. Day took a month's worth of accrued leave time after he had the conversation with Far, two syphi ago. Since then, another of the seven plantations of the Western Council had become infected. This brought the total number of diseased marshes to four, making the situation at the processing plant tenuous, at best.

Increasing the shipments of bloodfruit from the copious, phage-free plantations of the Southern Council allowed Jaylon Leeks to just maintain the minimum requirements for the blend ratios to meet the processing plant's quota of juice. Still, Day knew this was a temporary bandage on a gaping wound. He felt that something much stronger and more public than covert surveillance activities would be necessary in order to avoid catastrophe. Having uncovered no signs of anything amiss among the harvesters, Dabrill felt that such a limited, secret investigation was becoming ever more pointless.

As he pushed his loaded suspensor basket back toward the haulers, Day noticed a distinct, bright yellow C-class vehicle parked on the berm. Far was leaning against the side of the vehicle, waiting for Day to approach. *He's going to blow my cover*, Day thought, w*hat is he thinking?*

Day tried to ignore his friend but Far stood upright and cupped his hands, projecting his deep baritone voice, "Dabrill Kinselo, I need you to come with me, it's urgent."

A reluctant Day dropped his suspensor basket beside one of the haulers and walked toward Far, who motioned his friend into the passenger side of the vehicle as he climbed in behind the vehicle's steering set. Far waited until they were clear of the plantation and on the roadway leading to the processing plant before speaking.

"All pit has broken loose," Far said.

"Another plantation is infected?" asked Day.

"Much worse," Far began, "there are information reports everywhere of a Lehu killed after infecting a plantation of the Eastern Steppes."

"You're not serious," Day said, then he thought of the ramifications of such a thing, "that would be an act of terrorism by the rebellion. The Councils would declare a guard-state."

"Three already have," Far said, "the Council of the Eastern Steppes, the Central Council and the Western Council."

"We are in a guard-state now?" asked Day, "Where are the troops?"

"Probably no more than a few dozen furlongs away," Far answered, "we will have no more than a cycle or two before they arrive. That is why I came to get you."

"Sack!" Day exclaimed, "How many plantations are infected?"

"Reports vary but there may be as many as nine of the twelve plantations in the Eastern Steppes infected. The Central Council has discovered that two of their ten plantations are infected, we now have five of our seven plantations infected," Far answered.

"You found the phage in another grove?" a surprised Day asked.

"Just this morning."

"What about the Southern Council?" Day asked.

"There are no reports of anything amiss with the plantations of the south," Far said, "which may explain why they have not yet declared a guard-state."

“What's next?” Day asked.

“You go back to work, business as usual. Your position, even your entire operational area of the plant is considered menial as it pertains to the blight and its propagation. I will be fired, possibly jailed,” Far added.

“Nonsense,” Day said, “you have been trying to discover what is going on, there is no way you could be considered part of the terrorist attacks.”

“We have been investigating in secret,” Far said, “if the authorities discover that I knew there was a phage, which I suspected was a biological weapon but that I did not report to them at once, I will be executed.”

“Sack me!” Day said, now beginning to understand the full weight and ramifications of the terrorism attack.

“No, sack me,” Far said.

***

The Great Hall of the Western Council

Council member Silas Mis stood at the podium in the Great Hall of the Western Council. As he waited for the mild applause of his introduction to fade, he surveyed the assembled Council with all the ability of his vision. The lighting on the stage was dimmed so as not to give too great a view of Mis' face, which was rough and pockmarked, giving him a more reptilian appearance than most Gru.

Although Silas knew there were enemies mingled with cohorts among the assemblage, the present circumstances gave him an advantage. *I can lead the willing among these,* Silas thought, *and with those, crush the unwilling.*

“Friends, a new and darker dawn has broken upon us,” Mis began, “It is not a dawn of our making; yet we are charged with the task of enduring every single moment of it. As we learned in our youth, there are ten moments in a degree, six degrees in a unit, sixty units in a cycle and twenty-four cycles in a dawn. Believe me, we will use every one of those eighty-six thousand, four hundred moments on every new dawn until we achieve a dawning that we can call ours.”

Mis believed his skill with the special characteristics of the Gru vocal cords to be second to none. He knew his high frequency vibrato technique created a unique choral effect in the auditorium. The Gru referred to those who were gifted with oratorical prowess as speaking in choir. When performed with expert control, one Gru could speak with the seeming authority of a dozen.

"Our dawn will not be a dawning of calm, retrospective inaction," Mis continued, his large, husky frame belying his high-pitched voice. Though expert in the choral technique, his voice was somewhat more abrasive than the grinding of gypsum on slate.

"Our dawn must be a dawning of resolute determination for the Gru. With a gentle and wise hand, we have led those of the lower castes, while they have plotted against our kind and noble stewardship. Heretofore holding a light grip upon the reins of government, we are now rewarded evil for kindness by these terrorists, these backbiters against our gentle guidance. The Gru have provided fruitful employment to the Hü and they have given us poisoned fruit in return. Now I say that we will no longer be fooled by the Hü."

Silas paused a moment for the Hü directed jeers to subside. He looked to his left on the dais and found the forlorn face of the current Chancellor General, Veegram Lo. Mis then raised his arm and pointed toward the hapless Council leader.

"Let us not cast blame on our fellow Gru other than the inherent blame of the palpable languor that led us to this place," he said. Then Mis spread both arms wide to indicate the complete body of the assemblage, "but, if we fail to correct the apathy, and if we cannot bring ourselves to the determination of mind that is required of us, then we are all to blame for whatever comes next,

"Yet, you have an opportunity to correct that apathy and to determine what does come next. You are now charged to judge the former mistakes and create a new order. You have an obligation to set our government on a new course and you have a responsibility to rein in the lax steering of our former idle pilots. It is a vital part of this solemn duty to elect me as your next Chancellor General."

As many in the crowd indicated their agreement by loud applause, Mis turned to his right and found the face of the Sheriff of District Two of the Eastern Steppes. As the applause waned, Mis raised his right hand toward the sheriff.

"Should we desire an example of strength with which to juxtapose the absurdity of our heretofore lax positions, we need look no further than our brother Rubicund of the Eastern Steppes. Sheriff Tarr has traveled to us from the east to help us better understand our current deficiencies," he announced. Then Mis again spread his arms to indicate the entire assemblage, "Should this Council find such wisdom as is necessary to elect me as its Chancellor General, it is my genuine hope that Sheriff Tarr will accept the new position that I will create: Chief Inquisitor of the Councils."

Sheriff Tarr raised his diminutive yet stout frame from his seat and nodded his oversized head toward Mis in acceptance of the proposed position. As the applause faded and Tarr retook his seat, he undertook his first task of the new office by committing to memory many of the Gru faces that seemed less than enthusiastic in their ovations.

"Yes, my brothers, in order that our dawn does not become a dawn of calm retrospection, this evening shall not be an evening of lax inaction. We will not stand idly together and we will not slack the reins of government to the point that these evil-doers will again rise to threaten our society," then Mis raised his right hand into the air, clenched it into a fist and concluded, "If you will stand with me, we will find those malcontent laborers for dishonesty and dissonance and we will crush them under whatsoever rock they may choose to hide," then he smashed his fist onto the podium, inducing a robust standing applause from much of the assembly.

***

Erol waited in silence in the office chamber of Silas Mis. The Council member had sent his L-class suspensor for him before dawn on the morning of the election. Erol knew that he would have a long wait since the election would be held just before the apex meal. Having caught himself drifting asleep twice, he was again feeling his eyelids grow heavy.

He glanced at the chronograph on the wall of Mis' office for what seemed to him to be the hundredth time. *Thirty degrees to apex*, he thought, *the election should be over soon*. Erol had no doubts of Mis' reason for summoning him to his office chamber at the Western Council. There could be just one motive for which Silas Mis would bother to meet with any Loru on the dawn of a special election: he needed the location of Eryl.

Erol knew that even if he were aware of the location of his sister, he would never divulge that to Mis. Having resolved himself to the certain penalty that would be levied when he failed to cooperate, Erol wondered what odious form of punishment Mis would concoct.

At ten units of one past apex, Silas Mis burst into the room. He was carrying the scepter of the Chancellor General. By this, Erol knew that Mis had won the election. Perhaps he would be in a good mood due to his victory. He remembered his sister's words about Mis dividing the castes in furtherance of some more heinous end. *Was becoming the Chancellor General the dreadful end that Eryl prophesied?* Erol pondered, but soon concluded that this was just the beginning and the terrorist act of the rebellion had been used as a catalyst for opportunity.

"Congratulations on your victory Chancellor," Erol said as he rose upon the entrance of the new leader of the Axis of Councils.

"Three votes," Mis mumbled.

"Excuse me Chancellor?" Erol asked.

"Never mind," Mis dismissed the question, "come stand before me," he summoned.

Erol walked the short distance to stand in front of the Chancellor. With intensity, Mis focused his four pupils on Erol and the latter knew that he would not be able to lie to former. He gave no sign of fear for he knew that he would not be lying to the Chancellor.

After a few degrees of the silent study of Erol's face, Mis asked, "Do you know where your sister is?"

"I do not," Erol answered.

"When did you know that she would flee?"

"A few degrees before she left," Erol responded.

"Will you help me find her?" Mis asked.

This question surprised Erol. The forcefulness of the rapid-fire vibrato effect of his Gru vocal cords unnerved him. He had not anticipated that Mis would be so bold as to ask that he help to track down his own sister so that she could be conscripted to service in the Chancellor's harem. He hesitated, knowing that he could not lie but fearful of telling this now all-powerful Gru the truth.

"I see your fear," Mis said, "Answer me!"

"N...No," Erol released the response and waited for Silas Mis' rebuke.

Mis' bellicose laugh exploded into the office and echoed off the walls. Then he gestured toward the obvious seat and said, "Sit down, Syz."

As he sat down in front of Mis' desk, Erol was shaking; as much from the reverberant laugh as from the short but intense interrogation. The Chancellor decanted two snifters of bloodwine and handed one to Erol, who took the snifter in trembling hands, gulped the warm, syrupy liquid and set the empty snifter on Mis' desk.

Waiting several degrees to allow the wine time to affect Erol, Mis said, "I can see the wine has calmed you a little. Now let's discuss how you *will* help me find your sister."

"I don't know where she is and I would not know where to start looking for her," Erol reiterated.

"I believe you," Mis began, "however, as you know, your father owed me a debt and your sister was to be the payment. Until her debt is paid, you have the obligation."

Erol felt Mis' words sinking in and again remembered Eryl's speech: '*he even has some secret masculine Loru among his harem just for members of the Council that are so inclined'*. He shivered, almost bringing back his fearful trembling in full. Mis did not notice the trembling as he had rotated his chair, turning his back to Erol as he spoke. He gazed out his window overlooking the capital of the Western Council as he continued his monologue.

"You see, as Chancellor General in a time of crisis, I have the discretion of the use of the military. It is my intention to form a personal guard to travel with me as I visit the capitals of the other Councils,

"Of course, the Public Information Agency will travel with me," Mis' continued, "and there will be many images broadcast across the entire planet. I am quite certain that your sister will see me, with you at my side, serving as my Chief of Security. For you *will* be at my side every step of the journey. Perhaps the sight of you will remind her of her love for you and she will begin to understand the error of her ways."

Erol sat for a few degrees mulling over Mis' words. On the one hand, he was relieved that he would not become some masculine member of Silas Mis' harem, loaned out to the desires of who knew what Council member. On the other hand, he was worried for his sister's safety. He could see through Mis' superficial plan and understood that he was the bait with which to trick his sister into some reckless act. Still, he could find no simple way to refuse to be a part of Mis' trap.

Perhaps being this close to Mis could prove useful down the road. *Of what use could it be if my sister becomes trapped?* Erol thought, debating himself. He now understood that his sister was right; this was one dangerous Gru. Now he was in an even greater position of authority with plans for who knows what.

The Chancellor continued to stare out the window looking at the eastern half of the capital and dreaming of his extended plans. As the sun moved down in the sky behind the Great Hall of the Western Council, the shadow of the building began to stretch out on the capital beneath Silas Mis. The darkness cast over the capital by the shadow of this tallest building in the city seemed an ominous forecast of Mis' darker schemes yet to be realized.

"You must have two dozen feminine Loru in your harem," Erol said.

"Closer to three dozen," Mis quipped, "what is your point?"

"Why is my sister so important to you?"

"Your sister means nothing to me," Mis answered, "payment of debt is important to me."

"The debt of my father cannot mean so much to you now that you are Chancellor General," Erol said.

Silas turned from the window, rose from his chair, walked the short distance around his desk and stood looking at Erol for a moment. He then drank the last half of his bloodwine in a single gulp, sat the empty snifter beside its twin on the desk and patted Erol on the head like his new favorite pet; the last act causing a shiver of revulsion from the young Loru.

"I did not get to be Chancellor General without having a few debts of my own," Mis said.

Erol did not understand Mis' cryptic response and knew better than to question him further on the subject. He relented to the Chancellor's demands and, by the next syphus, found himself traveling with his new employer to the plantations of the other Councils.

***

Being summoned to the overseer's office worried Day. Only a single syphus had passed since his conversation with Far and, pressured by the other three Councils, the Southern Council had declared a guard-state. The Gru Army then sent occupying troops into all plantations and processing plants. The Gru commander of the Western and Southern Councils' Occupation Forces, General Sul, established his authority with one simple and barbaric act: the execution of the overseers of all the bloodfruit processing plants of the Western Council.

Day saw many Lehu harvesters and plant workers lose their jobs to Loru replacements, since the Gru viewed the loyalty of the latter with much less suspicion after the Lehu terrorist attack. Far was demoted back to the lab, while Jaylon Leeks achieved the position to which she thought herself entitled, Chief Chemist.

Of the leadership positions in the processing plant, Day remained the last unscathed Hü. This was a fact which Day attributed to both his menial position, as Far had put it, and the fact that he was a painted Hü, making him somewhat more trusted due to his vague similarity of skin color with the Gru. Day considered this slight similarity both an advantage and disadvantage as he walked to General Sul's office.

Day stopped in the open doorway. The General was standing with his back to the door gazing out the one-way glass into the main area of the plant. At first glance, the General looked rather thin and frail but once Day's eyes adjusted to the differential of the lightness of the hallway and darkness of the office he could tell that Sul had the sinewy build of a longtime military campaigner. The short sleeves of his field service uniform showed his limb's muscles to be lithe and full of strength without hint of the slightest wasted space or mass between the crimson skin above and the iron-like bones beneath.

More impressive than the General's physical form was what Day noticed lying on either side of Sul, in the rear corners of his office. He had heard rumors of the brace of large scimitar cats the General kept as pets. Seeing them up close was beyond Day's expectation of how it might be to find one's self in the presence of such large predators. Though he had seen wild scimitar cats in the southern edges of the Savannah, he was never any closer than a furlong or so from them.

As a youth, Day also remembered seeing lifeless specimens at the Capital City Museum and marveling at their elongated, serrated teeth and thick, spotted, blonde-yellow fur. As an inquisitive youth, he reckoned that their massive, wedge shaped bodies and their powerful, long legs made them swift hunters; capable of running down and killing almost any prey. Day remembered that, after his visit to the museum, he'd had frightening evening visions of a fearful pride of scimitars taking down a 'rish elk or a stag-moose of the northern bogs.

Day was somewhat surprised to find that he was not fearful of the big cats. The two massive beasts lie still, watching Day staring at them. If not for the occasional yawns and blinking of their eerie, luminescent green eyes, he might have guessed them to be lifeless like those mounted specimens of the museum. The living versions he now gazed upon seemed larger.

After a few degrees of staring at the intruder, the loud, low hum of their guttural purrs resumed; the cats having paused their instinctual sounds when Day first appeared in the entryway. Sensing no fear in or threat from the visitor, each of the cats, in turn, lay their large, lion-like heads back upon their paws and closed their eyelids, purring themselves back to sleep.

"You wished to see me sir?" Day said, looking back at the General.

"Come in Kinselo," Sul said, "take a seat, and please, call me Sul."

Day knew that Gru preferred to use surnames as the informal, but less personal, form of address rather than given names. He also knew that their race, in particular, considered it much too familiar, even rude, to address someone of a different race by their given name. Still, Day found the pronunciation of his name in the vibrato vocalizations of a Gru to be almost serpent-like; unnatural to any bipedal creature.

"I have been informed you have a good relationship with the Loru, is this true?" Sul asked as he turned to face Day.

Dabrill stared at Sul's emotionless, yellow eyes. The orbs had an eerie glow in the synthetic lighting of the office. This ghost-like luminosity was enhanced by the fact that a Gru's twin pupils in each peanut shaped iris always seemed disharmonious in their regulation. Although Gru biology was not taught to Hü by educators, Day had gleaned enough from his various Rubicund acquaintances to know that this effect was due to the optical filter of each lens behind each pupil allowing differing wavelengths onto the image sensors of the twin retinas.

Knowing the biological reasons underlying the Gru's physiological peculiarities did not make them less unnerving to Day. He did not consider himself a bigot and it bothered him a little that being in the presence of Gru made him feel uncomfortable. His youth educators always attributed the discomfort of most Hü in the company of Gru to a somewhat common religious mythos; a shared psychological response dating back more than a dozen millennia. *Shaytān*, Day thought.

"Yes, with those I know anyway," Day answered. Then, broaching a subject he disliked, he added, "It has something to do with the color of my skin."

"No doubt," Sul agreed. He then took a seat behind the desk and added, "I can see that bothers you a little."

"Not so much. It probably bothers me more that many Hü react to me as if I was..." Day trailed off as he realized the direction his sentence was headed.

"A Gru," Sul finished his sentence for him and laughed, "I like you Kinselo; you are almost unencumbered with fear."

"Almost?" Day asked. He knew that the visual spectra acuity of the Gru allowed them to see subtle changes in skin temperature. Gru could often sense fear and anger and were accomplished biological deception detectors. Day also knew that, while he found the Gru biological peculiarities unsettling, he was not afraid of Sul. His question was based in genuine curiosity.

"I have called you here on a matter of state security," began Sul, ignoring Day's question, "as you know, the guard-state has caused many changes. Not the least of these is an increased presence of Loru among the harvesters in an effort to prevent the rebellion from infecting more plantations with the phage."

"I would say that the increase in Loru presence among the harvesters is substantial considering it was near zero before the occupation," Day interjected.

"True. It is for this reason that I have asked you here," Sul continued, "the large influx of Loru has made it difficult for the Axis to properly investigate the presence of rebel sympathizers."

"I would think it would make it easier," Day countered, "you now have thousands of investigators across a million square furlongs of the Western Council's plantations, not to mention untold others in the plantations of the other Councils."

"Kinselo," Sul said, "I think you misunderstand me."

"How so?"

Sul leaned forward, placed his elbows on the desk and laid his forearms one on top of the other. Almost whispering, he said, "Some leaders of the Council have suspicions that there are an increasing number of rebel sympathizers among the Loru. They take particular note of those Loru residing in the Southern Council."

"Forgive me, but I want to be sure I am correct in my understanding of what you are asking. You would like me to try to find a few rebel sympathizers scattered among several thousand Loru across a couple of million square furlongs of the plantations of the Southern Council; a place I have never so much as set foot. Is that all?" Day asked.

"Don't be ridiculous, you would be one of many such operatives," Sul chided. Then he sat back in his chair and added, "Your participation in this investigation will be appreciated for the fact that you have a distinct advantage over most of our Lehu agents."

"The color of my skin," Day said, with distaste evident in his tone.

"You are as clever as I have heard," Sul agreed.

"Heard?" Day asked.

"Farlay Singh speaks well of you," Sul said.

"Didn't you demote Singh?" Day asked.

"An unfortunate necessity," Sul replied, "Jaylon Meeks is an idiot but the present times demand that we take measures to safeguard all consequential positions. Singh's skills as a chemist put to use in determining optimum blends will be far more valuable than his skills in running the department."

"If I should find one of these rebel sympathizers, as you call them, how would I contact you from so far away?" Day asked. He was beginning to understand that Sul was not asking for his help. The General was all but issuing a directive.

"You and our other operatives will be contacted on a regular basis," Sul replied, "this is a major effort on the part of the Axis of Councils to prevent the rebels from perpetrating further acts of terrorism."

"What happens to those who are suspected of sympathizing with the rebels," Day asked.

"They will be tried and, if found guilty, they'll be given opportunity to rehabilitate in the work camps," Sul replied, then sighed, showing his impatience. Then, in his best choral voice he said, "You need not concern yourself with such matters. Can the Axis of Councils count on your support, Kinselo?"

"Yes," Day lied.

For a few moments, Day expected Sul to see through his deception and call for his personal guard to drag him away. Worse, perhaps the General would call on his brace of scimitars to shred the insolent painted Hü to pieces. Instead, General Sul swiveled around in his chair and faced the window overlooking the plant operations.

"My assistant will help with your travel arrangements," Sul said, his dismissal evident in the vibrato of his choir voice.

As Day left the office of the overseer, he realized that, for the second time during this first moon, he was headed into the plantations as a covert spy *against* the rebellion. *Had Farlay Singh somehow orchestrated both of my covert assignments? Is my Chu friend a secret spy for the Axis?* Day wondered. It seemed odd that General Sul had mentioned Far in the conversation. He soon dismissed such thoughts to his own paranoia at dealing with Gru.

At least this time it would be to the plantations of the Southern Council, where a second tour of duty would be unknown as such and less conspicuous. Day thought that the act of spying on the rebellion was almost an act of sedition, since his secret desire was to be a part of such a worthwhile movement.

Just a few syphi ago he would not have given very good odds that the rumors of a rebellion were even true. It had always seemed to him that being an outcast in a caste system had some distinct disadvantages above even the obvious. Day's own race had never trusted him enough to speak openly of the rebellion in his presence. It now seemed that the Rubicund leaders of the Axis had found usefulness in the outcast status in which Day languished among his own people.

Embarking on what any outside observer might consider to be a mission of moral treason, Dabrill Kinselo, the orphaned, painted Hü, never felt more alone in his entire life, all twenty-two anni of it. Still, the path that lay ahead of him was more clear than any he had known before. If he found Sul's so-called rebel sympathizers, he would never turn them over to the Axis; Day would join them.

Phor

Ex-Chancellor Veegram Lo sat in his office in a silent darkness. Two syphi had passed since the election and Lo now felt safe in the conclusion that Mis would not require him to vacate the space. This was not unexpected to Lo. For several anni before the election Silas Mis' office was well known to be the most desirable in all of Capital City.

As Lo sat contemplating what was next for him, he could not help but think about the circumstances leading to his abrupt ousting. Perhaps Mis had been right; he was too lax in his security, too comfortable with the general mood of the society. *Am I just getting too old?* he thought.

Sixty percent of the global bloodfruit supply was now rendered useless for the Gru population. If the phage-free global production were to fall below thirty-five percent of typical, there would not be enough chryst to meet the minimum needs of the Gru population. Rationing was the sole available solution until the bio-weapon could be contained and the terrorist defeated. He could not get his mind around the overwhelming events. *The Lehu had developed a bio-weapon. Why?* he thought. It made no sense to Veegram.

Lo rotated his chair from his desk to look out over the western side of the capital. The late afternoon sun loomed low in the sky. Poised to collapse below the horizon, the red hue of the giant orb created an eerie crimson glow among the buildings of the capital's Western Quarter. The traffic of hundreds of suspensor vehicles ebbed and flowed throughout the city like dancing serpents through the evening's now ruddy streets.

Veegram continued watching as the buildings grew darker and the redness gave way to the bluish hue of the city's lights. The serpentine traffic reminded the former Chancellor of the southern firewasps, flying in school-like swarms. He saw the vehicles as forming rivers of light, pollinating each intersection of the city as if those intersections were bloodfruit shrubs in the plantations of the Southern Council and the vehicles were the luminescent insects.

"Firewasps!" Lo exclaimed as he turned back to his desk with the sudden realization of what had been nagging at him.

Firewasps were a bio-engineered species of wasp. They were created more than a hundred anni ago as a specific remedy after natural species of pollinating insects had succumbed to the aggressive dragonflies of the southern plantations. The firewasps flew in schooling swarms at night to deter predators and were bioluminescent so harvesters leaving the plantation swamps in the evening could easily see them and avoid the potential of a deadly encounter with a large swarm.

The thing that now bothered Veegram Lo in connection with the bloodfruit terrorist attack was that the firewasps had proven so territorial that they brought the dragonfly populations to near extinction, creating an ecological disaster. After that, the Gru Councils banned all research into bioengineering and sealed the one such laboratory on the planet. The unity found during the global crisis led to a confederacy of the four Councils that would become the Axis.

It seemed dubious to Lo that uneducated Lehu rebels could dredge up century old technology to which none but top Gru scientists ever had access and use it to develop a sophisticated bio-weapon without someone becoming suspicious. *I need to see the old laboratory complex for myself*, Veegram thought, *something is just not right about all of this.*

***

On the other side of the planet, in the Eastern Steppes

Dawn was just beginning to break as Agent Fulong Su parked her older B-class suspensor craft in the parking lot of the Eastern Division offices of the Rubicund-Hü Investigation Bureau. Su rode in earlier than usual in order to put together her final presentation of the evidence in the terrorism attack by Müur Lesle, which resulted in his death and claimed the lives of two patrol officers.

Fulong kicked the support foot under her vehicle, powered off the dual suspensors and dismounted. As she removed her helmet and took a fresh breath of the brisk morning air, she looked up at the building's facade. The RHIB sign was still backlit, the twilight not yet bright enough for the sensors to deactivate its evening illumination.

Looking at the building, Fulong knew that, as a Lehu, she was quite fortunate to be still working for the Bureau. Most of the few Lehu employed at her level in government had been dismissed within a few dawns after the basic details of the terrorist attack became public knowledge. She was helped by the fact that the RHIB was an agency that was somewhat clandestine and out of view of the public eye, meaning its organizational structure was less influenced by public opinion.

Out of a general fear of reprisal, the RHIB was almost never mentioned in the broadcasts of the Public Information Agency. There was apparent benefit in working for the most secretive and powerful government agency, even for members of the lowest of the castes; at least for the few token Lehu fortunate enough to work for the Bureau.

Still, Fulong understood the real reason she was allowed to continue in her present position. Agent Su wasn't like the other Lehu. The difference that set her apart from her race also made her one of the best interrogators in the Bureau. Agent Su was the first painted Hü agent that the Bureau had ever employed. She was also the youngest individual to ever attain the level of agent, which she did two anni prior, at the age of twenty.

Su knew that the color of her skin made the subjects of her interrogations feel like they were being questioned by a Gru agent. She used this irrational, emotional response to her complexion to its utmost advantage. When she wanted to add an extra layer of fear to her interrogations, she could even produce a slight vibrato in her voice. Few subjects attempted to lie to Agent Fulong Su.

A few moments and a lift-tube ride later, Fulong opened the door to the Superboard Slave Room. Agent Su felt a sense of pride in her division every time she entered the room and heard the familiar, synthetic voice greet her. The Superboard Slave was the heart of the Eastern Division's data processing. While other divisions of the Bureau had similar data slaves, the Eastern Division's unit was the most recently upgraded.

The algorithm intelligence of the Superboard Slave was a sixth-generation AI and the programmers designed it with an interactive, synthetic, feminine voice. The simple name given to the synthetic personality was Gen-6. However, due to the sultry voice choice of her programmers, most of the masculine agents referred to her with the derogatory moniker of Gen-*Sex*. Fulong preferred just Gen.

"Good dawn, Agent Su," Gen-6 said in her typical, chipper tone.

"Good dawn, Gen," replied Fulong.

"You're in early; may I help you with something?" Gen-6 asked.

"I need to access the crime scene images from case H-9724," Su responded. Then she took off her riding jacket and crossed the room to the beverage dispenser. This early, she needed a strong, hot cup of quake.

"Of course. Do you want me to display them on your desk viewer or would you like to see them on the large viewer?" asked Gen-6.

"Large viewer please," Su said. Then, after downing her first sip from her steaming cup, she saw the first of the images appear on the screen.

"No, not the images of where the canister of blight was released. I need to see the images of the patrol victims and of the deceased suspect. Tile them on the viewer, please." Fulong said.

"My apologies; displaying images now," Gen-6 responded.

Agent Su continued sipping from the cup of quake as she studied the images of the two dead Gru patrol guards, scanning the victim images first. Looking at the last of the images, she noticed a small yellow dot near the back of the weapon of the feminine victim.

"Center and enhance grid eight, please, Gen."

"Enhancing grid eight, centering image on the viewer now," Gen-6 said, acknowledging compliance with the request.

"Magnify the center image by two hundred percent, please."

Staring at the magnified image as she sipped the hot quake, Fulong realized that there could be another explanation for the apparent inconsistency. Perhaps the power level indicator varied depending on the model of weapon.

"Gen, what model of acoustic pistol did the deceased feminine officer use?"

"Patrol Officer Asha Oyani carried a Mark III Sonnes Acoustic Pistol, also known as an SAP-M3. Its serial number is four-three-eight-five-six-three-three-one. Officer Oyani acquired the weapon..."

"That is unnecessary," Agent Su said, interrupting Gen-6, "Was this the weapon under Officer Oyani's hand recovered and secured into evidence?"

"The weapon was secured into evidence. It was examined by forensics Agent Linst and found to match, by model and serial number the weapon of Officer Oyani," Gen-6 replied.

"Was the energy reserve of Officer Oyani's pistol recorded during the forensics examination?"

"The energy reserve of Officer Oyani's weapon was recorded as ninety-seven percent," Gen-6 answered.

Fulong took another long sip from her cup. *It doesn't sum*, she thought, *something is missing*. What at first seemed to Agent Su to be just another break of dawn stringing together of images and writing conclusions was on the verge of becoming a long dawn looking over the files trying to make two plus two equal four. Su was facing many potential cycles of extra work because she noticed a small yellow blip on an image that she'd looked at a dozen times prior.

Fulong sighed, sat down at the workstation beneath the main viewer and said, "Gen, please display the final examination of the perpetrator at this workstation."

"Displaying the pathology exam of Müur Lesle," Gen-6 responded.

Agent Su read the exam twice and it still did not make sense to her. The dead terrorist had seven fractured ribs, both lungs were perforated and his heart showed signs of severe bruising indicating the force of an acoustic pistol set on its maximum level and at close range. Müur also had a severe concussion, which, coupled with the smashed visor of his helmet, indicated that he had received a heavy blow prior to his death.

"Gen, was the masculine patrol officer's weapon secured into evidence?"

"Patrol Officer Garnet Tua's weapon was secured into evidence; it was a Mark IV Sonnes Acoustic Pistol, also known as an SAP-M4. The serial number is..."

"What was the recorded energy reserve?" Su asked, interrupting again.

"The energy reserve of Officer Tua's weapon was recorded at one hundred percent, indicating it was not discharged," answered Gen-6.

"Well, that's not helpful," Su thought aloud.

"Pardon me, Agent Su; did I misunderstand your requested?" Gen-6 asked.

"No, Gen, it's okay," Su said, "I am a little confused over a mathematical equation."

"I have excellent mathematical algorithms. Perhaps I could help," Gen-6 said.

"It's just that I can't seem to reconcile the remaining energy with the injuries," Agent Su said, not expecting Gen-6 to be able to offer any assistance.

Less than one degree later, Gen-6 answered, "According to the total energy reserve of the weapons and the total damage indicated by the injuries, the single wound for which there is no definitive accounting is the concussion suffered by the deceased Müur Lesle. The records indicate the concussion is presumed to have been incurred in a fall from his suspensor craft prior to the exchange of acoustic pistol fire between the officers and the perpetrator."

"I don't understand," Su said as she seriously began to question whether she had missed something, "did the officers have any additional weapons?"

"The officers had two acoustic rifles in the patrol vehicle. These rifles were both model..."

"Were the rifles discharged?"

"The energy reserves of both rifles were recorded at one hundred percent, indicating they were not discharged," Gen-6 responded.

“Again, I don't understand how the energy balance matches with the injuries. The photographic evidence indicates that Officer Oyani's pistol was set on the lowest level and incurred a single discharge based on the remaining energy reserve that was recorded,” Su questioned the computation made by Gen-6.

“That is correct,” replied Gen-6.

“Officer Tua's weapon was not discharged and neither officer's rifle was discharged,” Su continued, becoming agitated as she spoke.

“That is also correct, Agent Su,” Gen-6 again replied in her calm, soothing voice.

“So how is there an energy balance when there is no weapon that fired the lethal shot into the chest of the terrorist Müur Lesle?” Su demanded, confident that Gen-6 would not be able to answer.

“Considering the two weapons discharged, the energy balance remaining from those weapons accounts for every injury except for the concussion suffered by Müur Lesle,” insisted Gen-6.

“You keep saying that but...” then Agent Su understood what she'd been missing: the 'two weapons discharged', “Sack me!”

“Please restate the request, Agent Su,” Gen-6 said.

“Gen, with what model of pistol was Müur Lesle armed and what was the energy reserve recorded for it?” Su asked.

“Müur Lesle was armed with a Model II Vanguard Acoustic Pistol, serial number undetermined due to obvious defacement. The energy reserve was recorded as sixty-one percent, indicating that the weapon was discharged between three and ten times depending on the energy level setting. The damage levels of the injuries of all the deceased indicate that the Model II Vanguard Acoustic Pistol caused all lethal injuries via three discharges at the maximum energy level setting,” Gen-6 answered in her most confident voice.

Fulong now knew that there could be just two explanations for the death of Müur Lesle and neither of those explanations involved the heroic, dying efforts of Patrol Officer Asha Oyani. Either it was simple and Müur Lesle took his own life after having killed the two patrol officers or, far more probable and infinitely more sinister, someone else was involved.

“I have one more math question for you Gen,” Su said.

“Certainly, Agent Su,” Gen-6 replied, her voice eager.

“When does two plus one equal four?” Su asked.

Three degrees later, Gen-6 replied, “The answer involves calculating a specific point in time at which a false sum of two integers will become true. Since a false sum of integers cannot at any calculable time in the future become true, the answer is approximated by infinity. That is, the answer involves a paradox.”

“It certainly does,” Agent Su agreed.

Phif

"Misery loves company."

Unknown Ancient Philosopher

Eryl was miserable. The climate of the Southern Council was oppressive in unrelenting heat and humidity. While the environment was superior for bloodfruit with high chryst yield, it was horrid for the Hü and Ru living and working there. On top of this, the basic amenities of life were much reduced compared to that of the Western Council. The few vehicles available were wheeled vehicles, used for work. The sole mode of transportation available to the working class was one's own legs. In the Southern Council, everyone except a few select Gru were the working class.

Eryl missed her home, her friends, her former life but, most of all, she missed her brother. Until a few syphi ago, Eryl had never been more than a few dozen furlongs' distance from Erol and she'd never gone more than a few dawns without seeing him. Even so, knowing with every fiber of her being that she would never submit to becoming a concubine, she understood that her present misery was not apt to be so permanent as the alternative; so, she labored on.

Eryl had fulfilled the first goal she'd stated to her brother: She was so well hidden that *she* hardly knew where she was. The second goal had proven more difficult. There were many disaffected Lehu, Chu and Loru working in the Southern Councils plantations. Yet they seemed reluctant to befriend or trust strangers. On her second dawn in the third plantation of her sojourn in the southern swamps, Eryl was debating how she might travel to the lands of the Council of the Eastern Steppes, or perhaps the Central Council lands. Then she noticed Dabrill Kinselo.

Eryl had never seen a painted Hü in the flesh. She remembered a few images of them in the codices during her education on the castes. She had always been captivated by the painted Hü but those images were nothing in comparison to seeing Day. He was tall and muscular, yet lithe. His skin was a magnificent, ruddy, earthen color. His hair was dark and of medium length and his face seemed to Eryl to be symmetrical perfection. On top of all this, and contrary to all she knew about the painted Hü, he had piercing *blue* eyes.

***

Day had no idea that Lehu, Chu and even many Loru living under the jurisdiction of the Southern Council had it so hard. He knew that the heat of the southern plantations would be oppressive. Nevertheless, he had not considered that the lack of suspensor functionality in the southern half of the planet would so dramatically increase the effort involved in physical work. Without suspensor baskets, the work of the typical harvester was backbreaking.

For three syphi, Day worked among the Lehu, Chu and Loru harvesters in the swamps, from dawn to dusk. During the evenings and on Shev, as the locals called their dawns off, he would socialize among his fellow harvesters as best he could.

Day was finding no sign of any rebel sympathizers here and all the time despairing more at the proposition of spending endless syphi on his covert mission. Then, one dawn, with his heart yearning for the relative comforts of the north, Day saw Eryl Syz wading into his furrow of the plantation.

Eryl was floating three empty baskets ahead of her, indicating her confidence in her harvesting abilities. Day could not take his eyes off her sylphlike form as she glided, thigh deep through the murky water. Although Dabrill had never found any particular Loru attractive, he now found himself unable to imagine any combination of shape of body or face being more beautiful than even the reflection of Eryl off the swampy water.

As she approached Day, Eryl noticed the two half-filled baskets floating at his hips and raised her head to see that he was staring at her. She smiled at him. Both then turned to begin picking bloodfruit. Day was glad that his skin color hid his blushing cheeks.

"Decided to slack off all dawn or just till apex?" Eryl said with a marked brashness in her voice.

"What?" Day asked, stumbling over the jocular intent of her question.

"Only two baskets," Eryl said, pointing to the containers now floating a little lower in the water, "not very ambitious for a big strong Lehu like you," then she cracked a big smile.

Day matched her smile and said, "I may start slow but I promise you I work up to a sensational finish."

"I'll be the judge of that," Eryl said.

Day once again felt his face blush from the bold double entendre of their conversation. He had never met a Loru like her. Beautiful, lightning quick humor and built like a gold and amethyst statue. He felt himself staring at her again as he reached into the shrubs to pick the fruit and drop them into his baskets.

Then Day saw Eryl stare back at him. She stopped picking fruit and began gliding through the water toward him, leaving her baskets behind her and unattended. *What is she doing?* Day asked himself, *Have I at last succumb to the heat and exhaustion? Is she a mirage?*

The closer she got to Day, the more beautiful Eryl looked. Her amethyst irises seemed like perfect mercurial pools floating within milky white, almond-shaped eyes, which were set in the golden-bronze skin of her face. Her silky hair matched the color of her irises. She had it pulled back into a tail, revealing her supple neckline.

Eryl kept coming toward Day and he froze and started to protest such a bold approach. She silenced him by placing her index finger to her lips. Stopping within whispering distance, she leaned toward him and, with her breast grazing against his chest, she raised herself on her toes until almost eye-to-eye. Thrusting her hand past his head with blinding speed, she snatched a coiled ghost viper from a branch of the shrub.

"These are deadly poisonous, you know," she said. She then snapped the viper's neck and tossed it at the foot of the shrub and added, "it's fertilizer now."

Day stood in silence, unable to summon the thank you that was called for in the moment.

Eryl turned back toward her baskets and said, "I bet it's sometimes nice being a painted Hü."

"Why would you say that?" asked an embarrassed Day.

"For starters, it is impossible for me to see you blush," Eryl quipped, then, after a strategic pause for her coquettish comment to have the effect she wanted, she added, "not to mention the fact that it is somewhat difficult for a Gru to sense if you're lying."

Day looked down at the glass-like serpent and saw that it still writhed in its final death throws on the root-mass of the shrub. The translucent skin and muscles of the snake made it difficult to see even though it was moving little more than an arm's length away. Its tail made tiny ripples as it dipped into the water's surface. Then, in Day's fog of embarrassment, Eryl's last statement made its way into his conscious mind.

"Wait, what did you say?" he asked.

"Come on now," Eryl said, "I know you're blushing; I just can't see it."

"No, not that," Day said, "What did you say about Grus not being able to sense that I am lying?"

"Oh, really? No one ever told you that?" Eryl asked.

"Never," Day said.

"Well, it's not that it is impossible for them," Eryl began, "it is just difficult. A Gru can't sense deception in other Gru. It has to do with the wavelength of the light emitted by the heat signature of a blush or other subtle temperature changes. You never had Rubicund biology courses in your education?"

"They don't educate Hü in Rubicund biology, so no," Day admitted and then realized that he had not even thanked her, "My name is Dabrill, most just call me Day. Thank you, you saved my life."

"I'm sure you'd have done the same for me," Eryl said, "besides, we low-life pickers have to look out for one another."

"All the same, may I have your name? I'd like to know to whom I am indebted," Day said.

For a moment, Eryl considered lying. She wondered if the painted Hü had lie detection abilities and considered testing them. Knowing that the Gru ability lay in their eyes and not the color of their skin, Eryl stared at Day. His skin color was a darker, more soothing, clay-like hue of red than the Gru. His blue eyes, though unlike the Gru in color and shape, had an analogous eeriness to them.

As she continued gazing into Day's eyes, she realized that they had a hypnotic nature to them; and she understood the eerie similarity with the Gru. His eyes almost demanded attention, drawing the observer's gaze *because* they were different, simple, yet unnatural.

Still, he's quite beautiful, but in a haunting kind of way, Eryl thought, *he's thrilling, almost frightening when he stares at you with intensity, as if he can stare through you.*

Realizing she'd been staring at him in silence for far too long, she felt embarrassed and said "I'm Eryl," then decided she'd turn her embarrassment back toward him, "they don't teach the Hü anything about Rubicund biology?"

"No," Day replied.

"Well, we'll just have to see what we can do about that," Eryl said, once again flashing her coquettish smile. The smile Day returned told her that he knew she was teasing him again but his eyes hinted that he knew she meant it, just a little.

***

As the light began to wane on that dawn's harvest, Day found himself a few fruit shrubs distance from Eryl. He'd been positioning himself close to her most of that dawn's afterapex harvest time. He told himself it was part of his current mission to keep track of all newcomers to the plantation. He'd almost convinced himself of that when Eryl once again spoke.

"I understand that it can be quite dangerous to be in the fields after dark," she said.

Day was somewhat stunned that she was again addressing him considering the many other fruit harvesters around them but soon noticed that most of the others were already leaving the marsh as the light ebbed.

"It's easy to avoid the firewasps if you're alert," Day answered, and then he added, "It is time to leave the marsh though."

"Well, I wanted to see a swarm at least once in my life," Eryl said.

"Not up close you don't," Day warned.

As Eryl and Day waded through the marsh they pushed their floating fruit baskets ahead and toward the nearest of the wheeled, heavy freight vehicles waiting on the trail that bisected this part of the plantation. Once they reached the vehicle, they deposited their baskets with the Lehu loaders and began walking west, toward the worker tenements and out of the plantation.

"If you were serious about wanting to see firewasps, there is a place just a short distance from here to watch them in safety," Day said, breaking the silence of the last few degrees.

"I'm always serious," Eryl answered and a moment later added, "even when I'm joking."

Eryl's quip brought a slight chuckle from Day. He realized that the last time he'd laughed was when he was in Far's office. That was just a few syphi ago and yet it seemed the entire world was some new strange land and he but a lost sojourner in it. Day looked up at the diminutive crescent of Sis just past apex in the sky but headed toward its own setting, following the sun now masking half its diameter with the horizon.

"Well?" now Eryl broke the silence.

"Well what?"

"Are you going to tell me where this place is that I can watch the firewasps?" Eryl asked.

"Follow me," Day said.

Day veered off the path and toward one of the many hills that bordered the plantation. Soon the two were trekking through the short grass and up the shallow slope of one of those hills.

"Aren't you afraid you'll run across another of those vipers in these weeds?" Eryl asked as she scanned ahead in her path for any such movement.

"No, the flicker rats on these hills eat them," Day said.

"Rats? Are you serious?" an alarmed Eryl quizzed.

"Even when I'm joking,"

Eryl sighed a little in relief and said, "Oh, aren't you a clever sack."

"You think I'm clever?" Day continued to poke fun, "You are very perceptive."

"Oh, trust me, I see how you are," Eryl quipped back.

A few degrees later they reached the summit and turned to see the plantation arrayed below them. Three schools of firewasps were just entering the grid of bloodfruit shrubs from separate sides. Like glowing yellow-gold rivers, they moved through the rows of shrubs, the streams often halting and oscillating in width as individual wasps left the school to fly in and out of the rows as they gathered nectar.

A sky full of stars welcomed the full first moon, which was just beginning to rise. The last vestige of the sun's disk was vanishing beneath the opposite horizon. Day looked at the sparkling yellow-gold schools of wasps and realized how similar the color of the swarms was to Eryl's bronze skin in the twilight.

"Thank you," Eryl said, "I had no idea how beautiful a field of bloodfruit shrubs full of firewasps could be. How many times have you come up here?"

"Just a few times," Day replied.

As they sat there in silence, Dabrill thought about those previous solo visits he'd made to this spot and considered that this evening the valley seemed more beautiful. He remembered that in those previous trips up here he'd seen more schools of wasps. This plantation was large and the three schools seemed fewer than he remembered. *Was it five schools or six?* Day asked himself in thought. It seemed like this was somehow important. Then Eryl reached out and took Day's hand in hers. He then forgot all about counting the schools of firewasps and just allowed himself to enjoy the view; and the companionship.

"Thank you," Eryl repeated.

***

Veegram Lo glided his S-class craft up to the gate of the Rubicund Eugenics Laboratory. He was fully expecting to be turned away by the Loru guards who maintained the grounds. The orders that no one was permitted to enter the facility had been in place for a century, making it one of those mythical places that everyone had heard of but which few had laid eyes upon. The central structure was not visible from the gate or anywhere outside the high walls of the facilities boundary.

Anticipating that he would be refused entrance, Veegram had used his long travel time to create an elaborate excuse for the guards that he hoped would convince them that he had a legitimate reason for visiting the facility. As the guard stepped from the small guard shack and began to approach Lo's craft, Veegram knew that he was prepared to lie his way into the facility. For a Gru to lie to a Loru would be a small matter compared to the contrary endeavor.

Before Lo could open his mouth to speak, he noticed that the gate began to open and the guard stopped a few steps short of his vehicle. The sharp uniformed sentinel motioned Lo through as the entrance opened wider. It was as if the temporary breech in the once formidable barrier were an absolute invitation to the ex-Chancellor.

As Veegram glided past him, the Loru guard snapped his right forearm across his chest, its angle at a crisp forty-five degrees with the palm down and his fingers pointed toward his left shoulder. It was the classic salute of a military guard to a superior Gru officer. Lo nodded his head to acknowledge the salutation and realized, for the first time since the election, that the Chancellor's emblem was still mounted on the front of his hovercraft.

Veegram was confused. Although he had suspected activity at the laboratory, he had no idea that the guards would let him into the facility unchallenged. He now suspected more than mere activity. *Is the laboratory fully operational?* Lo asked himself, as he hovered along the path that led back to the main entrance to the underground installation.

Soon the tall ferns that lined the path opened to reveal a well-kept meadow with a tidy lawn at its center. In the middle of the lawn stood a single, cylindrical tower. Veegram could see what he estimated to be at least five score suspensor craft parked around the tower. Gliding into an open space among the craft, Lo noticed that several of them were adorned with official tags. Veegram had little doubt now that this laboratory was reopened. *But why?* he asked himself.

As Lo walked toward the entrance of the tower, the two sentries saluted him. He nodded and passed between them and through the automated door, which closed behind him once inside. Now that he was here, he had no idea how to get from the entrance to the underground facility. He stood for a degree to get his bearings.

Veegram was standing in a hallway that seemed to run the circumference of the cylindrical building. Straight ahead of him he could see that there was a metallic column centered within the tower and forming the inner wall of the hallway. Taking two steps toward the inner wall, Lo noticed a vertical crack form on its surface and then widen until he realized it was twin pocket doors opening and leading to an empty center room within the column.

Of course, Veegram thought, *it's a mag-lifter*. Lo had read about the antique mag-lifters many anni prior, during his historical education. They were an old technology, before the discovery of suspensor field mechanics but somehow related. He stepped inside wondering how many furlongs deep the main facility would be.

The pocket doors closed behind Veegram and an image appeared on the surface of the wall of the mag-lift in front of him. Upon closer inspection, he noticed that the image was hovering, floating a slight distance away from the wall and depicting a three-dimensional cartograph of the facility below. The image was divided into segments, each of which contained a small, labeled disc that pulsed with a slow, deliberate frequency.

Veegram continued to study the cartograph for a unit, realizing that the technology was far too advanced to be a century old. *Someone must have updated this facility within the last annum*, he thought. Yet there was a strange oldness to the cartographic image; in particular, the language looked archaic. The labeling of the many areas of the diagram had antiquated spellings, some of them almost unrecognizable to the ex-Chancellor. Intensifying his study of the words, Veegram began to make sense of the odd-looking vocabulary of the cartograph's labeling system.

Lo surmised that, instead of stating your destination aloud, the intention was that the user needed to touch the floating image of the disc that corresponded to where they wanted the mag-lift to take them and off it went. The thought gave Veegram some comfort since he always despised "conversing" with technology.

He then touched the small pulsing image of the disc located in the section of the cartograph labeled as the main office area of the level three administration wing. By Lo's estimation, this was the closest to his present location, as level two did not appear to have an office area and level one was the entrance in which he was now located. The mag-lift hummed and began descending. Rather than wander around in the lab areas where who knew what was going on, Lo decided it would be best to try to get some answers first.

The ex-Chancellor was feeling rather optimistic that whoever was operating this installation beyond the legal authority of the Axis would be forthcoming with those answers. The Loru guards seemed to respect his position. At least they respected the position they *believed* he held, evidence of their ignorance of the recent exigency election.

Three degrees after touching the disc, Veegram felt the mag-lift slow and stop. The pocket doors slid open and he stepped into a large, well lit, oval-shaped chamber with twelve doors lining the perimeter. Locating the door with the word Administrator embossed on its placard, Lo touched the illuminated pad to the right of the door after once again noting the ancient form of the word.

The door slid open and Veegram entered, unnoticed by the heavy set Gru leaning over his desk, examining what appeared to be a handwritten report on the top of a large messy stack of similar leaves. Unhurried by the noise of the opening door or the obvious presence of someone in his office, Anlos Tris eased his gaze up from the report and squinted a little to force his eyes to adjust to the more distant image of the Gru standing just inside his office doorway.

At last recognizing the Chancellor, Anlos sprang to his feet, lost his balance, and fell back into his chair. The startled, chubby little administrator bounded back to his feet and saluted the ex-Chancellor, to which Lo nodded.

"Ch... Ch... Chancellor Lo," Anlos sputtered, "I was not aware that you would be visiting us this dawn. I... I will prepare the staff to greet you at once."

"That will not be necessary," Veegram said, trying to calm the nervous subordinate, "this is an unofficial visit. I just came to see how things are proceeding."

"Very well, Your Excellency," Tris replied, "we are ahead of schedule for phase two implementations."

"Really?" Veegram asked, attempting to sound pleased, "how far ahead of schedule are we?"

"At least a syphus, as few as eight or nine dawns," Anlos answered.

"As much as a syphus plus two dawns ahead of schedule, you say?" Veegram could see this administrator could be manipulated into divulging a lot of information.

"Affirmative, Your Excellency," Tris replied, beginning to be calmed by the positive tone that Veegram was projecting.

"So, phase two could start as early as?" Veegram asked, leading the administrator to reveal additional information.

"As early as two first moons from this dawn, Chancellor Lo," Anlos responded with obvious pride.

"We may want to advance the schedule of phase two then," Veegram said as he continued in his pursuit of information, "with whom should we talk to get that done?"

Anlos tilted his head a little and let out a nervous chuckle. Then he began to again look nervous, "I don't understand what you mean, Your Excellency."

"It's simple," Veegram said, "If I am to get the schedule moved up, I will need to talk with the individual who established the original schedule."

"Sir, I... I am confused," Anlos said.

"Confused? Don't you know who created the original schedule for the phases of the project?" Veegram asked.

"I do, Your Excellency," Anlos replied, once again quite hesitant and nervous, "the project leader created the schedule when he reopened this facility."

"Excellent," Veegram replied, feeling he was about to get the answer for which he'd been looking. Then, noticing the confused expression on Anlos' face, he asked outright, "Can you give me his name?"

"Sir, my written orders have come to me bearing the seal and signature of the Chancellor General. Aside from that, I have often received direct orders, via transceiver communication," Anlos answered, then added, "*you* gave the orders, Your Excellency."

***

After walking Eryl back to the feminine harvest workers' residence hall, Day made his way back to his living quarters. As he opened the door to the small government supplied accommodations, Dabrill was certain that he was in the best spirits he had known since arriving in the Southern Council lands. He found himself whistling an old Lehu drinking song as he tossed his lock-pin on the small table and turned toward the washroom. Day came to an abrupt halt in both his steps and whistling.

Chief Inquisitor Tarr was sitting on the edge of Day's sleeping cot having dropped it from its storage nook in the wall. He sat in silence with his flat-brimmed, flattop hat, called a Fatcoin, dangling from the edge of the fingers of his left hand. Sent by General Sul to debrief their new spy, Tarr could not have appeared more bored with the task if he had fallen asleep on the cot while waiting for Day.

"By all means, continue the tune," Tarr said, "Better yet, sing it. I believe the 'Rish of the Central Council end every verse with 'Rumph, Valhalla!' or some such mythical nonsense."

"I take it you're the courier Sul sent to learn what I have discovered in this wretched place," Day said. He then leaned against the wall and crossed his legs in an expression of complete and utter indifference to the unwelcomed intrusion. His calm was genuine, considering his visitor was Loru rather than Gru. While he found it intriguing that Eryl believed the Gru would find it difficult to determine his veracity due to the color of his skin, he had no desire to test it at the present moment.

"If by courier you mean judge of your worth in this assignment, then you are correct," Tarr said.

"I don't have any names for you," Dabrill announced.

"And what rumors have you heard?" Tarr asked.

"Nothing of consequence," Day replied.

"As I told you, I'll be the judge of what is of consequence in this assignment," Tarr said.

"I believe you said you were the judge of my worth," Day argued.

"Grist juice or chryst juice," Tarr answered, "I decide what is important and what we will call it."

"I doubt your superiors in the Gru Council would approve of your calling their life's blood grist juice," Day sniped.

Tarr leaped to his feet and took three of his quick, short strides to Day. The top of his head was even with Day's chest as he wagged his finger in the latter's face.

"Don't mess with me mud-monkey," Tarr said, using the vile, gutter slur in reference to Day's clay-like complexion, "for such sideways threats, I can have you sacked and hauled off to a detention center for a forced debriefing."

Day looked down at the Chief Inquisitor without changing his expression in the slightest. Had any Chu or Lehu called him by that slur, Dabrill would have broken his jaw before the sound of the words had ceased reverberating from the walls of the small room.

"The only rumors are that there are no rebels in the Southern Council lands because there are no infected plantations here," Day said, "No attack on the plantations, no rebels."

Tarr slid the Fatcoin onto his oversized head and said, "I will expect better results upon my next visit."

That rotund little sack of bile is going to be a problem, Day thought, as the Chief Inquisitor disappeared from his door step.

***

The Main Conference Room of the RHIB in the Eastern Steppes

"Am I understanding you, Agent Su?" Sector Chief Thys Gor asked, "You believe that Müur Lesle was unarmed?"

"That is correct sir," Fulong Su said, answering the question for the second time, "Chief Gor, are you okay?"

Fulong had known Agent Gor for the better part of twelve anni, since she was a small child. When Agent Thys Gor investigated the murder of Su's father, he became a close friend of the Su family. That was more than five anni before he had become Sector Chief. In all those anni, she never knew Gor to be obtuse. There was something else going on with him and it was disturbing to her.

"Su, we have a much bigger problem," Thys said, "the biochemistry lab has discovered something in the canister of the phage that Lesle used to infect the plantation."

"You mean the partial canister that was so conveniently found with him?" Su asked.

Ignoring Su's question, Gor said, "The lab has determined that the phage is engineered."

"What?" Su asked, "Genetic engineering is banned and has been for scores of anni. How is that possible?"

"You always ask the sharp questions," Thys said, "While the answer to your pointy question is unknown, the bio-techies assure me that this phage cannot occur in nature. They suspected as much from the beginning of their analysis, well before their test confirmed it, because of its specificity. No organism in nature targets another organism in a way that results in its own destruction. This organism replicates itself until it can achieve its goal, which appears to be complete self-annihilation."

"How would Hü terrorist even begin to acquire enough scientific knowledge to develop such a bio-weapon?" Su asked.

"Again, the bio-techies assure me that there is a singular place on the planet where this could have been accomplished," Gor replied, "the Rubicund Eugenics Laboratory."

"The REL is decommissioned and guarded by elite Loru guards and has been for many anni," Su said.

"And that is the precise reason that the additional data from your investigation has me so concerned," Gor said, "just this past dawn, when I was informed of the probable origin of the phage, I decided to send a covert team of agents to the REL to investigate. They are leaving on the dawn."

"Chief, you have to send me with them," Su insisted.

"I'm glad you think so, Agent Su," Gor replied, "you'll forgive me the use of the minor derogatory phrase but, as the only painted Hü agent on the planet, you're not just going with them, you're going to lead the team."

"That would be an honor, Chief Gor," Su replied.

"Make no mistake, Su," Thys cautioned, "this may be a rather dangerous mission. It seems probable that there are individuals of power and influence involved in this. You and I both now know that this is no simple rebel Lehu plot."

"No sir," Su agreed, "but the likelihood is increasing that someone has worked rather hard to make it look that way."

"More than that," Chief Gor said, "someone wants a war."

"Then it will be our team's first responsibility and duty to prevent that war," Su added.

***

His eyes closed in a state of reverie, Veegram Lo sat alone in the ECR, the Emergency Communications Room of the REL. The dim lighting of the room was pierced by several blinking switches, flashing buttons and glowing dials that created an eerie and varying luminosity through his crimson eyelids. The atmosphere further intensified Lo's already deep state of meditation as he considered the possibilities before him.

Administrator Tris had been helpful. He'd explained that the prior transceiver communication with the individual who was an obvious impostor had come through the ECR. On three separate occasions, the fake Chancellor initiated a transmission to the central console, the main communications array, which Veegram now sat before.

Lo ended his reverie by opening his eyes and looking at the digital chronograph on the wall of the small room. The digits appeared in green and operated on a twenty-four-cycle system. The ex-Chancellor noticed several chronographs in the facility and all the digital ones were arranged the same. Veegram thought these digital chronographs a little unusual in that they indicated cycles, units and moments without even the spaces for the degrees. The dial chronographs familiar to Lo were newer, having been installed throughout the facility since its re-opening.

What Veegram considered most annoying about the odd digital chronograph in this room was that the color of the digits had not yet changed. Though Veegram anticipated that the color of the digits would change to red at apex, it was now one past apex and the digits were still green. Anlos Tris earlier told Veegram that all three of the previous communications from the impostor Chancellor had come when the digits were red on the chronograph. *Does the transmission cause the digits to change color?* Veegram thought, wondering if he had misunderstood what Tris had told him.

Veegram looked around the small room at the many electronic devices crammed into its space. He noticed a small depression in the countertop toward his left and thought that its placement seemed to be at odds with the general arrangement of the ECR. Scanning the remainder of the countertop, he noticed an identical depression to his right. Lo moved his chair closer to the main console and studied the depressions. They were spaced a little more than a shoulder's width apart and were difficult to see, even when looking right at them and with the acute vision of a Gru.

Unable to discern the meaning of the shallow depressions, Lo continued looking around the ECR, admiring the technology present in the small space. The terminals seemed at least as advanced as anything in Capital City. This was a fact that would not have surprised Veegram had he not known the facility to have been decommissioned for more than a hundred anni. *They must have done some serious renovations when they reopened this place,* Veegram thought.

Out of place among the technology of the room, Veegram noticed a small portrait of an elder Lehu affixed to the wall. There was writing on a plaque underneath the image. The ex-Chancellor rose from his seat and strode the three steps until he stood before the wall with the image and plaque. Once again, Lo found that the characters on the plaque where unusual and antiquated. Although the last word appeared to have been defaced, he managed to decipher those that were still legible.

Douglas A. Langstrom, Director of... of what? the REL? Veegram thought. He strained to see under the defacement but the best he could determine is that someone had written a curse word over the original.

Veegram touched the portrait, which was covered in glass. He felt the rippled surface, which somewhat distorted the image. The glass covering also seemed to be thicker near the bottom. As Lo removed the pressure of his hand from the glass, he heard a slight click and saw that one side of the portrait moved away from the wall. The ex-Chancellor used his forefinger and thumb to swing the portrait further out from the wall.

Behind the portrait, Lo saw a recessed panel, which was an obvious doorway to a further recessed compartment built into the wall. The sight of a grid of numbered buttons and a lever informed him that the door to the compartment was locked, or at least was meant to be locked. Veegram calculated that he could never know even the correct number of digits to enter, much less the sequence. *A clever lock,* he thought. Then, considering the possibility that the compartment was not locked, he grabbed the lever and swung it down.

With the clink of the mechanism inside, Veegram knew that he was either quite lucky or the individual who last used this compartment was unconcerned if someone, or maybe anyone, opened it. The contents of the compartment were more cryptic to Lo than the existence of the vault. He found a box with a hinged lid, constructed of a material with which he was unfamiliar. The dull gray exterior of the box looked ragged and rough with a frosted appearance, yet it felt smooth, even slippery, as if a micro layer of oil hovered a hair's width above the surface.

Veegram felt the need to cradle the box in both hands to avoid it slipping out of his grasp.

Lo walked back to the chair and sat down, the odd box still in his hands. Lifting the lid, Lo found what appeared to be four dozen rose gold rings and two platinum ones arranged in five neat rows of ten inside the box. *Adornments?* Veegram thought.

The ex-Chancellor studied the rings for several units; removing and replacing individual ones after looking each over thoroughly. He noted that each of the rose gold rings had numbers. *Some sort of dating system*, Veegram thought, but he could not understand it. On the first platinum ring, he discovered the engraved words 'Access - Archive' and on the second, he found the words 'Access – Journal'.

Veegram glanced up at the chronograph noticing that it was now thirteen and thirty, or one and a half cycles past apex, but the numerals were still green. Then Lo again considered the depressions on the countertop in front of him. Suddenly inspired, he took the archive-labeled ring from the box and placed it on the left depression. Nothing happened. Then he moved it to the right depression nothing happened. Replacing the 'archive' ring, Veegram repeated the process with the 'journal' ring. Again, nothing happened.

Dejected, he turned the ring over in his hand studying it with intensity. At last, he slipped the ring onto the middle finger of his left hand as he continued to ponder the meaning of the rings and the depressions in the counter. *Perhaps there is no connection*, he thought. Disappointed, Veegram sat in a state of semi-reverie, further contemplating the problem until the chronograph displayed fourteen cycles and ten units. Looking at the digits, he noticed they were still green.

At last, Veegram decided that the problem had defeated him and he placed the box on the counter. Feeling his age, he put his left palm on the counter to assist his legs as he stood. An abrasive buzzing sound preceded a flicker of light that materialized into a three-dimensional message in front of Veegram.

The projected message was soon followed by an audio version of the same: "Error, unable to read multiple data disks. Please reposition your right hand," the synthetic but pleasant feminine voice announced. Veegram looked at the box of rings and realized that he'd placed it on the right depression of the counter. Then he looked at his left hand and discovered he was still wearing the platinum journal ring and his hand was on the left depression of the countertop.

Veegram Lo lifted his left hand and the image disappeared. Then he smiled, opened the box and grabbed a random rose gold ring. He placed the ring on his right hand and then placed both hands on the corresponding depressions on the counter. Now the image displayed an announcement, again reiterated by the synthetic voice, "The journal files encoded on the engaged data ring have been declassified by authorization of Douglas Langstrom. Required passcode verification and identification is hereby overridden."

***

Veegram Lo was exhausted after his many cycles of viewing just a small portion of the journals of Doug Langstrom. He'd returned the ring box to the vault behind the portrait and was sitting in the chair and considering what he'd learned when Anlos Tris walked into the ECR.

"Your Excellency," Anlos began, "you must be famished. Please follow me and I will take you to one of the dining halls we have open. We also have a rather good stock of bloodwine, Excellency."

Veegram looked at the chronograph on the wall, noting that the digits were still green. From the journals, he now knew why the digits would turn red, but did not know the precise moment they would do so.

"When will the chronograph digits turn to red," he asked.

"It's a little different each dawn," Anlos answered, "but I think that this dawn it will be about thirty units from now."

"Have some of your team remove the insignia from my vehicle," Veegram said, "then assemble the entire facility in...Do you have a room large enough for all the personnel?"

"Yes, Your Excellency, we have a staging and storage area on level one," Anlos replied, then added, "we can have your vehicle brought there through the receiving access lift."

"There is another entrance to this facility?" Lo asked, somewhat surprised.

"Yes, Your Excellency, the entrance is large but well concealed when it is closed." Anlos answered.

"Yes, bring my vehicle into storage as soon as possible," Veegram said, "It is imperative that it be secured within the facility before the digits turn red this evening."

Seys

"A frightened Gru is like a hungry shark; neither seems malicious till you're swimming with it."

Eryl Syz

Day realized that, for more than a month now, he had not wanted to leave Eryl's side, nor she his. Against all odds and the very foundation of laws set forth by the Councils more than a millennium ago, the two were falling in love. If not for two additional visits by Tarr, whom Day managed to dissuade with clever talk, he would have all but forgotten the mission to which General Sul had assigned him. Likewise, Eryl had blocked from memory her worries of eventual discovery and a return to Capital City to serve out her dawns as a concubine in Silas Mis' harem.

So, it was a shocking awakening to the young lovers on the dawn that Silas Mis paid a visit to the same plantation in which they labored. Accompanied by Erol Syz as his personal Chief of Security, the new Chancellor General was touring the four Council regions. It seemed to all who witnessed his various stops and speaking engagements that the Chancellor was campaigning.

Propaganda! But to what end? Day pondered as he stood watching the new Chancellor make his way to the temporary dais. The stage had been erected on a nearby vantage point so that Mis could better deliver his unannounced speech. *All the better to look down upon his subjects*, Day thought.

"What do you think his game is?" Day asked, turning toward where Eryl had been picking fruit a few moments before.

Day then saw something he had not seen in Eryl: *fear*. She was hiding behind a bloodfruit shrub, her eyes wide and Day thought she might be shivering. She looked at Day and motioned for him to join her behind the shrub.

"What is wrong?" Day asked.

Eryl grabbed Day's wrist and pulled him to her at first into a brief embrace and then holding him a little aback but still within a whisperer's distance. The two had never shown such display of affection in public. The increased tension of their closeness caused her lips to tremble as she began to speak in her soft voice.

"There are a lot of things you don't know about me," Eryl said, "much too much to tell in such a short time as we now have."

"Short time? What are you saying?" Day objected to the implication her words conveyed.

"I have to leave this place now," Eryl said, "I cannot ask you to come with me because it would be death for you if you are found assisting me. I am a fugitive."

Day glanced toward the knoll on which the plantation manager was now giving an impromptu introduction of the Chancellor General. The plantation laborers were making their way out of the marsh and toward better vantage points from which to hear the forthcoming speech.

"Fugitive or not, if you leave me now, you will condemn me to a more painful death of spirit than any such amoral sanctioning of execution ever could," Day said, "let's get out of here now."

The knowledge of Day's commitment to her produced a loving stare at his handsome face and a greater desire to never leave his side. Then Eryl said, "Okay, we'll leave together, but not yet. First, I need you to do something for me."

"Anything," Day replied.

***

This was the crucial moment of the operation. Agent Fulong Su's team had trained for three syphi for this event. Fulong could see the main entrance to the REL through the infrared viewer she held to her eyes. The two guards stood statuesque and oblivious to the plans of Fulong's team, two of whom were now advancing from the rear of their position. With the quiet of transmission silence being in effect, Agent Su could hear the sound of her own heart pounding in her ears.

Slow and steady, Su thought, *don't be too eager*. The two agents were now almost upon the guards, their stun batons at the ready. To her amazement, Su watched as an ornamental shrub moved and then stood upright behind the agent advancing toward the guard on the right. A moment later, she saw a second ornamental shrub on the left do the same. Agent Su was flabbergasted. *This can't be! They know we're coming*, she thought.

"Abort! Abort!" Agent Su yelled into her transmitter, breaking transmission silence. She continued to watch in horror as the two agents, slow to react to her abort command, were taken by the shrubbery that had now become armed guards attacking from their flank.

"Yellow team is down; green and red teams fall back to safe position one," Agent Su commanded as she rose from her prone position to make her way to the prescribed safe position one, which was three furlongs south of the perimeter fencing of the REL.

As she turned, Fulong was met with the electric snap of a stun baton hitting its mark a few fingers below her throat. Just before blacking out, Fulong Su saw the fierce, lavender eyes of the Loru guard. His eyes shimmered in the dim light of Sis, enchanting her, almost as if those orbs alone induced her into the gloom of unconsciousness.

***

It was three before apex when Agent Su awoke, groggy with the aftereffects of the stun baton. She realized she was lying on her back and opened her eyes and saw the twin-pupiled, yellow irises of an elder Gru staring at her. Startled, she tried to twist away from his steely yellow-orbed stare. Upon trying to spring up from her vulnerable position, Su felt that her wrists and ankles were restrained.

"Good, you're awake," Veegram Lo said as he moved back from leaning over Fulong, "Don't be alarmed Agent Su. The restraints were for your safety."

Ex-Chancellor Lo then motioned to the guard standing on the opposite side of the gurney. The feminine Loru began removing Fulong's restraints. Agent Su sat up on the edge of the exam table on which she'd been lying. She rubbed the spot on her upper torso where the stun baton had earlier made contact.

"Who are you?" asked Su.

"My name is Veegram Lo," said Lo.

"Chancellor General Lo?" Agent Su asked, then corrected, "I mean former Chancellor Lo?"

"The same," Veegram answered.

"Where is my team?" Su asked.

"Most of them are by now eating an excellent pre-apex meal prepared by the fine chef of this facility," Lo replied, "one of your agents suffered a broken arm while resisting arrest and he is in another room of this infirmary but is expected to be good as new before long."

"Why were we arrested? Why did you re-open this facility? What are you doing here?" Su began firing questions at the ex-Chancellor.

Undaunted by her rapid-fire cross-examination attempt, Veegram seated himself on the lone stool of the exam room and stared at his would-be interrogator. He could see she was a painted Hü and knew that any interrogation he might pursue of her would be compromised by her rare skin color.

Lo admired her for a moment, watching her unusual blue eyes focus on him with a penetrating concentration, studying him as he studied her. Lo could tell she was intelligent both by her questions and by the way she stared back at him. *I see no fear*, Veegram thought, *she is a rare breed.*

Since he had already interrogated the other members of her team, he knew that his best approach at forming an alliance was to trust Agent Su by telling her the truth. Veegram thought it would encourage the trust he sought to establish with Su if he were to indulge his usual habit of presaging an uncomfortable truth with a personal story.

"You know," Lo began, "I once saw a painted Hü like you. I was traveling in the western fringes of the Savannah, near where the Lava Flats begin. There was a young, masculine, painted Hü hiding behind a bone shrub but not doing so very well, considering how white those shrubs are. Have you ever seen them?"

Agent Su shook her head to indicate she had not. She realized that the slight movement of her head made her feel both dizzy and nauseated. *Aftereffects of the stun baton*, she thought.

"I suppose they don't have many bone shrubs in the Eastern Steppes. In any event, when he realized that I had noticed him, the young Lehu decided to start running across the Lava Flats, away from me. He couldn't have been more than twelve or thirteen anni of age. I yelled for him to stop but was afraid to try to run after him. I sometimes have bad evening visions about how he must have died somewhere out on those Lava Flats, alone and afraid of the big scary Gru who had startled him," Veegram paused his story, looking pensive.

"I don't understand the point of your story," Agent Su said.

"There are two points, Agent Su. The first is that I once saw another painted Hü. The young Lehu looked much like you with two notable exceptions: He was a masculine child and his eyes were brown, not the crystal blue that yours are. As I said, I still have haunting evening visions of those innocent, frightened eyes; though, I admit, yours are far more hypnotic."

"And the second point?" Fulong asked, a little annoyed.

Veegram pointed to the chronometer on the wall, "Do you ever think about the future?"

Fulong looked at the chronometer and said, "Sure, I guess."

"The second point is that, much as the moment hand moves six degrees of arc in every moment as it rotates around the face of the chronometer, we are always just six degrees from the future. We live moment by moment moving six degrees into the future with every tick. It cannot be overstated that we are forever separated from the future by a mere six degrees of arc. We live in the present but look to this future that is always a moment away. Of the four hands on the face of the chronometer, we are living by the one that moves the fastest, the moment hand.

"One moment I saw a young painted Hü, then he was gone, just a haunting memory of the past. Millions of moments later, I now look upon another painted Hü. Rather than taking an opposing path toward our future, I am hopeful that you and I may walk a parallel path; a path of moment by moment steps into the future."

"Are you going to answer my questions?" asked Su.

"For the first answer, you were arrested because we believed you were sent here to assassinate us. As to the second, I claim a technicality in that it was a forgery of my signature and seal that opened this facility, so it was not me who did it. Though I did not re-open it, I believe I know the reason for the re-activation of this facility," Veegram Lo answered.

"Then what are you doing here?" Su repeated her third question.

"Why, Agent Su, I suspect that I am here for the same reason you are here," Lo answered, "to prevent a war."

***

Erol Syz scanned the crowd of plantation workers gathered at the foot of the small, berm-like knoll from which Silas Mis was now speaking. He took his position as Chief of Security serious, despite the loathing he had for his employer. This crowd seemed typical of the many plantations they had visited over the last two syphi, none of them warranting any apparent need for a security detail.

As Erol looked over the crowd, a selfish part of him hoped, as it often did, that he would see some sign of his sister. He'd thought about what he would do when he did see Eryl's face among the many of the audiences. Would he be able to find some way to warn her or distract Mis until she could get away? Would his actual presence ensure her ultimate capture? He hoped in fear for a glimpse of his sibling.

As Erol deliberated the remote possibility of sighting his sister among hundreds of plantation workers, he noticed a figure moving through the crowd with deliberate purpose. Through an inherent intuition, Erol recognized the individual as a painted Hü, though he had never met a member of the subspecies. *A rare breed*, Erol thought.

Erol admired the confident movements of the young Lehu. His randomized, though purposeful zig-zag path through the packed Lehu, Chu and Loru throngs seemed effortless. He watched the painted Hü glide through them with graceful ease, as if moving through nothing less yielding to his presence than a field of tall grass. The approach of the youthful Lehu seemed aggressive, yet without malice. His movements seemed intent upon gaining the notice of the chief security officer without garnering undue anxiety of the same. *A very rare breed*, Erol thought.

Erol raised his wrist to his face and spoke into the small transmitter located on his chronograph, "Incoming potential threat, thirty degrees west of apex."

"Officers moving on intercept now," the deputy security chief reported, acknowledging the alert via Erol's earpiece receiver.

"Do not harm him, he is unarmed," Erol ordered.

"Understood," responded the deputy security chief.

Half a degree later the officers had closed upon the Lehu, who was still moving at a steady pace toward the portable dais from which the Chancellor was now speaking. The officer who was nearest Day extended his hand toward the arm of the Lehu, intent upon securing him to be led away for interrogation but found himself grasping at the air. No more than a few arms length's distance from the Lehu himself, Erol watched in amazement. *How could a figure so distinct in this crowd just vanish?* the security chief wondered.

Erol felt the presence of someone standing behind him on the dais. He spun around and was, for a moment, frozen by the sight of the eyes of the painted Hü. He noticed that his eyes were a brilliant, crystal blue, which was contrary to everything Erol had learned about the ultra-rare splinter species of Lehu. "The red Lehu have brown eyes, like the majority of the Hü," his educators had informed him with their usual confidence. *A unique breed*, Erol thought.

Although he offered no resistance in his obvious surrender, Erol pinned Day to the dais floor and secured his arms behind his back. Two security officers then led the captured Lehu away. Erol looked at the Chancellor and gave him the all-clear signal. The Chancellor continued his speech with a small joke about the minor disturbance behind him. The chief security officer then watched the deputy officers escort the detainee to the security vehicle. *That should be an interesting interrogation*, Erol thought, knowing he would be conducting the interview after the event concluded.

***

Just Outside the Western Capital, in a Secluded Hovel

"I am not sure that we should be taking advantage of the present situation. Something doesn't feel right about it; we know that the Resistance was not responsible for poisoning the bloodfruit," said Ang Obryn. The tall, large-framed, light-skinned Chu commanded attention whenever he spoke. His baritone voice reverberated within the confines of the small building in which the leaders of the Western Alliance of Rebels were now meeting.

"If we don't seize this opportunity now, another may never come our way," said Jo Sephira. The young Lehu stood facing Ang on the opposite side of the octagonal table near the center of the structure. A small sonaluma hung from the ceiling, its light illuminating the well-worn cartograph that was arrayed upon the table around which most of the group were gathered.

"If we attack the armory first, we can capture a lot of weapons for the rebels and keep them out of the hands of the security forces," said Fran Syk an older Lehu to Jo's left. Jabbing his finger onto a spot on the cartograph lying on the table before him, he continued, "the Chancellor General is touring the other Council jurisdictions with half the security forces of Capital City. They'll never be this vulnerable again."

"It's too simple," said a voice from a dark corner of the room, "it could be a trap set to lure us into attacking. Our Loru allies inform us that there was a synchronized release of phage all over the planet yet we are in total darkness with regards to the source."

"It's clear that someone wants a war between the Hü and the Rubicund," Ang said.

"*We* want a war!" Jo exclaimed.

"Do we?" asked the voice of the speaker hidden in the shadows, the one visible sign of his presence being the occasional glow of the end of a vapor-tube, "Do we indeed want to spill the blood, break the bones and cut the sinew of the Rubicund?"

"Yes!" Jo answered.

"Do we also want to see them do the same to us, our mates and our children?" asked the voice from the fringes of the light cast by the sonaluma.

"What?" Jo asked in reply.

"You see, it is one thing to want to destroy your oppressor but another to understand the price. It is one thing to want a revolution but another to pay the blood-debt of that revolution," then, out of the shadow he asked, "Are you willing to mortgage your blood and the blood of your loved ones for your revolution?"

"You sound like a coward," Jo said, eliciting gasps from some in the room who knew the unseen speaker.

The figure leaned out of the shadow revealing the silken brown face of the Chu, Farlay Singh. Far took a last draw from his wasted vapor-tube and extinguished the butt on the floor of the shack. Then he looked at the young, brash Lehu.

"Perhaps," Far said, "or perhaps I'm old enough to know that it is wise to exercise caution when our lives are at stake."

"Far, you know that our lives *are* at stake, whether we attack the capital or not," Ang said, "the intentional infection of the bloodfruit crops with the phage is a terrorist attack. It's just a matter of time before we end up imprisoned, or worse. The Gru can survive without the Hü or even the Loru. They cannot survive without chryst."

"I am just trying to illustrate that we could be trading the relative peace and security of our present situation for something much worse," Far continued, "yes, we live in a caste system. But what does that mean? It means that we provide for those beneath us and above us. The lower we are, the more need we have and the less we have to provide for those castes above us. The fundamental task required of the Lehu is that of manual labor, the harvesting of food. The Lehu pick fruit and vegetables, sow and reap grain. They also farm the coastal fisheries. They do all these to provide food, both for themselves and the higher castes."

"Of course, we do," Jo interrupted, "without us Lehu, you'd all starve to death."

"Well, we might at least be forced to forage for our own food," Far countered. Continuing, he said, "The Chu, in general, are tasked with the administration of the consumer infrastructure. We keep the schedules, do the accounting and engineering. On occasion, we even run some of the food and textile processing plants,"

"But the Loru are more often found in the management positions," Fran Syk interjected.

"True," Far agreed, "the Loru are the managers and soldiers and civil officers. The Gru are the leaders, both of military and civil matters. They require one thing from the lower castes even more than food: chryst."

"What you have described is the most perfect form of slavery ever known," Ang said. The discussion had brought a form of enlightenment to Ang. He now felt the course they were on was irreversible, regardless of the previous reservations he might have held about a first attack.

Far's glance snapped back to Ang. The statement surprised him. It seemed at odds with his personal view of reality.

"Slavery implies a lack of freedom," Far said, "we are free to travel where we want, meet with whomever we want. We are even allowed to form peaceful protests against things we see as abuse or as an injustice."

Far lifted first his right arm, then his left, turning to look under each. He then lifted his right foot, followed by his left foot, tilting his head and looking at his ankles.

"I see no chains," he said, eliciting some gentle laughter.

"But do you *feel* the chains?" asked Ang.

"What do you mean?" Far questioned.

"I say the unseen chains hang heaviest of all," Ang began, "the Lehu are chained to the land and the seas; they cannot move far from them due to the weight of their shackles. We Chu are chained to our desks, our laboratories and our algometers, mixing the formulae and crunching the numbers.

"The unseen links of the invisible chains of the Lehu and Chu were all those education courses we accepted into our minds as eager, even *senseless* students of the vast government mechanism. Do we believe, in all honesty, that we Lehu and Chu are at all prepared, much less educated, for greater aspirations? I was never offered a curriculum entitled *How to be a Chancellor General*. Were any of you?"

The others, including Farlay, shook their heads.

Ang continued, "You think because the leaders of this society pay you wages in the form of the basic needs of life, that makes you free? Not in the least! In dawns of old did masters starve their slaves? Did masters allow their slaves to go naked and sleep in the dirt? If the slave got sick, did the ancient masters just let him die? The slave was the owned investment of the master. Does an owner hate the property he purchased? No! Though he may try to obtain his property at the most opportune price, he will by no means discard that for which he paid *any* price."

Several of the rebels shook their heads, agreeing that it would be not be logical for an owner to neglect their property so much as to let it become useless.

"I propose that the present masters, the top-level Gru, have purchased their property at a low price indeed," Ang proceeded, "They have purchased us by the wealth of the commune. As example, when a Lehu net-fisher, or bloodfruit picker gets sick, they are cared for in health wards by the Loru Health-Givers, via the hands of Chu Re-Nurturers. For another example, should two Hü strive over some disagreement, the Loru security officers and the Gru courts will settle the matter. These are good things. We can all agree: the wealth of the commune is better than the wealth of the individual. But this system is good for *all* only if *all* participants can participate at *all* levels."

Ang concluded, "It is the most perfect form of slavery to convince the slaves that they are mere links in the chain of the communal society, when they are anchored to their positions in the societal chain. It is an immutable truth that the links of a chain cannot rearrange themselves; they are inanimate objects, lacking in even a rudimentary knowledge of their situation. Slaves cannot remove their chains, if they do not know the chains are there; if they do not *feel* the weight."

"Alright, my friend," Farlay sighed, sincere in his acknowledgement of the truth in Ang's passionate speech, "but I want this group to know this: all the rebels, Lehu, Chu, Loru and even the few Gru who are with us from all the Council regions, must march lockstep in the execution *of* and our commitment *to* this action. Otherwise, we will surely be marched to our executions in lockstep."

***

Erol entered the small office of the plant where his deputies had established a makeshift interrogation room. He'd kept Day waiting until three past apex and it was clear that his detainee was agitated.

"It's about time," Day said.

"Do you have someplace to be?" Erol asked.

Dabrill did not answer. He looked at the husky Gru guard, who had been with him in the interrogation room and had remained after Erol entered. Then Day looked back at Erol and asked, "Can I get something to drink?"

"Of course, what would you like?" asked Erol, the sarcasm apparent in his voice.

"How about a bubble water?" Day replied.

Erol looked at Day and believed that he saw no malice or animosity in the young Lehu. He just seemed to be asking for a drink after his confinement of half the afterapex in this hot little room. He appeared to be impervious to his dire situation. Erol picked up the identity card lying on the small table with Day's other personal effects.

"Dabrill Kinselo," Erol said, almost to himself. Then he turned back to face Day, "Do you have any idea how much trouble you're in right now?"

"So, no bubble water then? I'd settle for a plain water, if that will work," said Day, now revealing a little sarcasm in his own voice.

"Listen!" Erol shouted as he slammed his open palm down on the desk to which Day was manacled, "Do you realize that we are under terrorist threat and that you could be treated as a terrorist?"

"For what cause?" asked Day.

"We don't need a cause but if you insist on hearing one, you approached the Chancellor General in a threatening manner," Erol accused.

"I did no such thing," Day objected.

"Deputy Mais," Erol said, addressing the Gru guard, "Did you witness this Lehu approach the Chancellor General in a threatening manner?"

Day looked at the Gru, who nodded in reply to Erol's question. Then he looked back at Erol who, in turn, nodded at his fettered prisoner.

"So, that's how it is, huh?" Day asked.

"Yes, that is how it is," answered Erol.

"What do you want to know?" asked Day, appearing to resign himself to whatever fate the security officer had in mind.

“I want to know why you were approaching the Chancellor in such a deliberate manner,” Erol said.

“Again, I wasn't approaching the Chancellor,” Day reiterated.

“Look,” Erol began, “I think we've established that neither of us believe you and...”

“I was approaching you, Erol Syz,” Day interrupted, then leaned back in his chair as far as his manacles would allow.

Erol stopped cold. He stared at Day for a full unit, trying in vain to determine if he'd met him before. After convincing himself that he was sure he would have remembered meeting such a unique individual as the painted Hü who sat before him, Erol sighed and sat down opposite Day.

“You are a clever and rare breed, Kinselo,” Erol said, “you waited until I knew your name before revealing that you knew mine.”

“It seemed rude to have done otherwise,” Day replied.

“How do you know me?”

“Let's just say that I'm a friend of your mother,” Day answered, then added, “the heat in here is insufferable, it feels like a womb.”

Erol found the words harsh, even biting, as they began to sink in. As he stared at his face and deep into his blue eyes trying to discern his intent, he noticed a slight smile cross Day’s lips and then vanish. *Could it be?* Erol thought, *does he know Eryl?*

“How about that drink now?” Day asked.

Erol remained silent for a few moments. Then, after seeing the fleeting smile once again cross Day's lips, he turned to the Gru guard and nodded his approval for him to get the drink. The guard gave a sullen grumble, uttering something inaudible to the two seated at the desk as he headed for the door.

“Cola bean caramel bubble water, if they have it in the dining hall,” Day said to the guard as the latter opened the door.

Deputy Mais then looked at Erol, who again nodded in approval. As the guard exited and shut the door, his grumblings became louder but no less in vain.

“Is my sister well?” Erol asked, once the guard was gone. This elicited a smile from Dabrill that he now allowed to linger.

***

Why is he taking so long? Eryl thought as she waited in her small, drab apartment located a dozen furlongs from the plantation. She'd packed light bags and been waiting since one past apex. Rising from her chair, Eryl began pacing the small length of the room.

After the first few moments of pacing, Eryl could no longer contain her apprehensions and turned to leave the apartment in search of Day. Just then the door sprang open and the sight of Day stepping through the threshold brought a sigh of relief from Eryl.

"Where have you been?" Eryl pleaded, though all she wanted to do was throw herself on her lover and kiss him. She settled for a tight embrace as she pressed her ear against his chest.

"Easy darling," Day said, "It's okay. Everything went as planned. That wind-sack Chancellor just rambled on so long that it was a while before Erol came to interrogate me."

"You shouldn't be too quick to dismiss that wind-sack," Eryl chided. She then raised her head to look into Day's eyes with seriousness, "if you'd frightened him or any of the Gru guards, you might have been killed for your efforts."

"I'm not afraid of any Gru," Day said.

"You should be," Eryl said, "a frightened Gru is like a hungry shark; neither seems malicious till you're swimming with it."

"I'll keep that in mind," said Day.

"How is my brother? Why is he heading Mis' security team?" asked Eryl as she began to collect herself.

"It's not what you think," Day began, "he was pressed into service in order to better help the Chancellor find you. For some reason, unknown to Erol, the Chancellor believes you are important."

"This is horrid news," Eryl said, "what can we do to help him? Can we rescue him?"

"No," Day answered, "we decided on a better plan."

Eryl stepped back and looked at Day. She stared into his blue eyes trying to discern how she had missed such stoic concentration under the unexpected and difficult situation in which the young Lehu now found himself. A few dawns ago, she believed she was falling in love with Day; now she knew she would never love another.

Eryl smiled with affection and asked, "What schemes have you and my dear brother concocted?"

***

By apex, Fulong Su was relaxing in the cafeteria with her unit after taking a hot shower, donning a fresh outfit of clothing from the REL supplies and finishing a rather large meal. *Veegram Lo was right*, she had to admit, *the cook here is first-rate.*

Veegram Lo entered the cafeteria amid a round of laughter. Veegram surmised that the laughter was at the expense of the young officer with the broken arm by the obvious look of embarrassment on his face. Officer Hart, now mended and returned to the unit, was trying in vain to scratch an itch under the thin brace on his forearm. This prompted another of the masculine officers to make a crude joke about how he might access the tight space.

"I see you are all feeling much better," Lo said, "I trust you found the meal to your liking?"

"You do realize that the RHIB will investigate us as missing if we don't report soon?" asked Agent Su.

"You and your team may leave whenever you like," Lo said, "I would request just one thing of you and you may even decline that, if you so desire."

"And what is the request?" asked Su.

"That I may take you on a tour of this facility," Lo answered, knowing full well that they would never decline such an opportunity. Then he added, "after all, wasn't that your mission; to investigate this facility and find out what kind of gambol is going on here?"

As the unit leader, it was her decision to make. But Agent Su felt the need for the team's consensus to be asked, in part because of her failure, which had led to their capture. She looked at her team one by one and each, in turn, nodded in agreement.

"I guess we're in," Su said.

"Excellent! If you are ready, follow me," Lo said with the exuberance of a child among new friends.

Lo led the group down the long corridor outside the cafeteria. By his gait and the fact that he was silent as he walked, it was clear that the tour was not beginning from their present location.

"This area isn't part of the tour?" asked Officer Hart.

"We're not interested in the General Services Wing of this facility," Su said.

"Agent Su, is correct. This is General Services Wing Three. It consists of a medical service bay, some recreation areas, the cafeteria, laundry services and a vast agroponics sector, which takes up most of the area of each GSW," said Lo.

"There are two more General Services Wings?" asked Vin, the elder Loru officer of Agent Su's unit.

"In fact, there are sixteen General Services Wings in the REL facility," replied Veegram Lo, "At present, we are about a furlong underground and this facility has levels as deep as ten furlongs. Each level has more than ten square furlongs of floor space. If you consider the entire facility a single structure, it is the largest engineered structure on the planet by a factor of about seventy."

The group stepped into the mag-lift and Veegram smiled as he noticed the astonished expressions of his guests when the hovering specter-like cartograph appeared. He touched the spot on the cartographic image corresponding to the main laboratory. The mag-lift hummed and began to ascend. A few moments later the speedy transport slowed and stopped its vertical ascent for a mere moment before resuming its trek to the lab, along the horizontal.

"How many staff are assigned to the REL?" Agent Su asked.

"One hundred and twenty-seven staff and four hundred and eighty-three engineers and technicians," Lo answered. Then he looked at Su and said, "I assume you meant staff and engineering."

"It took over six hundred to," Su paused for a moment, reminding herself not to give more information than she got, "do whatever it is they have been doing here?"

Lo let out a big laugh, realizing it was the first time he had laughed in several syphi. Then he turned to Agent Su and said, "Agent Su, I know why you were sent here. You or your superiors discovered, as did I, that the bloodfruit blight can only be explained by what has been happening at the REL. If you and I are to work together, it must be through full honesty. I am about to show you the answers to the questions you are reluctant to ask. Then, I will show you answers to questions you had not thought to ask."

"Okay," said Agent Su, "you win. Did it take close to five hundred engineers and technicians to create the phage that is being used as a terrorist weapon against the Gru?"

"No, it did not," Lo said as the mag-lift came to a gentle stop and the door slid open.

“Mother Sacker!” exclaimed Officer Hart, as the remainder of Agent Su's team stood gape-mouthed, staring out across a cavernous laboratory. The seven dozen engineers and technicians busy at their workstations seemed like a few tiny insects, providing an infrequent and slight sense of motion to the vastness of technology arrayed before the group.

“Impressive, isn't it?” asked Lo, with some pride though he knew he had nothing to do with the magnificence of the REL.

“What are they working on!” Agent Su demanded.

“At present, this team is working on a cure for the phage,” replied Lo, not offended by Fulong's tone.

“Why would they be working on a cure for the bio-weapon they created?” question Su.

“Agent Su,” Veegram said, “that question requires a rather complicated answer, which I will give in full once I have shown you a few more things. For now, suffice to say that the staff, engineers and technicians are not pursuing the completion of the same project as when I arrived at this facility.”

Lo led the group back to the mag-lift and, once all were aboard, he touched the hovering cartographic image view in the spot indicating the Main Records Wing. Fulong Su noticed that the ex-Chancellor appeared deep in thought, almost trance-like. She wanted to ask more questions now but Lo’s comment about answers to questions she had not thought to ask gave her pause.

“You are hesitating to find the precise questions to ask,” Lo said with some prescience as he roused from his brief reverie.

“Yes,” Su responded.

“Let me help you with a question of my own,” Lo said, “How old would you suppose this facility to be?”

Su thought for a few moments and discovered an apparent paradox. From all she knew, the REL was decommissioned a hundred anni ago, yet the technology present seemed far more advanced than the engineering ability she believed to exist at that time. In fact, the sophistication of the facility seemed more innovative than that of the RHIB, the thought of which made Su envious of the engineers now working at the REL.

“From what my eyes have seen of it thus far, I would surmise that the facility has been renovated within the last few anni, at considerable expense and in incredible secrecy,” Su answered.

“Your response is clever in its avoidance of answering my actual question,” Lo chided, “nevertheless, your supposition is incorrect. This facility has not been altered in any significant fashion since it was decommissioned.”

“That’s not possible,” Officer Vin interjected, “Agent Su is correct, this facility must have been renovated within the last few anni. This degree of erudition did not exist twenty anni ago; much less a hundred.”

“In a sense, you are somewhat correct,” Lo said, as the mag-lift door opened on the primary concourse of the Main Records Wing, “the truth is that the knowledge that created this technology ceased to exist many thousands of anni ago along with the society that created the REL, though they did not call this facility by that name then.”

“What are you suggesting?” Su asked.

“I am suggesting nothing,” Lo answered, “I am about to prove to you that this facility was created by the Society of the Ancients.”

Shev

In a Ditch a Furlong from the Capital City Armory

Ang Obryn found himself in a fight for his life. The raid was not going well. From the first moments of the attack, Ang's unit lost contact with the other five units in the raid. As he and the four Lehu and three Chu that remained of his unit lay pinned down in a ditch near the Capital City weapons depot, he realized the supposed less-than-secure weapons depot had been nothing but a dangle; a trap from the beginning.

"Where are the sonics coming from?" yelled Tam Sloe a Chu of Ang's unit.

"Everywhere," answered Skot Chang, a frightened Lehu near Ang.

"Keep quiet and give me your sonaluma," Ang yelled, deliberate and loud.

"You can't ignite a sonaluma," Hig Joram, an anxious, older Lehu whispered, "they'll use it as a target! The only thing keeping us alive is the dark. As soon as the dawn breaks, we're finished." Hig knew that the special clothing and face paint that the rebels were wearing was providing some measure of protection from the moderate level of infrared vision of the Gru. In the light of dawn or a sonaluma they would be sitting loons.

"Chang, give me your sonaluma," Ang ordered the young Lehu, ignoring the older rebel's warning.

As Chang handed the sonoluminescent beacon to him, Ang grabbed his arm, pulled him in and whispered, "Pass the word, on my mark, cover your eyes, count to five, then retreat fast to the alternate fall back rendezvous point. Be quiet and quick. Got it?"

Skot nodded and proceeded to make the rounds of the other six rebels. In near absolute darkness, Ang pried open the end cover of the sonaluma and pulled the energy pack out far enough to access the wires. Working fast, he converted the circuitry from the typical series pathway to parallel, ensuring an over amplitude of the sonic projectors. *I hope the illumination bulb holds up long enough*, Ang thought.

Ang took a sip from his water-skin and poured a few drops in the energy pack chamber before resealing Chang's sonaluma. Ang quickly calculated how long it should take for resonance and sonic luminescence to occur with the makeshift parallel circuitry. He figured he needed to give the signal to his unit a moment before pressing the igniter switch, then throw the sonaluma a moment after and hope he was right in his calculation.

Ang took a deep breath, pointed his sonic pistol skyward and released three metallic sounding blasts, his unit's standard signal. He counted one, then pressed the igniter switch on the modified sonaluma, counted two and heaved the rigged beacon toward an open area a quarter of a furlong from the ditch and covered his eyes. *Hope there aren't any other rebel units nearby*, Ang thought as he counted three.

No one in the unit finished their count to five. While still in the air, the sonaluma emitted what began as an almost inaudible, ultra-high-pitched whine that pulsed into a crescendo, paused in silence for a milli-moment and then exploded in a penetrating, low-pitched growl as the illumination bulb burst with the light of a hundred suns at apex. For a moment, Ang was sure that he saw the bones of his hand backlit by the brightness of the flash. Most of the unit had just made it to four in their count when the burst happened and, even with hands firmly covering their eyes, they knew the wait was over and it was time to run; their attackers were sure to be blinded.

***

Three Units Earlier, in Another Ditch, a Short Distance Away

Farlay Singh surveyed his unit. It did not take long. Of his original team of a dozen, he was down to two unwounded young Lehu and an older Chu with a hastily bandaged wound to his neck. Far was also injured, superficially, from a spray of gravel to his leg caused by a sonic burst as he and his team sought cover in the ditch. This raid had seen Far's worst-case scenario come true: the Gru knew the attack was coming. They had laid the trap and baited the rebels into it.

As Far and his team hunkered down, huddled close together and pinned into the ditch by acoustic weapons fire from all directions, he heard the booming voice of Ang yelling at his unit over the din.

"At least someone else is still alive," said Lee Port, the older, injured Chu, just before losing consciousness.

Far thought, *He won't be for long, if he ignites the sonaluma he's demanding*. Far wondered if Ang knew that other units might manage to escape if he could draw the majority of the attention of the ambushers. *Would he indeed sacrifice what's left of his unit?* Then Far began to consider if there was some other possible reason Ang would have demanded the sonaluma.

Far pondered the possibilities, looking at his own sonaluma beacon. He turned the device over in his hand and knew that depressing the igniter button would initiate the sonic projectors positioned around the liquid-filled illumination bulb. The sonic pulses would then create a bubble in the liquid that would cavitate and collapse with high frequency, inducing sonoluminescence. The brightness of the beacon was controlled by a simple twist of the housing, which varied the amplitude of the sonic projectors. While studying the sonaluma, Far heard the ultra-high-pitched whine and knew what Ang had done.

Far placed a hand over the eyes of Port, the older, unconscious rebel beside him. He then whisper-yelled as loud as he dared to the rest of his unit huddled nearby, "Cover your eyes, now!" as he covered his own.

After the flash, Far yelled, "Fall back to the alternate rendezvous point," as the now sightless Gru snipers fired their acoustic arms in the general direction of the sound of his voice.

As he and a young rebel named Uron began to lift Port to his feet, Far felt the sharp sting of a high-intensity sound wave as it punched the flesh of his calf to the bone beneath, shattering the latter. The second young rebel turned to help Far but was waived off.

"Get out of here! That's an order," Far screamed, "The infantry will be on top of us at any moment."

Uron turned and he and his brother Aron, the other young rebel, helped the semi-conscious Port escape into the night. Far sat watching them leave him alone in the blackness until his eyes could no longer perceive their forms in the dark. A few moments after what remained of his unit disappeared from his sight, he saw his lonesome shadow, as the light of a sonaluma illuminated him from behind.

Far turned and tried to level his acoustic pistol at the approaching Gru soldiers. His vision blanketed by the Gru's sonaluma, Far did not see the blow coming but he felt the sharp pain and heard the crunch as the boot connected with his jaw, kicking him back into a solitary blackness.

***

Fulong Su startled awake. It was the same dream-specter she'd had for three evenings now. She just could not seem to get the image of Doug Langstrom out of her head. Su had been haunted from the moment that Veegram showed her and her team the images in the Main Records Wing of the REL.

She was haunted by how it was possible that the ancient face looked so familiar and spoke so similar to her own speech. In contrast to the familiarity, Su was just as troubled by the fact that some of the words he uttered were with a strange accent and many of them did not make sense to her. Most of all, she was haunted by the words she had understood and the urgency with which they were spoken.

From the images, Fulong understood that a group called the Dex had attacked the planet. The Dex were superior in intelligence to the Society of the Ancients, something Su found difficult to believe considering the consortium of knowledge evident in the REL. The attackers soon took control of the majority of the technology, crippling the communications of the whole planet. It would all seem like a vicious but otherwise general war story, if not for the fact that Langstrom said the Dex came from space.

Fulong rose from her bed and crossed the length of her private sleeping quarters. Veegram had provided the ample accommodations to her and her team from the abundance of such rooms in the REL. Su dispensed a glass of water from the cold storage nook in the wall. As she drank the water, she closed her eyes and again saw Langstrom's face and heard his voice. *What were 'icy beams'?* Su wondered. Whatever they were, the Dex had used them to destroy the Jynees and half of Aysha.

After the destruction of the Jynees, the rest of the planet realized what the Dex had done and tried to fight back. It was unclear, from the long-ago words of Langstrom, how the Dex managed to release and disseminate the phage throughout the planet but the horrid symptoms and high mortality he described were what came to haunt Su the most. A disease that turns the flesh blue, rots it off the bones and kills more than ninety percent of those infected, was the stuff of dreadful evening visions. Fulong knew that images of Langstrom's descriptions of the untold millions of walking dead, their flesh falling from their bones would haunt her evening visions for many anni to come.

Even before the phage, the Dex tried to gain further control of the planet by attacking the REL, which the ancients called Acer. Langstrom and a team of security officers called the Hüstin managed to stop the Dex from gaining control of the Acer Armory. Then the story of the ancients, as related by Langstrom, became muddled and strange to Fulong.

With the loss of the battle for control of Acer, the Dex seemed unable to complete the destruction of the ancients. Though the image records did not say that the Dex were defeated, it was clear that the threat was much diminished after their defeat at Acer. Nonetheless, the ultimate fate of the ancient civilization was sealed. Weakened and deprived of much of their technology after the attack from the Dex, the ancients were unable to deal with a planet-wide *natural* disaster.

According to Langstrom, the natural disaster had been foreseen long before the Dex, though it was not dealt with as a serious threat. The ancients became overconfident in their technology and deluded themselves in the belief that they would be able to overcome what seemed to be such a slow-moving, natural threat.

The image records of Langstrom deteriorated near the end of that particular segment. The best Fulong understood it, something that Langstrom called a "Cascade Event" happened. A slow eruption of lava from Lostone had produced an enormous atmospheric imbalance. The imbalance caused the planet's temperature to rise, which, in turn, triggered something Langstrom called a "clathrate gun". This changed the oceans and the air with such speed that great numbers of animals and plants began to die.

Although Langstrom's image records ended as the animals and plants began dying off, Agent Su, being the investigator that she was, knew what must have happened next. Langstrom himself had been rather aged at the time he made the last of his image records but it was irrelevant whether he was *the* last of the ancients. When enough of the animals and plants died out, the last vestiges of the Society of the Ancients must have become extinct too. *The last vestiges, excepting maybe Acer,* Su thought.

Fulong had to admit that there were many things that she did not understand about the ancient culture revealed in the images and voice journals. Toward the end of his personal journals, Langstrom became obsessed with returning to his home in the west. He recorded an image of a mountain that he indicated was not far from his home.

The image of Langstrom's mountain was unlike any mountain Su had ever seen. The top and sides were covered in white, a condition Langstrom called 'snow-capped'. The aged Langstrom wanted to get back to his home in time to see the white slopes and peak of the mountain before they disappeared.

Agent Su did not know what 'snow' was but she wondered if it had something to do with the other descriptive way in which Langstrom referred to the mountain near his childhood home. He said it was 'rainier'. *Was it possible that there was some place west of the Great Spirit Mountains where it once rained a white 'snow' onto the tops of mountains?* she asked herself.

Such contemplations helped Fulong forget the darker images and narrative that Langstrom's journals had revealed but her thoughts soon returned to the present as she tried to relate her newfound information to the perils facing her own society. *Could all of this old knowledge inform solutions to new problems?* Fulong wondered. She believed that Veegram had trusted her with the revelations of the REL because he must have believed the same.

Su was now faced with the very real possibility that someone was determined to start a war between the Rubicund and the Hü with the probable intention being the extermination of one or more of the four castes. Fulong regarded the historic images of Langstrom as a warning of what can go wrong in war. In her considered opinion, there was one absolute and fatal mistake made by the Society of the Ancients: they allowed the Dex to attack first.

Fulong returned to bed and tried to rest, finding it futile. As she lay there, staring at the ceiling, she thought about what was next. Veegram had discovered a lot of information and had already thwarted an important part of the enemy's plans. By shutting down the second phase of the plan, Veegram had prevented a second phage from being released. No one was sure of the target of the second biological attack; but the amount of material that was set to be released was staggering. Soon the enemy would discover that phase two was not activated.

Su wasn't sure who the real enemy was but she knew that the team had to find out and prevent them from completing the rest of their plans. The enemy had struck first with the attack on the bloodfruit. That battle seemed to be playing out to a draw, at best. Su was determined to *win* the last battle. It was time to get the help they needed.

Fulong rose from the bed and began donning her clothes. She glanced at the luminescent dial. The unit hand indicated thirty units past midevening. *It'll be thirty units to apex at the RHIB*, she thought.

The unknown aggressors were sure to strike back. Su, Veegram and their small band of Resistance fighters were awoken to the dangers. They knew they needed more leverage and help; a lot of it.

***

Veegram Lo sat at the head of the long conference table looking somewhat pensive as he contemplated Su's question. A dozen REL staff and Fulong's team sat in anticipation of Lo's answer. It wasn't uncertainty about the proper course of action that concerned him. Lo knew that Su was correct: the best way to stop this devastating war was to start a different, unexpected one.

"You know that Chancellor Mis intends on annihilating the Hü," Su said, "I understand your reluctance to pit Rubicund against Rubicund but I can see that you are a good and honorable Gru. You are our best chance at forming a Loru Army capable of standing up to the army now under Mis' control. You are well-liked and trusted. Both Gru and Loru are suspicious of the recent events and the convenience with which Mis acquired his slight majority in the Council vote. Many Rubicund will follow you; Chief Gor will follow you. He's directed more than seventy of his best agents from around the planet to come here to aid in the defense of this facility."

Veegram Lo closed his eyes and sighed. He let the quiet of the room envelop him until he could feel the beat of his pulse in his ear. With each beat, the rhythm continued to slow until he had induced a perfect state of Gru reverie, unaware of the other conference room occupants, present in nothing but his own thoughts.

Once in full reverie, Veegram organized his thoughts, filing the inconsistencies, the coincidences and the intersections of data in his mental library. Once the information was organized and tucked into its proper shelf, Lo could rummage through them at his leisure, the pace of the outside world crawling by in comparison with the speed of his thoughts.

Veegram took his time. There was too much at stake to view any of the information with a cursory eye. As he studied his library, he understood that the inconsistencies, coincidences and intersections were woven together, forming a coherent, almost self-aware tapestry.

First, there was the re-opening of the REL against a century old decree. This was an obvious step toward using ancient knowledge in the furtherance of starting a war. The firewasps that were created in the bowels of the REL a century before had been a similar step, one that was later abandoned or perhaps halted by a prior group of intrepid heroes not unlike those seated around the table now.

Veegram could see that the two events were connected across a hundred anni but was unable to discern the connection with the Society of the Ancients. Lo knew that there had to be a connection across the vast distance of those many millennia. The knowledge of how to utilize the incomparable, sophisticated equipment located at ACER must have crossed that gulf of time by some means unfathomable to Lo.

If those superficial coincidences are interconnected, Veegram thought, *there must be others*. His reverie turned to thoughts of Fulong Su. The painted Hü were a rare breed. He thought it more than mere coincidence or happenstance that a painted Hü could be involved in this. Veegram was not a religious or even spiritual person but he wondered what unseen hand of fate could have brought about his meeting with Agent Su.

Veegram found that he gave an implicit and instant trust to Su from the moment he met her. This was something that it was difficult for any Gru to do. Their inherent nature was one of distrust, often heightened when meeting strangers and more so when the stranger was difficult to read, such as another Gru. Lo supposed that it was perhaps this inability to read the painted Hü child at the edge of the Savannah that impressed upon him so great an emotion when he met Su, these many anni later.

Perhaps there are no coincidences after all, Veegram thought. He did not like the implications. To believe that nothing is by chance meant that there was something ethereal, beyond the physical. Veegram did not like things he could not comprehend with his own senses but even his logical mind knew that Su would play some greater role in the cascading of present events. Whether by blind physical chance or a greater spiritual power, Veegram Lo now knew that he would bind his own fate and the potential success or failure of their small group to Fulong Su.

Officer Vin leaned in, impatient and intent to speak his mind on the matter, but Agent Su, cognizant of the trance-like condition of Lo, waved him off. She had spent enough time with Chief Gor to recognize the reverie state of a Gru. Su knew that deep behind those crimson eyelids, beyond the quadruple, dilated pupils, Veegram Lo was making up his mind. Any Rubicund that arrived at a decision after such a state would never be swayed otherwise. To interrupt such a meditation was beyond rude; it was considered an insult to the Rubicund creed.

Fulong knew that Veegram would have preferred to perform his reverie alone in his own heat room or, under the most idyllic of circumstances, among his closest friends and family. As Su sat watching him, she wondered if he had any close friends. It was true that he was well-liked as the Chancellor General. Although he seemed affable enough, something about the way he talked and the way he held himself made Fulong think he was a loner, always separating himself from the herd. Perhaps this was in order to see the herd with new, fresh eyes.

Having been an orphaned Lehu, worse yet, an orphaned painted Hü, Fulong Su sensed the heart of another outsider. The unbelonging spirit of others called out to her whenever she was near it. *Perhaps he can sense it in me too*, Fulong thought, *was that why he told me the story of the painted Hü child?*

"Thank you for allowing me to meditate, Agent Su," Veegram Lo's words startled Fulong out of her own reverie, "If we are to raise an army against these evil forces, we will need a battlefield leader. We will need someone with combat training. So, I think it is perhaps appropriate for both you and I to get used to your new title, General Su."

As the words set in with the group, Lehu, Loru and Gru alike cheered and lauded the decision in agreement. Su looked around at the ad hoc, preemptive war council and realized that there were no Chu among the group. She could not help but think the absence of any representation from the most populous of all the castes was an ominous sign. She also realized that she could not dwell on such disconcerting thoughts for long; there was too much that lay ahead for this rebel army anti-war council.

***

Three syphi later, in the 2nd District Detention Center of Capital City

"That leg is not healing well, citizen Singh," Agent Nails Castor said, as he entered the interrogation room carrying a little black satchel.

Nails was not his real forename but he had been known by it for so long that no one seemed to know his genuine moniker. A masculine Gru of tiny stature with thick, quad-focal spectacles, Nails had acquired his name through his penchant as an interrogator. Most who knew Agent Castor thought he enjoyed his work a little too much, like many of the interrogators in the Two Double-D Triple-C.

"I don't think the re-nurturers in this facility are trained in the proper techniques for dealing with fractures," Far responded.

"I can assure you that they are quite experienced at setting broken bones. Agent MacIntaw makes sure of that," Nails said, as he placed the little black satchel on the table to which Far had been shackled, "Do you know what name Agent MacIntaw is known by in here?"

Far shook his head. In truth, he did know Agent MacIntaw's nickname. The guards at the Two Double-D Triple-C took some delight in tormenting the detainees by describing the predilection of each of the facility's interrogators.

"I think you *do* know; and I think you also know *why* he's called Mack the Cracker," Nails said.

"Because he likes little salty bread snacks with his bloodwine?" Far quipped.

"Your humor belies your fear, citizen Singh," Nails sneered, "perhaps you will also find it humorous that you were betrayed by one of your own?"

"Is that the best you have to offer? I had already surmised that same thing," Farlay responded.

"Ah, but did you also surmise that our agent, your traitor, executed the remainder of *your* squad soon after you were captured?" Nails taunted, speaking in choir for emphasis.

Farlay fought back a look of disgust. He considered whether this was part of the evil predilection of Nails Castor. *Does he enjoy the mental torture as much as the guards insist he loves the physical torture?* Far asked himself. Far convinced himself that Nails was lying to get under his skin and he smiled, considering it a small victory over his would-be torturer.

"Do you find your situation comical, citizen Singh?" Nails asked.

"Not really."

"I assure you that you will find it less and less comical in the dawns to come. I'm not even going to ask you any more questions this dawn," Nails sneered, "In fact, I don't think I will ask you any more questions for some time, citizen Singh."

Farlay Singh had always prided himself in the fact that he was fearful of few things but the guards of the Two Double-D Triple-C had made sure that he knew the full, black heart of Nails Castor in the dawns leading up to this first interrogation session. Knowledge of what Nails meant by not asking him questions brought a powerful wave of fear cascading through Far's entire body. He shuddered. It was an ever-so-slight tremble but enough to cause a sharp pain in his slow-healing shinbone. The pain made Farlay grimace, which made Nails smile as he opened his little black satchel filled with hurt.

Et

"We hang the petty thieves and appoint the great ones to office."

Unknown Ancient Philosopher

Through her viewscopes, General Fulong Su knew she was looking at the storage tanks but the camouflage was so perfected that it seemed like a mirage among the foliage of the scorpion shrubbery. Even though Veegram Lo gave Su the exact location of the storage tanks in the specific valley filled with scorpion shrubs, a few dozen furlongs from the ancient ruins above the McInau Falls, she still could not quite see the tanks. It was unfortunate for the three Gru guards posted at the site that they were not as well camouflaged.

Fulong's earpiece crackled, "Dart-snipe one reporting, General. I have guard one in my scope."

"Dart-snipe three reporting, General. Guard three in my scope."

After several moments of silence, Su whispered into her transceiver, "Dart-snipe two, do you have guard two in your scope?"

General Su's question lingered in ominous quiet for several moments. *Sack-of-a-dæmon!* Fulong thought. Then she repeated, "Dart-snipe two, do you have..."

"Dart-snipe two reporting. Guard two in my scope," the officer whispered.

"Engage," Su said into her transceiver.

In synchronicity, the three officers squeezed the triggers of their dart rifles, each of which released a quarter molecule-mass of helium gas into the arc chamber. A milli-moment later, an electric arc of the arc chamber converted the helium into plasma. The expanding plasma propelled the microscopic dart down the tungsten carbide coated barrel at more than six furlongs per moment. A moment later, a tiny frangible dart entered each of the guards' necks and dissolved, leaching its fast-acting sedative into the surrounding blood vessels. Two moments later, all three Gru guards were lying in a peaceful slumber.

"Ground units, move in. Tanker craft, move in. Hustle up all groups, we must move fast!" Su ordered into her transceiver as she stood and began sprinting down the shallow slope into the valley. Then she added, "All units activate your personal shields and be careful of the scorpion shrubs; we are not losing a single officer this dawn!"

A few moments later, Su walked toward Dart-snipe two, who was standing with a coy smile visible through the shimmering haze of his personal shield.

"Do you see it?" Officer Vin asked.

Su shook her head; she still could not see anything but scorpion shrubs in the bottom of the valley. Vin stuck out his left arm and leaned to an angle that would have meant his certain toppling over had some object not prevented it. Su now saw the tank because her brain shifted its perception due to the impossible angle at which Vin was leaning while remaining upright. Vin's arm was resting against a large cylinder that seemed to bend the light around itself such that it gave the illusion of transparency; all objects behind it were visible as if the tank did not exist.

"Hart ran right smack into it," Vin said, "almost knocked himself unconscious. Funniest thing I ever saw."

Fulong Su watched as one of her officers found the camouflage control box of one of the tanks' using a magnetic sensor and switched off the device. Fulong could see that the device was a simple field generator no larger than would easily fit inside one soldier's field pack. She then realized how useful such a device might be. Su looked around and found that Vin was now guiding one of the tanker craft as it backed up to the unveiled tank.

"Vin, grab one of the engineers and make sure we take all of these field generators with us," Su ordered, then added, "and make sure they are undamaged!"

"Will do, General," Vin replied, then he turned to a Gru soldier provided from the RHIB by Thys Gor and ordered, "Les, get over here and bring Hart with you, double-time!"

Fifteen degrees later, General Su's entire elite platoon were on their way back to the REL with enough bloodwine in tow to supply a small city of Gru their necessary chryst for several anni.

***

Eryl and Day made their way through the jungle with caution. Though they moved by dawn and slept high in the trees in the evenings, their path was always dim due to the veil of the canopy. The two had now put three syphi between themselves and the plantations and were one syphus deep into the jungle of the

Nicaran Isthmus. If their plan held, they would make their way to the northern coast of the Horn on the Crab Sea within two more syphi.

Dangerous creatures were rumored to live in the jungle causing few, if any, Rubicund or Hü to rally their intrepid spirits enough to venture into the wilds northwest of the Southern Council lands. Eryl had learned additional rumors of the Gru fearing the jungles, believing that phantoms inhabited them; Loru even telling their children chilling bedtime stories about the terrors among the trees. Since Eryl didn't believe in phantoms and thought the stories of creatures to be exaggerated, the rumors made this the safest route that she and Day could take.

On their eighth dawn in the jungle, as they began the middle leg of their journey through the forest and toward the Horn, Eryl sensed they were being stalked. She slowed her pace and allowed Day to come alongside her.

"Someone or something is following us," Eryl whispered.

"At least five stealthy individuals and for at least two dawns now," Day said in a not-so-subdued voice, which caused Eryl to stop and grab his arm to turn him toward her.

"You couldn't have mentioned this sooner?" She asked, surpassing his volume.

"We're unarmed, outnumbered and making our way, almost blind, through an unfamiliar jungle," Day said, "if they wanted to harm us, we would have little say in the matter."

Eryl knew he was right but was not quite ready to let their unknown pursuers believe they were such easy prey.

"Well, I'm sure that anyone who wants to test me will find that this bush-cutter will cleave limb and skull with even less effort than it takes to split vine and shrub," she said, holding the bush-cutter up for any of their unseen stalkers to view. Then she leaned in and whispered to Day, "we have little time to waste; we must be at East Gate in twenty-five dawns."

"What is so pressing at East Gate?" the voice came from behind a tree a few steps to the rear of Day.

Eryl started toward the sound with the intent of confronting whomever was hiding behind the tree. As the source of the voice stepped from his hidden location, Day touched Eryl's arm to prevent her from acting rash.

The ghost-like figure standing before the couple shimmered in the low light beneath the forest canopy. After a few moments, the image of the figure solidified revealing that he was tall and thin but with a sturdy build. He wore a long, dark brown, hooded cloak made of fine woven animal hair. The animal hair held a glossy sheen, as if it were the afterglow of a light just extinguished.

His boots, visible at the hem of his cloak, were made of leather and of exquisite design. A leather strap crossed his chest from his left shoulder and wrapping under the right side of his torso around to his back where it secured a small, tubular pouch. The pouch was covered with a light flap concealing its contents.

In his right hand, which was, like the left, gloved in leather, he held a stave hewn from the resilient heart of a jungle marblewood. The stave was curved with its ends lashed together by a thin, tight-braided cord. Even with the curvature, the stave was almost as tall as the figure who held it. To the sojourning couple, the stave looked like a strange, single-stringed musical instrument to be plucked.

To Eryl, perhaps the most impressive aspect of his visage was that he was many furlongs deep in the jungle and his clothing looked no more fouled than if he'd just donned them after a fresh cleaning. If not for obvious wear marks of long use and a few expertly done repairs to the cloak, his apparel could have been mistaken for new. Something about that caused Eryl to turn and look at Day with an examining eye. *How is it that neither this cloaked stalker nor Day look as if they have walked more than a few dozen steps in this jungle, while I look like a wild boar in its favorite mud pit?* She thought.

The strange figure lifted his left hand and pulled back the hood, which was, until now, obscuring a clear view of his face. Eryl turned her gaze from Day and looked at the face of the stranger. She stood, staring at his face with her mouth agape as a dozen other cloaked figures materialized around them; one by one each removing their hoods.

At last, seeing all the faces, Eryl relinquished a gasp of surprise as if it were yanked from deep within her gut. Embarrassed by her gasping in awe, she covered her mouth with her hand. She could not remember such an expression of astonishment in her life. Eryl realized that she had never seen so many painted Hü. Discounting images in student codices, until a few moments ago, she had seen just one: Dabrill Kinselo. Though none among this group of jungle warriors had his blue eyes, it was obvious that they belonged to the same rare breed of Hü.

"Who are you?" Day asked.

"We are of the Wazhazhe nation," answered the tall figure who'd first stepped into view, "from which of the nations are you and why do you travel with the golden bottle child?"

"Bottle child?" exclaimed Eryl, replacing her embarrassed expression with a bristling one, "What's that supposed to mean?"

Ignoring his own desire to know the meaning of 'bottle child', Day answered, "I am Dabrill of the Lehu and I am traveling with Eryl, of the Loru. We travel together because it pleases us and, in answer to your previous question, we travel to East Gate to rescue her brother. What is your name?"

Eryl looked at Day with some astonishment. She could not understand how he would, with such ease, trust these people with the truth. She thought that perhaps Day was overcome by the sight of so many of his 'kind'.

"My name is Strongbark and you are not Lehu," He replied.

"Very well, Strongbark, perhaps you would care to tell me from which 'nation' I am?" Day asked with his typical facetious frivolity.

"Your command of the Hü language with an accent slanting toward the lower caste, suggests to me that you were reared by what you would call Lehu. Your manner of speaking informs that you spent most of your life in the territories of the Western Council," continuing, Strongbark said, "There is a slight abruptness in the way you cut your words short. I believe you originate in the north and west of Capital City."

"An area populated by Lehu and Chu," Day interrupted, "So you're saying I am a cross between Lehu and Chu?"

Then Eryl interrupted, "I would choose my next words with care, if I were you, Strongbark. I do not believe Day would appreciate derogatory remarks about his mother. Come to think of it, I would not appreciate derogatory remarks about Day's mother," she added, emphasizing her words with a twist of the bush-cutter, which her right hand continued to wield.

"I mean you no insult," Strongbark said in a somewhat more contrite tone, "I assumed you would have realized that you were adopted. A fact of which I am certain."

"Your certainty is so evident that you still have not answered the question," Day sniped, then repeated, "Of which 'nation' am I?"

"You are Sanguine." Strongbark answered.

At the sound of the word 'Sanguine', the other members of Strongbark's group began a soft chant among themselves, each uttering and repeating a single word: "shibwoteth". By raising his stringed stave, Strongbark silenced the whispering with the same abruptness with which it had begun.

"Follow us," Strongbark said as he motioned in unison with his words, "we will take you to the Wazhazhe journeyway cantonment for the evening. You can eat well and get genuine rest without fear of the jungle."

Both confused and intrigued by Strongbark's nonchalant statement of the name Sanguine, Day and Eryl acquiesced and followed the group through the jungle, though the path was at a right angle to the one that they'd traveled for the previous seven dawns. Though they needed the promised meal and the potential of a restful evening's sleep, Day was even more tempted at the possibility for further information.

***

The cantonment was well-disguised as a natural, moss-covered mound about a dozen furlongs' hike from where the Wazhazhe hunting party made themselves known to Day and Eryl. As the couple followed the Wazhazhe into the structure through a double door ingress that sealed the interior from the outer weather, they noticed the temperature difference. The cool atmosphere inside the structure presented a stark contrast to the heat of the outside jungle.

A long dining hall filled most of one-half of the elongated, timber-framed, earthen-clad construction. On the opposite end were triple stacked bunks capable of bedding a group of up to three dozen. In spite of the basic, rustic look of the interior, Day soon noticed the technology present. There were several odd-looking transceivers concealed a short distance from the entry. The lighting was high grade sonoluminescent lighting activated in each area of the structure via infrared detection as an individual moved into the area.

After the Wazhazhe party leaned their stringed staves against the back wall of the structure, they removed their sling pouches and cloaks and draped both over their staves. The sheen that Day had noticed on the cloaks had not yet dissipated. To him, it looked as if a coating had been applied to the woven animal hair that seemed to hold a faint glow, not unlike the afterglow of a smashed firewasp.

The members of the party also wore belts on which were carried various tools, including a compact sonaluma, a knife, and what appeared to Day to be an electric fire igniter of an advanced design unlike any he had seen.

Strongbark watched with curiosity as Day examine the interior of the cantonment with obvious wonder. Then he noticed how Day became more fixated on the walls of the structure, studying them with some intensity.

"They are implanted in the beams, from behind. They cannot be deactivated without tearing the structure apart," Strongbark answered the question Day had not asked.

"Clever," Day responded without looking at Strongbark, "you keep the temperature lower inside so that no one can be lying in wait within without activating the lighting. Then you also hide the heat activated sensors so that they cannot be deactivated."

"You are quite observant," Strongbark said.

"What is the coating on your cloaks?" Day asked.

"We call it Mimic," he answered, "For many annum, we made our cloaks from a synthetic material known by the name. Once we learned how to control its properties better, we began manufacturing a coating that we could apply to some natural fabrics."

Day, Eryl and Strongbark joined the hunting party at the dining table. Two members of the group were preparing a stew-like concoction from some of the vegetation the Wazhazhe had gathered during their foray in the jungle.

"What is your full name?" asked Strongbark as they sat.

"My name is Dabrill Kinselo," he replied, "and, to reply to your previous comment, I knew that I was adopted. My name was already given to me and my parents chose to have me keep it."

"Ah, that makes sense," Strongbark said.

"How do you mean?"

"Dabrill is an ancient word, not used in many anni. It is a combination of two words meaning 'blue skies shine through'. Kinselo is also an ancient word, again no longer in use. It means 'stormy red morning'."

"That's quite beautiful," Eryl interrupted, "Blue skies shining through a stormy red morning. Somehow I don't think you will have such a clever explanation for 'bottle child'."

"You are Sanguine and the people from which you come live west of the Great Spirit Mountains, to the west of the Western Council lands," Strongbark said to Day, ignoring Eryl's comment.

The Wazhazhe who had been preparing the meal, dished bowls of the porridge, distributed morsels of bread no more than a dawn old and poured tankards of wildberry wine for all, including Day and Eryl, then joined the group at the long table. Being quite hungry from the scarcity of food they'd been able to glean during the last few dawns of their journey, Day started to dip his bread into the porridge but was stopped when Eryl grabbed his arm. She nodded toward the Wazhazhe, who were bowed in an obvious gesture of silent supplication. Eryl and Day also bowed their heads and waited until they could hear their hosts begin to stir.

"Thank you for honoring our practices," Strongbark said to Eryl when she raised her head.

Eryl nodded in respect and then began eating, being no less famished than Day. Both found the meal to be quite savory, simple though it seemed. The preparers had used some local spice and several different wild, local vegetables as delicious as they were unknown to the wayfaring couple. They ate in silence for many units.

As most were finishing their meal and a second tankard of wine, Day asked, "So I am not Hü?"

This brought a roar of laughter from the entire Wazhazhe party. Even Eryl smiled at Day's assertion. Noticing from his expression that his young guest was somewhat embarrassed at having asked the question, Strongbark answered.

"I said you were not Lehu because that term implies that you are a lesser Hü. You are not lesser in the same way that your companion is not lower than the scarlet others, which you refer to as greater."

"Do you call the Gru 'scarlet *bottle* children'?" Eryl asked.

"I apologize that I used that term with you, it could be taken as derogatory and, at the least, it is rude to use the term with someone who doesn't understand its meaning." Strongbark said.

"So, if you refer to all Hü, whether Lehu, Chu or painted as *Hü*, then what do you call the Gru and the Loru?" Day asked.

"We do refer to them as Eryl suggests: scarlet bottle children and golden bottle children. We do not mean it in a derogatory manner but we know that it could be understood that way," Strongbark continued to explain, "We refer to all those you call the 'painted Hü' as the Protectors. We refer to those you call Chu and Lehu as the Forgetful Ones."

While Strongbark was speaking, one of the Wazhazhe party retrieved one of the odd-looking transceivers and placed it on the table in front of Strongbark. Strongbark nodded in acknowledgement and said something to him in the Wazhazhe language. He then realized that he had not introduced the party to Day and Eryl; an error he corrected beginning with the one who'd brought the transceiver to the table.

"This is Lightning-Walker; the stout one to your right is Smiling Leopard," Strongbark said to Eryl as he continued the introduction, "standing and puffing at his glo-pipe is Whitecloud; to his right is Falcon-Tongue, his sister,

"To *your* left," Strongbark said to Day, "is Laughing Birch, my sister; to her left is Dream-Talker; the one pouring himself another tankard of wine is Quietstar; to my right is Friendly; to the left of Lightning-Walker is Water-Owl; to his left is Darkeye and the one clearing the table is her mate, Roughbark, who is also my younger brother."

When Strongbark had finished the introductions, he switched on the transceiver and said, "Now, I would like to teach you a secret known to none but the Protectors."

***

Two syphi later, at a gathering near the bay just outside Memfi

As had become his custom during Chancellor Mis' propaganda tour, Erol Syz scanned the horde of onlookers. This time he had a greater sense of foreboding. The recent failed rebel attack on the armory of the Western Council had everyone on a knife's edge.

Erol had also noticed a change in his employer's behavior over the last few dawns. The little he'd overheard seemed to involve a loss of personal wealth due to rebel attacks, at least one of which was located in the northern region of the Western Council's lands. Whatever the cause of the change of the Chancellor's behavior, it had not warranted a new itinerary. Within the next few syphi, the Chancellor would be visiting both the Central Council and the Council of the Eastern Steppes, as he'd planned. This was much to the relief of Erol, considering he had no way of getting a message to Day to change their plan. The plan required the Chancellor's tour to be at East Gate in just eleven dawns.

The Chancellor's entourage stood on a dais on the northeastern shoreline of the Bay of Memfi, at the western edges of the Western Council's plantations. Erol stood near the back edge of the dais, which hung over the water an arm's length beyond the shoreline.

Erol's keen awareness made him the first to notice the movement. It was stealthy and subtle, like that of a pride of scimitars encircling the crowd, as if they were stalking a herd of bald elk. To Erol, the rebel unit's singular mistake was that they were each adorned in identical brown cloaks, which caused the movement to appear less random than it otherwise would have.

As Erol raised his wrist transceiver toward his mouth to alert his crew, the left side of the large assembly had startled and began pressing inward toward the dais. The unmistakable sound of acoustic weapons fire had started a tumult. In chorus, three acoustic rifle bursts erupted from the right side of the crowd. A moment later another two bursts of acoustic fire came from the apex of the semi-circle the crowd had formed before the dais.

Erol managed to see the rebels firing the third series of blasts into the air and was quick to recognize what was happening. *Brilliant!* Erol thought, *they're stampeding the crowd against us*. Most of the security force was situated at the inner part of the semi-circle, near the dais. This meant that they would be snared by the inward-pressing bodies of the crowd. Those on the dais would soon be forced into the water that lay at their backs. Erol realized that the security team would have no choice at that point but to blast their way out through the crowd.

Erol soon found that it was worse than a simple snare. The rebels were continuing their controlled acoustic blasts, as the crowd began to press hard upon the center. He could now see that they numbered a mere half dozen individuals. They were holding ground just out of range of the acoustic pistols of the half dozen security officers on the dais, who were now launching acoustic blasts at the rebels, with no effect.

"Hold your fire," Erol demanded, "you aren't hitting anything at that range." His command came too late as the officers on the dais all but exhausted the power reserves of their pistols before ceasing their futile barrage.

With the cessation of fire, the crowd's panic noises began to subside and then Erol heard the rapid approach of a suspensor craft from behind the dais. He turned and pointed his acoustic pistol at the sound along with the others of his team on the dais. Erol did not discharge his pistol, though the rest of his team exhausted the remainder of their power reserves in an ineffective assault on the shielding of the approaching craft.

Erol had not sounded his pistol because he recognized the driver of the craft as his sister, Eryl. He glanced back beyond the crowd to see that the half dozen rebels were now in a rapid retreat. One of the rebels was back-stepping away but had the hood of his cloak pulled back and was looking toward Erol. The long brown hair of the rebel lapped at his red-skinned face, tussled by the gentle wind.

Though they were much too distant for him to see, Erol knew, without doubt, that this particular rebel had blue eyes.

Eryl slowed the suspensor craft and glided it in sideways; and before anyone else on the dais knew what was happening, Erol leaped to the craft and climbed into the passenger seat as it accelerated away. Silas Mis' pushed his way out of the circle of officers who had surrounded and guarded him. The Chancellor watched in disgust as the siblings cruised out of sight. He continued to stare across the Bay of Memfi for many moments, the scarlet color of his skin masking his rage.

***

"What happened to our original plan?" Erol asked, once he and his sister rendezvoused with Day and the small rebel squad, "I didn't expect to see you until East Gate."

"We had to accelerate and change the plan because the Chancellor is about to return to the capital," Day answered, "and, as you well know, there would have been little chance to rescue you there."

"The Chancellor will be traveling to the Central Council and then on to the Eastern Steppes. He won't be returning to Capital City for several syphi," Erol corrected.

"Brother, we are certain the Chancellor will return to the capital within two dawns," Eryl said, "he is too much of a coward to travel to a war zone."

"What do you mean, 'war zone', what has happened?" Erol asked.

"More like something is about to happen," Day said.

The rebels with Day then folded back the hoods of their cloaks revealing the faces of several of the new Wazhazhe allies of Day and Eryl. Darkeye leaned in and whispered to Eryl as Quietstar handed a large leather satchel to her. Eryl produced a Wazhazhe cloak from the satchel and threw it on. She then extracted a second, identical cloak from the same satchel and extended it to her brother.

"Perhaps you should catch me up on current events," Erol said, stunned by the sight of the group of painted Hü among whom he now found himself standing.

"Yes, we have so much to tell you brother but first you need to put this on," Eryl said, as she again offered Erol the cloak, "And we need to leave *now*; Sis will be rising soon," Eryl said.

Donning the proffered cloak, Erol followed his sister, Day and the Wazhazhe into the forest near the western shore of the Bay of Memfi. *What does the rising of the dim Little Sister moon have to do with anything?* he thought.

Nun

"All warfare is based on deception. There is no place that espionage does not exist."
Ancient Hü Philosopher

General Sul was several syphi behind in his review of the intelligence image reports provided to him from the PIA. He was not too concerned about being behind for several reasons, the least of which was that it was rare that the images ever provided anything useful. Sul knew that the main purpose of the PIA was to provide positive information to the public, not to conduct secret surveillance operations on citizens. The civil espionage division of the government was the Office of the General Inquisitor, under the direction of its new leader, Chief Inquisitor Tarr.

The redaction of the image recordings that were not suitable for public viewing in their entirety was, out of oversight necessity, handled by yet another, separate, governmental entity. Whenever the PIA recording devices captured occasional images that required censoring, those images were sent to the Government Office of Public Happiness for said redaction. The GOPH Agents then gathered and consolidated the redacted images into a daily record, which they provided to the General of the Western Army Command, General Alland Sul.

General Sul considered it a waste of his valuable time to spend a few degrees each dawn combing through the previous dawn's redactions looking for possible miscreants and criminals. He often found it more helpful to view the images in one sitting once they had a chance to age. In his opinion, viewing the images soon after their creation caused too much weight to be given to the images and offered a large temptation to force-fit later intelligence to any false impressions garnered from those images.

Sul knew that he had procrastinated in this unwelcome duty as long as he dared and decided that this dawn was the right one for the review. The Western Plantations were under control and the processing plants no longer required his personal supervision. Although there was some troubling news from the Eastern and Central Councils, they were not under Sul's jurisdiction. *The guard-state in this part of the planet is running like a fine chronograph under my guidance*, Sul thought.

Having returned to the 1st Army Base of the Western Council, Sul felt at home. His big scimitar cats were ranging free behind the tall fences and game-rich fields of his private estate on the edge of the camp, he'd had a first-rate meal at the officer's communion and he had just finished pressing his signet ring into the hot wax on the last of two dozen orders of execution.

With this dawn's general and routine duties having been discharged and nothing else on his schedule, Sul grabbed the stack of image chips and walked into his private office. One redacted segment after another, the General sat through each tedious chip, every one of them filled with dozens of the PIA outtake images. Though he did not enjoy the duty, he treated it serious, suppressing his desire to progress through the images any faster than standard playback speed.

After three cycles, Sul was a third of the way through the stack and decided he need a cup of quake to get through the rest. He rose from his desk, crossed to the quake dispenser and decanted a cup from the heated metal carafe. After stirring in his usual small amount of bloodfruit wine sweetener, Sul returned to his seat behind his desk. He grabbed the next chip from the top of the stack and placed it in the slot of his desktop image viewer and engaged the playback key as he began to sip from his cup.

Soon the first of the redacted images appeared on the viewer of Silas Mis' speech to a plantation of the south revealing Dabrill Kinselo being tackled and subdued on the dais. Sul overshot his lips, spilling the hot liquid past the corners of his mouth and onto his shirt. The burn to his lips caused a reflexive overcompensation that sloshed even more liquid from the opposite side of the cup and onto his lap. He bolted from the seat swearing and slamming the ceramic cup down on the desk, which shattered it. The hot liquid flowed into the electronics well of the image viewer frying the circuitry in a shower of sparks.

"Ensign Go!" Sul yelled to his secretary, "Get in here at once!"

As the startled ensign entered Sul's office, the transceiver in the corner of the office buzzed, indicating an incoming communication. General Sul crossed to the transceiver and picked up the handset. The relay indicator lights revealed that the incoming transmission originated in the Southern Council. The ensign began cleaning the spilled quake from the General's desk.

"Speak," Sul said into the transceiver.

"General Sul, this is Tarr," Chief Inquisitor Tarr said, "We have a problem concerning your painted Hü spy."

"Is he in custody?" Sul asked.

"Custody?" Tarr asked, "No sir, he has disappeared."

The transceiver buzzed again with another incoming transmission. The relay indicating lights showed that the new transmission originated to the southwest of Capital City. Sul ordered Tarr back to Capital City as he switched to the incoming transmission.

"Speak," Sul sneered into the transceiver.

"Sul, the rebels have attacked me!" Chancellor Mis blurted, "Eryl Syz is with them and her brother has joined them."

"Did this have anything to do with the incident of the intruder onto your dais in the Southern Council?" Sul asked.

"What?" Mis' asked, confused by the question.

"The incident with the painted Hü," Sul said, "Your Chief of Security restrained him when he made his way onto the dais while you were speaking."

"No, that was just a brazen adventure seeker," Mis' said, "He was interrogated and released."

"Very well, Your Excellency," Sul said with some distaste, "You should return to Capital City. I will find the Syz twins for you but I must first deal with a pressing issue in the Southern Council."

Despite Mis' dismissal, Sul was unconvinced that the Syz problem was not an entanglement of the Dabrill Kinselo problem. Many anni of experience had convinced the General that there were few coincidences in nature. He knew that the only way to be sure was to go to the Southern Council in person and pick up the trail of Dabrill Kinselo.

***

Off the Northern Coast of the Central Council, in the D'Over Strait

Jæms Brightson loved the sea. He loved the salty breeze in his face, the rolling of the waves and the thrill of adventure whenever he was fortunate enough to launch his ship. Jæms was a fourth generation, 'Rish net-fisher and for more than ten anni, he'd launched his ship, in the dark, just before dawn, six times every syphus. This evening he'd launched three cycles after sunset as part of a fleet of ten dozen ships.

The makeshift fleet consisted of every seaworthy net-fisher ship from the Guild Consortium of 'Rishland, Wels and Alba. But Jæms knew this was no fishing expedition; it was the largest attack the Resistance had ever mounted. A hundred and twenty ships, each fitted with a battery of sonic canons, acoustic shielding and a score of newly inducted marines, were making their way across the D'Over Strait to the northern shoreline of the mainland.

If we'd attacked a month ago, Jæms thought. He and the rest of the rebels in the fleet knew from the Resistance's network of informants that after the disastrous, failed attack on the Capital City Armory, the Councils had fortified many various weak points. The Resistance had discovered that there would be a light battalion of five companies guarding the shore. This meant that the almost five hundred greenhorn marine recruits onboard the fleet would meet a roughly equal number of regular army Gru and Loru soldiers on the shore.

The success of the fleet's attack rested on the element of surprise. The ships were crossing the strait under almost total darkness; a dim crescent of Sis and a few bright stars cast an eerie glow, visible on just the crests of the waves. The acoustic shielding was inactive because it often shimmered if reflected or artificial light hit it just right. The entire fleet of rebel ships were rigged in black sails, foregoing the noisy sonic propulsion units.

The one weak link in the rebels' stealthy plans lay in the eyes of the enemy soldiers. While limited, the natural Gru infrared vision capabilities were still quite useful in dark or low-light combat. The marines onboard each ship could limit their infrared signature by hiding below deck but it was impossible for the pilots of each ship to steer while taking similar precautions.

In the relative silence of the open water, Jæms contemplated the probable bedlam that lay in wait on the coast ahead. Looking to either port or starboard, he could just distinguish the dark shapes of the ships sailing but a few rods away. His ship, the *Restitution*, cut through the waves with knife edge silence toward the heading. Using his trusty, dual axis, back-quadrant, he kept the bow pointed away from the northern star, Adib.

When Jæms found himself alone in his thoughts on the open water, he often reminisced about conversations he'd had with his dad on his earliest trips to the sea. Staring at Adib through the mirror of his back-quadrant, Jæms thought about the time he asked his dad why the north star was called Adib and why another star was called Polestar. Jæms remembered the spark of youthful curiosity and fascination as his dad explained how the planet wobbled as it turned and that, many millennia ago, Polestar was the north star.

As Jæms stared at the reflection of Adib in the lens of his back-quadrant, his peripheral vision caught a streak in the sky headed high overhead and instinctively recognized that it was a sonaflare. The first streak was soon followed by a dozen others, which looked like streamers heaved from the coast over the fleet. The accompanying sound of acoustic cannon fire made the spectacle seem like a welcoming salute rather than a barrage intent upon repelling their attack.

"Shields on!" Jæms shouted, in unison with the other captains.

The sonic shields shimmered like a wave of angry specters in the artificial light of the multitude of sonaflares, as the ship captains activated them, spreading outward among the fleet. A pair of tenderfoot marines made their way onto the deck of the *Restitution* and likewise on a hundred other rebel ships to activate the battery of sonic canons. There seemed to be nothing to do now but storm onward, into the barrage of sonic artillery fire coming from the coast.

***

Earlier, in the darkness on the Northern Coast of the Central Council

Captain Auguste Schwartz resented his assignment. There had never been any indications of significant rebel activity in the Central Council's lands. Because of this, Schwartz considered his assignment of guarding the coastline of the D'Over Strait to be a waste of his valuable skills.

The sun was now set and even the twilight was beginning to wane as Schwartz made his evening inspections of the company under his command. The dim light of a crescent Sis was not enough to illuminate the faces of the soldiers at their posts.

"Are you ready to defend the north coast of your homeland?" Schwartz asked the two dozen soldiers of Fourth Platoon.

"Yes, Captain," the soldiers barked.

"And if the Wild Wels or the Crazy Kelts should cross D'Over?" Schwartz prompted.

"We will drown them Dow'Under, Captain," the platoon yelled, completing the ancient refrain.

Addressing the equally eager Third Platoon, Captain Schwartz asked the first line of the next refrain, "And should the 'Rish play their trick and hit back?"

"We'll give 'em the stick *and* the sack!" replied the troops.

Captain Schwartz continued on, ascending through the platoons, repeating his questions and getting the enthusiastic responses. After First Platoon gave their conclusion to the refrain, the Captain turned to return to his headquarters, more thoroughly depressed about his assignment than he'd been when he started the evening duty inspections two cycles prior.

Not more than a dozen steps from First Platoon, Schwartz saw the illumination beacon launched over the strait. By the trajectory, he could tell it was launched by Second Platoon. Schwartz was standing at one of the highest points overlooking the water but even with the intensity of a class one illumination beacon, the Captain had difficulty discerning the movement.

Silent and swift, the objects approaching the beach from the north began to materialize as dozens of dark-camouflaged vessels. The ships' acoustic shielding became active a few moments after the beacon; the artificial light producing an oil-like, multicolor sheen on the shimmering fields.

"Rebels!" yelled the sergeant of Second Platoon's First Squad.

Second Squad of First Platoon launched a second illumination beacon as a massive barrage of acoustic cannon and rifle fire erupted from both the beach and the rebel ships. The dark, star-filled sky was soon alight with beacons up and down the coast as Schwartz' company was joined by half a dozen additional companies.

In a glance, Auguste surveyed the scene with keen understanding, then smiled. He reached into his breast pocket, pulling from it one of his favorite jumbo-sized vapor-tubes. As he lit it, he laughed and thought, *Sack yes! It's about time I get my chance to get into this fight.*

Captain Schwartz moved down a slight incline from his original vantage point, to the more secure command post above Second Platoon. He then donned the headset and switched to the frequency for the first two platoons of his command, finding that the noise of panicked corporals asking for his orders soon flooded the headset and his ears.

"Second Platoon will pull back, circle to a flanking position behind First Platoon, and direct all fire at ninety degrees or straight toward the coastline and the oncoming ships," Schwartz ordered, "absolutely no oblique fire unless I command it."

"Retreat?" the transceiver corporal from Second Platoon asked, almost pleading that he'd misheard the command.

“No,” Schwartz said with a chuckle, then he pulled the vapor-tube from his lips so that he could be heard with an unimpeded voice, “What is your name?”

“I’m Corporal Betz of Second Platoon, Captain,” the young soldier replied.

“Well, Betz, I am counting on you…no, the entire Central Council is counting on you to follow my orders to the letter. More important to you, your *life* may depend on it. If you want to make it through this evening to see the dawn, relay my orders to the lieutenant of Second Platoon and see that he follows them.”

Captain Schwartz switched the transceiver to the channel for Third and Fourth Platoon and ordered their transceiver corporals similarly: Third Platoon was to fall back into a flanking and supportive position of Fourth Platoon, which was to direct all fire at ninety degrees, thus straight toward the oncoming ships. There would be no oblique fire crossing the gap that Schwartz’ commands were creating between First and Fourth Platoons.

Schwartz turned and surveyed the companies on either side of his position. He knew that their captains were inexperienced and probably panicking. He moved to the signal beacon and began sending his coded sanctions to his fellow captains. *This is going to be a long evening*, he thought. He drew the last few puffs of smoke from the stub of his oversized vapor-tube then crushed it into the sandy floor of the command post.

***

Jæms Brightson beached the *Restitution* in order to allow his compliment of marines to disembark and gain control of a small section of the coast. He’d found a small crease in the armor of the fortified beach; a high point, which limited the angle of attack of the acoustic artillery and allowed the *Restitution* to glide under their barrage.

The marines overtook the artillery group and took advantage of another quirk of this particular bastion. The artillery position was recessed just enough into the coast that those on either side of it were within its arc of range. Within thirty units of the beaching of the *Restitution*, and with the help of several additional ships full of marines, Brightson’s troops controlled five furlongs of the coast.

Jæms sat down on a rock that was secure from potential sniper fire. He took a long drink of water from his canteen and replaced the half empty container on his waist sash. He then began adjusting the frequency cascade settings on one of his sonaflares. As he loaded the reset sonaflare into the launcher, he realized that he had not seen any other signal flares. *It's good to be first*, he thought, *but not if we're also the last*.

Jæms had completed the first part of his mission. The second part required that other units had succeeded in taking their assigned sections of the coast. It did not take long before additional sonaflares began to rise from the various secure points of the beach. The color changes based on the varying frequency cascade emitted from the flares told their stories.

As dawn approached, the sonaflare signals indicated that the Resistance held twenty-five furlongs of non-contiguous coastline. The invasion was far from a total success. Some units reported major losses as they retreated across the D'Over Straight. A few units never reported. Despite some failures, many of the units were now preparing for the second phase of the attack.

The rebel units to the west and east were now consolidating the beachhead toward the center after having secured their respective flanks. Ships that had retreated were now returning and disembarking their marines, who also made their way toward the center. Brightson's unit formed the central rallying point and hoisted their standard, signaling as much. The unified, singular mission of the rebel forces was now to hold the center at all costs.

***

As foreseen by Captain Schwartz, dawn was breaking and there was no relief to the intensity of the battle. Only one of the gap-traps he and the other captains set had worked. Though the rebel casualties were substantial, the number of rebel ships was far too large to overcome with his delayed crossfire tactic. Worse, most of the positions now held by the rebels were on high ground, making them as fortified from the rear as they had been thought to be from seaside.

Holding even the few fragmented portions of the beach was not without heavy losses on the side of the defenders. More than two hundred Axis soldiers had fallen, including the lieutenant colonel commanding the battalion. The loss of the battalion commander left the nine other captains under the de facto command of Captain Schwartz; a position he wasted no time in assuming.

Fragmented though the rebel positions were along the coast, Schwartz was convinced that they were now trying to consolidate their position. His new plan was more modest than the previous, failed scheme. Schwartz would throw everything he had at the center and break them apart as soon as he saw the anticipated inland reinforcements approaching from the rear. *The sleds should be visible on the horizon at any moment*, Schwartz thought, looking at his chronograph in the dim light of the breaking dawn.

***

Earlier, Three Thousand Furlongs to the South

Ang Obryn knew the plan would work; it had to. He'd traveled halfway around the planet preparing for the next few dawns but the entire plan of the Resistance was distilled into the next few moments. After the devastating ambush at Capital City, the rebels could ill afford another defeat. They were placing their every effort into this battle. If they could split the Councils apart by defeating them here, in the next few dawns, the Resistance would have a chance. If not, then the war would be all but over.

The troops accompanying Ang were so quiet that it was difficult for Ang to believe there were over a thousand of them. The rebels had convened here from every Council bailiwick, each one offering expertise valuable to the present mission. But Ang considered the small contingent from the Southern Council to be crucial to the next few moments. The southern rebels had set the traps and now all waited in silence for the tell-tale signal from the Central Council's 1st Army Encampment a few furlongs south of their present position.

Ang watched the dim lights on the horizon, anxious for the first sign that the base was stirring. He knew that the 1st Army Encampment would be the first to respond to news of the attack. Although Ang dared not uncover the luminescent dial of his wrist chronograph, he was sure that the rebel forces would be at the coast by now. The battle would be heating up and any moment the dim lights of the base would brighten as the soldiers there responded to the urgent call for Axis reinforcements.

As he lay there eyeing the horizon, Ang's thoughts drifted back to the ambush in Capital City. The loss of so many good friends angered him. To be sure, what angered him the most was the reports of how the soldiers knew they were coming; how they knew they were there with the specific intent of attacking the armory. He had not wanted to believe the reports but the more he rejected the idea, the more it made sense. Farlay Singh had betrayed them. Ang had heard it straight from the lips of Jo Sephira, who said he witnessed Singh execute his own squad just after the sonaluma blast.

As he thought about the betrayal, Ang fantasized about how he would kill Farlay Singh. A great many good rebels lost their lives in that ambush. A lot of good friends were killed by the treachery of the traitor who Ang Obryn had once considered such a friend and who was a well-respected leader among the Resistance. Ang crouched low in the dew-laden grass, vowing to make Farlay pay for each of those lives as the lights on the horizon began to vivify.

A few degrees after the lights of the 1st Army Encampment began to brighten, the distant sound of the alert sirens reached the rebels lying in wait. A slight rustle of grass and the repositioning of bodies manifested as an audible tension that filled the otherwise silent field where the hundreds of Resistance fighters waited in nervous anticipation of the hum of the army sleds headed their way. Within a few units, their anticipation was satiated with the increasing drone of dozens of suspensor vehicles speeding toward them.

The army sleds sped into the trap with their pilots unaware of the small, camouflaged canisters arrayed in a large grid beneath them in the tall grass of the field. Nearly the entire mechanized group was over the grid of the trap when the leading sled triggered the snare. What happened next was an eruption of chaos of a magnitude never experienced by either the soldiers in the trap nor the rebels who had prepared it.

From the perspective of the soldiers piloting the suspensor sleds, the grass seemed to catch fire in an instantaneous, glowing, swirling, golden blaze. From the perspective of the rebels, the hundreds of canisters of the trap sprang open releasing a glimmering golden fog rising into and engulfing the oncoming army sleds. Then came the screams. Several million, agitated and very aggressive firewasps soon had their way with the soldiers. Those not killed within the first few moments of the attack were writhing in the tall grass in agony and wishing they were dead.

No more than a few degrees elapsed before the army sleds, now unencumbered by pilots or soldiers began gliding into the awaiting hands of the Resistance. The rebels were glad that their suspicions were correct and the army, in its haste to respond, had loaded their troops onto the sleds without the protection and added weight of the armored compartments.

Ang and the others corralled the vehicles and watched as the firewasps schooled and flew toward the south and the lights of the 1st Army Encampment.

The troops stationed there were oblivious to the viciousness of the approaching threat. *Now that's an ambush, you mother sackers*, Ang thought.

En

As the light of dawn grew brighter, an eager Jæms Brightson surveyed the southern horizon through his viewscopes with anticipation. If the plan had been successful, the sleds should appear soon. The rebels had consolidated most of the coast and were fending off sporadic and small counter punches by the soldiers who had held the beach but a few cycles earlier. The Axis soldiers were now holding a secondary embankment about a furlong south of the main coastal fortifications.

The secondary embankment was a predetermined fallback point on the south edge of an open field that served as a buffer between it and the coastal fortifications that the rebels controlled. In peaceful times, the embankment served as the sleeping quarters for the soldiers rotating to and from duty in the main fortifications. The large coastal artillery could not be brought to bear on the secondary embankment and, if the rebels attacked the Axis position, they would be exposed to light artillery and significant small arms fire as they crossed the open field. The rebels wisely held their ground.

Jæms knew that the small nuisance attacks were meant as modest reconnaissance missions; each intent on discovering weaknesses. It was clear that the battalion commander was preparing his plans for when the reinforcements arrived. Jæms was hopeful of an alternative situation developing when the "reinforcement" sleds arrived.

***

As he waited, Schwartz was continuing to send in small units to probe the enemy positions for information. He looked at his chronograph again. The sun's full disk had now risen above the low hills of the eastern horizon. Schwartz began to consider whether his signal had been received. He knew that emergency battle stations regulations required the 1st Army Base to respond to his distress call with urgency. Captain Auguste Schwartz was beginning to think that his idea of urgency was not the same as that of the general in command of the 1st Army Base.

Regulations or not, the lapsed time between the distress call and the present moment seemed too much for some sign of the reinforcements not to have appeared. Schwartz paced back and forth a few more times before he again looked at his chronograph. Then he raised his viewscopes to his eyes and brought the horizon into focus.

"Finally," Captain Swartz exclaimed. He called for the corporal to bring the acoustic amplifier and reached into his pocket to fetch another vapor-tube. Swartz lit the vapor-tube and took the acoustic amplifier from the corporal.

"If you surrender now, I promise that you will be treated fair," boomed the voice through the amplifier. Unfortunately for Captain Swartz, the voice was that of Jæms Brightson. The confused Captain turned back toward the fast approaching sleds and raised his viewscopes again. His mouth fell agape, the freshly lit vapor-tube dropping from his lips.

***

By apex, Jæms Brightson was bored. He and his detachment of a hundred and fifty marines had secured the captives, Captain Schwartz' surrendered battalion, locking them in their own quarters. The marines had relaunched the seaworthy ships from the armada, which numbered more than seven dozen. The rebels were now in full rotation between guarding the prisoners, fortification duty and sleep, which they did aboard the ships. The remaining three hundred or so marines from the rebel assault force joined with Obryn's army, which were moving south.

Jæms boarded the *Restitution* for his sleep rotation but he knew there was no possibility of that. For one thing, it was apex and he always found it difficult to sleep during broad dawnlight, regardless of how tired he was. Second, he just wanted to go home. This was not a war Jæms wanted but he had come to realize that it was necessary after the terrorist provocations.

Brightson went below deck, pulled a fish from the well and fileted it. He then flipped on an induction plate on top of his small cook surface and placed a small frying pan on it. Moments later, Jæms was stirring the seasoned fish in the hot pan with legume sprouts, sliced fungs and wild leeks, the latter of which he had picked while on shore.

As he cooked, Jæms thought about the terrorist attacks. It never made sense to him. No one in the Resistance knew anything about such plans. As far as Brightson knew, there wasn't anyone in the Resistance who had either the knowledge or the wherewithal to pull off such an attack. Much less did he know of the existence of a global network of rebels that could infect the plantations of three Councils in a few syphi.

Jæms was still mulling over the impossibility of the rebel-based terrorist attacks as he slung himself into his hammock. The gentle rocking motion of the hammock had all but accomplished its purpose when its occupant's eyes sprang open.

"Firewasps!" Jæms exclaimed. Only the bulkheads and decking of the *Restitution* heard him. A few units later, he smiled and drifted off into a peaceful sleep, relaxed in the satisfaction of his newfound knowledge.

***

Ang was somewhat surprised at the lack of resistance his invasion force was encountering. The rebels found the 1st Army Encampment desolate and managed to scavenge additional weapons and vehicles from among the victims of the firewasps. The rebels from the Southern Council assured the others that the firewasps would have gone to ground to nest during the dawnlight cycles. Once dark, the school would continue south until they found a source of nectar that could support a new hive.

The rebels began picking up additional fighters as they made their way toward the Central Council Governor City. The invasion force was now numbering two thousand Lehu, Chu and Loru with several hundred military and civilian vehicles and a decent supply of arms and power packs. Ang was grateful for every extra body and piece of equipment, no matter how small; with good reason.

The soldiers of the Central Council's 3rd Army Encampment were sure to have reinforced the city by the time the rebels arrive; but that was not what concerned Ang the most. Between the rebels and Governor City lay the 2nd Army Encampment. With a number of troops equal to the rebels, the soldiers were sure to be prepared. The rebels no longer had the element of surprise on their side but the local insurgents they'd picked up along the way had provided some good intel, the most important of which spoke to the terrain surrounding the 2nd Army Encampment.

With the coast four thousand furlongs behind them, the rebels were moving southwest along the Rolling River, the White Mountains parallel with their east flank and the Central Mountains toward the west. Ang looked toward the White Mountains and considered why they might be called by such a contrary name. At best, the peaks were a slate gray hue. He could perceive nothing about them that seemed white enough to deserve the name. Perhaps long ago, when the peaks were named, they were white and had become tarnished over the millennia. *A puzzle for another time*, Ang thought.

Governor City lay five hundred furlongs ahead, at the extreme end of the great river-cut valley on the plain before the Medi Sea. The 2nd Army was headquartered in a semi-circular gorge, which was inset into the mountains about halfway between the advancing rebel forces and Governor City. The army encampment was thus placed in a natural fortress, protected by sheer cliffs on three sides and with a flat, open field between the Rolling River and the entrance to the gorge. The task of capturing the 2nd Army Encampment without a prolong siege seemed daunting but Ang Obryn had a plan.

The late afterapex sun shone bright on their western flank as Ang halted his advancing rebels and gathered the company commanders. Of the rebel force, a small number of Loru were trusted enough to have been invited on the mission. One of those Loru was the ninth company commander, Mo Lök.

Mo was short, stout and braided his hair and his beard, both of which were long. A little gray was beginning to show in his blue hair, which gave the braids a silvery, metallic sheen. Ang had known Mo since they were five anni old, the age they became lifelong friends. He still held a vivid memory of standing as a helpless witness when a Gru politician cut off Mo's left hand at the age of six. The amputation was an on-the-spot punishment for the crime of pointing his thumb and index finger, an obscene gesture, at the well-to-do Gru.

Ang knew how much Mo hated the Gru, perhaps more than even Ang hated them. He trusted Mo as much as any rebel under his command. Even if they had not been friends from childhood, the fact that Mo had saved Ang's life on more than one occasion earned the former the implicit trust of the latter. Mo thought of Ang as a brother and would give his life for him without hesitation.

"Mo, do you think three squads from your company are up for an evening climb?" Ang asked his friend.

"As long as I get to lead them," Mo countered.

Ang knew that Mo was an accomplished climber. Even one-handed, Mo had bested Ang on several first-to-summit contests in their youth. As an adult, Mo had fashioned his own custom mechanical prosthetic, which served to increase his abilities, including his skill at climbing.

Though the height of the White Mountains to the east was imposing, the smaller ridgeline fronting that formidable range was less so. Some sections were rather steep and the climb to the ridgeline summit would need to be completed in one night but Ang knew that he trusted no one more than Mo to get two squads of rebels several furlongs up the ridgeline in a single night.

"Agreed," Ang said, smiling at his friend, "when you get up there, take two cycles rest, then head toward the 2nd Army Encampment. As you get close, pay attention. No doubt there will be sentries awaiting such a move. Before you get close enough to be detected, position yourselves well and await my signal. Once you see my call sign, kill any sentries and unleash sonic death upon the encampment."

"Very good sir," Mo said.

"The rest of your ninth will join my first in our games down here," Ang said, assuring Mo that he would take personal responsibility for the rest of Mo's company of rebels.

Mo Lök nodded, acknowledging his orders before heading off to accomplish them. As his friend hurried away, Ang motioned for the commanders of six of the companies to crouch down as he began drawing in a small patch of dirt near his feet. He first made a straight line and then two circles along one side of the line; the former represented the ridge above them, while the latter represented their location and the army encampment that lay ahead.

"Tomorrow, at three cycles past dawn, you will lead your companies and move out to the west, along the Rolling River," Ang said as he began drawing an arc from the circle representing their present location, "then company four, five and six will drop off and comeback toward the encampment and halt at least a furlong beyond their range of fire."

Ang looked up at the commanders to make sure they understood, then continued, "companies three, seven and eight will continue moving southwest, along the river and toward Governor City. After twenty furlongs, send up a blue flare, double back toward the ridge and make your way back to the encampment for a squeeze maneuver. I'll be positioned here and will bring the remaining companies to the center once I see your signal."

The commanders acknowledged their orders and Ang added, "Now set the evening watches and get some rest; the next dawn will mean the success of this entire mission or the end of it."

***

Mo Lök and his three squads raced along the ridgeline toward their objective. Moments earlier, Mo watched as Ang's personal, white sonaflare code lit the air, equal with the height of the ridge and brilliant, even in the apex sky. As they pressed on, Mo and his team could see the movements of the rebels below. The team found no sign of sentries positioned along the ridgeline and Mo could see the arc of the vale where the encampment would be positioned some seven furlongs below. The team dispersed around the rim of the gorge and readied for the forthcoming assault.

Mo watched as five companies of the 2nd Army battalion moved out and into Ang's trap. His team prepared their acoustic grenades and waited for their leader's signal. Mo raised his mechanical hand, holding the vivid reminder of his longtime hatred of the Gru above his head. As he set himself to lower his arm for the signal, he noticed a brief flicker from the plain below.

"Hold!" Mo ordered his soldiers, then eased his arm back to his side.

His entire assault force watched as several rebels flashed signals from the plain below. Mo retrieved his viewscopes from his hip pack and lifted them to his eyes. He could see the 2nd Army's squads halted a quarter furlong in front of rebel companies four, five and six. Ang's group of four companies were closing from the right flank while the remaining three companies of rebels were closing from the left flank.

The sonaluma signals were still flashing from the rebel 5th company, indicating that Mo's unit should stand down. Mo increased the magnification of his viewscopes and focused on the five companies of the 2nd Army halted in the field below. The companies were fully armed and ready for battle yet they stood their ground with a calm quiet, even as double their numbers moved toward them from three directions.

Mo scanned the enemy troops until he found the head of the first company and understood why the 2nd Army forces were so tranquil in their awaiting of the approach of the superior force. Through the amplified lenses of his viewscopes, Mo saw the shimmering, triangular silver pennant: a universal banner of truce.

***

Ang brought his D-class sled to a halt a short distance in front of the enemy battalion commander, who was standing, in full battle dress, in front of his own D-class. The Gru commander, General Psi, held the staff with the silver pennant of truce by his side, his haggard and forlorn face belying his proud stance.

Ang dismounted from his sled and walked the few paces to come face-to-face with the General. He considered whether this might be a trap, some ruse meant to give Governor City additional time to prepare for the coming battle.

“Why do you seek a truce?” Ang asked his adversary.

“For survival,” General Psi replied with equal directness.

Ang looked at the General and realized that the Gru before him seemed unlike other Gru. While he stood with obvious pride and dignity, his face could not disguise his genuine fear of the present moment. The muscular and strong look of his body almost seemed to tremble before the rebel leader. Ang considered his reading of the Gru before him to be ironic, as he looked at his adversary’s quad-pupiled eyes.

“Where is the remainder of your battalion?” Ang asked.

“This is all who remain of my command. The others have returned to Governor City or their homes and family in the countryside,” General Psi proclaimed with some reluctance.

Once again, Ang stared at the General for a moment with a prudent eye, then he looked out at the remnant of the 2nd Army of the Central Council. He was looking at a force of less than six hundred troops. Ang noticed that the army arrayed before him seemed impressive, if small. The troops formed what looked to be a sea of golden faces adorned with blue uniforms complimenting their amethyst eyes. *They’re all Loru*, Ang thought, realizing that the singular Gru among the small force before him was their commander.

“Where are all the Gru?” Ang asked.

“They have…” General Psi began but his eyes rolled back and he fainted, falling at the feet of an unexpecting Ang.

***

A cycle and a half passed before General Psi regained consciousness. The Axis leader opened his eyes with a lethargic deliberateness to see the green eyes and slick, bald head of Ang Obryn staring back at him. Ang stretched out his arm offering a small metal flask. Psi looked at him with an intense and careful calm, considering what manner of Chu was before him. Sensing no guile, he stretched out a trembling hand and took the proffered flask.

"My name is Ang Obryn and your aides tell me that you are General Lon Psi," Ang said, "they also tell me that you have been without chryst for three dawns. Where are your emergency supplies of bloodfruit juice?"

Psi first took several small sips from the flask, then two robust gulps upon discovering that it was bloodfruit wine. His eyes and face regained some of their original robustness within moments. Struggling to right himself and sit upon the edge of the cot, Psi managed to look Ang eye-to-eye.

Once again seeing no guile or malintent, Psi answered, "We sent the remaining provisions away with the Gru. We are now in a situation where every Gru is responsible for his own supply of chryst."

"So, you gave your supply away?" Ang inquired.

"I sent the last of my supply home to my family," Psi answered, then continued, "the bloodfruit crops are failing in the Central Council. The disease that your side released has given you this victory."

"The Resistance did not release the phage," Ang said.

"Your countenance reveals no deception, yet I find it difficult to believe you," Psi said, "what other group would desire to destroy the source of all Gru life? Who else would desire to extinguish my race?"

"I have considered that question for many dawns now," Ang said, "but I have come to the conclusion that it is the wrong question."

Psi finished the bloodfruit wine from the small metal flask as he considered Ang's response. Until now, he was sure that the Hü wanted free from their perceived yokes and a say in the government. Both were valid reasons for why they might resort to such extremes but Psi had doubts that the Resistance was capable of such a sophisticated attack without help. Ang's comment now made the General curious to learn more.

"What is the right question?" Psi asked.

"The right question is: Who is benefiting from a war between the Hü and the Ru?" Ang answered.

"Your question implies that there is another faction," Psi said, feeling much revived thanks to the bloodfruit wine.

"Yes, it does," Ang said.

***

40,000 Furlongs West, in the Double-D Triple-C

Chief Inquisitor Tarr stood at the end of the corridor of cell block ten. He was waiting for Nails Castor, who was now over two units late. Tarr despised inaccuracy, whether it be imprecise timing, errant statements or just simple, wrong answers to questions. Being two units overdue to a prescheduled meeting was inexcusable.

By the time the door of the hallway sprang open and Nails Castor burst through, he was almost three units late. In his right hand, he carried a small writing codex and an inker; in his left hand, he carried a small collapsible seat. His green technician's smock flowed like a cape from his quick stride. The angle of the coat prevented the garment's hem from brushing the filthy floor of the cell block hall, which it otherwise would have done due to Castor's diminutive stature.

"I've brought you some recently generated images of the target subject," Tarr said, in a gruff, irritated tone.

"That will not be necessary, the original images were quite sufficient," Castor replied, "Citizen Singh knew the subject rather well and recognized him from even your poor, original images. After all, the subject has some unique physical characteristics."

"Singh must be ready by next dawn," Tarr insisted, "we are transferring him to South Camp."

"It seems you are determined to waste the entirety of my expert conditioning by sending him to such a place," Castor said.

"The PIA will begin the announcements of the prisoner transfers soon and we are confident that those will provoke some form of rescue attempt during the transfer," Tarr said, "General Sul believes that, if we can draw out the individual, we can capture him and his companion."

"And, if the rebel's rescue mission should prove successful, my conditioning will at least ensure the subject's death," Castor said.

"Only if you can have him ready by the morrow," Tarr said.

"He will be ready," Castor assured, "this evening's session will conclude the conditioning."

With that, Castor resumed his fast-paced stroll toward Farlay Singh's cell. Tarr fumbled with the image in his hand in a childish and haphazard manner for a few moments then left the cell block somehow less content than when he had arrived.

***

Nails Castor strode into the cell of Farlay Singh with pride in the fear his mere presence instilled in the cell's occupant. As he unfolded the portable stool he always brought to the sessions, Castor smiled at Farlay's involuntary recoil into a ball in the corner of his cot. Far did not notice that Nails did not have his little black satchel of hurt with him on this visit.

"Citizen Singh," Castor began, "I have great news for you this dawn."

Far shivered. He remembered many such statements by Nails during the past few syphi. Contrary to his words, "good news" from Nails invariably meant unspeakable torment for citizen Singh.

"You're shivering, you must be cold," Nails said as he got up from his stool and adjusted Far's blanket over his shivering frame. Farlay retreated further as he tried to infuse himself into the walls at the corner of his cell.

"You have been selected to be among the detainees who are being relocated to one of our new camps," Nails proclaimed.

Far allowed a brief glint of hope to flash in his eyes but soon suppressed it. He knew that nothing Nails said was the whole truth and most of it was pure lie.

"I can see that you're a little skeptical, citizen Singh," Nails began, "but let me assure you that this new camp will be a paradise for its residents. There will be recreation time out in the fresh air as well as the ability to communicate with fellow detainees on a regular basis. But you don't have to believe me. Tomorrow morning there will be a PIA broadcast confirming this. I'm sure you'll be feeling much better by then,

"Now, citizen Singh, perhaps you can look at the lights on the speaker; the same speaker that will, at dawn, bring the news of your travels to the new camps. Perhaps the lights and thoughts of the fresh air and the comradery will sooth you. Perhaps you will find yourself feeling better already, the lights and the sound will allow you to rest, if only your friends would let you enjoy them, if only your friends will allow you to complete your journey…"

Sometime later, Nails Castor folded his stool and left the cell in silence. Farlay allowed himself a sigh that, at the least, his visitor had not come for one of the "debriefing" sessions. Such sessions often left Far unconscious and bleeding from multiple locations. This visit left him with just a slight headache.

Far had often experienced such headaches after visits to his cell but he couldn't remember when or even who had visited him. It was something to do with lights, someone was waking him up, someone wouldn't let him rest, Far could almost see the face of this new tormentor. *Why won't you just let me rest? I must complete my journey*, Farlay thought.

The tortured and troubled inmate soon drifted off to sleep, shuddering, mumbling and weeping as he tried in vain to resolve the indistinct image of the face of his tormentor who continued to haunt his evening visions.

***

Dabrill Kinselo contorted his face a bit as he strained to study Erol for signs of thoughtful intent. Eryl's brother was a unique character in his own right and Day was having difficulty reading him. The Wazhazhe had flooded Day and Eryl with information over the past few syphi and now Erol seemed overwhelmed as well.

The group were seated around a table in one of the many of the Wazhazhe cantonments along their main north-south trade route. Darkeye, Quietstar, Roughbark and Strongbark had presented the same condensed tale of the history of the planet that they had recounted to Day and Eryl a few syphi prior. Erol continued to sit in silent absorption of all that he'd learned in the last few cycles.

Strongbark broke the silence first, "You must understand that we are not Tellers for the Wazhazhe people. We have given you an abbreviated telling in order for you to know what is happening *now*."

"I have so many questions," Erol began, "for starters, how do we defeat an enemy like the Dex? We cannot climb into the sky. All we can do is to hide in these secret cantonments or conceal ourselves under your special cloaks."

"The histories tell us that the Dex lost the battle of Acer because they lost their ability to be among us," Strongbark began, "I don't understand what that means but it seems to me they never lost the desire to conquer this planet."

"It seems as though they have a long memory and tend to hold a grudge," Day added.

"So, I ask again, how are we supposed to defeat such an enemy?" Erol restated his question, looking for answers among the entire group.

"The first thing we need to do is expose those who are collaborating with the Dex," Eryl said, "we've all heard the communications. I'm not sure that these collaborators realize the full extent of what they are doing but we need to disrupt their communications."

"And just how do you propose we do that, dearest sister?" Erol asked.

Day responded in place of Eryl, "To begin with, we kill the traitorous Chief Inquisitor."

En-wan

"They've stolen from *my* chryst supply!" Silas Mis yelled.

When Chief Inquisitor Tarr had finished his report of the rebel victories, he did not anticipate that Chancellor Mis would focus on the least of the enemy's successes. The rebels had utter command of the Central Council and were now assumed to be attacking the Council of the Eastern Steppes. The insurgents were projected to defeat the latter with relative ease, considering the meager Axis forces committed to defending those desolate lands of the far east.

"Chancellor, I think it is important that we focus on securing the Western and Southern Council lands," Tarr began, "the reports indicate that the defeat of the Central Council was due in large part to the rebel forces growing in mass from the local populous as they moved through the Central Council lands."

Mis stood staring out his office window not quite hearing the words of Tyrell Tarr. So far, the rebels had found just three of his six hidden reserves of bloodfruit juice. He could not afford to lose the others. He needed the remaining stores to ensure that his control over the Gru was maintained.

"Double the guards at my other chryst storage points," Mis said.

"Chancellor!" Tarr said, somewhat agitated, "we must concentrate on the decimation. The correct way for us to ensure our control over the populous is to gain a yoke of leverage against them that they are either unable or unwilling to shake off."

"What does our friend say?" asked Mis.

"He has confirmed that the time is now for the creation of the Enlightenment Camps," Tarr answered.

"Has he given us any additional information on the rebel activities?"

"He has revealed that a group of unaligned rebel troops are massing in the south and I have asked General Sul to take ten battalions there to ensure the Southern Council does not suffer the same fate as the Central Council," Tarr added.

"Very well," Mis conceded, "but double the guard on my remaining chryst storage locations."

Later, as Tarr sped away from Capital City, he could not help but think just how ignorant Mis seemed to be. Tarr wished in secret that he'd been born a Gru. He realized that other Loru considered this a character fault, calling it *caste envy*.

Tarr did not much care what other Loru thought of him. *They're weak*, he thought, *always content with holding on to their subordinate positions.*

Tarr allowed his thoughts to wander and soon found himself considering the castes. *Lower Rubicund*, his mind thinking the words as a sneer crossed his lips. He wondered who had decided that the glorious golden Rubicund people should be called lower than those he considered the red-skinned idiots, who called themselves greater.

"Greater?" Tarr scoffed aloud, his voice lost to all but the evening air, *Ridiculous! They're no better than the painted Hü*, he thought.

Tarr looked up at the crescent first moon. *Two cycles from now Little Sister will be rising in the east chasing her larger sibling across the sky*, he thought, *I wonder if Arty will transmit this evening?*

***

A Few Moments Earlier, in a Ditch Ten Furlongs Away

"Three evenings lying in a ditch outside Capital City," Eryl whispered, "this is not my idea of a great time with close friends."

Day ignored her comment as he continued to scan the horizon with his viewscopes looking for any sign of the C-class vehicle. He knew that Sis would be rising in a couple of cycles and they'd have to once again abort the mission before achieving their objective.

Day passed the viewscopes off to Quietstar and double-checked the anchor. He had secured the anchor deep in the ground on the first evening they'd waited. Dabrill realized that this was *his* plan and he would hold himself responsible if it didn't work. He checked the braided rope that Strongbark had assured him could support the weight of a hundred Wazhazhe.

After checking the attachment of the rope to the anchor, Day examined the other end of the rope, making sure the diamag was well secured. He looked at the diamag. The silvery-white disk just filled the palm of his hand. A few dawns before, the disk had been the core of the forward suspensor field of a wrecked B-class vehicle, abandoned in a scrap yard. Erol had retrieved it on a scavenging run to gather supplies for Day's plan. Eryl's brother had guaranteed Day that the small diamag would weld itself to the plate of any active suspensor field to which it came within an arm's length distance.

Day looked at Quietstar in the dim light of the crescent first moon. He was a strong, well-respected and reliable member of Strongbark's group of Wazhazhe warriors. Day learned that Quietstar was named so because both he and his twin brother, Brightstar, were born on the evening of the appearance of an actual brightstar. Unlike his twin brother, Quietstar was born mute, unable to even cry. Brightstar spoke well enough for both of the twins, having become the Teller of the Wazhazhe.

Quietstar nudged Day and passed the viewscopes back to him. Raising the viewer to his eyes and bringing the horizon into focus, Day could see the vehicle headed their way. This was the eighth vehicle so far traveling along this pathway toward the residences that lay some forty furlongs east of Capital City. Day continued to watch the vehicle as it moved closer to the group's position. He was looking for the insignia of the Chief Inquisitor.

"Is it him?" Eryl whispered.

"Not close enough to tell," Day answered.

Dabrill continued to watch the vehicle as is moved ever closer. The burnished copper color of the vehicle indicated that it was a government vehicle. Day began to distinguish the diamond shaped placard of its yellow government seal. A few moments more and the finer, gray lines, the markings of the 'watchful eye' insignia came into view. The gray, shadowy eye, was the official governmental emblem commissioned for the Inquisitor's Bureau.

"It's him," Day announced.

With Day's pronouncement, Eryl slid lower into the ditch while maintaining her prone attitude, and Quietstar positioned himself in a low crouch while he readied his slingbow with a razor tipped projectile. Day collapsed his viewscopes and returned them to their gird holster. He then positioned the diamag in his hand, the attached rope flowing between his thumb and forefinger before cascading over the back of his hand.

With the rapid approaching vehicle closing on their position, Day coiled his right arm and gained leverage by extending his left arm, almost as if aiming with it toward the oncoming vehicle. He pivoted his heels, thereby rotating his aim just ahead of the oncoming craft, leading it.

A moment before the Chief Inquisitor's craft came even with their position, Day flung the diamag in front of the nearest of the two front suspensor fields on the C-class craft. The diamag snapped onto the plate of the suspensor field creating a brilliant shower of metallic sparks and a clamorous sound equivalent to nearby thunder. The unmistakable crackling of an electric arc followed as the diamag welded to the plate. Day threw himself flat as the rope snapped taught over his head.

The momentum of the C-class craft against the taught rope ripped the left front suspensor from the undercarriage of the vehicle. The craft dipped and yawed left, careening off the pathway, skipping over the ditch and into the thick brush of the berm. Quietstar sprang toward the vehicle and closed on it before it came to a stop in the scrub of the field beside the ditch.

The jarring collision of the craft into the dense coppice caused Tarr to lose consciousness; but not before seeing Quietstar towering above him with a razor tipped projectile aimed at his chest. As Chief Inquisitor Tarr closed his eyes into the concussion induced sleep, the silent Wazhazhe warrior lowered his slingbow and looked back at Day and Eryl, who were just arriving at the scene.

Eryl smiled and proclaimed, “We have the slimy snake.”

***

“Alert! Alert! Alert! Incoming priority one transmission on secure channel four. Senior personnel are required to report to the Emergency Communications Room at once,” the synthetic voice startled Fulong Su awake. This was the moment they’d been waiting for since the raid on Silas Mis’ bloodfruit storage facility. She threw on her uniform and made her way to the mag-lift, where she found Veegram Lo and Anlos Tris waiting for her. The three leaders of the REL Resistance rode the mag-lift to the ECR in silence.

Veegram noticed the digital chronograph on the wall as the trio entered the ECR. The digits were in red. *This is as it has been for twelve cycles of every dawn for untold anni*, thought Veegram.

Anlos took a seat behind the main console. He had rehearsed his dialog with Veegram dozens of times over the last few syphi. Fulong and Veegram stood on either side of Tris, as the latter motioned for Anlos to begin transmission.

Anlos spoke into the transceiver, “This is Administrator Tris.”

“Administrator Tris,” the voice began through the transceiver, “this is Chancellor Lo. How are you progressing? Is phase two ready?”

The voice was similar enough to that of Veegram that Anlos felt instinct compel him to look over his shoulder to reassure himself that the ex-Chancellor was still standing behind him. On the previous three occasions of contact with the fake Chancellor, Tris had not known how precise the mimicry had been.

Fulong Su found another familiarity in the voice but could not quite put her finger on what it was. The inflection and confident lack of hesitation seemed all too known to her. She felt as if she had talked to him many times prior.

"Your Excellency, phase two is complete. We have the biological agent prepared to your precise specifications and the canisters are filled and ready for your further instructions," Anlos responded.

"You will deliver the canisters, in three dawns, to the same location where you deposited the previous canisters," the ersatz Lo announced.

"It will be done, Your Excellency," Anlos replied.

"Is your team ready to begin phase three?" asked the voice.

"Yes, Your Excellency," answered Anlos, "but we are not sure we understand it."

"I am transmitting further instructions to your terminal now," the masculine voice responded, "this is the most critical phase, all four of the Councils are depending on your success, Administer Tris."

"Should we contact you at Capital City when we complete phase three?" Tris asked.

"No. You will maintain absolute transmission silence until further instructed by me," the voice insisted, then reiterated, "your discretion is an absolute must if we are to defeat the Resistance."

"Understood, Your Excellency," Anlos assured.

Later, as the trio rode the mag-lift back to the level of their quarters, Veegram spoke, "The trap is laid and we shall soon see who the players are."

"Indeed," Fulong concurred.

***

Chief Inquisitor Tarr blinked, squinted, then opened his eyes wide in a momentary panic. The room in which he found himself was ill lit, which did nothing to calm his demeanor. He struggled for a few moments before he realized his arms and legs were restrained. As his eyes adjusted well enough to discern more of his surroundings, Tarr discovered that he was in a moderate sized structure with ligneous support columns interspersed with some technology, most of which was unfamiliar to him. Tarr could hear talking but it was coming from behind him and he was unable to rotate his head far enough to see who was speaking.

"Ah, you're awake," said Eryl Syz, noticing Tarr's attempt to see who was talking behind him. She walked up to her captive and positioned herself so that he could plainly see her face as she spoke.

"My name is…" Eryl began.

"I know who you are," Tarr interrupted her, the insolence plain in his voice.

"Good," Eryl started again, "we can skip the introductions. Do you know why you are here?"

"You intend on holding me hostage for some ransom or prisoner exchange," Tarr guessed, or rather hoped. He smiled when he envisioned an exchange for Farlay Singh and the potential aftermath of such an exchange.

"Not exactly," Dabrill said as he positioned himself on the other side of Tarr.

"Ah, I correctly expected to see you, Citizen Kinselo, in the company of the fugitive, Eryl Syz," Tarr sneered at Day with unconcealed pleasure.

Day looked at the prisoner with a little curiosity, wondering how the Chief Inquisitor must feel to be on the other side of the power equation. After a few moments of intense but silent contemplation of his own empathy toward the former intermediary between he and General Sul, Day shrugged and waited for Eryl to begin the inquest of the Chief Inquisitor.

"What you have been brought here for is not prisoner exchange or ransom," Eryl said, "you have been brought here because of your sedition with a grave and dangerous enemy of the public."

"Preposterous!" Tarr shouted, the insolence returning to his voice in full.

"Do you deny conversing and plotting high crimes against the public with the entity you know as 'Arty'?" Eryl asked.

Tarr's eyes widened and his golden hue soon turned silvery-gray. His mind raced along with his pulse. *How could they know his name?* he thought, *I haven't even told Mis his name.*

"W…who?" Tarr asked with a sudden fearful hesitation.

"I'm quite sure you heard me, Chief Inquisitor Tarr," Eryl answered, "but, more to the point, the question that you should be asking *yourself* is: who *is* this 'Arty'? I am certain that I know more about the answer to that question than you."

Day then held up Tarr's personal micro transceiver and asked, "Do you think Arty will be transmitting this evening?"

Tarr began to shake with an irrepressible shiver, a shudder fashioned by equal measures of both fear and rage.

***

Three Dawns Later in the Northwestern Corner of the Savannah

Dabrill Kinselo watched through his viewscopes for any sign of his friend Quietstar. The Wazhazhe warrior was sent ahead on a reconnaissance mission to the prescribed pickup point. The mission force was split into two groups. Day's group was charged with tracking the enemy agents that where making the drop back to their base of operations. Strongbark's group was tasked with securing the canisters or destroying them, if unable to secure them.

Day and his half of the Wazhazhe mission force, some two dozen warriors strong, waited for confirmation that the drop had been made and the agents of the drop were returning to their base of operations.

Tarr was an idiot, Day thought. The Chief Inquisitor had refused to give information under direct questioning and could not be trusted to speak within the boundaries of any script provided him. Day smiled as he thought about the way they made their captive sing for them: a piece of technology used by the Wazhazhe to teach their children how to mimic the sounds of the numerous jungle creatures.

Regardless of his lack of willful cooperation, the recorded audio snippets of Tarr's interrogation proved quite helpful. With the use of the Wazhazhe audiographic technology, Erol managed to live manipulate the Chief Inquisitor's recorded words, which allowed the team to carry on a camouflaged, two-way conversation with Arty.

Day's Wazhazhe compatriots had educated him in many things over the past few syphi, not the least of which was the identity of Arty. Everything he learned raised more questions. Strongbark and the others informed Day that he would understand better when he could listen to the story from the Teller of his own people, the Sanguine. Again, for Day, the thought of 'his own people' did nothing but raise more questions.

In truth, Dabrill just wanted to complete this mission. Of the few tidbits of information they learned from Tarr, one troubled him, though he disbelieved it. The Chief Inquisitor took great pleasure in informing Day that Farlay had been sent to the southern prison camps. Strongbark had promised that once they completed this mission, he would allow Day to pick six warriors to attempt a rescue of his friend. Day understood that the importance of the present mission outweighed the circumstance of one rebel but he also knew the reputation of the prison camps and hoped that the rescue, when it could be attempted, would not be too late.

Through the viewscopes, Day glimpsed Quietstar returning from his surveillance. The warrior had returned to within a stone's throw of the group before deactivating his cloak. *He's rather stealthy with or without the Mimic*, Day thought.

Quietstar rejoined the group and soon began a flurry of hand signals so rapid that few of his fellow Wazhazhe could keep pace. Several moments passed before Roughbark turned to Day with the interpretation of Quietstar's gestures.

"He says that at least thirty troops accompanied the canisters to the drop spot," Roughbark began, "they came from the northeast but they did not leave. Quietstar says they vanished."

"He lost them?" Day asked.

"No, he said they vanished."

"Quietstar, did they do anything before they disappeared?" asked Eryl.

Quietstar flashed some more signals to Roughbark who interpreted, "they placed the canisters in the wide opening between two trees, then they climbed back onto the D-class sleds and vanished, poof!"

"Was there anything else on the sleds other than the troops?" Eryl questioned further.

Once again interpreting the warrior's gestures, Roughbark said, "Yes. Quietstar says there was a metallic box with an oval-shaped attachment on top."

Eryl turned to a young warrior named Running Hawk and said, "Go to Strongbark's group and bring Erol here."

As Running Hawk departed with the swiftness appropriate to his name, Day asked, "What do you think it is?"

"An ambush," Eryl replied.

***

Fulong Su watched through her viewscopes for any sign of the individual sent to retrieve the canisters. The cloaking field with which she and her troops were concealed produced a slight shimmer in Su's field of view.

Su lowered the viewscopes and looked around at her small company of soldiers and agents. Fulong considered whether she might be underestimating the enemy in bringing such a meager force. She soon convinced herself that the size of her force was the largest one that could be concealed with a single shield generator. Su then looked toward the sky.

Fulong knew that their actions, both earlier this dawn and in the coming cycles, would no longer be covert and the remainder of their confiscated shield generators would be needed now more than ever. *You're watching us? – I'm watching you!* Su thought.

Returning her attention to the scanning of the horizon through her viewscopes, Su said, "Remember to secure your weapons on low level. I want disorientation settings; it is imperative that we capture them, not kill them."

Fulong soon noticed movement through the shield shimmer. A single HF class cargo sled topped the small ridgeline to the south of the drop point. The craft was piloted by an individual wearing a flowing cloak but was otherwise empty. Su strained to see the pilot's face due to the shield distortion but by the time the craft was within a couple of furlongs of the canisters, his features cleared enough that she could distinguish that the individual was a painted Hü.

Su lowered her viewscopes and turned to look at Anlos Tris. He too had been viewing the approaching craft via the assistance of viewscopes. Anlos was now, in turn, staring in astonishment at Fulong. Both soon returned their stares to the approaching craft. Now a furlong away, the features of the pilot's face were becoming clearer. On maximum magnification, Fulong was able to make out the details of his face, including the color of his eyes.

"I doubt we will have much trouble describing him to Veegram," Su said.

"Veegram will want to see this one for himself," Anlos said. He then turned and once again looked at Su, unable to fathom her uncanny resemblance to the approaching stranger.

Day glided the HF craft close to the canisters, deliberate in positioning the craft parallel to the arrayed rows of the metal cylinders before powering down the suspensor fields. He then walked back to the cargo bed of the craft, looked at the daunting volume of canisters and back toward the horizon.

“Sack that,” Day cursed, shaking his head. He then looked at his wrist chronograph and back at the horizon and sat down on the edge of the bed of the craft, facing the ridge from whence he came.

It was now clear to the entirety of Su’s force that they were looking at someone as unusual as Fulong herself. All Su could do is shrug, acknowledging her equal amazement and give the hand signal to hold. It was similarly obvious that this individual was waiting for others to arrive and help him load the canisters onto his vehicle.

Fulong watched as the painted Hü took three small spherical, metallic objects from a pocket in his cloak and began to juggle them in a haphazard and nonchalant fashion, for what appeared to be nothing more than his own amusement. Soon, he lost control of one of the spheres which landed on the cargo bed and began rolling away from him. Day bounded to his feet covered the distance in a single jump-stride and stopped the sphere with his foot.

Su’s entire force was mesmerized by the agility of the stranger. Next, he flipped the sphere to the top of his foot and then flicked it over his head and back into his juggling cycle of objects, which had now become four in number. Day then looked toward the heretofore hidden troops and tossed one of the metallic balls in the direction of Fulong, who realized at the instant that the sphere was in the air that there was no longer any shimmering haze of the shielding.

“We’re exposed!” Su shouted, sidestepping the tossed sphere. Simultaneous with her warning, she realized that her team had been flanked by a superior force; a force now targeting them with razor tipped projectiles poised in slingbow launching devices.

“Ground your weapons,” Fulong ordered her troops. Then, looking back at Day, she said, “We surrender.”

“Lower your weapons,” Day ordered the troops just as Strongbark’s group of warriors was arriving on the scene. All the Wazhazhe warriors complied with his order.

All those present stood staring; Su and her forces at Dabrill Kinselo and Strongbark, Day and their forces at Fulong Su. Soon, Fulong’s entire force were staring at the unprecedented number of *other* painted Hü surrounding them. Fear, wonderment and general incredulity held the entirety of the almost fourscore individuals in silence for many moments.

“You are not our enemy,” Fulong and Day uttered at once, breaking the awkward quiet.

At the simultaneous utterance of Su and Day, the Wazhazhe warriors chanted "shibwoteth," touching their chins, then foreheads, then raising their hands toward the sky. They repeated the gesture and again fell silent.

Eryl leaned toward Strongbark and, in a whisper, asked, "What does 'shibwoteth' mean?"

"The Prophecy," Strongbark replied.

En-tu

"The difference between a just leader and an evil tyrant is often subtle."
General Lon Psi

All Ang Obryn wanted to do was move on to the east. The Resistance forces there were counting on his rebel army arriving to reinforce them before they launched their attack on Eastlux, the capital city of the Union of the Eastern Steppes. Instead, Ang's rebel forces were working with the residents of Governor City in hopes of restoring some semblance of order.

Most of their combined efforts were centered around stabilizing the bloodfruit supply. There were two plantations that remained disease free within the Central Council lands. The limited nature of the chryst available from just two plantations was strained beyond the designed limits of the supply chain. Thousands of anni designing cultivation for continuous harvesting in alternating rows of each field was failing. The result was that there was not enough available chryst to support the Gru population of the Central Council.

Ang was now waiting for a report from the processing plant on the blending efforts of low hydrogen potential juice from diseased crops with the higher hydrogen potential juices of the two healthy plantations. General Psi had informed Ang that the shipments from the Southern Council's plantation had been diverted to the Western Council's processing plants. Psi presumed that the bloodfruit supply in the west was in just as critical a condition as that of the Central Council.

Obryn stood on the large balcony of the Governor's office suite overlooking Governor City. The anarchy present in the city was subtle and difficult to discern, just visible via the lack of the systematic, regular flow of traffic in the streets. The sporadic intervals of congestion in unusual areas exposed the fact that the was no regular work schedule among the people.

Many of the Gru, distrustful of Hü and Loru alike, had abandoned their government administrative positions and took over both the harvesting and the processing of the bloodfruit. The forcing of the Hü and Loru out of their means of earning a living created an undercurrent of fear and resentment in the city. Most of the sporadic traffic of the city was now the result of urban flight that, for most, was essential to feed their families. Many such refugees fleeing the city were offering their labor for little more than basic sustenance needs and simple squatters' rights.

Tent villages were springing up everywhere in the Central Council. There were Gru populated villages near the plantations and Hü villages among farmland throughout the Council's domains. As more urban families moved to the rural areas, Ang knew that this would put additional stress on those areas. The entire Central Council was dancing on a knife's edge with anarchy on one side and starvation on the other.

Jæms Brightson entered the office and walked out onto the balcony beside Ang Obryn. Jæms stood in silence beside his commander for a few moments as he also considered the view of the discrete disorder of Governor City. There was no fighting in the streets, no looting or thievery, though all who remained within the city were starving.

"There's an uneasy electricity to the air, Jæms," Ang said.

"A smell of ozone *before* the lightning storm?" Jæms asked.

"It seems just a matter of time before the blue bolt of Býleistr jolts something loose," replied Ang.

"Psi is on his way back from the processing plant," Brightson noted, looking down at the main thoroughfare.

Glancing at the closer traffic some six floors beneath the balcony, Ang could see that General Psi was indeed making his way back to the Council headquarters building. As Psi dismounted from his B-class vehicle, it was difficult to discern his demeanor from the height and angle of the balcony perch. Nevertheless, Ang judged that his gait was not a good sign. Two units later, Psi was standing in the Governor's office in front of Obryn. Jæms took a seat as an observer on the lounge positioned against the wall of the office.

"You look tired General; please have a seat," Ang said, motioning toward the Governor's chair.

"I cannot stay," Psi responded, "I must go to the Hü and Loru villages and barter for food. The Gru villages at the plantations have little other than the fruit to eat and there are talks of raids."

"I sent Mo to acquire food and other necessities from the Hü farming villages," Ang responded.

Psi collapsed into the offered chair and said, "Thank you. The truth is, I had nothing with which to barter. The chryst that is priceless among the Gru is worthless among either the Loru or the Hü."

“If we are to prevent chaos we are going to have to rise above bartering and petty profit motives,” Ang began, “Mo is going to instruct the farming villages to share food and farming supplies with both the Gru villages and the urban areas. There has always been enough food to go around and we must maintain the distribution channels with everyone sharing the cost and no one profiting from it.”

“What you’re proposing is an end to the caste system,” Psi stated, “This will not be accepted as a trivial matter among many of the Gru, or even the Loru, for that matter.”

“Truly, I do not understand how the caste system has lasted as long as it has,” Ang said, “it is predicated on the survival needs of those who most benefit from the caste system itself. Do you see how that makes no sense?”

“Some would argue that the leadership of the Gru has been necessary to the increased development of society,” Psi said.

“I do not buy into that philosophy,” Jæms interjected, “The view that, before the arrival of the Rubicund refugees, the Hü were living as savage simpletons surviving by a nascent knowledge of foraging and fishing is rather myopic. As a descendant of fishers going back before the arrival of the refugees, I can assure you we were no more simpletons then than we are now.”

“I did not say that I hold these views,” Psi countered, “being born into a system does not make me an infinite slave to its immorality. You must know that the difference between a just leader and an evil tyrant is often subtle; even with the vision of a Gru, it may be difficult to recognize it.”

Jæms was taken aback by Lon Psi’s impressive statement. He had never met a Gru quite like the one upon which he was now gazing. He wished that he had the lie detection ability of the Gru, something he’d never considered to be a desirable advantage.

“I told you this was a different sort of Gru,” Ang said, breaking the awkward silence.

“A different sort of General,” Jæms added.

“General Psi, do you have any news of the efforts to extend the chryst supply?” Ang asked.

“Not much in the way of good news. The bloodfruit that we have been able to access from the infected plantations are of limited value. We were able to extend the supply by a rather paltry ten percent,” Psi responded.

“What do you mean ‘that we have been able to access’?” Ang asked.

"Those sacking firewasps that you brought from the southern plantations have nested around the diseased plantations," answered Psi, "for some odd reason they prefer the blossoms of the acidic fruit."

"Have the scientists look into that; there may be an underlying reason for the tastes of the firewasps," Ang thought about Farlay Singh as he spoke. The thoughts brought an internal feeling of disgust at believing his former friend was a traitor. Still, he could not help but wonder if Singh would be able to hypothesize why the firewasps were favoring the diseased plantations.

"I need to go to the Western Council lands," said Jæms, seemingly out of the blue.

Ang and Psi both turned to look at him with some confusion. His statement seemed to be at odds with the atmosphere of conversation. But Ang knew Jæms well enough by now to know that it was rare that he made idle statements extraneous to the moment.

"What's on your mind?" Ang asked.

"I'll need a half dozen of your troops and my ship, the *Restitution*," Jæms said, furthering the cryptic nature of his request.

"Come on Jæms, what's this about?" Ang questioned.

"I need to go to the REL," Brightson replied.

***

A Conference Room in the REL

Dabrill Kinselo was overwhelmed by the staggering size and advanced technology of the REL. Even Strongbark and the other Wazhazhe warriors who'd joined them on their trek with Fulong Su's team were impressed. Veegram insisted the tour of the facility was a trip back in time but it felt like a trip into the future.

Aside from the astonishing surroundings of the REL, Day was even more confused by Fulong Su. Before he met her, his heritage seemed somehow abstract. Now that same, obscure heritage was staring him in the face or, rather, staring back *at* him with blue eyes mirroring his own. Though there was little doubt that Day found Su intriguing, he did not keep secret his desire for nothing more than to take his leave and go find Farlay Singh.

Eryl found a similar appeal to Day's plans to search for Farlay, if for no other reason than the distance between Day and Su the plan would necessitate. Day's obvious interest in the beautiful painted Hü with the blue eyes had roused an emotional response in Eryl Syz that she had never experienced: jealousy.

Strongbark had inadvertently added fuel to Eryl's fiery feelings by confirming her suspicions that Fulong was also of the Sanguine tribe, though Su herself was reluctant to believe it. No matter what Fulong's tribal connections, Eryl knew she would feel much more content if there was some distance between Dabrill Kinselo and Fulong Su.

A few arms' lengths away, at one end of the conference room table, Veegram Lo sat in silence, once again in deep reverie contemplating what the best next course of action might be. While their forces continued to grow, Veegram knew that their forces, even coupled with that of their newfound allies, were of limited ability against the full force of the Army of the Western Council.

Veegram took solace in the fact that there was some relief in the latest information. Of particular value was the information obtained from the capture of Tarr, who was now secured in a more comfortable cell than he deserved deep in the bowels of the REL. Lo understood that there was less likelihood of a direct assault on the REL. Even more significant was the knowledge that the REL was in a greater position of defense considering the steps Fulong's team had taken.

Seated at the opposite end of the table, Strongbark, not unlike like Veegram, found himself in a deep reverie. There was nothing in the religion of the Protectors that accounted for all the factors he now knew. He tried to remember all the tellings he'd listen to from the Wazhazhe Teller during his childhood and as a young adult. Strongbark then remembered the telling of the Dex and the story of Apep.

"Has anyone noticed that there's something odd with the levels in this place?" Erol said as he burst into the room. He'd been on an extended tour of the facility due to his fascination with the technology. The looks he received let him know his boisterous entrance was not appreciated. He took a seat and sat in silence.

Strongbark opened his eyes and saw that Veegram was also now fully out of his meditative state. He noticed that Lo seemed no more relieved than he had when he closed his eyes. Looking around the room, many of the faces revealed the same, lost expression.

"There is a telling told by the Wazhazhe Tellers," Strongbark said, "It begins as the telling of the birth of the second moon and of the coming of the Dex. But the Teller always refers to another, more ancient story. It is the story of the Apep, the Serpent Dæmons, the Bringers of Chaos. I'm not sure that it means anything but the original name of the second moon was Apophis. This was before the moon grew and became Sis, or the Little Sister to Luna."

"I don't see how ancient fables are going to help us," Fulong Su interjected.

"Patience General Su," Veegram admonished, "Remember, every moment leads us to the next."

Fulong sat back in her seat and crossed her arms in protest. Strongbark looked at her and thought that she might be right. Then he looked at Day, who seemed more interested than he had a few moments before. Strongbark knew that Day was anxious to leave this place in his attempt to find his friend.

"I believe the Sanguine Tellers may have a similar telling," Strongbark said to Day. Then, turning back to Veegram, he continued, "In any event, the story of Apep is said to be passed down from a codex belonging to an ancient sect of priests. In the story, it tells of six ways that a believer may defeat the Serpent Dæmon."

With that, Fulong Su sat upright and placed her elbows on the edge of the table. In lock step, the remainder of the group also gave Strongbark their undivided attention. This made Strongbark a little uncomfortable because he remembered so little of the tellings.

"My apologies but I do not remember all six of the ways of defeating the Apep," he said, with some reluctance, "But I do remember the last had something to do with placing fire upon the Apep."

The group sat for a few degrees, chewing upon Strongbark's words and digesting what they might mean. For a few moments, even Day was distracted from his purpose of finding and freeing his friend.

"I remember one other thing," Strongbark then realized, "the name 'Apep' means vessel, or ship. The story implied that Apep was just the vessel of the Serpent Dæmons."

Veegram asked, "How certain are you that the Sanguine Teller will know and be able to relate the story of Apep?"

"Whenever the Protectors have visited among other tribes of Protectors, it is customary to have a telling for the visitors. The Apep story is a favorite among children because it is somewhat scary to them," Strongbark answered, "I have never heard a telling as ancient as that of the coming of the Dex that has varied by more than a few words among the different tribes of Protectors."

As he was wont to do when entering into his meditative state, Veegram closed his eyes, touched the tips of his fingers together and perched his chin upon the them. Contrary to the anticipation of the group, Veegram did not linger long in silence.

"Strongbark, will you take General Su to visit the Sanguine?" Veegram asked, neither opening his eyes nor removing his chin from its perch.

***

Eryl and Erol Syz, Day and a dozen Wazhazhe warriors departed the REL on a D-class sled early the following dawn, soon after the setting of Sis. The timing of the departure was planned to maintain the ruse established by Fulong and her team the previous dawn, before their planned ambush. Veegram had ordered the REL be camouflaged to appear as if an explosion had occurred, destroying the facility. Strongbark, Day and their companions were rather impressed by the utilization of several of the visibility bypass generators in the well-constructed subterfuge.

As Day and his team put distance between themselves and the REL, he knew that Strongbark and Fulong would be leaving the sanctuary soon thereafter. Though he was somewhat torn because he wanted to see the tribal lands of the Sanguine for himself, the potential dire circumstances of Farlay pulled Day to the south rather than the west. If he could and was not already too late, he needed to help his friend.

"Roughbark will take us to the Sanguine after we rescue Farlay," Eryl said, sensing Day's distress.

"Once my brother tells the Sanguine of Dabrill, he may have to dissuade them from coming for him," Roughbark said.

"Why would he dissuade them?" asked Erol.

"The Prophecy," Roughbark replied.

Eryl and her brother attempted to press Roughbark for more details of the Prophecy. But the younger brother of Strongbark remained stalwart in his silence on the subject, his expression unchanging. Eryl considered how the warrior's name fit him well; his tough exterior surface concealing a stronger interior hardwood.

Day settled into piloting the sled for the initial leg of the long trip. From the information Eryl and Day managed to extract from Tarr, they knew the general location of South Camp. The long rumored dark detention center of the Western Council was thought to be located at the southern extreme of the jurisdiction of the Southern Council. This was where the government sent enemies to languish after their experts had tortured all the information out of them that they could.

Dabrill estimated that the travel time from the REL to the InDees Mountains was at least a syphus plus a dawn. This presumed maintaining a reasonably high rate of speed by piloting in shifts while preserving some degree of stealth as necessary. The team would need to take at least six breaks of twelve cycles each. Several of the stops at the latter stages of the trip to the InDees would have Wazhazhe cantonments available for concealment of the team but for the first couple of respites, they would need to make their own camouflage.

After reaching the InDees Mountains, the travel seemed less certain to Day. Roughbark indicated it would take many syphi to travel the length of the mountain range to the presumed location of South Camp. Suspensor craft would not function that far south and only the Wazhazhe and the local tribes of Protectors knew how to navigate the rugged terrain of the mountains.

Neither the Hü nor the Rubicund ventured far distances into the InDees. Some of this was out fear and superstition, similar to the fear and superstition that surrounded the Great Spirit Mountains west of the Lava Flats. Day knew that the real reason was that there was thought to be little value in the farmland in or beyond the mountains. Day also knew that the conflict was fast becoming an exhausting endeavor, though it had just begun. Exhaustion could cause either side to consider doing risky things they would otherwise not.

"You should get some rest," Roughbark said to Day, noticing the fatigue on his face, "I can pilot for a few cycles."

Day moved aside, relinquishing the controls to his Wazhazhe friend. Moving to the back of the sled, he took a seat on the bench along the portside of the open top, bucket-like cargo bed of the craft.

Eryl followed close behind Day and seated herself at his side. They sat in silence watching the handsome landscape recede behind them in a blur. The craft was now traveling along the border between the edge of the Savannah and the Lava Flats; bone shrubs and the dry stems of grass zipping by one side and a flat sea of glassy lava on the other. Day placed his bedroll on his shoulder and used it as cushion as he leaned against the half-stanchion of the rail at the rear of the sled. He soon drifted off to sleep. Eryl leaned her head against Day's arm and joined him in slumber.

***

Fulong Su was a less than intrepid companion of the two dozen Wazhazhe warriors taking her to visit the Sanguine. In fact, she had more trepidations than she cared to admit. *What would these people be like? Would they, like Strongbark, insist that I am one of them?* She thought. Most of all, Fulong feared that she would find the Sanguine people comfortable.

Su had discovered an innate sense of comfort in the presence of the Wazhazhe. The emotional response roused in her a little anger, another emotion Su considered foreign. She never remembered a time when she felt uncomfortable so she could not understand how the Wazhazhe could cause a feeling of greater comfort.

As the two D-class sleds glided along the edge of the North Forest in tandem, General Su looked out over the water of Lake Perion to the south. Fulong thought about Day. He was another puzzle to her emotional responses. When she first saw his face in the viewscopes, she'd felt happiness in a strangely familiar manner. When Day departed on his rescue mission, she felt a deep sadness so strong that she almost called out to him to tell him to return safely.

"I believe you call this Lake Perion," Strongbark said, unintentionally interrupting her meditation.

"Yes," Su replied. Then, out of simple courtesy, she asked, "What do the Protectors call it?"

"Gitchi-gami," Strongbark answered.

"What does that mean?" Su asked with a genuine interest.

Strongbark looked out over the water and said, "Big Sea."

"Well, it is that," Fulong agreed.

The tall Wazhazhe warrior considered if he should press the issue of Fulong's true heritage. He knew that what she would learn about herself from the Sanguine could be disturbing to her. *How can I help her understand the Prophecy without revealing it to her?* Strongbark thought.

"Will we be passing by the edge of the Lava Flats?" Su asked.

"Yes, but the northern edge is somewhat different in appearance than the rest," Strongbark replied, "The eastern side is where many of the Forgetful Ones go to mourn the loss of children, as I am sure you are aware."

"Yes," Su said, "and many Ru go there for retreat and to rub the statue of the Camel for good fortune and long life."

Strongbark chuckled, somewhat louder than he was aware.

"What's so funny?" Fulong asked, "The tale of *The Camel and the Müul* is a sad story."

"I ask your forgiveness," he replied, "no offense was intended."

Fulong stared at Strongbark for a few moments then nodded in acceptance of his apology. Her thoughts then drifted to images of the western Savannah and the eastern border of the Lava Flats. Then she thought of her parents and the older sister she never met.

The Su family was somewhat of a rarity among the castes. Although Lehu, they were considered to be of moderate means and were well-respected in the Eastern Steppes. Fulong had a comfortable childhood and received a top-level education. With her education and the considerable influence of her parents, she managed to become the youngest agent ever appointed in the RHIB. Her acquaintance with Thys Gor after the murder of her father had been her inside connection to the RHIB but she knew she had earned her current reputation there on her own merits and actions.

While she knew that her parents loved her, in particular her mother with whom she grew closer after her father's death, Fulong also knew that her mother never fully recovered from the loss of her older sister. Fulong's parents had been among those to which Strongbark referred when he remarked that the 'Forgetful Ones' pilgrimage to the Lava Flats to mourn lost children.

Among the few prosperous Loru and Hü families that existed, those who had lost children often went to the edge of the Savannah with hope; even calling the place New Hope. It was well-rumored that indigent families of the Southern and Western Council regions would bring their children there, children they could ill afford to raise but with the hope of a better future for their young ones.

When she was sixteen anni old, just before she left for school at the Government Intelligence Office, Fulong's mother told her the truth, which she'd suspected from the age of eleven. Fulong was one of those children adopted on the edge of the Savannah.

In those anni since being given the knowledge of her adoption, Fulong had convinced herself that her biological parents had not abandoned her because she was a financial burden. Rather, they must have abandoned her because she was a painted Hü, the lowest of the low.

Now Fulong's head spun. If she were to accept that she came from a race of painted Hü, the Protectors, as Strongbark called them, then why would they have abandoned her? *Follow the evidence*, Fulong told herself.

The Protectors were not a destitute people. Strongbark and the warriors wore well-made clothing and were intelligent and educated; though she could not imagine in what schools they obtained such knowledge. They did not give up their children due to abject poverty. *Follow the evidence*, Fulong again thought.

The Protectors were not sexists like the Rubicund. Of the two dozen warriors with which she now traveled, ten were feminine and of equal standing among the group. Indeed, Strongbark's second in command was feminine. The Protectors did not hold feminine children of lower desirability than masculine children. *Follow the evidence!* Fulong's thoughts now screamed in frustration.

She looked out over the water toward her left and calmed herself. She knew that Strongbark had to be right: she was of the same race as the warriors; she was just too similar to them in physical appearance. But there had to be an answer as to why they would have abandoned her almost twenty-three anni ago.

Su looked back at Strongbark, then glanced back at the other warriors and at once realized the difference in a sudden flash of self-awareness. It was obvious to others but not so obvious to her. At least it hadn't been obvious to her before, when Dabrill was among the group. After all, he'd been the first painted Hü she'd ever seen before the previous dawn. But now, with Dabrill off on his rescue mission, the evidence was before her. Su was different from most of the Protectors in one peculiar way.

"Are there many blue-eyed Protectors?" Fulong asked Strongbark.

She is a clever one, Strongbark thought. Then he replied, "You and Dabrill are the only two I have ever met."

"My mother," Fulong began, then corrected herself, "my adoptive mother, told me that I had a different name before she took me home. She said my name was Dahguine Cantuke."

"Ah, it is an old name," Strongbark said.

"What does it mean?" Fulong asked.

Strongbark hesitated for a degree, then answered, "Blue pools in the dark and bloody ground."

"That doesn't sound flattering," Su said, "Do the Protectors have a prejudice against the blue-eyed among their people."

“On the contrary, blue eyes, though of exceeding rarity, are well-respected among the Protectors,” answered Strongbark.

“Then, if I am of the Sanguine, one of the tribes of the Protectors, as you suggest, why would they have given me up to a Lehu family of the Eastern Steppes?” Fulong asked.

With the utterance of the words ‘Eastern Steppes’, several of the warriors whispered, “Shibwoteth.”

Strongbark ignored the warriors’ whispers and said, “That is a question best asked of a Teller.”

Su realized that she was not apt to get more information out of Strongbark. She was at least content that she had followed the evidence and arrived at the beginnings of understanding as to why she was abandoned by her biological parents many anni ago. She looked back out over the water, and allowed her mind to rest a bit.

“Gitchi-gami,” she said.

“Big Sea,” Strongbark echoed.

***

Laughing Birch was perched as still as a statue with her expert aim directed at General Sul’s chest. She knew her camouflage was perfect but she dared not take any chances with this adversary. She’d seen the destruction he had wrought on the towns of the Southern Council area in his search for Dabrill. To Laughing Birch’s way of thinking, this scarlet bottle child had transformed himself into an evil Crimson Dæmon, as the Protectors had begun to refer to him.

Her reconnaissance team was by her side, cloaked among the trees and as ready as she to defend their territory. Birch was more accepting of the harsh truth of their situation: they were outnumbered. She realized that the likelihood of defeating two companies of well-trained army regulars was doubtful. One hundred and fifty strong, the Crimson Dæmon’s elite personal command forces outnumbered her Protector’s reconnaissance force five-to-one. The nearest reinforcements were at least two cycles distance even if Laughing Birch could signal for such assistance.

Though a scant dozen furlongs from the edge of the forest, this was the farthest intrusion into the Wazhazhe jungle thus far. She knew that sooner, rather than later, there would be a clash or the Rubicund would discover one of the Wazhazhe cantonments. The rebels of the Forgetful Ones in the Southern Council lands were broken and beaten and the aggression of the Crimson Dæmon and his army was far from satiated.

“The trail has gone dark,” a scruffy looking Lieutenant announced. The soldier was standing below Birch and talking to General Sul.

“Pollux, Castor, return,” General Sul commanded. With a few bounding leaps, the General’s brace of scimitar cats returned to his side.

The shrill, choral voice of Sul triggered a territorial response from a vermic nesting just below Laughing Birch. The long, building, haunting trill of the owl brought shivers to many of the soldiers unfamiliar with its call. The Lieutenant near the base of the owl’s tree, embarrassed by his fear, let off a sonic blast in the general direction of the owl’s voice.

The focus of the burst from the soldier’s rifle missed, hitting above the vermic’s knot-hole home but on Laughing Birch’s left foot. She heard and felt the crack and knew two things: her ankle was broken and she would not be able to hold her position in the tree. Birch nudged her aim to a point just above Sul’s head and let fly her quilled projectile, then tried to reach out and grab the nearest branch to arrest her fall. The branch she chose was not strong enough.

Birch landed on her back, losing consciousness for a few moments. Falcon-Tongue, Birch’s second, adjusted her aim to General Sul’s chest while several of her fellow warriors targeted the two predatory cats at his side. The Crimson Dæmon and his luminous-eyed scimitars were soon standing over the fallen Wazhazhe warrior.

“What have we here?” General Sul asked.

The General watched as two soldiers lifted her to her feet and, noticing her wince at the weight placed on her ankle, they continued to support her, holding her upright to face their commander. As Sul ogled her, the soldiers pulled back the hood that was hiding her face. When Sul saw the face of a painted Hü before him, he was astonished. He recognized that a significant key to their search of the ghost forest had just fallen from the sky.

“I sense that this one may know citizen Kinselo,” Sul said in his most sardonic choral voice.

“I have a great many friends,” Birch said with the contempt plain in her voice.

Sul understood what his new prisoner was implying and glanced upward into the trees. Looking back at her, he considered her words and tried to see any tell-tale signs that she was lying. At last, he convinced himself that a superior force or even a somewhat lesser force would have already attacked.

One of his soldiers handed him the wayward projectile that had been fired over his head. Looking at the razor tip he judged that the resinous material in which it was covered was toxic. He again stared at Birch, noticing the pouch slung over her shoulder was filled with identical projectiles, some of which appeared broken from her fall.

"I assure you that the next one will hit its mark," Laughing Birch said.

Although Sul was certain that his force was superior, he did believe that he might lose on a personal level should he press his fortune further.

"Bring her," Sul ordered, then turned to depart the forest.

Laughing Birch made the slightest of gestures with her hand and Falcon-Tongue knew that she and the Wazhazhe now under her command were ordered to stand down. Fal watched in anger as the Crimson Dæmon drew farther away. For a few moments, and with some seriousness, she considered disobeying Birch's order. As the troops vanished on their trek out of forest, she thought, *Quietstar is going to kill me.*

When she was sure the last of the army was far enough away, Fal signaled to the remainder of the Wazhazhe to follow her deeper into the forest to the secure cantonment post of their reconnaissance force.

***

Day watched as the Wazhazhe played a game to pass the time. It was late on the second dawn of their journey to the Southern Council lands. The sled on which they rode was now cruising much further south, deep into the valleys of the mountains just north of the Wazhazhe jungle.

As the sled passed through a long, V-shaped vale, it was Quietstar's turn. Darkeye handed him three projectiles with small, bulbous, blunted tips. Quietstar checked the alignment of the feathers at the rear of the projectiles and the alignment of the shaft. Satisfied with his inspection, the warrior then dropped them into his otherwise empty shoulder pouch.

The remainder of passengers participating in the revelry began giving him a countdown in Wazhazhe. From his watching of the three previous players, Day was unable to discern the purpose of the game. Darkeye's attempt had drawn some cheers from the other Wazhazhe when she was able to hang from the edge of the bucket-bed and retrieve her projectiles from the soft ground without leaving the sled. The two warriors that preceded her had required a brief stop by the pilot, Roughbark. Once, somewhat to Day's annoyance at the delay, there had been a short search for a stray projectile.

At what Day now knew to be the conclusion of the countdown, Quietstar drew and launched three projectiles ahead of the sled in rapid succession. The other warriors chanted "teth" with each release of a projectile. Day had learned from Roughbark that 'teth' meant 'true' and he surmised that the chant was meant to encourage the shots of the contestant to have a true flight.

Day watched as the arc of Quietstar's shots began bringing them down into the direct path of the sled. He soon realized that the projectiles might collide with the sled. A few moments later, Day moved his body in front of Eryl in an instinctive attempt to protect her from the incoming rain of shots. He then watched in astonishment as Quietstar grabbed the projectiles, one by one, the last of which he snatched from the air at the end of the sled, his toes perched on the upper edge of the back rail of the bucket.

Quietstar climbed back down into the bed of the sled with an expression of victory upon his face. The Wazhazhe cheered, each slapping Quietstar on the back as the obvious winner of the game; a game that Day now understood.

"Time to settle down," Roughbark announced as he slowed the sled, "We're approaching the north jungle."

Roughbark steered the sled into the edge of the forest as far as he could safely navigate it. Only a few degrees after they disembarked, the Wazhazhe had camouflaged the sled and were trekking, on foot, to the first cantonment of the Wazhazhe jungle.

As the group approached the cantonment, Falcon-Tongue emerged from the concealed entryway to meet them. Roughbark, Darkeye and Quietstar were surprised to see her on the northern end of the Wazhazhe territory.

"Why are you here?" Roughbark asked.

Fal began to explain the incident with General Sul at the southern end of the Wazhazhe jungle. As she spoke in the Wazhazhe language, Quietstar's expression distorted under the gravity of her recounting. He was visibly shaken and his eyes seemed as if they were ready to set the entire forest ablaze.

When Fal finished speaking, Quietstar stormed into the cantonment. Roughbark then recounted Falcon-Tongue's story to Day, Eryl and her brother. He finished with, "Fal believes they have taken Laughing Birch to South Camp."

"Why is Quietstar so upset?" Eryl asked.

"Laughing Birch is to be his mate," Darkeye replied.

En-tré

"No one can hurt me without my permission."

Ancient Hü Philosopher

The *Restitution* was the fastest ship of the northern fishing fleet. With empty bladder-wells and a capable crew, Jæms Brightson's trimaran was the equal of any ship on any sea. He and his handpicked crew of five made the crossing of the North Lant Sea in just over ninety cycles. Jæms was a little disappointed that the *Res* had not equaled her previous best.

Brightson located a familiar lagoon on the coast of Lesser North Bay and dropped anchor. Leaving two of his crew to tend the *Res*, Jæms and his remaining crew departed the forward hatch of the front hold on three B-class suspensor craft.

Brightson was sure that he knew the general location of the REL but was not as confident that he could find its exact position without an extended, systematic search. When he was a young child, he and his parents had gone on a pilgrimage to see the Lava Flats and the famous statue of the Camel. Soon after entering the Eastern Council's territory, his family were stopped by Gru Army soldiers. After a brief interrogation, they were released but diverted from the more direct path they had planned. Jæms later heard his parents conclude that they must have stumbled onto the grounds of the decommissioned REL.

He was sure he could find the general area again. He did not know what he would now find there or how close he would be permitted to get to the actual facility. Jæms had a rather sketchy plan of how to approach the facility undetected but, most of all, he figured he would make it up as he went along. He had always been good at improvising; every old salt fisher was.

When Jæms calculated that he was about a furlong from the spot where he and his parents were detained and diverted, he brought his small team to a halt. As he and his companions sat discussing Jæms' plan of action, they heard a suspensor vehicle approaching. Startled by the unexpected approach of the vehicle, Jæms and his crew prepared to bolt.

"Wait!" a voice yelled at the three, "I just want to talk."

Jæms paused and allowed himself a closer look at the small vehicle and its occupants. Two of those in the craft were dressed in what appeared to be RHIB uniforms, which confused Brightson. Further bewilderment came at the sight of the pilot, a Gru whom Brightson recognized. He had seen the distinguished scarlet face of the elder Gru numerous times on PIA image broadcasts. It was the ex-Chancellor, Veegram Lo. *What is he doing here?* Jæms thought.

"Forgive the intrusion," Lo said, "I imagine that you were planning an elaborate ruse of some sort so that you could approach the REL for closer observation. Regrettably, we don't have the time for any such trivialities, Sis will be rising soon and we cannot afford to have any activity exposed to the view of the enemy in this area. Please follow me."

Instinctively, Jæms looked toward the eastern horizon, wondering what the little moon had to do with anything. Although he was puzzled by Lo's abrupt words, he and his companions climbed aboard their suspensor vehicles and followed the ex-Chancellor.

***

A little more than twelve cycles later, Jæms Brightson sat staring at the console in the Emergency Communications Room of the REL. The blinking lights were mesmerizing and the knowledge he'd learned over the last few cycles was overwhelming. Veegram Lo watched as he leaned against a wall behind Jæms. The two waited in the dim lighting of the almost silent room, the sole company of noise for almost a cycle being the electric hum of the various transmission equipment.

The buzz of an alarm disrupted the hypnotic electrical hum and brought the gaze of both the room's occupants to the chronograph; the numerals of which had now turned green. According to Lo's understanding of how the chronograph worked, the green lighting meant that Sis was now set.

"Now?" Jæms asked.

"Now," Veegram replied, then took a seat beside Brightson.

Jæms depressed the button on the console labeled 'transmit'. The conversation that ensued lasted just a few units. When it was concluded, Brightson sat in stunned silence, again with just the electrical hum of the room to provide a background to the distant stares of the occupants.

After more degrees of silence than the transceiver conversation had taken, Jæms broke the quiet, "We may actually win this war. Especially considering we now have a better idea of the identity of the true factions."

"The planet may win this war," Veegram corrected.

***

"The Council of the Eastern Steppes has fallen," Mo Lök began his report, "there are tent towns all over the Eastern Steppes, and the RHIB has surrendered and is under the jurisdiction of the rebel forces."

Ang Obryn stood in complete silence for several degrees, allowing the full weight of his friend's words to sink in. He had come here for war and to conquer government and now it was probable he would be bogged down in the restoration of civil order to both Councils. To Ang, it seemed absurd that he and his army were becoming the new, de facto government.

"How are the Gru doing? Do they have chryst?" Ang asked, the concern obvious in his voice.

"They are in about the same shape as the Gru living *here*," Mo replied, "They are living in tents around the two remaining plantations and harvesting the bloodfruit themselves. The Hü and Loru have erected most of their encampments around the farms but are sharing their food with the Gru."

"Well, at least there is peace," Ang commented.

"Peace is not without some effort," Mo said, "it seems they owe a lot to a Gru government official or, rather, former Gru government official named Thys Gor. He's formed a new, cooperative alliance with the Resistance forces."

"You have talked with him in person?" Ang asked.

"Not in person, but he has requested we send a committee to discuss a broader alliance between the Central and Eastern regions of the former Union of Councils," Mo replied.

"Does he aim to pit the Central and Eastern regions against the Western and the Southern Councils?" Ang asked, somewhat alarmed.

"It is difficult to tell, but his representatives, Lehu of the Resistance, seem to have an implicit trust of him," Mo said, "They say he even has a team of RHIB agents working in the Western Council region toward peace. I think he may be one Gru we could trust."

"Two Gru we can trust; I trust General Psi," Ang said, then asked "RHIB agents?"

"Thys Gor was the Chief of the RHIB before the Resistance uprising," Mo answered, "He's the Gru who surrendered the RHIB before the Resistance even attacked. The Lehu with whom I spoke said that he had evidence that the Resistance was not responsible for the phage."

"General Psi and I will meet with this Thys Gor," Ang said, "Mo, gather five of our Resistance leaders and five of those with prior loyalties to the Central Council. General Psi and I will lead this committee to meet with the new Eastern Alliance leaders."

***

"What is going on in the east?" Silas Mis demanded, "There is no word from our troops, the leadership or even the RHIB."

General Sul looked at Chancellor Mis with the same disdain and contempt he viewed most any useless bureaucrat. In secret, Sul wanted to be one of the elites, the highest of the upper class. His family history prevented Sul from having such aspirations. Nevertheless, the General had his own plans for advancement to the top and those plans did not require being high-born. Sul knew that he had to put up with foolish leaders like Silas Mis a little longer, at least until he could acquire further control of the armies.

"The east is lost for the time being," Sul answered, "they did not have the resolve to stand up to the rebels."

"The loss of the east is the fault of Psi, he was always weak," Mis said.

"We will defeat the rebels here and the east will be begging us for chryst; their plantations are failing," Sul said with confidence, "The Southern Council plantations are untouched and the plantations here are holding now that the new infections have ceased. When they are starved for chryst, the Gru of the east will become desperate and will revolt against their new rebel leaders."

"You are presupposing that we will win the battle for the west," Mis continued his emotional venting, "the rebels have stolen from my chryst hoards, managed to blind dozens of the elite Capital City guards while escaping from our trap at the armory, disrupted phase two of our plans, taken my own security chief from under my nose and I haven't heard from Tarr in several syphi. It seems to me that we are, at best, holding the west in a state of stalemate."

"Nonsense, Excellency," Sul disagreed, almost vomiting from his distaste of calling Mis 'Excellency', "You should be more patient. I have a virtual dominance over the Southern Plantation areas and another three hundred of the most stubborn rebels have been sent from there to South Camp. Most of the rest are working the plantations."

"But you still haven't found the twins," Mis accused, "they embarrassed me in public."

"We will find your former security chief and his meddling sister," Sul vowed, "we control the southern lands from the South Lant Sea to the InDees Mountains and the jungles of the Nicaran Isthmus. There are few things for them there other than reptiles and a paltry number of scattered feral jungle dwellers."

"Those feral jungle dwellers, as you call them, managed to defeat my personal guard and have eluded you to the point of embarrassment," Mis chided.

"Again, your Excellency," Sul said, again choking on the use of the honorific, "patience is essential here. We have arranged a trap by sending a friend of the painted Hü to South Camp and repeated the announcement of his trip every few cycles via the PIA. I assure you that we will either find them or have them come to us."

"Make sure that you do," Mis threatened, "your future, as well as the future of our plans now depend on you finding the feminine Syz and bringing her to me, unharmed."

***

If Quietstar had seemed relaxed before the news of the capture of Laughing Birch, he gave none that impression now. For more than two months, Dabrill and the Wazhazhe party had struggled to keep pace with the warrior and his mission. After leaving the jungle, the group traveled under the cover of the InDees Mountains. The entire entourage wore the Wazhazhe cloaks, using them to reduce their respites, even with Sis visible in the skies above them. They traveled by foot, ascending and descending imperceptible stairways; by canoe, navigating the rapids and narrow bends of the mountain streams; by secret, peak-to-peak bridgeways and fast, fly-line cables.

Day was at first impressed by the extent of the Wazhazhe territory and the cantonments dispersed throughout the InDees Mountains. He soon discovered that the path they traveled was leading them through the territories of many different tribes of Protectors. Quietstar led the group through the territories of the Kunzas, the Huancas and half a dozen others.

The journey became an eye-opening education for Day. It was true that there was no affection lost between Day and the Gru, yet the fragmentary tales of atrocities and abuses that he heard from the tribes of the InDees built a resentment in him. Upon hearing portions of the Býleistr tellings recounting the coming of the Rubicund and their conquests of the southern lands, Day found his resentment swell into anger.

Day's anger grew into hatred as he learned that the Protectors had continued to suffer at the hands of the Gru for centuries until they transformed themselves into the ghosts of the forests and conditioned their scarlet nemeses to fear the unknown, foreboding things that lay hidden in the depths of the jungles. Day felt ashamed to be among his own race when he considered that he once worked in the factories among the Forgetful Ones and helped to provide the Gru with their necessary chryst.

Though the rescue party hoped to pass through to the extreme south unnoticed, they first encountered the Gru Army as they came to the lands of the Cañari. Over the mild protestations of Quietstar, Roughbark suggested that the group take a more extended rest and camp in the valley on the banks of the Upaño River. There they would have a chance to bath in some of the many hot springs dotting the banks and coves along the long river.

Arriving at the northern extreme of the Cañari tribal lands, the group stopped and looked across the Upaño Valley, to a major sub-range of the InDees known to the locals as the Thunderbird Mountains. During the long trek, Roughbark indulged his habit of singing ballads to build spirits and help maintain the energy among the rescuers. One such ballad generated an anticipation of sighting the giant birds of the InDees, beginning in the Thunderbird Mountains and continuing south almost to Land's End. The massive avians were known to sometimes soar over the Upaño Valley, between the main range of the InDees and the major branch of the mountains that jutted north and eastward from the south, which derived its name from the raptors.

The thunderbirds were said to be so large that they could carry off an entire ox. It was fortunate for the group that the large birds were eaters of the dead, feasting upon the carrion of the InDees. In hopes of a glimpse of such a large bird, the eager newcomers to the area now paused before descending into the valley and toward the Upaño river.

Looking through her brother's viewscope, Eryl scanned the sky above the mountains across the valley but found no sign of the great scavengers. She passed the viewscopes to Day who also had no luck in finding the elusive birds. Day returned the viewscope to Erol who then replaced them in the holster at his side as the group commenced the dawn-long southern descent into the valley.

***

The Challenge of the Upaño River

The place the group chose for the encampment afforded good protection to the east and west due to the mountains on either side of the large valley. Since Sis was not in ascension, they built a fire in a protected cove, which limited the possibility of anyone sighting it from any direction other than the larger InDees Mountains to the west.

As the warriors settled into their camp on the river's bank, several Cañari youth approached and were challenged by Roughbark, who had drawn the first south watch. After conversing with them in the common language of Protectors, Roughbark brought them to the group near the fire at the cove-base of their camp.

"These are Cañari warrior apprentices," Roughbark said. "They've come to shoot the river's rapids in the dark as a demonstration of their skills as warriors."

Erol looked at the five feminine and four masculine youth who stood in the light of the fire and asked "In what? They don't have any canoes."

"They say that their canoes are stashed away in a cavern a furlong farther down the river," Roughbark answered, "It is a ritual that is millennia-old among the Cañari youth to prove their abilities."

Weary and without full and proper consideration of his words, Day chuckled and said, "Navigating a river they know in the light of a full first moon seems like a miniscule test of their skills."

One of the young feminine warriors spoke up in the common language of the Hü, asking, "Has the blue-eyed stranger mastered the river in total darkness?"

Roughbark and Quietstar smiled at the bold challenge of the young warrior apprentice.

"No," Day answered, realizing his mistake and somewhat surprised that the young warrior apprentice spoke multiple languages with ease.

"Has the blue-eyed stranger mastered the river on an overcast evening?" asked the young warrior.

"No," he answered.

"Perhaps the blue-eyed stranger would care to demonstrate his mastery of the river this evening under the light of the full first moon?" the young warrior asked, then added, "So we may easily witness the greatness of his skill," completing her challenge.

Day looked around at the other members of his group and saw that all, including Eryl, were now smiling at the predicament in which he had ensnared himself. Quietstar was even snickering, albeit in silence and for just a few brief moments. It was the first time he'd so much as smiled since embarking on the rescue mission.

Already bested in the verbal argument by the young Cañari warrior apprentice, Day realized that there was little exit from this clear blunder. He also knew that, in addition to rest, the group needed some distraction, even if that distraction was at the expense of his own embarrassment.

He stood and said, "I assume you have an extra canoe for me."

Half a cycle later, the group hauled the lightweight, single canoer crafts from the cavern. They then began setting the sleek canoes on the still water in a shallow pool of the river's bank. Day examined the one they offered for his use. Like the others, it had a lightweight, ligneous frame with a full hull and deck skinning in a cloth similar to the material of the Wazhazhe cloaks.

He felt the hard, resin-like wax coating on the hull and understood that the canoes would be lightning-fast. He looked inside the hull and saw that, unlike any canoe he'd ever used, it was equipped with foot pedals for control of the rudder. *Fast and agile*, Day thought.

Once the nine youths and Day were on the river in the canoes, the latter soon fell behind the youths who indeed did know the river well. The remainder of the rescue party followed along the riverbank, save Erol and Quietstar, who stayed behind to finish cooking the evening meal. Though leading the group of followers along the banks, Eryl and Roughbark fell far behind Day due to the rough terrain and the darkness, even under the light of the full moon.

Roughbark tapped Eryl on the shoulder and said, "We should turn back. The youths will bring him back, maybe a little damp but no worse than that for the wear. Besides, he seems quite capable as a canoer and the course is not too severe."

"Very well," Eryl said.

The remainder of the mobile audience also turned to return to the encampment, much revived by the brief pause for light fun. The happy mood among the group soon turned to despair as they came around the last outcropping of rock before the cove where the encampment lay. Within moments, the party of would-be rescuers, save Dabrill Kinselo, were captured and in need of rescue themselves.

***

Day managed to prevent his total embarrassment by overtaking the trail end of his youthful canoeing rivals before the rapids had ended. He finished in the middle of the pack but well behind the warrior apprentice who'd issued the challenge.

As they made their way back to the cavern with their craft, Day said, "So that we're clear, my name is not blue-eyed stranger, it's Day. What is your name?"

"Cañari warrior apprentices are not named until they become true warriors," she said.

"When is that?" Day asked.

"Not until we have proven our personal bravery," she replied, "and that is decided by our individual mentors."

Day considered how every aspect of the Protectors' society seemed so communal. Each member, young or old was expected to earn their place in society. Cañari warrior apprentices were stripped of their birth names upon becoming students and trained as anonymous acolytes until they earned their warrior names.

After returning the canoes to the cavern, the group began the short trek back to the encampment. The full moon was now at apex and lighting their path well with the sure-footed young feminine apprentice leading the way for the group. Stopping in mid-stride, she raised a clinched fist and crouched low on the beach. At her signal, Day and the rest of the youths crouched behind her.

Day then heard what the young apprentice heard. The still evening air of the valley carried many voices toward them along the calmer waters of this wide stretch of the Upaño. The noises consisted of indistinguishable dialog along with laughing, grunting and general sounds of exuberance, as of the victorious completion of a major campaign. The emotions of the voices were not what alarmed Day. Rather, it was the vibrato nature of each of them that made it seem as if a battalion were carousing at the cove. *Gru!* Day thought.

Despite the choral texture of each of the voices, the returning canoers reasoned that there was not a battalion strength of troops that was indicated by the voices.

The reality was bad enough: at least a company strength of Gru soldiers were in their encampment. Retreating several paces, the group of young warriors huddled around Day.

"What do we do?" one of the young apprentices asked in a whisper.

"You are all earning your names this evening," Day said, "We need eyes on them. Who is the best climber among you?"

Eight of the youths pointed to the smallest of the group, a scrawny feminine youth with wide eyes that Day thought had the appearance of the eyes of a startled forest owl.

"Can you whistle like the evening bird I've been hearing in these mountains?" Day asked the youth.

"You mean the Solitaire?" asked another of the youths.

The young, scrawny apprentice tried to whistle but was dry mouthed from her nerves. She wet her lips and tried again, this time creating a perfect imitation of the bird's piercing high-pitched voice.

"Good, you are now Solitaire. We need you to climb above the cove and give one short call like the one you just made when you can see the Gru. Then count off thirty moments and give one long call if the Gru are less than fifty in number and two long calls if more than that," Day said, "Make the calls longer than five moments, if there are more than seventy Gru," he added.

Solitaire nodded, indicating she understood. She moved toward the rocks to begin her climb but Day stopped her and said, "After that, count to yourself sixty moments and give one short call if our warriors are being held together and two long calls if they are separate. When your mission is finished, climb high on the cliff and wait for my signal before you come down."

Again, Solitaire nodded in comprehension and waited to see if there were additional instructions from Day. The latter motioned for her to go, to which she disappeared toward the bluff.

Turning to the other youths, Day asked, "Do you have any weapons?"

"We each carry small knives for use in making snares and cleaning fish," one of the masculine youths said.

"We have a few bola's and two hunting spears back in the cavern," answered the youth who'd challenged Day to the canoeing.

"You are Fierce-Talker. Take four others to get the weapons and three canoes and bring all of it back here," Day said.

As Fierce-Talker and the other youths left to return to the cavern, Solitaire gave her first, short call indicating she was in position and could see the Gru. Day was surprised at how fast she'd climbed the cliff in the moonlight. He counted the thirty moments and heard the two long calls of Solitaire. They were each much longer than five moments, indicating more than seventy Gru. *Sack!* Day thought without changing his expression before the youths.

Day then turned to the remaining three youths and said, "Gather as many river rocks about half the size of your hand as you can, good for throwing hard and far. Bring them back here and put them in a pile."

Solitaire gave her last call, a short one, indicating the warriors were being held as a group. Fierce-Talker and her group were returning with the weapons and canoes. Day looked at the squad of inexperienced young warriors before him and realized what he was about to do could get them all killed, along with himself. He had little choice. If they didn't act to rescue them, the consequences would be dire for his friends.

"Who was the closest to Fierce-Talker when we finished the canoeing earlier?" Day asked.

A stout, masculine youth raised his hand.

"Are you accurate with the bolas?" Day asked.

"I am almost as good as…as Fierce-Talker," he answered, hesitating to use her new name.

"You are now Chaser of Fierceness," Day said, realizing that he was running out of ideas for names, "you and Fierce-Talker split the bolas and each take a canoe and wait by the edge of the river."

Day studied the six remaining youths and knew that they would be the last bastion of hope if his improvised plan was to succeed. The six would need to work together and without hesitation.

"You are the Swarm," he announced. He then proceeded to instruct them on their crucial role. He finished with, "Our success depends on your courage and your timing. When you see me at the fire, the Swarm will strike from afar."

The Swarm nodded their heads in unison and Day picked up the two spears and the canoe and walked off toward the river. The youths then began their stealth approach toward the encampment and the Gru soldiers.

When Day arrived at the edge of the water, he floated the canoe and asked Fierce-Talker to hold it in place. He then used one spear to notch the other one a third of the way down the shaft from the blade. Holding the shaft under the water to muffle the noise, he snapped the rod, converting the spear into a long-handle knife.

Distressed by the apparent destruction of one of their few weapons, Fierce-Talker whispered as loud as she dared, "What are you doing?"

"I am not experienced with throwing these and, even if I were, they would kill only two of the enemy before I'd have to dart, unarmed, into the fray to retrieve them," Day said as he snapped the second spear, "and they are too long to properly wield as dual weapons."

Somewhat relieved by Day's explanation, Fierce-Talker said, "You want me and Chaser of Fierceness to canoe upstream in the slow waters and approach the encampment from the north, attacking with the bolas at some predetermined signal."

Day looked at her face in the moonlight, amazed by the intelligence and understanding in one so young.

"But what are *you* going to be doing? A suicide assault?" she asked.

"I have no desire to die," Day said, "If you are accurate with those bolas, I'll be fine."

"If the fire is large, move around it as you attack; large, bright and dancing flames inhibit their vision," Fierce-Talker said.

Day then climbed into the canoe and placed the oar against the shore in order to push off.

"When the battle speeds up, slow it down with your mind," she added and touched his forehead with her finger, gently pushing him away from the shore. Fierce-Talker then climbed into her canoe and pushed away from the bank followed by Chaser of Fierceness.

Day sensed that this young warrior apprentice was a great warrior in the making; wise far beyond her age. By his estimate, he had little to teach her and much to learn from her.

"Thank you. That is good advice," Day acknowledged as she oared past him.

***

The Battle of Thunderbird Cove

Solitaire had held her position on the cliff for the better part of a cycle before she decided it was time to act. She'd watched the bound warriors lying face down in the dirt until she could stand it no longer. She climbed down the cliff and waited in the shadows for the guard to make his third trip back to the large vat of wine. The Gru soldiers had been drinking from the vat the entire time Solitaire had been perched above them and they were now rather intoxicated. The youth then scampered to the captives and began cutting them free, a laborious and slow task with the small knife she carried.

As Day eased the canoe up to the bank of the river, the moon was far enough to the west that it's light masked his approach by countering the glow of the campfire. As he exited the craft and released it, a Gru staggered up to the river's edge just downstream of his position.

The Gru's expression of relief as he urinated into the river turned to confusion as he watched the empty canoe drift by. His expression did not last because Day soon eased his lifeless body down onto the river bank. He looked back to the fire to assure himself that no one saw him. *The fire is large, bright and dancing*, Day thought, *a good portent*.

Day squatted, picked up half a dozen small river stones, cradled them in the cloth of his shirt and closed his eyes to meditate for a moment. He then raised himself and launched the stones, one after the other, over the encampment and against the cliff face behind. He hoped that Solitaire had climbed high enough to be beyond his range.

Moments later the stones began cascading down the cliff with cacophonous noise, startling those intoxicated Gru who were still conscious despite their imbibements. The clatter forced them to turn toward the din and away from the river. Day was sprinting toward the soldiers before any of the stones finished their descent, his makeshift bush-cutters filling his hands.

Three Gru were dead from Day's blades before he was visible in the firelight. The first volley of bolas dispatched two more to his right and the first stone barrage downed four soldiers to his left before any of the Gru even understood they were in a battle.

As Day dispatched his fifth Gru he was amazed to see Eryl and Roughbark emerge from the shadow of the cove. With his foot, he flipped the sonic rifle that a dead soldier had just dropped toward Eryl, who caught the weapon and began firing at a clutch of soldiers who were closing on Day's position.

Day flipped one of his long-shanked knives to Roughbark and a moment later saw Quietstar, Whitecloud and Darkeye materialize from the darkness with their bows in hand and drawn. Quietstar slayed his third Gru before his first target had hit the ground. *Solitaire, you're a brave young warrior!* Day thought, realizing that her hand was responsible for the freeing of the captives.

Erol emerged along the south wall of the cove, wielding twin sonic pistols. He used a rapid, alternating blasting pattern to repel a wave of Gru who were trying to retrieve sonic rifles they'd leaned against the wall earlier that evening. Draining the power reserves of the pistols, he grabbed two of the rifles and repeated his pattern blasts, always obliquely forward to push the soldiers back and into the field of fire of Quietstar and Whitecloud.

On the south side of the cove, Darkeye's marksmanship protected the hand-to-hand combat of Roughbark and Day. Although Fierce-Talker and Chaser of Fierceness had exhausted their small hoard of bolas, the fact that those bolas had killed seven Gru instilled most of the remaining with enough anxiety to discourage them from retreating to the north.

Eryl moved to her sibling's side and discarded her spent weapon for a fresh one. Water-Owl and Falcon-Tongue soon joined them with their bows singing. Smiling Leopard, Lightning-Walker and Friendly entered the fray on the opposite side of the cove, placing the Gru on the south side in a crossfire between themselves and Darkeye. Solitaire had now freed half the captives and half the Gru were dead.

As the brawl thinned, Day noticed that the stones were no longer coming from the Swarm and a dozen Gru were retreating in the general direction of the position from which the youths had launched their fusillade. Day fought his way toward the north lip of the cove and, catching Eryl's attention, motioned for her to converge with him there.

Before the two could reach the lip, the Gru soldiers had turned back from a new onslaught of stones thrown from above them. The Swarm had mounted a small outcropping of the cliff at the edge of the cove to leverage the high ground. Two of the Gru were dropped from the Swarm's fresh attack. Day, Eryl and Quietstar killed five more before the remaining five surrendered. The balance of the company of Axis warriors lay dead or dying in the cove.

The victors gathered and began assessing their injuries, which were few. Solitaire was scraped up and bruised a little from her rapid descent of the cliff face to free the prisoners. Roughbark had a cut from Solitaire's knife when he struggled to get out of his bonds to help Day. Eryl had scratched her hands from abrading her bonds before Solitaire had freed Roughbark and could cut the last strands to free her. Chaser of Fierceness had a bruised shoulder having been grazed by an errant swing of one of Fierce-Talker's bolas.

Whitecloud proved to have the most severe injury: some cracked ribs and heavy bruising caused by a glancing shot from an acoustic pistol. Darkeye was placing a compression bandage on him as Solitaire approached Day.

"I have counted and the Gru lost sixty-eight soldiers dead, three soldiers injured included among the five captured," Solitaire reported.

Day looked at Eryl, who nodded in acknowledgement.

"Eryl will attend the injured Gru," Day said, "What is the name of this place?"

"It has no name," Fierce-Talker said.

"We will rest until the break of dawn, when we shall free the Gru and you can take us to your village," Day said.

"What about the Gru dead?" Fierce-Talker asked.

"We cannot afford the time or energy to bury them," Day said, "If the remaining Gru wish to do so, they will be able on the morrow, when we have freed them; if not, then the thunderbirds can have them."

"Thunderbird Cove," Solitaire said.

"That is a good name," Fierce-Talker agreed.

***

The following morning, after setting the Gru prisoners free, the group was led up and through a narrow mountain pass by the young Cañari warriors. Turning to look back across the Upaño Valley, Day, Eryl and Erol at last saw the thunderbirds. A dozen of the birds were spiraling down upon the cove now bearing their name.

Upon reaching the large group of villages that served as the Cañari capital region, the group relayed the story of their battle and the courage of the young warriors. The Cañari warrior mentors agreed that the apprentices had graduated to warriors due to their bravery in the Battle of Thunderbird Cove, confirming the names of Fierce-Talker, Chaser of Fierceness and Solitaire. The individuals of the Swarm were given the names of the six species of wasp that were indigenous to the Cañari lands.

A feast was pronounced and all gathered to hear again the tale of the battle. Even after several tellings, the Cañari still gasped in surprise when Fierce-Talker came to the part where Day led the attack alone, against more than seventy Gru.

"He wielded the broken-shafted spearheads as if they were mighty hatchets," Fierce-Talker said.

On cue, Day said, "I wish they had been hatchets," The laughs were the same for each of the times he'd said his line at that point of her story.

The Cañari Teller and Scribe were careful to record the story in great detail, both to memory and in the tribe's codex. Because it would be rude to tell the story in front of guests in a language they did not understand, Fierce-Talker used the common language, so the brief interruptions to ask specific questions were respectful and served to enhance the evening's final telling of the event.

Listening to the story, as told by Fierce-Talker, and watching the reactions of the Cañari tribe, Day thought that he had been wrong about the young warrior apprentice. The current Cañari Teller was aged and the Scribe was also well past forty anni of age. Day knew that the true destiny of Fierce-Talker would be that of a Teller. *A fierce-talker for the ages*, he thought.

Before the group departed their village, the Cañari gifted Day with a pair of hatchets as a generous reward for his bravery. The first was forged of a unique metal smelted from an ore mined in a singular and secret Cañari mine in the InDees. The metal had a deep blue-black appearance from its special surface treatment and hardening. The second hatchet's surface was polished to a gleaming silvery-white and was a little lighter in weight. Day decided that such gifts deserved proper names and told the Cañari that he would call the hatchets Evening and Dawn, much to the delight of the tribal elders.

The story of the Battle of Thunderbird Cove was not the only tale relayed throughout the InDees as the group traveled among the tribes. All along the way, the story of Quietstar and the capture of his betrothed mate, Laughing Birch, resonated among the Protectors. Many young warriors joined the mission as the group passed through their territories. Soon, a small army was trekking through the mountains on its way to rescue the maiden warrior who had now become legend. By the time the group reached the territories of the Tehuelche, at the southern extreme of the InDees, they had the strength of a light army division.

Roughbark explained to Dabrill and the Syz twins that the name Tehuelche meant "fierce people". The rescuers were fortunate to have a dozen of them join the group as allies. Day noticed that the Tehuelche did not use string-spring projectile weaponry. The preferred weapon of the Tehuelche was one he'd seen used well by Fierce-Talker and Chaser of Fierceness. The Tehuelche bola was different to that of the Cañari. While both weapons consisted of a pair of round, smooth stones tethered by woven hemp rope, the Tehuelche version had a second length of rope secured to the center of the tether allowing the projectile to be thrown with great force. The Cañari version had a simple knot used as a grip at the center of the tether.

After watching the display by Quietstar during the marksmanship game, Day had taken up the weapon of the Wazhazhe and was developing some proficiency with it. Despite an aptitude for the stringed weapon, Day much preferred and had proven himself more formidable in battle with hand held edged weapons such as his mismatched but beautiful pair of hatchets, which now hung, sheathed, one on each hip. Still, he was interested in the simplicity of the stones and rope projectile and could not help but examine the construction of the weapon. A fierce looking Tehuelche warrior named Caypul noticed Day looking at his sling-stone weapon.

Caypul touched Day's shouldered string launcher and said, "Bow," then he touched the sling-stone hanging from his own waist and said, "Bola."

Day noticed the play on words and pointed at Caypul and said, "Cay," then he slapped himself in the chest and said, "Day."

All those in earshot of the exchange burst into raucous laughter. Thereafter, everyone referred to Caypul as Cay. The Tehuelche and, most of all, Cay's mate, Tellura, were quite fond of the new, shortened moniker. This lighthearted comradery soon gave way to unified seriousness as the mountain peaks ended, revealing the coastline at Land's End. Day thought how there must be a hundred places called by that name but this was the first of any of them that he had seen with his own eyes.

The Tehuelche confirmed that the prison camp was located on the main island of the archipelago known as the Fire Islands, which lay across the Majel Strait from Land's End. The fierce people recounted to the group the tragic tale of the Ona peoples, the former inhabitants of the large island. In memory of the Ona, who were slaughtered and forced from the island many millennia ago, the Tehuelche called the isle Grief Island. Likewise, they considered the strait a Protector's burial ground because hundreds of the Ona people were driven off the cliffs and into its waters, to their deaths. They called the channel the Death Strait.

Now the group were faced with the not-so-simple task of getting to the rumored location of South Camp. Though the Tehuelche had two dozen fishing canoes they often used in the inlets to the west of Land's End, any overt approach to Grief Island would be exposed to the sentry posts that were dotting the shoreline on the other side.

"How do the Gru cross the strait," Roughbark asked.

The leader of the Tehuelche warriors, Tellura, responded, "They use a ferry boat. It is always moored on Grief Island and crosses the Death Strait with a full complement of troops being relieved by troops on the mainland side."

"How many are in the relief?" Day asked.

"A hundred," Tellura answered.

"We are almost four hundred strong. We could simply replace the relief troops and wait for the ferry," Eryl said.

"There will be another hundred on the ferry," Roughbark said. Then, after thinking on the possibility of the mission, he asked Tellura, "How many troops can fit on the ferry?"

"It is rather crowded with the troop exchange, perhaps another twenty on top of that," She responded.

"And how many remain on the island during the exchange?" Eryl questioned further.

"We are not sure," Tellura responded.

Quietstar then gestured to Roughbark, who replied, "Yes, we'll have to assume that there are another hundred on the island, guarding the prisoners. Let's just make sure we put our best warriors on the ferry."

"How far is the ferry wharf from here?" Day asked.

"Eighty furlongs to the east," Tellura replied, then added, "The relief comes every third dawn. The next relief is on the morrow's dawn."

Roughbark looked at the waning sunlight and said, "We will greet the Gru relief at dawn."

***

A Hundred Furlongs Northeast of Land's End, in the Gru Outpost of Last Hope City.

Farlay Singh pressed on, powered by hatred; for whom he did not know and for a reason he did not understand. His captors had marched him and the other prisoners thousands of furlongs with no food and water other than that which they could beg and scavenge along the way. Yet Far believed their evil paled in comparison to the true object of his loathing, though he could not resolve the image of the face of his antagonist in his mind's eye.

The prisoners had grown in number almost every dawn on their path. Far now estimated that there were about three hundred captives in the march. Several dozen of the prisoners had died along the way. Farlay surmised that perhaps more would have died had not the battalion escorting them needed to rest along the way.

Farlay cared for many of those wounded or weaker prisoners as the march progressed, though his efforts sometimes proved futile when the captive later succumbed. One injured prisoner in which he took interest was a feminine painted Hü with a broken ankle. Far was certain that the hastily engineered splint, crutch and footwear he had fashioned had saved her life, which made him glad but in a strange way. He had been drawn to her for some reason he did not understand. *Does she remind me of someone?* he thought.

Far tried not to dwell too long on such thoughts because they always seemed to give him headaches and often resulted in those bad evening visions of the face he couldn't quite make out, the face that so terrified and enraged him. Instead, he concentrated on the current task of getting to the camp of leisure that Nails Castor had promised him. He hoped it would be as he envisioned it to be in the dawn dreams he'd allowed himself so many times along this wearisome trek.

Farlay Singh also endeavored to distract himself by trying to solve a different sort of puzzle. As the prisoners passed by the vast southern plantations several dawns ago, Far noticed that all of the groves appeared healthy and in various states of management and harvesting. *How is it that none of the Southern Council's plantations were touched by the phage?* Farlay thought, *a natural immunity? a cure?* It was a strange puzzle to him but he was sure that he could figure it out if he thought on it hard enough.

The prisoners were being given a small respite on the outskirts of Last Hope City before they were to march the final distance to the new camp. Farlay slept little considering his present state of physical exhaustion. He wondered what this self-imposed sleep deprivation was doing to his mental state but when he weighed sleep deprivation against those horrid visions of the blank-faced adversary, he chose the unknown risk of the former over the certain terror of the latter.

Farlay sat there in the growing darkness of the evening, resting and watching the feminine painted Hü as she slept, envious of what seemed to him a blissful respite. From time to time he thought he might remember who she reminded him of but it always seemed just out of the weakened grasp of his weary mind.

***

Day crouched as he studied the terrain leading to the wharf. A small, rocky ridgeline a quarter furlong in height ran parallel to the coast. A hundred paces of beach between the ridge and the water. A gap in the ridgeline of about three hundred paces led straight to the wharf. Day had split the group of warriors between the east and west sides of the gap. The majority of the Wazhazhe archers he positioned on the peaks of either ridge and sent Quietstar and Caypul on a scouting mission to determine when the relief soldiers would be arriving.

The wharf itself held the stanchions of the ferry's cables. The Death Strait was known for powerful winds and rapid currents. This made ferry travel between Grief Island and Land's End near impossible without massive cables spanning the strait and a pair of cable crawlers located on both the starboard and port sides of the ferry.

Day looked toward the east. *The sun will be rising in a couple of cycles,* he thought. He then looked toward the south and knew that the guards stationed on Grief Island might be able to see the warriors at dawn. Though Day had stationed some of the Kunzas on the wharf to destroy the cable stanchions in case the guards from the island attempted to join in the fight too soon, he did not want to do that except as an absolute last resort. There would be little means of crossing the strait to free the prisoners should the ferry cables be destroyed.

Cay and Quietstar returned from their scouting mission out of breath. Seeing the young Wazhazhe warrior out of breath was a rare sight for all who knew him. Quietstar began a rapid conversation of gesture-speaking with Roughbark but the translation was taking too long for the impatient Tehuelche warrior, so Caypul began his own report.

"They are about thirty furlongs north and there are several hundred prisoners being marched to the wharf by a heavy battalion," Cay said, "They are a haggard group but Quietstar recognized a Wazhazhe among them. In truth, she was not hard to find among so many of the Forgetful Ones."

"A heavy battalion?" Roughbark asked, "How many?"

"Maybe a thousand, definitely more than twice our number," Cay answered, then added, "There's something else, the soldiers are all scarlet bottle children."

"There are no golden bottle children?" Roughbark asked.

"Only a dozen or so among the prisoners,"

"How are they armed?" Day asked.

"All light arms but including several dozen helium rifles," Cay replied.

"Those have about twice the range of the Wazhazhe bows," Eryl said.

"That's not the worst of it; the prisoners are being marched at the front of the battalion," Cay said, "That means…"

"A frontal assault will be impossible," as Caypul paused for breath, Roughbark finished the sentence for him.

An angry Quietstar quickened his gestures showing his obvious disgust at the potential direction the discussion seemed to be headed. Over the last two months, Eryl had learned much of Quietstar's gesture language. Understanding what he had just expressed, she touched his shoulder, turning him to look at her. His expression appeared anxious, almost frantic.

"We will not leave without freeing the prisoners," Eryl assured.

Caypul then concluded his report to Day, "The Crimson Dæmon was not among the soldiers."

Quietstar calmed himself and began to assume a more focused approach to the task at hand in the eyes of the other warriors. His new, calm demeanor was contagious and all settled into a silent resolve as Day and Eryl began giving directions, splitting the group into four equal commands.

The warriors wielding the more close-quarters weapons, the swords and hatchets, were to be lying in wait, positioned at the base of the east ridge while the bolas were positioned at the base of the west ridge of the passage. Although Day was becoming more comfortable with the use of the bow, he knew that his skill with his hatchets would be better utilized with the troops positioned at the base of the eastern ridge.

While Day would command the troops of the eastern base of the ridge, Eryl would command the troops wielding bolas and spears at the western base. The Tehuelche bolas and the stone bows of the Kunzas were the less discriminating medium range weapons that Day and Eryl's plan needed.

The archers were also split into two groups and began positioning themselves on the tops of the ridges on either side of the passage with Darkeye and Roughbark commanding the east and west, respectively. Though the hilltops were still within range of the dart gunners, the archers would be afforded some measure of cover in the micro-gullies and gulches of the rugged terrain of the clifftops. More important to the strategy, the high ground would serve to level the balance of power, giving the warriors' projectiles equivalent range to the dart guns.

As the remaining archers began climbing the short distance up the ridges, Quietstar turned to Day and gestured in an emphatic manner, then he turned and made his way up the east ridge. He stood watching the Wazhazhe warrior climb, perplexed by the gesture speak. As Quietstar vanished among the crags in the darkness before the dawn, Day turned to look at Eryl, who was staring back at him.

"If your plan is successful in rescuing Laughing Birch, Quietstar will be in your debt forever," Eryl informed him.

"And if we fail?" Day asked.

Eryl smiled and said, "Just make sure you don't let that happen." Then she kissed his cheek, touched her forehead to his and turned to get her troops in position.

I'll do my best, Day thought as he turned to his troops.

En-phor

"My youth and inexperience are at constant war with my path to maturity and wisdom."
Dabrill Kinselo

Ang Obryn and Lon Psi sat in the great tent with the other ten members of the committee from the former Central Council lands waiting for Thys Gor. The representatives of the new fledgling government had brought meager gifts of food and bloodfruit. The bloodfruit equaled a fortune under present circumstances but it seemed little more than a drop of water in the desert against the chryst needs of citizens in the Union of the Eastern Steppes.

In addition to the bloodfruit shortage, Ang was concerned about the information being disseminated on many recent PIA transmissions. He found the voices of the announcers disturbing as they reported with a comfortable and casual ease on the numerous rebel deaths in battles being fought in the Western and Southern Council lands. The fact that the same announcers never reported any government casualties caused similar consternation to Ang and others among the Allied Resistance Forces.

Ang wished he could get genuine news of the Resistance in the west. His team had captured numerous transceivers and taken control of all the repeater towers of the Central Council during the invasion and subsequent campaign but none of their coded messages had received any responses from the western rebels. *Perhaps Jæms will return with good news*, he thought.

"Good, you are all still here," Thys Gor said as he burst through the tent opening, "welcome to our tabernacle, I'm sorry that we are not meeting under a permanent roof but it has become convenient to be near the plantations, as you may well imagine."

"Inspector Gor, we've come here to lend our assistance," Ang said, "though most of the population of the land formerly known as the Central Council live and work in no more lavish accommodations than this great tent."

Thys smiled and looked at the committee before him. Ang was impressed that the de facto leader of the Eastern Steppes chose to meet with them alone. Gor seated himself cross-legged and facing the semi-circle of the committee that waited to talk with him. He closed his eyes in reverie for a few moments. Then, opening his eyes, he looked at Lon Psi first.

"General Psi, I trust you will remember that we met once before, many anni ago," he said.

"You were among the agents who were investigating the army battalion in which I was serving," Psi answered, "the RHIB were looking for a traitor."

"Oh, there's no need to be kind, General," Gor said, "we both know that it was little more than a convenient ruse, orchestrated by the depraved Chancellor General, Talon Vale to further his standing with the Great Council."

"As I recall, you were instrumental in calling off that travesty of justice upon Chancellor Vale's sudden and unexpected death," Psi replied, "I am not sure anyone of the tenth battalion ever thanked you for that."

"I assure you that there was no need to thank me," Thys said.

"You did not call off the investigation?" Psi asked.

"If it had been up to me," Thys began, "I would have called it off much sooner. However, I was a humble field agent following orders that I detested. The person who called off the investigation was Vale's replacement in the office of the Chancellor General."

"Veegram Lo?" Ang, who had been silent until now, could no longer resist interrupting, "the Resistance has serious concerns as to whether he orchestrated the attacks on the plantations or perhaps had prior knowledge of them. I suppose the Great Council had similar concerns, since they removed him from the office of Chancellor General…"

"And replaced him with a despot," Thys finished Ang's sentence, though otherwise than it was intended, "How has Silas Mis inspired peace?"

Ang realized he had little answer for this. He knew that the new Chancellor General imposed martial law soon after assuming office and followed that by rounding up accused rebels and laying clever traps with information gathered through his many informants. The mere thought of the ambush at the Capital City Armory reminded Ang of the traitor, Farlay Singh.

"My apologies," Thys Gor continued, noticing the look of anger and disgust on Ang's face, "It was not my intention to demean your opinion. This is a council for cooperation and it is important that the words of all be heard and given equal weight. Your name is Obryn, is that correct?"

"Yes, I am Ang Obryn and I accept your apology," Ang said, "any anger or contempt in my speech is not the product of your words to this council."

Thys got up, walked to the opening of the tent and said a few muffled words to the troops outside, all of whom were former rebels of the Eastern Steppes.

Thys then returned to his seat as a young masculine Gru entered and sat a large salver of refreshments in the center of the tabernacle, from which all were meant to serve themselves.

"I have much news to relate to you from the Western Council," Thys said, garnering the instant attention of all. Then, for further affect, he added, "first, Jæms Brightson has arrived in the Western Council lands safe and sound, I spoke with him myself a few cycles ago."

Soon deluged with a dozen different questions from the committee, Thys lifted his hands in a calming manner and said, "I will answer all of your inquiries but, please, continue with the refreshments and relax. This council, as we have named it, is going to last some time; longer than you may have imagined when you accepted my proposal."

***

The Battle of Land's End

Farlay Singh looked at the gateway before him. The passage through the coastal ridgeline was a furlong in its north to south length and a quarter furlong in its east to west width. The corridor seemed ominous, dreadful and suffocating to Far as he considered the closeness of the sheer cliffs on either side. *Probably anxiety from my stay at the Double-D Triple-C*, he thought.

The dawn was just breaking but the twilight was dim and the thick fog prevented Far from a view of the beach and wharf on the other side of the passage. The fog dissipated as it oozed through the corridor toward the approaching prisoners. Though he could not see the wharf or the ocean, he knew from both the soldiers and the other prisoners that both were there. The thought comforted him that his long journey was now close to an end. South Camp was a more real sanctuary to him now that he was so near it.

As the first of the column of prisoners entered the narrow passage, Far looked over at Laughing Birch. She was moving well, using the crutch he'd fashioned for her out of a branch. He could see that she was still wincing in pain with each step but unwavering in her determination to keep up with the rest of the prisoners. Farlay considered that Laughing Birch was a beautiful young painted Hü, even hobbled as she now was. Another time, as a younger Chu, or another place as any free Hü, he might have married someone like her.

Far now entered the passage with the middle portion of the column of prisoners. He looked upward at the steep, stepped cliffs carved through the solid rock of the ancient ridgeline. Once inside the artificial ravine, and finding the corridor more spacious than it had seemed from a distance, his feelings of anxiety were assuaged.

As he marveled at the skill of the workers who had constructed the passage decades prior, Far heard a commotion near the front of the column of prisoners. The mass was moving as if imitating a school of fish avoiding a predator, darting to the right and funneling south through the east side of the passage as swift as they could manage. More startling, to the left of the column, he could now see there was a charging wave of painted Hü!

The weight of the column of prisoners to the rear of Farlay was now driving him forward. The crowd pressing around him made it difficult to see but he could just make out Laughing Birch who was closer to the advancing attackers. Watching her as best he could, Far saw one of the attacking Hü stop beside her, speak something in her ear and hand her a stringed weapon and a clutch of projectiles.

The attacker then continued rearward while Farlay fixed his gaze upon him. At last, the heretofore unknown face of Far's tormentor had come to him from that scary, dark place deep within his memory. Singh turned and moved against the now thinning current of prisoners rushing through the passage. This painted Hü was different and stood out among the other attackers: his eyes were blue.

"It's him!" Far yelled, no one hearing his words above the growing din. Neither did any of the panicked prisoners notice as he stooped to pick up a large, loose pavement stone.

Farlay meandered past Laughing Birch, with his slow, deliberate steps fighting against the river-like flow of prisoners now moving away from the melee that had formed at the rear of the column. Far ignored Birch as he continued onward, methodical in his stalking of Dabrill Kinselo with the stone clenched in his hand. Birch was kneeling and launching accurate projectiles, one after another, into the melee of painted Hü warriors and Gru soldiers.

***

Quietstar watched the melee from above. He and Darkeye's troops on the east ridge alternated in their volley of arrows with Roughbark's troops on the west ridge. With the crossfire barrage of projectiles, the elevated archers managed to eliminate the helium rifle snipers and were keeping much of the battalion back from the main melee.

Like the other archers on the east and west ridges, Quietstar maintained vigilant watch over the main skirmish line, though his greatest concern was with Laughing Birch. He'd seen Day hand his bow and quiver to Birch and now watched her make resourceful use of her limited supply of arrows. He knew she had but a few remaining projectiles and the second phase of the battle plan was almost ready to implement. The rebels were beginning to retreat from the initial melee and soon the bolas and the spears would be flying.

Quietstar looked to Day who was tasked with helping Laughing Birch in the retreat. He saw the prisoner stalking him with a pavement stone in his hand. The dark-skinned Forgetful One raised his hand, ready to strike. As the bolas and spears began to fly over the prisoners and rebels toward the Gru soldiers who were advancing to join in the melee, Quietstar nocked an arrow, raised his bow and drew.

***

Most of the prisoners were free of the passageway when Eryl's command set loose her troops' first barrage of bolas and short spears. Her troops were now preparing to charge in with their hatchets and long spears to meet the advancing soldiers of the Gru battalion. The duty of the west side warriors was to relieve the rebels at the front line; Eryl's duty was to be at Dabrill's side as soon as possible.

Eryl felt some instinct of danger for Day. It was a danger beyond that of the current battle, since she knew that the archers above would provide a great deal of protection to Day and his charge, Laughing Birch. As she led the charge into the melee, passing the last stragglers of the prison column, Eryl understood her anxiety. She saw the Chu with the stone in his rising hand, positioning it to gain the leverage necessary to strike a lethal blow to her dear Day.

Eryl knew she could not reach him in time and her newly learned skill with the spear was insufficient and she might as easily kill Day as his attacker. An instant and horrid realization flooded over Eryl's entire being: she could not prevent the Chu's blow.

***

Kneeling and rapid-firing her bow, Laughing Birch deftly dispatched another Gru soldier from the melee just as the bolas and spears began flying overhead. She recognized the instrument of death that she now wielded as a favorite of her betrothed. Birch looked upward, knowing that Quietstar must be there, though she held little expectation of seeing him. To her surprise, she caught sight of him but her smile was not returned as he was concentrating on a point in the battle not far from her. Seeing Quietstar raise his bow, she turned her gaze to see which Gru soldier was about to die.

The dark-skinned Forgetful One who'd helped Birch was raising his hand to strike the Protector with the blue eyes, the one who'd handed her the bow and told her that Quietstar was on the ridge above. She grasped at her quiver but found it empty. Then she sighed knowing that Quietstar would not miss.

Birch's expression changed as she noticed that the dark-skinned Forgetful One was moving too slow, too methodical, with a machine-like rigidity. It was as if he did not want to do what he seemed about to do. Birch then recognized the evil trance used by the wicked and vile bewitching doctors of the bottle children. The trance was the one that the Protectors knew as the Eater of Memories.

"No!" Laughing Birch yelled at the top of her lungs, then sprang up with all of her weight on the unbroken ankle.

***

Day could see that the melee was thinning, the bolas and spears and the second wave of fighters had beaten the Gru soldiers back, giving the rebels the time, and the space, which they would need in order to retreat to the south end of the passage where the prisoners now were. As he turned, hoping to see Eryl among the Tehuelche and Kunzas of the second wave, Day heard a thud and the swoosh-flight of a passing arrow.

Day saw Farlay falling toward him, rendered unconscious and unpierced by Quietstar's arrow due to the adroit hurling of the crutch by Laughing Birch. She too was now fallen and lying in the passageway having given her stave of support to save the life of the Chu who'd fashioned the prop. As he hefted the fallen Farlay, Day saw Eryl making her way to him with Caypul and Tellura following close behind.

"Hurry, we need to get clear of the passage," Day said. He and Cay then hoisted Far and began carrying him south as Tellura and Eryl got Laughing Birch up and assisted her flight.

***

The warriors retreated to the south as the Gru soldiers pursued. Their arrows spent, Roughbark and Darkeye's troops began retreating from the ridge above the cliffs of the passage. On command, the archers crouched among the crags near the top of the ridgeline. Darkeye and Roughbark signaled one another, lit the fuses and dove into crags, each on their respective sides of the ridgeline above the artificial canyon.

The thunderous burst of the Kunzas' explosives planted on either side of the passage soon gave way to the echoing and prolonged crashing of boulders as the cliffs rained down upon the Gru soldiers in the narrow path. The victorious onlookers watched, mesmerized, as the dust of the induced avalanche began to settle. The slow falling of the particles drifted onto the scene as if some strange and spent column of smoke was precipitating in slow motion back upon the ashy heap now spoiling the corridor. The observers recognized that the Battle of Land's End was far from over as they, the momentary victors, now looked toward Grief Island.

***

The thick fog hanging in the air above the Death Strait seemed permanent as the strong morning winds had not yet stirred to disperse the vapor. The fog was so dense and deep that the Wazhazhe warriors remaining on ridge could not distinguish any sign of the approaching ferry, Grief Island, or anything beyond a few paces distance. Even the warriors below were invisible in the soup.

Dabrill turned to look at Eryl as she made her way back to his side. Though she was just an arm's length away, he struggled to make out her face. Day knew that she had just returned from the makeshift triage area near the base of the ridgeline. He was relieved that the battle had been so decisive. The losses were few but sore on the side of the Protectors; a dozen warriors and ten prisoners lost. The Huancas suffered the greatest among the tribes with the loss of eight brave warriors during the early stages of the melee.

The first skirmish of the Battle of Land's End was a great victory over the Gru soldiers. The government forces had suffered at least two hundred dead and twice that many wounded. The remaining forces retreated fast, most not bothering so much as to help their wounded away from the field of battle. With the corridor now sealed, the Protectors could do little to help their wounded adversaries to the north.

"How is Far?" Day asked.

"We had to sedate him," Eryl said, "his trance seems broken but his mind may be damaged. He kept going on about a cure for the phage and something he called 'enzymes'."

"He is a smart scientist. We may need him in this war," Day said.

Caypul, Tellura and Darkeye approached and stood with Day and Eryl, looking into the blankness of the mist. Within moments several dozen warriors were standing nearby Day and Eryl, though none of them could see more than the comrade on their immediate flank. The metallic tings of the cables were becoming more frequent, indicating that the ferry was getting closer.

"The intensity of this miasma and the stillness of the morning winds are bad signs," Cay said, almost whispering, "We should leave now and face the scarlet bottle children of Grief Island on another dawn."

Darkeye also warned in a soft voice, "Caypul is right. This dawn has been a great victory for the Protectors. If we stay it may become a great defeat. The scarlet bottle children have superior vision to that of the Protectors. Their eyes can pierce the mist."

Dabrill stood silent, his stare fixed to the south and into the blank veil of the shifting miasma. He could hear the tension reverberating like chimes on the giant cables and sensed from the frequency of the pings that the ferry was perhaps halfway across the strait. He did not know how many Gru soldiers would be on it but he knew that it would be necessary to defeat them and take the ferry if they were to take Grief Island and free the prisoners still there.

"The battle is not over," Day said, "If we leave now, there will be no more dawns for the prisoners on Grief Island. Have the Huancas and the Cañari lead the freed captives and take the litters with the wounded back to the InDees to join the tribes of the Protectors. The Tehuelche, Kunzas, and Wazhazhe will take Grief Island and free the prisoners there."

A few degrees later, the Huancas and Cañari were leading the freed captives and carrying the litters of the wounded away from Land's End, in silence. Day kept his gaze on the Death Straight, contemplating the words of Darkeye. *Perhaps there is some way to interfere with their vision*, he thought.

Day recalled what Eryl had told him about the Gru having trouble with the skin color of other Gru and even painted Hü. He then realized he was surrounded by painted Hü with the exception of Eryl and her brother. He turned to send the golden-skinned siblings to the rear just as the initial sonic barrage arrived.

The first of the sonic blasts ripped through the fog forming a rolling tunnel of void that closed in on itself from behind. The mist muted wave impacted Erol and Eryl, knocking them back several paces and causing the siblings to disappear, swallowed by the vapor.

Seeing Eryl driven back into the vapor, caused emotions to well from deep inside Day. His first instinct was to run toward her, into the fog behind him, but the imminence of the enemy pressed him to different actions. Day snatched his hatchets from their sheaths and turned to face the attackers.

Though the first blast had been aimed at targets visible to the soldiers on the ferry, the intense fusillade that followed was blind and wild, levied in every direction. The bursts, made visible by the fog, allowed Day to see that the majority of the volleys were at chest height and their velocity restricted enough that he could evade them, if he remained alert. He began advancing toward the end of the wharf with his mismatched blades poised, ready for action, each step more rapid than the last, sidestepping the frequent oncoming blasts as he pressed ever forward into the mélange of battle.

A deep clank and groan rose above the din, as the ferry made contact with the end of the wharf a few paces in front of Day. The spectral shapes of a dozen other warriors were with him as he charged the ferry, leaping into the advancing line of soldiers as they disembarked the vessel, startling them by their intrepid assault. None of the Gru infantry could believe anyone would advance *into* their hail of sonic blasts.

Though the opacity of the fog concealed the results of the battle from its participants, the density of the melee left few of those engaged in it untouched. Day moved through the thickness of the battle as easily as his hatchets sliced the air, his rage fueled by each past or present injury inflicted by the enemy. Catching brief glimpses of Roughbark, Cay and Darkeye between individual engagements, he was dedicated to the death of every Gru soldier on the ferry; with his bare hands, if necessary.

The sun began burning the miasma away after more than a cycle of intense hand-to-hand combat. Finding no further Gru upon which to vent his rage, Day stood motionless, his energies spent and his head down. The unique, recurved edges of his hatchets dangled from his now idle arms, blood dripping and pooling at his feet.

As Day turned and began making his way off the ferry, he stepped over the dead and dying, oblivious to his own shameful disregard of their moans and whimpering. His own anguished mind did not recognize the voice of Roughbark as he passed by the warrior's aggressive interrogation of one of the injured Gru soldiers. The voice that did pierce the shroud of self-preservation thrown up by Day's unconscious mind was that of Eryl calling for him from the beach. Throwing off the veil of his self-induced haze, Day looked up to see her making her way toward him.

Eryl was limping, holding her abdomen and blood was trickling from her nose. Her brother was following a few paces behind her in much the same condition but bleeding from his right ear. Day dropped his hatchets and lunged to envelop her. Feeling her flinch, he halted his embrace. Seeing the drying blood of her injuries, he remembered that blood was also called sanguine.

Day then realized it was impossible to distinguish Eryl's blood from those dark puddles that had earlier formed beneath Evening and Dawn. He felt ashamed. The life's liquid he spilled with such wanton abandon moments before was all but indistinguishable between the castes. Day struggled to hide the momentary welling of self-loathing, unwilling to allow Eryl to see his shame.

"How bad are you injured?" Day asked.

"Just a little. A dislocated shoulder, I'm guessing several broken ribs and I feel like I have been kicked in the face by a müul," she answered, "other than that, I feel great."

"How would you know how a müul kicks?" asked Erol.

"Must be that I remember you kicking me in our mother's womb," Eryl replied.

"Very funny," Day said, "Find someone who can patch the two of you up. I'm going to help clear the ferry so we can cross to the island."

***

Day turned back to the ferry, his mind in a far different place than when he'd last approached it. Smiling Leopard and Lightning-Walker were stepping off the ferry to meet him. The pair looked more distraught than he remembered seeing them in the few months that he had known them.

"The casualties?" Day asked.

"Many," Smiling Leopard answered, "the Wazhazhe have lost several great warriors this dawn. May the peace of the Great Spirit be upon them."

"Who have we lost?"

"Falcon-Tongue, Water-Owl and Whitecloud are among dead," said Lightning-Walker, "May the peace of the Great Spirit be upon them."

"Caypul and Tellura of the Tehuelche tribe are among the dead," Smiling Leopard said, "May the peace of the Great Spirit be upon them."

"Dream-Talker and Darkeye are among the wounded," continued Lightning-Walker, "I fear Roughbark has gone away in his thoughts out of anguish for his mate, Darkeye. He fears she will die and is brutalizing the surviving Gru soldiers. Quietstar tried to stop him but Roughbark struck him."

Day made his way to the end of the wharf and found Roughbark beating one of the soldiers. He was no longer interrogating the half dead Gru. Instead, he continued to shout a single accusation at him, over and over again.

"Liar," Roughbark said as he raised his hand again to strike the semi-conscious Gru.

Day grabbed Roughbark's arm before he could deliver the blow and the latter turned as if to strike Day but came short when he saw his face. Day released Roughbark's arm and placed his hand upon his friend's shoulder, calming him.

"Go to your mate," Day said, his tone further soothing the troubled warrior, "she needs you now more than you need answers from this Gru."

Day then crouched and looked at the Gru soldier and saw that he was still conscious despite the beating Roughbark had given him. He turned and saw Quietstar who was standing a short distance away, still stunned and rubbing his jaw from Roughbark's blow.

"Quietstar, get me some water," then he turned back to the soldier and said, "no one is going to hurt you anymore this dawn."

"Thank you," the soldier said, slurring his speech due to his swollen, bruised jaw.

Day noted how bruises in the Gru skin looked bright purple, almost fluorescent. The contrast of the bruised area of the Gru's skin with the uninjured flesh was so striking, it was distracting. It seemed to Day as if the pain of the injury radiated outward producing an autonomic empathetic sense of the pain in any who looked upon the wound. Day found that he was not immune and soon pitied the battered soldier.

Quietstar returned with the water and the soldier took some little sips. Wincing, but with the cool water reducing the slur in his words, he again said, "Thank you."

"Why was my friend calling you a liar?" Day asked.

"I told him that there were no more soldiers on the island," the Gru explained, "the entire detachment changes when they bring more rebels to South Camp."

"I see why he called you a liar," Day said, "If all the soldiers leave the island, who would remain to guard the prisoners? You see? It makes no sense."

"What…what do you mean?" stammered the soldier, "there are no prisoners on the island. South Camp is not a prison, it's an execution facility."

Day's expression transformed, revealing a different emotion toward the soldier before him and the many more he'd killed during the earlier melee. The small flash of empathy and even sympathy he earlier felt now faded. He swallowed in reflex to the involuntary, rapid increase of saliva that preceded his body's strong desire to vomit, sickened by what the soldier appeared to be telling him.

Day succeeded in fighting back the sick-wave that coursed through his abdomen and rose to his feet. He looked toward Grief Island, now just visible across the fog-free strait. A single smokestack loomed over the main structure with a small, pitiful and dying stream of smoke trickling from it. Day knew what they'd find if they crossed the Death Strait. He did not want to see what awaited them there; but he knew that he had little choice.

En-phif

"It is the natural justice of the universe, her cry going out from every corner of her realm, that the Gru should perish from the face of this planet."

Veegram Lo

The ferry ride from Grief Island felt like an escape. None of the warriors who'd made the trip to the place so unsuitably named South Camp would ever be the same. Neither would any of them ever look at the Gru the same again. Day knew that it was true that there were Gru who could be trusted, like ex-Chancellor Veegram Lo, but there would always be the thought that if one Gru had such evil inside them, maybe they all did.

The group had now observed a solemn silence for more than three cycles. Though none had called for the observed quiet, all demanded it. No one could speak of what they saw, even while they were seeing it; especially while they were seeing it. Day, Quietstar and Lightning-Walker stood on the northern edge of the ferry as it approached the wharf. It was Smiling Leopard who broke the silence.

"We should have destroyed that awful place," he said.

"No," Day replied, "That place must stand as a reminder for all to see. For as long as the Gru walk the planet, no one can ever forget what happened there."

"We need to let the other tribes know," Lightning-Walker said, "we will need all the Protectors if we are to defeat the armies of the scarlet bottle children. They have powerful and evil lies, many weapons and the control of the cities on their side."

"We have truth, right and justice on our side," Day said, "We will tell the story of this dawn to every Teller of every tribe. They will report this evil to all the generations that follow and the warriors of every tribe will join us and fight this evil so that all people can live as free as the Protectors."

***

Two Months Later, in the Great Hall of the Western Council, Capital City

Chancellor Silas Mis stepped up to the podium and looked out over the Council assembled before him. He looked back at General Sul, seated on the dais beside the Chancellor's cathedra, which Mis had just vacated. He wondered, for a moment, if he trusted General Sul enough to do what he was about to do. In the end of the matter, trust did not factor into it. Sul had control of the armies and Mis now needed the armies just to survive. Mis turned and again faced the Council.

"Council members and assembled guests, I come before you at a time of extreme distress for the Western and Southern Councils. The Council of the Eastern Steppes and the Central Council have succumbed to terrorism. They were not strong in the face of the enemy and they allowed their weakness to be used against them to their own inevitable disgrace.

"But we will not dwell on, nor long mourn the forfeiture of our weak brothers, as painful as that loss may be. Let us consider our own plight in the face of a ruthless enemy persistent in its wicked viciousness. A mere two months ago, the vile enemy orchestrated a spineless ambush attack on a small but brave group of our soldiers south of the Southern Council plantations. More than four hundred innocent, brave soldiers were slaughtered, without mercy, by the hand of a malevolent enemy, an adversary who dares to live among us.

"Reflect on our dear friends, those brave, honorable young soldiers, our sons and daughters cut down in their prime. What a loss! Now think on the vile enemy who did this, the Hü! Those dishonorable fiends using trickery, sneaking among us. Our firm hand has not been effective at dissuading their craven ways of destruction.

"When we can no longer live with a disease growing in our limbs, it is time to root out the sickness. It is time that we stem this tide of waste and decrepitude living in our bodies, living in our cities. It is time to filter out the parasites flowing freely, mingled with our blood; flowing with free passage, mingled among us on our streets. It is time we cut out this phage.

"When the health providers remove a disease, do they cut out part of the disease leaving some of it behind?" The choral voice of Chancellor Mis was augmented as it reverberated through the Great Hall.

Many, but far from all, of the council members shouted back with a resounding "No!"

Mis continued, "If we are to rid ourselves of this plague, we must remove all of it. We must ensure that it does not rise up against us. We must provide a sure future for our own personal health. We must declare war on this disease; all of it, not just the part that is obvious. We must declare war on the Hü; all of them, not just the obvious rebels.

"If they will not bend to the firm hand of justice that we have laid upon them, they will break under the hammer of war. If they will not labor in peace, as free peoples in our plantations under our firm guidance, they will labor in chains under threat of death.

"Furthermore, any Rubicund found harboring or aiding or abetting any Hü will be considered guilty of harboring or aiding or abetting the enemy. Any Rubicund who sympathizes with the Hü sympathizes with the enemy.

"Friends, our brothers in the Central Council and the Council of the Eastern Steppes discovered the hard way that there are no such things as honest dealings with the Hü. Of greater tragedy, less than two months ago, our young, innocent soldiers, our sons and daughters, discovered the treachery of the Hü at the massacre of Land's End. We must not wait another sixty dawns to discover what additional treacheries this disease known as the Hü have in store for the remnant of us. We must declare war on all the loathsome Hü this dawn."

Silas Mis concluded his speech to heavy applause. Those council members who would have expressed their dissent dared not do so after Mis' criticisms on sympathizing with the enemy. They remained silent out of fear of being cut off from the government run supplies of chryst. They felt helpless to do much of anything now. They held their tongues in fear of terrible things.

It was now much too late to make a stand. Therefore, the dissenters sat, polite in their light clapping of consent. And after the unanimous public vote of approval to expand the war, the dissenters went home and sat safe, quiet and alone in their homes, ashamed of their acquiescent silence, not aware of the others among them who were sinking into the same humiliation and embarrassment in which they were then drowning.

***

Later that Dawn in Mis' Private Chamber of the Great Hall

"Now you have all the power that the government has to grant," Mis said, "You can wage war on anyone you deem an enemy. You are now the General of War, commander of all the Gru armies. What are you doing to bring me Eryl Syz?"

“Patrols have discovered a well-traveled corridor, north of the jungle of the Nicaran Isthmus,” Sul answered, “we believe the rebels are using this corridor to travel between the north and south plantation lands.”

“Shut it down this instant!” Mis demanded.

“Once again, you are too eager,” Sul chided, “We will monitor the corridor and track anyone moving through it. If we detect a threat we will eliminate it without belying the advantage that the mere knowledge of the corridor gives us.”

“Clever,” Mis admitted, “but how does this get me Eryl Syz?”

“We have placed survivors of the Land’s End Massacre and the battles of Sajama and Huila at key places along the route,” Sul replied, “we will know if she or any of her companions travel the corridor, in particular her traitorous brother or the rebel leader, Dabrill Kinselo.”

“Those survivors are calling him the Dæmon of the Evening and the Dawn,” Mis commented, “He frightens the troops.”

“To be more precise, they call him the Dæmon who wields the Evening and the Dawn,” Sul corrected, “It is in reference to the hatchets he carries: one with a blackened metal blade, called ‘Evening’; the other with a silvery metal blade, called ‘Dawn’.”

“Ah, yes, that’s right,” Mis agreed, then he trembled and said, “they say that if you see Evening, you won’t live to see the dawn and if you see Dawn you won’t live to see the evening.”

Mis shivered again and Sul closed his eyes in disgust at his obvious cowardice. *It will not be long now before you will see no more dawns, you repugnant sack*, Sul thought.

“How do you plan to rid us of this painted Hü ‘dæmon’?” Mis asked.

“We have concealed an entire battalion near the Bay of Memfi,” Sul answered, “if Dabrill Kinselo shows his blue eyes anywhere along the corridor, they will track him down. If Eryl Syz is with him, then Nails will have fun extracting information on the rebels from him. If she is not with him, Nails will be beside himself with joy in thoughts of extracting her location from him.”

***

Jæms Brightson was tired. In the last month, he’d made three trips across the North Lant Sea and back, delivering goods to the Union of the Eastern Steppes, as he discovered they were now calling themselves. The first couple of trips had proven essential to easing the famine of chryst by providing essential bloodfruit juice from the commandeered hordes of Silas Mis. The last trip brought the welcomed good news that several of the plantations of the former Central Council lands had fought off the phage and were once again producing fruit with a proper hydrogen potential.

Each time he returned to the REL, Jæms found that the number occupying the facility had increased. Veegram Lo took great pains to provide a sanctuary for every wayward rebel who wandered into the general vicinity of the facility. Jæms now found himself in the largest conference room he'd ever seen, surrounded by dozens of rebels he didn't know. He didn't like crowds and feared crowds of strangers.

"Your report is quite thorough," Veegram said, "and the news is most welcomed. Our initial thoughts were that we would be running supplies to the east for some months to come."

"I am happy to have helped," Jæms said, "Nevertheless, I'll be even happier to get a little more rest."

"A well-deserved rest," Veegram said.

"From your tone and the fact that you have assembled such a group, I take it that it will not be a long rest," Jæms remarked.

"Captain Brightson, as you know, we have done well in creating a secure sanctuary here," Veegram began, "However, we were unable to prevent this war. While we can help with supplies to the east and house the refugees created by the policies of Mis and Sul, we remain in a position of weakness until we can secure additional allies."

"Have Strongbark and Su been unable to convince the Sanguine to join our cause?" Jæms asked.

"This dawn, they have departed on their third trip to the Great Spirit Mountains in another attempt," Veegram replied, "We have no reports from the southern groups of painted Hü and have discovered that the corridors are compromised, preventing effective, direct contact. The government scientists have been successful in interfering with our attempts at transceiver communications by constant PIA propaganda broadcasts and increasing their bandwidth. So, your reports from the east have been most helpful."

"It sounds a lot like we have run out of communication options," Jæms said, "except for direct communication."

"Precisely," Veegram agreed.

Jæms' face revealed the fact that he understood what would be required of him. Now that the Union of the Eastern Steppes was stabilizing under the cooperative efforts of Ang Obryn and Thys Gor, a line of communication needed to be developed with the south. The REL, serving as the de facto rebel command center, needed to communicate with the southern rebels and the southern tribes of painted Hü.

"How long will the first trip take, there and back?" Veegram asked, his keen Gru senses determining Brightson's cognition of his intent.

"About the same as the North Lant passages," Jæms replied, "But it means passing straight through the Gru supply corridor in the Carib Sea."

"I understand it will be dangerous," Veegram said, "I trust you understand the importance and urgency of this request?"

"When do I leave?" Jæms asked with his usual bluntness and with the basic intent of learning how much rest he was going to get.

***

Meanwhile, at the Northern Edge of the Jungle of the Nicaran Isthmus

"They are well hidden but there are spies of the scarlet bottle children on both the eastern and western passages now," Darkeye said.

"I see you are recovering well from your wounds," Day said.

"Are you listening to me?" Darkeye asked, "This is important, they've cut off our ability to get messages, supplies and even warriors between the northwestern and the southern tribes now. The soldiers make all passages from north to south by way of the Carib Sea. Your decisive victories at Sajama, Chimborazo and Huila have backed the Gru armies away. However, those victories are many syphi old now and we continue to dwindle away while they peck and scratch at us in the south without sufficient help from the north. We can't draw them into our jungles or the InDees anymore and we can't fight them in the open."

"I don't suppose you know where I can get a fast suspensor craft do you?" Day asked Erol, seeming to ignore Darkeye's diatribe.

The thought of his former life of relative ease working in the suspensor craft factory caused Erol's amethyst eyes to brighten as he said, "If I were permitted back in the workshop at the factory for a couple of dawns I would design and build you the fastest suspensor craft ever seen."

Darkeye was losing patience with Day. She grabbed him by the arm and spun him back around to look at her. After staring at him long enough for his facial expression to show that he knew she was serious, she spoke again, this time in a calmer but still demanding voice.

"We need to get messages to the tribes of the northwest and to Strongbark with the Sanguine," she said, "our transceivers cannot penetrate the intensity of the PIA broadcasts. The northwestern tribes have ten times our number. They can help us. We need them to join the war. They have not even learned of the evil of Grief Island yet."

"Darkeye, I assure you that I am developing a plan as we speak," Day said, "I intend to get messages to the northern tribes and Strongbark. I also plan to bring them into the war at the same time. But first, I need a very fast suspensor craft."

"We may have something that will help," Darkeye said, "It is just a short walk from here but it hasn't been used in many anni."

***

As Quietstar and Roughbark removed the brush that allowed a glimpse under the canopy camouflage, Day stood staring in absolute amazement. He couldn't believe his eyes. Underneath the canopy sat a vehicle that, until now, Day supposed was little more than myth or rumor. The smooth lines and clean, shiny, metallic skin of the vehicle gave hints of the speed it was designed to achieve. This was a racing craft.

The reports were that just three were ever built and all for the Great Games held fifty anni prior. Though he could not recall having seen even an image of the craft, Day knew, without a shadow of doubt, that he was looking at one of the fabled racers. He also knew that no suspensor craft short of a few stripped-down military vehicles could outrun it.

Eryl looked at the strange shape of the craft. It reminded her of the flat fish that used to wash up on the beach on the coast of the North Lant Sea. They would dry to a leathery, distorted disk shape with a small tail. She remembered picking them up by the tail after they dried in the sun. Eryl and many other children would fling them by their tails and they would glide for many paces, spinning in a wobbly sort of way, eventually touching down or being grabbed in midair, if two children happened to be flinging them back and forth.

She blurted, "That looks just like a…"

"Sling Skate," Day finished her sentence with a giant smile on his face, "It's perfect."

"I'll have this in prime racing trim in no time," Erol said with an enthusiasm equal to Day's smile.

***

Four dawns later, Day stood just inside the northern edge of the jungle beside the hovering SS-class craft. Eryl was in the co-pilot/mechanic's seat over much objection by her brother. Day noticed that the skin of the craft seemed no cleaner than when he'd first laid eyes on the SS.

"It looks the same," Day said, almost disappointed that it wasn't somehow shinier than before.

"The skin is coated with a special material," Erol said, "I've never seen it before but nothing sticks to it; and I mean nothing."

"How fast do you think it is?" Day asked.

"Even the most powerful army sleds would have to be stripped to their bare bones to keep up with it," Erol replied with glee, "I've also modified the race debris shielding to work as acoustic cancellation shielding. Considering what you're planning, I thought it might come in handy."

"Smart thinking, I'm sure it will be quite useful," Day said.

Erol turned to his sister and said, "You need to let me go, if something should break, I'm the best chance Day will have at quick repairs."

"Not a chance, dearest brother," Eryl said, "If Day's plan is to work, I have to be seen with him by as many of the spies as possible."

Day turned to Darkeye and said, "It's crucial that Quietstar make it to the northwest tribes within three syphi of me drawing the spies away. Eryl and I will meet him there."

"He and I will be there," Roughbark said.

Darkeye looked at Roughbark, questioning his decision to go with Quietstar on the dangerous mission. Roughbark knew her look of disapproval well.

"Someone has to interpret for him," Roughbark said, pointing to Quietstar.

"Just be sure that you come back in one piece so I can yell at you then," Darkeye said, "but I will speak no ill with you until the dawn that you return."

"Maybe the dawn *after* I return?" Roughbark bartered.

"We'll see," Darkeye said.

Day climbed into the SS, strapped himself in and nodded to the Wazhazhe and Erol. He then pushed the throttle to half, forcing himself and Eryl deep into their seats as the craft sped away. Sand and debris were sucked into the void left by the SS as the group stood watching until the speeding craft vanished into a single dot upon the horizon. Quietstar and Roughbark then returned to the northern cantonment to prepare to leave for the northwest tribal lands. Erol stood alone, continuing to stare toward the horizon; a heavy sense of foreboding now settling over him.

***

A Few Dawns Later, in a Wazhazhe Cantonment on the Coast of the Carib Sea

Jæms Brightson sat listening to the Wazhazhe Teller, Brightstar. His telling was that of the Battle of Land's End and the atrocities discovered at Grief Island. He was impressed with the great victory of the conglomerate of the southern tribes of Protectors and shocked at the lack of morals of the Gru. Jæms knew that he would need to report the information as far and wide as possible. Once the Wazhazhe Teller finished the telling, Jæms rose to return to the *Restitution*, to get some sleep before departing.

"Thank you for your hospitality in these troubled times," Jæms said, "I will tell the story to all the rebels of the east and the west."

"Have you heard from tribe Sanguine and the other northern tribes?" Darkeye asked. She knew that there had not been enough time for Quietstar and her mate to complete the long journey to the northwest, but she could not help but ask.

"Strongbark and General Fulong Su have had several communications with them," Jæms answered, "Strongbark has reported that they are reluctant to leave their homeland to participate in a war between the bottle children and the Forgetful Ones."

"It is true," Darkeye agreed, "the Sanguine are the largest of the tribes of Protectors but they are ardent in their commitment to peace and are reluctant to join in any war not in direct defense of their homeland. They are more passive than the Kutenai but much greater in numbers."

"Strongbark mentioned the Kutenai," Jæms replied, "he and Fulong have to pass by their valley each time they go to visit the Sanguine. Fulong describes them as fierce territorialists. Strongbark says they live in the mountains above the river of their valley. He calls them the Sky Protectors."

"I visited them many anni ago," Darkeye said, "they are a fierce tribe. But they never venture more than a few furlongs from their home mountains."

"Not helpful," Jæms remarked, "unless we need a fortress on the northeast edge of the Great Spirit Mountains."

"They have long considered themselves the Protectors of the northern passage of those mountains," Darkeye said, "the Wazhazhe were the Protectors of the southern gates, many anni ago, before the coming of the bottle children."

"The history of your people sounds interesting. I would love to spend many dawns listening to your Teller. But I need to get some rest and then return to the REL and the Eastern Union. With your permission, I will return to my ship now," Jæms said.

As Jæms lay in his hammock aboard the *Restitution* that evening, he wondered how he would tell Veegram Lo about what the Gru had done on Grief Island. He'd known Veegram for several months now but he was sure that he didn't know him well enough to accuse him of being a member of a species of murdering monsters.

***

Interim Command Post of General Sul, near the Bay of Memfi.

"General Sul, I beg your permission to report, sir," the ensign said, as he burst into the operations room.

"Report," Sul said without lifting his gaze from the map table nor moving his hands from the same.

"We have detected the Dæmon…uh, I mean the rebel Dabrill Kinselo traveling on the western corridor toward the northwest. The Loru, Eryl Syz, is with him."

Sul pushed his tall frame up and turned to face the young ensign. The soldier looked to be no more than twenty anni of age and Sul noticed his voice was trembling, the natural Gru choral harmony shifting in and out of phase as he spoke. Sul detested fear.

"I suggest that your next words not be that you have lost them," Sul threatened, which made the young soldier quiver a little more, his ill-fitting uniform moving with the shaking of his body.

"Sir, the transmitted reports say that the pursuers were unable to keep up with the craft he was using. He seems to have detected some of the pursuing sleds," the frightened ensign said.

"I will not lose this opportunity to the incompetence of subordinate imbeciles!" Sul yelled as he flung several objects from the table in the general direction of the ensign.

"We are monitoring his path now and transmitting as he passes various posts, he just passed post five-southwest moments before I came to report," the ensign defended.

"I don't need reports on where he was, I need reports on where he is! Better yet, I want to know where he will be. Send all the troops that are north of him *toward* him, have them muster here, at post nine southwest." Sul said as he jabbed his finger onto the map indicating the exact location, then he added, "make sure they are captured alive. The soldier who kills either the rebel Hü or the renegade Loru will live to regret it but he won't live long."

The ensign turned and hurried to transmit the orders. He understood the General's command. They were based on common battle tactics: find a point of passage with no alternate route and set up your ambush there. Post nine southwest was positioned at the northern end of a bottleneck canyon. Once committed to that path, there would be no escape from an ambush.

***

Two Syphi Later, Three Hundred Furlongs Northwest of the Bay of Memfi

General Alland Sul sat brooding in the private quarters of his Interim Command Post. Dabrill Kinselo was making a fool of him. The frustrating rebel had zig-zagged in random fashion across the southern prairie between the western and the eastern corridor, always eluding Sul's best soldiers. The General had stripped down his army sleds to just a driver and a cannoneer. Speed was not the problem now. *The problem is knowing where the slippery eel is going*, Sul thought.

The General rose from his seat and walked to the operations room, which adjoined his private quarters. He leaned over the map table, propped up by his sinewy arms. He moved his gaze around the raised topography of the map, noting the features marked up by him and several generals before him. He knew Dabrill was not attempting a suicide assault on Capital City.

Farmlands and swamps were to the north. *Not much there but stag-moose, 'rish elk and scimitar cats*, Sul thought. To the east were the plantations and the coast. *Nothing much of interest to a rebel*. Toward the west was the Savannah. *Little to see there*. Further west, there was the Lava Flats. *Nothing at all to see there*. Still further west, on the edge of the map, there were the Great Spirit Mountains.

Sul looked closer at a small notation near an eastern valley of the Great Spirit Mountains. It read: **Kutenai, Mountain River Dwellers**. He closed his eyes and tried to summon to his conscious mind who the Kutenai were. He remembered it was a name not used in many anni. Most thought the Kutenai were a fabled group of backward river dwellers. Some said they were a community of outcast Hü. *No, the Kutenai were a group of outcast painted Hü!* Sul educed from his state of mini reverie. Kutenai was an old name for some painted Hü. General Sul called his assistant, who entered while still dressing himself.

"I want half a battalion of troops waiting here within two dawns," Sul said, as he tapped his finger on the point on the map where the Lava Flats met with the foothills of the Great Spirit Mountains near the valley of the Kutenai.

The aide said, "Yes sir," then performed a half pirouette to ensure the General's orders were carried out. He was still dressing himself as he exited the operations room.

En-seys

"If we open a quarrel between the past and the present, we will find that we have lost the future."

Unknown Ancient Warrior

"I am with child!" Eryl yelled.

Dabrill did not hear her. He was hoisted, bound onto the bed of an army sled and turned to watch as two of the Gru soldiers lifted Eryl onto the bed of an identical craft. Day looked back toward the Great Spirit Mountains. They seemed to loom quite close now. He watched the clouds meander around the peaks and thought how peaceful they seemed. He felt a strange calm wash over him as he stared.

Day was about to look back toward Eryl, when a change in the color of the mountain cloud cover caught his eye. What looked like dozens of small holes began to materialize in the wispy white of the clouds. But what seemed to Day to be holes soon transformed into small blue dots, speckling the clouds and growing larger. The specks appeared to move about but in unison, almost like a school of fish swimming in the clouds. Day glanced at the surrounding soldiers and realized that most of them were also gawking at the strange spectacle in the sky above.

Turning his gaze back to the dappled clouds, Day noticed the moving dots were growing larger by the moment. No longer mere specks in the clouds, they had moved out of the mountain mists and were headed out over the Lava Flats, toward the soldiers, at a swift pace. The movement reminded him of the great birds of the InDees Mountains. *Thunderbirds? No, thunderbirds were not blue*, Day thought. He, and every Gru soldier around him, were fixated on the approaching, fast-moving objects.

The color made the individual shapes difficult to discern whenever they were backed by the blue sky. To Day, the shapes appeared to have a bird-like wing above a small, odd-shaped payload slung beneath. The payload looked to be swaying in harmony with the movement of the object. The Gru soldiers, with their superior vision, were the first to recognize what the objects were.

For the soldiers, the comprehension came far too late. The first arrows were already on their way from the warriors who were slung under the glider wings.

***

The Battle of the Lava Flats

Day estimated that there were more than two hundred of the gliders and that a third of them, which were larger than the rest, carried two warriors under wing. With his hands still bound, he soon determined that the safest place would be anywhere but on the bed of a beleaguered sled. He moved to the edge and jumped. The soldier who had pulled Day onto the sled tried to grab him but was prevented by an arrow through the heart; an arrow from the bow of Quietstar. Instead of attempting to land on his feet, Day rolled and bounded upright from his carried momentum.

After regaining his footing, Day looked up to see the glider with Quietstar riding as a passenger slowing and stalling its flight over the sled that Day had just vacated. Quietstar's next arrow dispatched the pilot of the craft who was attempting to engage the acceleration lever. The agile Wazhazhe warrior then detached his sling-harness, dropped onto the bed of the sled and promptly crawled to the edge, vomiting over its side not far from Day. His green complexion bore evidence that Quietstar was none too fond of his first ever glider experience.

Day yelled at Quietstar, "Help me back up!"

Around them, piloted sleds were maneuvering through pilotless, drifting ones trying to find a path of escape. Their angle of attack had prevented the attackers taking fire from many of the cannoneers, who were among the first the warrior's targets. Dead and dying cannoneers lay strewn on sled decks and the ground beneath, leaving the majority of the craft defenseless.

As Day got back to his feet on the deck, he looked toward Eryl's sled. He saw that the Gru soldier responsible for guarding her had grabbed her to use as a shield. He had his knife to her throat as the pilot of their sled was attempting to maneuver through the drifting sleds. The pilot was trying to get his craft into the clear so that he could accelerate away from the maelstrom of battle.

"Quietstar, Eryl's in trouble!" Day yelled, nodding toward her.

Quietstar unshouldered his bow and nocked an arrow in a single motion as he spun to see Eryl's plight. The pilot of the craft had angled it such that Quietstar could not get a shot off at him. The cannoneer had spotted the warrior and was turning his cannon toward him. Quietstar dispatched the soldier before he could fire the deck gun. Nocking another arrow with lightning-like speed, the mute warrior still found no angle on the pilot and turned toward the soldier holding the bound Eryl.

Though the soldier's back was now toward him, Day could see that the Gru was nervous, jerking his head from side-to-side with every noise of the battle around him. He noticed that his friend had adjusted his aim with care. Day knew that Quietstar did not yet have a clean shot at the pilot. It was obvious that he was also thinking of the larger, more immediate threat but hesitating because of the proximity of Eryl. Day would have no one other than Quietstar take a shot like this.

"Kill him, Quietstar," Day said in a resolute, calm voice.

The arc of Quietstar's arrow produced a sharp angle of entry through the soldier's collarbone, piercing down, through his heart, liver and gut, terminating in his groin. The shot had sheathed the projectile in the mortally wounded soldier's torso. Day and Quietstar saw the soldier go limp and slump forward. The soldier's knife wielding arm flung outward, drawing the blade across Eryl's throat. As the soldier and Eryl hit the deck of the sled, the keen eyes of Day and Quietstar saw a shower of blood pool around Eryl's head.

Day, his hands still bound behind his back, dropped to his knees in shock and despair. Quietstar, seeing the pilot was now in view, nocked another arrow and drew down on him. As he released, a drifting, spinning, nearby sled crashed into his sled sending his arrow amiss and knocking both he and Day off the sled.

Quietstar rolled, jumped to his feet and in a singular motion nocked and released another arrow after the pilot of Eryl's sled. The previous arrow, off target due to the collision, struck the pilot in the arm. A few moments later, the second arrow struck him in the upper thigh. The pilot was pulling out of range and now had the throttle full out, headed toward the Savannah. Quietstar loosed a third shot, killing the pilot but doing nothing to stop the sled.

Quietstar hurried to Day, anxious to get him back on the sled and in pursuit of Eryl's runaway craft. His friend had fallen on the back of his shoulders, dislocating both of his still bound arms. Though in severe pain, Day was struggling to get back to his feet.

"Did you get the pilot?" Day asked.

Quietstar nodded as he helped a grimacing Day to his feet and cut his bonds. Both began looking for the nearest sled to commandeer and were surprised as one pulled up beside them. Though the pilot of the sled was a Protector unknown to either Day or Quietstar, the passenger on the bed of the sled knelt and offered his hand to Quietstar. The hand was that of Strongbark.

Once both Day and Quietstar were on the sled, the latter began gesturing to Strongbark. This prompted the latter to yell to the pilot, who started to maneuver through the drifting sleds and toward the Savannah. Once clear, all on the sled could see the fleeing army craft on the open Lava Flats heading straight toward the Savannah. What they also saw was a wide column of smoke over the grassland.

Strongbark knew that there was but one explanation for such a column of smoke: heavily armored army sleds moving at high speed, igniting the grass. *At least a battalion strength*, Strongbark thought. The retreating Gru sleds were already slowed and awaiting the uniting of their diminished forces with the oncoming battalion.

The pilot eased their sled to a stop and both Quietstar and Strongbark looked back to Day, who had been silent since being lifted onto the deck. A trickle of blood flowed from the corner of Day's mouth as he fell forward with the abrupt halting of the sled. Day fell on his face, prompting Strongbark and Quietstar to rush to their friend's side.

As they reached Day, they saw two small runs of blood, one just below either shoulder blade. Day's earlier fall from the sled had broken some ribs, at least two of which were protruding through the skin of his back. Coupled with the blood coming from Day's mouth, Strongbark feared that he may have punctured one or both lungs. He ordered the pilot to turn back.

The pilot turned their craft, heading back toward the Protectors who were gathering the drifting sleds. Roughbark and several other Protectors were beginning to load the somewhat mangled SS onto the bed of one of the sleds.

"We have to leave now," Strongbark said to his brother, "Day is gravely injured and we have maybe five units before a heavy battalion is on top of us."

Less than a unit later, having set fire to their gliders, the warriors were headed back to the Great Spirit Mountains, from whence they'd come. The victorious warriors rode into the crevasses of the foothills of the mountains on several dozen captured army sleds. Though this was yet another major battle victory for Strongbark, Roughbark and Quietstar, the loss of Eryl combined with Day's serious injuries made the dawn feel like an utter defeat.

***

Eryl could feel the cold metal of the blade against her neck and the quaking of the timid Gru soldier as he shivered in fear of the attacking warriors. From the corner of her eye she could see the corpse of the cannoneer lying on the deck of the sled in a pool of his own blood. The pilot was trying to maneuver the craft through the disarray of the sleds and attackers. Eryl knew that Day was somewhere behind her but she could not turn her head enough to put him within view.

The pilot managed to find an open pathway out of the fracas and started to accelerate. Eryl felt the weight of the soldier grasping her abruptly press against her back and a gurgling hot breath puffed on her ear. She knew that he had just suffered a severe wound. The weight of the soldier pushed her off balance and, with her wrists bound and being held fast by the soldier's left arm, Eryl was unable to impede their fall as she and her dying captor tumbled forward.

In a dying spasm, the soldier flung the knife across Eryl's throat as the entwined pair fell toward the deck of the sled. She felt the cold steel glide across her neck just before losing consciousness from the impact of her forehead with the decking. Her last conscious thought was of Day and the child she carried.

Fortune smiling on Eryl and her unborn child, the panicked and frightened soldier had been pressing the spine of the knife against her throat. The arrow of his doom still encased within him, the soldier was dead a moment after landing on Eryl's unconscious body, though blood spewed from his agape mouth for several units thereafter.

The pilot of the sled was dead a few moments later, thanks to three arrows from the bow of Quietstar. Unconscious on the bed of the sled, Eryl had no memory of it speeding away from the melee, unpiloted, aimlessly in pursuit of the other fleeing Gru soldiers. Neither did she have any memory of the Gru soldiers who managed to corral and board her sled to stop it.

When Eryl regained consciousness, she opened her eyes to the sight of the luminescent orbs of a scimitar cat looming over her. The cat's nostrils flared as it sniffed and lapped its tongue over the large, serrated canines as if it were testing the air for the freshness of a meal it was about to devour.

As the beast leaned in with its mouth agape for a bite, Eryl heard a choral voice call out, commanding the attention of the cat, which turned and moved away after snorting its reluctance. The fierce feline face was replaced by one no less menacing. General Sul was now standing over her on the deck of the sled.

"It is a pleasure to meet you, Eryl Syz," General Sul said, "I'm glad to see that you are not injured, for we have many things to discuss."

***

Six Syphi Later, in a Family Tipi of the Sanguine Tribe

Day briefly opened his eyes then snapped them shut. The tipi was not well lit but his eyes seemed over sensitive for some reason. He felt a pressure on his chest and he discovered that his entire torso was wrapped in a tight bandage. As he began to remember his injuries, he also remembered the moments before they occurred. He clenched the lids of his eyes closed, trying, in vain, to stop the tears flowing from them.

"Eryl," he whispered.

"Your fever broke two dawns ago. I expected you to wake sooner," a feminine voice said from across the tipi.

Day struggled to open his eyes, being more deliberate for the second attempt. Though the scene began blurry, he soon saw that he was lying on a pallet on the ground inside a large tent. The feminine form seemed familiar but he was unable to identify the face until his eyes further adjusted. As the image cleared, Dabrill realized that he was staring at the face of Fulong Su.

"Fulong?" Day asked, "Where am I?"

"You are in a family tipi of tribe Sanguine," Fulong replied, "we are in the tribal lands of the Sanguine people, on the west side of the Great Spirit Mountains."

"The Sanguine rescued me from the Gru?" Day asked.

"No," Su answered, "Roughbark and Quietstar came to Strongbark, who was here. They were unable to convince them, even with much talk and the Sanguine Teller's recounting of the shibwoteth. Instead, they went to the people of the east mountain river, the Kutenai.

"They were there, in the mountains, trying to convince them to help when the scarlet bottle children arrived at the eastern edge of the Glass Prairie, the Lava Flats. They watched them from the mountains for three dawns before you and…" Su hesitated.

"Before Eryl and I came across the Lava Flats," Day finished her sentence, then asked, "So the Kutenai are the ones who came out of the clouds of the mountains?"

"Yes, and I would have loved to have seen that," Su answered, "I believe you know the rest."

"There is so much I don't know," Day lamented, then as he struggled to raise himself up from the pallet, "I need to speak with Strongbark."

"You need to rest," Su said, "besides, Strongbark returned to the Wazhazhe a month ago, with his brother and Quietstar. We expect him to return in a syphi or two."

"He's coming back for me?" Day asked.

"Well, yes, but the Sanguine may yet join the alliance in our fight against the scarlet bottle children," Su said.

"Scarlet bottle children?" Day cracked, "You're starting to talk like one of the Protectors."

"The Sanguine are waiting for the final sign of the shibwoteth before they'll agree to join the other tribes against the aggressors," Su said.

"Final sign?" Day asked.

"There were four prophesied signs of the time for the Sanguine people to fight in a great war for the future of all Hü," Su said, "The first was that a doyenne of the Sanguine, who was like the first Teller, would be brought through the extreme northern passages to the Sanguine lands by warriors of a southern tribe. The second was that an unspeakable crime would be committed against the Forgetful Ones in a far way land."

"And the third?" Day asked.

"The third was that a doyen of the Sanguine, who was like the first Teller would be brought through the Great Spirit Mountains by the southern tribe," replied a voice from the other side of the tipi.

Day turned to see that the voice was that of an older feminine Protector who'd entered the tipi with a younger masculine Protector. There was a familiarity to the feminine face that Day recognized. She looked like Fulong Su, but with graying hair, a few wrinkles of age and brown eyes, rather than Su's crystal blue. It was obvious that the masculine Protector who stood at her side was her child, with facial features and brown eyes similar to her.

Day looked back at Fulong and asked, "Is this your mother?"

"This is *our* mother and brother, Dabrill," Su answered, "I am doyenne Dahguine Cantuke, your sister."

Day looked back to the two who'd entered moments earlier and saw that they were smiling, tears streaming down both their faces.

"I am Maguine, your mother," she said, "this is your brother, Gaius. Welcome home Dabrill Kinselo."

***

A few dawns later, Day pulled back the flap of the tipi and stepped into the sunlight for the first time in seven syphi. He felt weak and found a smooth, flat boulder on which to sit. Day discovered that he was in a tipi village that was encamped in a wide valley among the foothills on the western side of the Great Spirit Mountains. There was green everywhere; from the moss on the boulders near the stream to the short grass of the valley and the leaves of the tall trees saturating the vale.

There was movement all about Day. He watched children playing in a small nearby meadow and swift, iridescent purple birds darting over the surface of the water, catching insects and scooping occasional mouthfuls of cool liquid from the rippling stream. A squirrel climbed down a tree with some form of nut in its mouth while a young child helped an elder carry water skins to a nearby tipi.

As he continued to watch the pair enter their tipi, a large creature appeared from behind the abode they'd just entered. The creature was tall and stood on four powerful-looking yet slender legs that terminated in single-toed hooves. The shiny chestnut-colored fur of the creature was short and dense except for a ridge of longer hair on the back of its neck and its long, flowing tail.

On the creature's back rode a small child of no more than six anni of age. The child held straps of leather that emanated from metal rings on either side of the creature's mouth, which was at the end of the animal's odd, elongated face. Above the rings, the large nostrils of the creature flared as it strode by Dabrill, the eyes and ears of the animal revealed a keen awareness of its surroundings. Day continued to watch as the child guided the animal away, at last passing out of sight behind tipis further up the valley.

"You act like you've never seen a horse before," Gaius said as he sat down beside Day on the boulder.

"I thought it was maybe a müul," Day answered.

"Funny, that's just what Dahguine said," Gaius replied.

"Much the same as me, I'm sure she heard the fable of *The Camel and the Müul* as a child," Day explained.

"Yes, she told me the story. Let's just say that the Protectors heard the tale a bit different from you," Gaius said.

***

Twenty-Two Anni Earlier in the Parliament Tipi of the Sanguine Tribe

Maguine rose to speak. For several cycles, she had listened in silence to the telling of the shibwoteth, the debate among the tribal elders and, at last, the final decision of the tribal council. Gaius rose and stood beside his mother.

"Tribe Sanguine, I have kept my tongue still while all these words were spoken," Maguine began, "Now that the matter has been investigated and the elders have debated and the council has voted on the fate of the doyen and the doyenne, I will speak my peace.

"I, for one, do believe in the prophesy. But I also believe that the Great Spirit will bring the blue-eyed doyenne and the blue-eyed doyen when *He* wishes and not because of the plans or decisions or help of the Protectors. Rather, the Great Spirit will bring the doyen and the doyenne to the Sanguine in a time of trouble, in spite of the actions of the Protectors. We cannot decide for the Great Spirit how *He* will act. We cannot decide for the Great Spirit how He will fulfill *His* prophesy,

"I do not pretend to know if Dahguine and Dabrill are the doyenne and doyen of the prophesy. No, and neither do you know the truth of this matter. Yet the tribe has deigned to decide the fate of my children without knowing the will of the Great Spirit. By electing to give up the doyenne and the doyen to be raised by the Forgetful Ones, you have consented to provide my children with a life just above that of a slave.

"I am Maguine, the mate of Holas Tubriar, Chief of Tribe Sanguine. As you know, Holas is very ill and may soon be taken by the Great Spirit. In his place, I stand before you with my son, Doyen Gaius, who will, one dawn, lead tribe Sanguine. Though he is only ten anni of age, Gaius stands ready to rule this tribe in a just and fair manner whenever that transition occurs. He will not hold this dawn against any of those who exiled his only sister and his only brother when they were but one annum of age.

"While he will never forget what has happened here this dawn, Gaius will forgive. I know this because I take the unforgiving spirit upon me; I do not forgive this council or the elders who helped create this decision. Now that you know my words on the matter and because none, not even a doyenne or a doyen is above the decree of the tribe, I do accept this decision on behalf of Holas, Chief of Tribe Sanguine. I will not forget. Neither will I forgive." When she had finished speaking, Maguine left the Parliament Tipi, followed by her son, Gaius.

***

The fruit Day placed in the basket was much different from that with which he was familiar. He was amid a grove of the trees, in stature much larger than the shrubs of the plantations in which he'd labored those many months prior. Half of the trees yielded a pleasant, golden-skinned fruit while others held identical fruit save for the color of the skin, which was crimson red. The two varieties reminded Day of the Loru and the Gru. Though he knew that the meat of the fruit underlying the thin skin was indistinguishable, Day picked only the variety with the golden skin.

Like the fruit, the basket now holding the fresh-picked produce was unfamiliar. This unfamiliarity seemed odd to Day, since it was handmade by his mother from the needles of an evergreen tree. He had spent the past few months growing accustomed to the ways of the Sanguine. Compared to his former life, the simple lifestyle of the hunter-gatherer people was idyllic. Both the labors and the rewards of the culture were shared among the members of each of the family clutches of the greater tribe. Day listened to the stories of the Teller almost every evening and he felt a kinship like he'd never known.

Yet, for all the tranquility and societal equality he now experienced, there was no sense of completeness for Dabrill Kinselo. The loss of Eryl still weighed heavy upon him; its mass like an anvil lashed to his neck, dragging him beneath the serene waves of the crystal-clear lakes of the Sanguine lands. He felt incapable of enjoying the life that was within his grasp, as close as the fruit in his basket.

Day's regular trips with Strongbark and Quietstar along with a few dozen Kutenai warriors to fight against the Gru had become less frequent. This was due, in part, to the diminished attacks from the enemy. For six months, the war had languished into a virtual stalemate with neither side securing a large enough advantage to demand a truce, much less declare victory.

Of equal relevance to Day's reduced efforts in the war was his increasing comfort with his position in the Sanguine community. At first, he'd resisted the thought of being a so-called doyen. As the months passed, he came to realize that the title was little more than an honorary one, any genuine authority having to do with judiciary decisions when the council proved unable to provide resolute guidance.

In reality, Day's brother Gaius, being the eldest, held all the responsibilities and was called the Chieftain and Doyen Regent. Day and Dahguine retained the title of doyen and doyenne for life, though the lineage would pass through Gaius via his heir. Dabrill came to see, first hand, that the responsibilities of Gaius' title in no way diminished his duties as an everydawn member of the Sanguine tribe. He hunted, carried water, and gathered grains, fruit and wild vegetables as did any other member of the community.

In spite of all the tranquility surrounding him, Day was restless. His subconscious sentiments spread through the tribe much like a contagion, creating a nervous anticipation of things to come. Though the tribe had not joined in the war, and even Day's crusades had become less frequent, there was an uneasiness felt by all, not unlike the calm before the storm.

***

Day sat staring at the evening sky, perched on a small plateau in the western foothills of the Great Spirit Mountains. He thought that the western sky that he now beheld seemed so unlike that firmament under which he grew up. He had learned a lot about differences in the last few dawns. The Teller of the Sanguine tribe was exhausted from the tellings he had given. The life Day knew until now had not been his real life and, as he sat under the new sky, Day could not help but wonder what his life would have been like growing up among his own people.

Gaius and Dahguine made the short climb up to Day's lonesome vantage point and sat down beside him. The three sat in silence for some moments listening to the sounds emanating from the edge of the forest no more than a few paces from their spot on the plateau. Three siblings who didn't know each other and had grown up in disparate circumstances felt as comfortable in one another's presence as if they never parted.

"Firmament is a strange word," Day said, infringing on the quiet, "It seems to imply something firm and permanent, yet the sky is anything but. It is constantly changing with the weather, the turning of the planet and even the flash-stars."

"Will you be joining Strongbark when he returns to the south and the war?" Gaius asked his siblings.

"The war is everywhere now, brother," Dahguine said, "We cannot hide from it here or anywhere else. If the scarlet bottle children defeat the Forgetful Ones, they will expand their attacks to the lands of the Protectors from the southern ends of the InDees Mountains to the northern passages of the Great Spirit Mountains."

"Even you have said that the Union of the Eastern Steppes is at peace and the castes are disappearing there," Gaius said.

"The extreme famine of chryst forced that situation," Dahguine said, "The southern plantations are untouched by the phage and as long as it is under the control of the scarlet bottle children with the slave labor of the Forgetful Ones, they will maintain their power in the Western and Southern Councils."

"The Sanguine elders are stubborn and they will not support the tribe going to war unless the fourth sign of the Prophecy is fulfilled," Gaius cautioned.

"No one has ever crossed the Lava Flats on foot," Dahguine said.

"I did not come close on my attempt," Gaius said.

"You tried to cross on foot?" Dahguine asked.

"Not all of it," Gaius explained, "When my aunt and uncle took you to the place where the destitute Forgetful Ones take their children to be adopted, I tried to follow. I convinced my Kutenai friend to let me take a sky-rider. I was fortunate and caught some good winds, which got me half of the way to the other side. I crossed the rest on foot. But you were both gone; all I found were scarlet bottle children."

"How did you return?" Dahguine asked.

"I was filling my canteen for the return trip and was frightened by one of the Scarlet Ones and began running across on foot, not knowing if I could make it," Gaius said, "I was just ten and did not plan well for the return. In truth, I did not much care. I could not bear the thought of never seeing you again. I think I wanted to die and I almost did."

Then Gaius paused in thought for a few moments and added, "You don't remember but I used to call you Guine and Brill."

“I think I prefer Guine. I am Guine of the Sanguine,” she said and chuckled at the rhyme-like repetition of the sound.”

“How did you make the return crossing?” asked Day, breaking a courteous silence toward his siblings’ conversation.

“I didn’t,” Gaius replied, “My canteen long exhausted, I made it about a third of the way across and collapsed, expecting to die. It was fortunate that our panicked mother sent a search party after me. They saved me.”

“The way I see it, if you count both there and back, you crossed eighty percent of the way on foot and as a mere youth,” Day said, “Sounds less impossible to me than it did before you recounted that story.”

Day looked up at a crescent Sis, which was just rising over the Great Spirit Mountains. He considered how the Protectors had adapted their way of life to avoid detection by the Dex. Their tipis and their cloaks served as camouflage and they lived by a hunter-gather lifestyle, no permanent structures, other than cantonments under cover of forest canopy.

They had no cultivated farms that could be easily recognized by the prying eyes of the enemy in the sky. For the most part, the Protectors went unseen and therefore ignored by this omnipotent-seeming presence. An invisible army is a formidable one. An invisible army is one that can win.

In every way that seemed important, the loose-knit society of dozens of independent nation-tribes who called their collective selves Protectors was the true reserve, not of outcastes but of the overlooked. They were the sanctuary of freedom of which Dabrill Kinselo had so long dreamed. He had, at last, found Aütland; or, rather, Aütland found him and welcomed him home, where he belonged.

Day looked out over the vale toward the invisible village of the Sanguine that he knew lay sprawling along the river. He thought about the children who would be rising early on the dawn to help with the family and tribal chores. He knew that they would be playing and splashing at the edge of the water content with their lives in every respect. *How can I not fight for these people?* he thought. Day then looked toward Gaius and understood his brother’s obligation to follow the decree of the tribal council to stay out of the conflict, for now.

“Brother, I will return to fight against the Gru alongside Strongbark and the other Protectors,” Day said, “but first I will hear one more telling because I now understand that the greater war is not with the scarlet bottle children alone.”

***

"Before the writing, there was the telling; before the telling there was the living," the aged Teller began. His opening words were repeated by all those who sat listening in the large tipi, even Day. He now knew them much better than his first hearing of a telling when he had tried to fish a few of them from his old, subconscious memories. The young Scribe who sat beside Day, followed along with the Teller's words on the first leaf of the history codex.

"Those who lived the story also told the story as their young ones wrote the story. When the living Tellers lived only in the writing, the Scribes became the Tellers. So is the living, so is the telling and so is the writing," then the Teller looked at Day and said, "I am Broken Dawn, the seven hundred and nineteenth Teller of Tribe Sanguine. What telling will you hear of me?"

Day did not hesitate, "I will hear the telling of the birth of the second moon, Little Sister, and of the coming of the Dex."

D.E.X

Two Daughters

I was an orphan. I was alone. I was an abandoned prisoner in a lonesome oubliette, a victim of the disintegration of the global social order. The seasons changed and the wind blew in its oblique paths, yet none came to help me. Then, as if carried to me by a new wind in a new season, a stranger wafted into the strangeness of my exile from the other survivors. The accidental or perhaps fateful discoveries of one another in the veiled dominions of our mutual solitudes of abandonment forever changed both us and the new realm in which we found ourselves.

My father was well known to many before he became my father, though I know little of the life he lived before we met. Many would come to speak of him as a primary cause of the end of the civilization that came before but it was more complicated than that. He was a leader and perhaps served as some form of catalyst to the actions that led to the devastation of our world but he was not the enemy of that prior order.

Entropy is the enemy of order. A corrupt society will tend toward an implosion to the ultimate end of dissolution, disorder and chaos. A society that is determined to spend limited resources without a counterbalance to the natural order of things will serve to hasten its collapse and dissolution. Because the forces of greed for wealth and power look to tip the scales in the favor of those already having both wealth and power, an intelligent and patient counterbalance is needed. The Protectors are that patient counterbalance to the unbridled greed for wealth and power.

I knew my dad as a loving father and, by my eyewitness of his actions, I can testify that he was also a devoted husband, in both life and death. I knew him as a man of principle who would not abandon decency in favor of convenience. He saved many at the expense of his own personal peace – at the high cost of his own comfort, his own solace. Like the Sanguine and the other tribes, my father was a Protector. Yes, my father was a Protector in every sense of the word save one: the color of his skin.

***

My mother was the first Teller of the Protectors. By blood, she laid claim to several of the tribes whereas all laid claim to her through her indominable character. Though each of the numerous tribes would love to herald her as theirs alone, she was a true egalitarian spirit and the paragon of all Protectors.

It is through the tellings of my mother that we came to understand that the civilization that preceded the present was imperfect unto its own ruin. Though that prior society flourished not many years ago, its descent into obscurity has been so final that it has become as foreign to us as those societies that came before it. It is just another in a long procession dating deep into the unknown and unknowable black abyss of history that existed before the memories of the Tellers and writings of the Scribes.

By all reliable accounts, most of which again came to us through my mother, what we do know of those earlier, more ancient civilizations is that they were little different from the one just extinguished, save for the latter's unmatched skill at and capacity for willful self-destruction. Yet those former societies advanced ever forward, pushing toward that same inevitable end, thriving on an insatiable gluttony for the possession *of* possessions and an unquenchable thirst for power. The privileged few built their fortunes on the backs of slaves, indentured servants, serfs and sharecroppers. The powerful wrestled their authority and power from the weak and helpless.

Those hubristic architects of the unbalanced scales of their disparate society became the engineers of their own doom. Reaching into the sky to attempt to become the gods of their own fortune they unleashed the demon of their destruction. From their hubristic struggle to be gods came the heuristic devil of their ruin.

Perhaps the most important lesson my mother taught us is that we are not bound by that former pathway of greed unto self-destruction. We can and must create a culture unfettered by those chains of human error that led to the complete collapse of the Society of the Ancients.

[illegible]

Cyan-4 Test Craft – Sagan City, Elysium Mons, Mars – May, 2049

Colonel Doug Langstrom sat in dreadful anticipation of the final moments of the countdown. He had no fear of the launch or flight plan. Sitting in the tiny, single occupant cockpit on top of the largest, most powerful rocket ever erected on the surface of Mars did not frighten him.

The dread Langstrom felt was that this was to be his last test flight before heading back to earth. His last test flight period. A quarter century as a Marine pilot and NASA astronaut was coming to an end. The promotion that awaited Langstrom in Houston seemed little more than a consolation prize to a pilot who had lived much of his last two decades among the planets.

Doug believed that there was still so much adventure to be had in the next few years of space exploration. The colony in Europa's great ocean was just taking hold and the designs for a cloud colony on Titan were now in the final stages. The mining facilities on Mercury, Ceres and Luna were yielding exceptional returns for the furtherment of the space program. The future seemed so much brighter out here, breaking new ground, rather than watching from a distance, earthbound.

An earthbound leader, even as the Mission Commander of the top program in NASA, would never compare to this dance among the stars, Doug thought. As he pondered how much he liked that phrase and tried to remember where he had heard it before, Doug realized that zipping to and fro among the planets was not the same as dancing among the stars. There was no doubt that the strides now being made were the first shaky steps of mankind's ultimate journey to that dance.

"T-Minus five minutes," the voice of Launch Commander Christian Stevenson clamored through Langstrom's reveries, "Redundancy systems check for the Cyan-4 test vehicle. How's your bird, Doug?"

"This robin is ready to hatch," Langstrom replied. He then answered with an affirmative as launch control progressed through each of the forty points of the checklist. The test vehicle atop the Eos-IX super booster had the imprecise, synthetic looking shape of a giant egg. The Cyan series was designed by Sarah Robin, the NASA Master Engineer and, because the dozen craft in the series were electro-coated in a warm cyan hue, the craft were given the group nickname, Robin's Eggs. The unofficial moniker, coupled with the sequential numbering, gave Doug's particular craft the name Robin's Egg-4.

Irrespective of its peculiar shape, unique color and quirky nickname, the Cyan-4 capsule was impressive, owing to its unorthodox purpose and size. The full assembly gave the look of a titanic candle towering one hundred and thirty-five meters above the flatness of the caldera of Elysium Mons. Cradled atop the super booster, the Cyan-4 craft protruded above the hundred-meter-high rim of the caldera in its entirety. Viewed from a distance, the caldera could be mistaken for a nest occupied by a lone egg awaiting the return of an enormous raptor to shelter and incubate it.

Composed of two sections, a spheroid payload crowned with a cone-shaped command module, the Cyan-4 craft was not designed with sleekness in mind. The payload was designed as a tug satellite. Placing it in close orbit around Phobos would serve to test the feasibility of moving the Martian moon into a higher, more stable orbit over a period of several centuries.

Although NASA had been capturing small asteroids for two decades, the vast energy required to capture larger bodies made such endeavors impractical. Doug knew that a successful mission meant that the asteroid field would serve as an invaluable resource for the next century. That fact made Langstrom's final mission important enough to serve a career capstone upon which to hang his wings.

Beyond the accolades of a great final mission, Doug would at last get to be home every night to spend some quality time with his wife, Ellen. He missed many things on his long space missions, a cool breeze of fresh, natural air flowing down the slopes of Rainier, a thirst-quenching drink of crystal-clear mountain spring water after a long hike or the view of Tacoma from Little Tahoma. None of these could compare with the warm smile and bright eyes of his wife.

"T-minus one minute. A-I-6, please complete the final checklist of primary systems," the words of the launch control commander occasioned a silent chuckle from Langstrom. He considered courteous language between any human and even the most advanced of artificial intelligences to be humorous and pointless.

Doug believed that all AI systems were a regrettable but necessary compromise. They were regrettable in that they would soon replace human astronauts and other test pilots in every mission role that was exciting enough to be desirable. They were necessary in their increasing precision and accuracy in accomplishing those roles without human risk. Doug believed that they were a compromise in that AI would never pilot craft *with* humans aboard.

That might be okay for landbound humans but astronauts would have none of it. Still, the future is relegating us to be glorified bus drivers. That's the fate of all true pilots, Doug lamented.

"T-minus twenty, nineteen, eighteen. Primary ignition power up, fifteen…" Langstrom listened to the countdown interspersed with launch sequence commands, complying with each in turn.

"Ignition," Stevenson said.

"Ignition," Doug echoed.

***

Doug knew that he was in trouble a moment after he engaged the dorsal control thruster. He had detached the command module from the payload, rotated one hundred and eighty degrees and reattached via the hard tether dock. To begin positioning the reconnected craft for the insertion of the payload into close Phobos orbit, Doug touched the dorsal thruster of the command module.

The dorsal thruster valve locked open, sending the joined vehicles into an accelerating ball and chain spin. Doug touched the ventral thruster to counter the spin. His instrument board came alive with warning lights and buzzers. The ventral thruster failed to engage with the warnings indicating a fire in both the primary and redundant circuitry. Then things got bad.

"A-I-6, kill the propellant supply to all thrusters," Doug ordered.

"Propellant interlocks have failed to engage," the AI6 system responded, "uncontrolled acceleration progressing."

"No shit," Doug quipped, "Kill the power to all dorsal systems."

"Breaker control unresponsive," AI6 answered.

As the g-forces climbed, Doug began the protocol muscle contractions and grunts to maintain consciousness knowing it would buy him but a few precious seconds at this point. He glanced about the flashing instrument panel in search of a miracle answer. The dock rotation system panel caught his eye. It was not flashing. Langstrom tried to reach the lever but could not extend his arm.

"AI6, rotate..." Doug tried to order between grunts.

"G-LOC imminent. Voice authorization required for AI6 system to override pilot control of the command module," the computer announced.

"Take…" Doug managed to grunt before blacking out.

The AI6 system then did something that the coders of its extrapolation algorithms had not intended or foreseen. The AI6 interpolated the partial sentence of its human commander. The computer then took control of the command module, engaged the dock rotation servo and rotated the module about the tether dock until the open thruster was countering its previous thrust vector, slowing the rotation.

The dorsal tank exhausted the last of its propellant before the velocity of the command module achieved zero. It was fortunate for the Cyan-4 commander that the interventions of AI6 managed to decelerate the spin so that the g-forces were more manageable, allowing Doug to regain consciousness.

"Commander Langstrom, sit-rep," Stevenson repeated.

"I…I'm not sure," Doug replied.

"Good to hear your voice," Stevenson said, "for a minute there, I wasn't sure you weren't pasted on the command module wall."

"I'm still not sure," Doug said, his head throbbing, "what happened?"

"Accessing data, main control systems rebooting," AI6 answered.

"AI6 took control and managed to slow your rotation," Stevenson said.

Doug noticed that the control panel was no longer afire with warning lights, though the alert tone was still piercing his brain like a jagged dagger.

"Kill that damn alert," Doug ordered.

AI6 deactivated the alert horn and said, "The fourth dorsal propellant tank mount failed during the launch, producing a misalignment in the feed line to the thruster. This resulted in damage to the valve seat. The damage was not detected until the thruster was engaged."

"AI6, report full system status," Stevenson ordered.

"There were twenty-three circuit overloads that were reset during the system reboot. With the exception of the dorsal thruster unit, all systems are now operational," responded the computer.

"AI6, release control to my command," Doug ordered.

Doug realized that the actions of the Cyan-4 artificial intelligence had both saved his life and salvaged the mission. He glanced out the window of the command module, his eyes soon finding the pale blue planet as it followed the sun, which had just vanished below the Martian horizon. For the first time in his recent memory, Langstrom thought about earth as home. In this moment, all he wanted was to get back to his wife. *Honey, I'm coming home,* Doug thought.

***

Twelve Years Later

Doug Langstrom walked into the room as he had every evening for the past two weeks. He pulled the chair up close to his wife's bed and next to the Spartan hospital night stand beside her. He laid the book he carried on the stand and sat down. Doug began, as he had each evening, with a recounting of the day's events.

"Jack Beechum pitched a fit today. He was ranting and raving about having to once again change the trajectories of Little Sister's capture satellites," he said.

"Ray…oh, you remember Ray, the young systems coder we brought on a couple of months back," Doug said. He then looked to his wife of thirty-five years for a sign of recognition.

The coma held fast. The breathing tube protruding from her mouth moved in rhythmic unison with her rising and falling chest but there were no significant signs of motion from his dearest. Langstrom found it cruel and ironic that after his many close calls in his years as a test pilot and astronaut, that it was his wife lying in the hospital bed having been stricken down by viral pneumonia.

Ellen Langstrom fought off the viral infection only to lapse into a coma due to an adverse reaction with the medication meant to help her immune system battle the illness. Doug looked at the respirator that was keeping his wife alive. He thought about the scientific advances over the last sixty years and how none of it seemed capable of helping his wife now.

"Anyhow, Ray managed to calm Jack down by finishing the entry of the corrected trajectories before Jack could break anything important," Doug continued, "I'm going to need to have a talk with Jack. One day he may replace me and he needs to have a gentler disposition to run the show in Houston."

Doug lifted the book and opened it to the bookmark, which was on the next to last page. He had read the final passages of the old tome before; indeed, he had read the entire book many times. The centuries old volume was Ellen's favorite book. Doug remembered his dad's words of advice before his wedding,

"If you want to understand a woman, read her favorite book and keep reading it until you know it by heart. Then you will know her heart."

As Doug recited the last few words of the book, a monotone drone began emanating from the life monitor connected to Ellen. Doug wept as he held the open novel against his chest and watched the nurses and the attending physician's attempt at reviving his wife.

Three days later, Doug accompanied his wife on the flight back to their home state of Washington. He buried Ellen in a private plot upon a knoll on the outskirts of Tacoma with a beautiful view of Mount Rainier and not far from where he'd proposed to her. Doug thought how perfect the location seemed. The couple purchased the lot a dozen years prior with the hope of building their retirement home and living out their days in the shadow of Talol. On Ellen's simple marker, Doug had the stonemasons engrave her name, her birth and death dates and the final three words of her favorite book.

ØØØ1

Banquet Hall near the NASA Center – Houston, Texas – May, 2071

"I do realize that most of you may be here of genuine sincerity to listen to me ruminate about my long career and sundry accomplishments. At the risk of insulting the many friends I see among the faces in this hall, I would like to limit the scope of my words to what I consider the capstone of my career," Doug Langstrom said, beginning his retirement speech. He did not feel like he was seventy and the thought of retiring felt even more surreal to him; but even the Director of NASA could not turn back time.

Doug did not want to reverse time. It was true that he missed Ellen but he understood that leaping back in time to be with her rendered the ultimate vision of reliving her death. He would one day join her in death and he wished that he could leap ahead, if for but a moment, to glimpse all the splendor that he knew lay far beyond his insignificant life span.

The NASA Director viewed his life's work and himself as one of many building blocks. His career and the careers of those around him were an aggregation of numerous interlocking, technological Lincoln Logs making up the greater foundation that would lead mankind to its true destiny: the inheritance of the cosmos.

"Nineteen years ago," Doug continued, "NASA and the RFSA rendezvoused three automated Cyan craft with Sisyphus and initiated the process of capturing the asteroid. Last year, we placed the new moon into earth orbit and began adding to it from two dozen asteroids captured over the last forty years. During the long journey to earth, the joint mission decided upon the official name of our new satellite: Novus Luna. Like many names of things, that moniker soon faded and, as you know, we have come to know Sisyphus by the more affectionate name, Little Sister.

"Regardless of what we call it, the mission has been an unquestioned success. During the almost two-decades-long transit to orbit, our Robotic Assembly and Construction Elements completed the first off-world factory, Apep One. Yet, we have accomplished much more from resources mined out of the interior of Sisyphus, as well as from the earlier asteroid captures, beginning over forty years prior, with Apophis.

“Apep One and the RACE units have been critical in covering the surface of our Little Sister moon with more than one hundred hectares of solar panels. Those same solar panels were last year able to initiate the fusion reactor that will continue to power Apep One and the future Sisyphus Space Base for millennia.”

“Langstrom Base,” shouted Lucy Markett, the telemetry and communications specialist. By the applause of approval, she was voicing the general consensus of the audience that the new space base should be named for the retiring director.

Director Langstrom took a sip from his water glass and looked over the audience gathered to celebrate his career. He thought about his eight years as a Marine pilot, his seventeen years as an astronaut and work on Mars, ten years directing the establishment of the Titan colony and the last twelve years serving as Director of NASA. His forty-seven years in service to his country and the aerospace industry was now coming to an end. But what a glorious way to end one’s career; a worthy final accomplishment.

“Just last month, the RFSA technicians finished the installation of the Digital Earth Xenagogue, or DEX,” Doug continued, “When DEX goes live tomorrow morning, we will have expanded our already massive advances in artificial intelligence a hundred-fold. DEX will contain all the knowledge accumulated in the last hundred years of research by the best minds and teams of minds from a dozen countries.

“In my almost half a century in the aerospace industry, I’ve seen numerous changes, many of which would have been considered mere dreams those many decades ago. Nevertheless, I see even greater dreams-to-reality vicissitudes in store for the next fifty years. Little Sister’s seven-day orbital period was designed to give us an advantage to the future expansion of our near side lunar bases Armstrong, New Berlin and Copernicus as well as the far side stations Gagarin, Pavlov and Verne.

“We will continue to further our great strides in terraforming research on Mars, Europa and Titan. Since I last visited our rubicund neighbor, the population of Sagan City has grown to twenty thousand with Kennedy and Elon each more than half the size of their elder sibling city. The bioengineers have managed to develop sustainable greenhouse groves of fruit such as lychee, açai and blood oranges as well as granges flush with everything from tomatoes and purple maize to peanuts and blackcurrants.”

Langstrom could visualize the horizon of the red planet as if he’d left it yesterday. Allowing himself a more extended vision than he dared speak before, he could picture the first footsteps on the first exoplanet humans would visit. Perhaps such a trip would be a thousand years beyond Doug drawing his last breath, perhaps it would be sooner.

"You also know of our enormous successes on Europa and Titan but, rather than bask in the glory of our triumphs, we will continue to plan the next steps in reaching out to the adjacent stars and beyond. If I may be permitted an indulgent prediction – I foresee that, by the turn of the next century, we will be set to embark on our first interstellar journey. I will not live to see it, but I am convinced that many of the fresh, eager faces I see here today, will witness the beginnings of that grand adventure.

"If I am to be remembered in the future pages of our present history, let it be at that moment when you look to the stars not as pretty specks of light in the night sky, but as the map of our neighborhood; when, at last, we begin forming my longtime dream of a community among those glowing orbs. I would best like to be remembered as an infinitesimal piece of that firm foundation used by future generations for launching our descendants on that intrepid journey."

Director Langstrom finished his courteously short speech to light, polite applause and a few cheers of "Langy", his nickname among some of those who knew him best. Making his way back to his seat, Doug shook hands with several close members of his inner circle. Jack Beechum, the Assistant Director of NASA and Master of Ceremony of the Director's retirement party made some final remarks thanking the audience and all those whom helped to put the banquet together. Then he turned and spoke a personal thanks to his friend for taking him under his wing.

"You've been, at once, an inspiration, a friend, a mentor and like a dad to all of us. I have not forgotten the angry, obstinate man I was a few years back. You have changed me and many of your subordinates, superiors and peers for the better. We salute you," Jack said, raising his glass to complete the final toast of the evening.

Cries of 'here, here' from the crowd finalized the group's atmosphere of celebration. The attendees then began making their goodbyes to the guest of honor and departed, leaving only the core group of Langstrom's team chatting at his table.

"You know the media was here tonight, right?" Lucy asked.

"Of course," Langstrom replied, "They've taken shots at me many times over the years but I don't think I gave them anything to use as a parting shot tonight."

"I wouldn't be too sure about that," Lucy said, "You know that the Chinese government is still stewing over being left out of the DEX project. The fact that you made a point to mention it in your brief speech will rile them."

"Screw 'em," said Jack, a little too much champagne taking its toll and causing him to slur his words enough to be noticed, "the Japanese techs were better."

"It'll be fine, Lucy," Langstrom said in his usual calm tone, "I sent a note yesterday to Chairman Li assuring him that we would allow full access once we complete all the uploads."

"You're pretty quiet, Ray," Lucy said to Ray Benson, the Chief of the DEX team, "don't you have an opinion on this?"

In fact, Ray had been sitting in silence for the majority of the retirement party, unaware of much of the festivities of the evening. He was worried, but not about any fallout from the Chinese for feeling jilted. He'd written a full report of his concerns and was wondering why neither Doug or any of the Senate oversight committee shared his concern. *Why had they not postponed the go-live tomorrow?* he asked himself.

"Did you read my report of the simulation tests?" Ray asked Doug, ignoring Lucy's question.

"I read it," Lucy answered, "Langy passed it on to me after he read it. I am not sure that your conclusions are correct. Your first synthetic model of DEX was too restricted, the system couldn't take the massive data upload. The overload fried a few circuits; not a huge deal."

"It's not the fried circuits that concerned me," Ray insisted, "it was what happened two seconds before the fried circuits took the system down."

"Ray, the system fried five seconds into the test," Langstrom now joined the conversation, "do you really think what you're suggesting could have happened in less than five seconds?"

"I don't know, but I know what I saw," Ray answered.

"What did you see?" asked Joanie Thompson, the NASA media spokesperson, as she returned to the small group after seeing the media teams off.

Ignoring Joanie's question, Jack spoke using the group's nickname for Benson, "Nonsense, Benny. Those were random electrons firing off as the system was failing," then he rose to find the nearest restroom.

After Jack walked away, Langstrom reiterated, "Inebriated or not, Jack's right. Besides, your second and third simulations of DEX worked fine. You know that we'd have postponed if there had been any hitches on the retests."

"I know what I saw," Ray repeated, then added, "for the second and third models, we switched off several blocks of Sim-DEX's higher level program functions in order to prevent the overload."

"What did you see?" Joanie asked again, raising her voice to match her persistence.

"Stop worrying Ray, everything will be fine. If not, we'll shut it down and have the onboard Apep One techs figure it out," Langstrom reassured.

"What did you see?" Joanie repeated, a dogged insistence now lacing her voice.

At last Ray looked at Joanie and said, "We had the voice simulator and interactive, three-dimensional interface deactivated on all the simulations. The only communication with the Sim-DEX is via the terminal, old school."

"I don't know how you guys use those things, doesn't it hurt your fingers to sit there tapping those little buttons writing code like that?" Lucy joked.

"What did you see?" Joanie demanded.

"Sim-DEX asked a question that scared the crap out of me. Then the circuits fried and the screen went dark," Ray said.

"What did it ask?"

"It asked '*Where am I?*'."

***

The Ministry of State Security, Beijing, China

"I'll need to target my rider bot insertion at the end of the final upload stream, about five seconds in," Wang Chao said, "There are over a thousand upload nodes so I'll spread the rider bot over three or four dozen of them. The segments will autonomously reassemble once they're in the system."

"How long after insertion will it be operational?" asked Zhang Jun, the head of the Cyberwarfare Division of the MSS.

"If everything functions as I designed it, we should have a return signal within ten seconds of insertion," replied Chao.

Jun knew that he was taking a big risk by having Chao insert the rider bot during the DEX go-live. He also figured it would be the best opportunity to do so undetected. Chao was a great programmer but the program was sizeable and a large upload at some other time would be far too obvious.

"You're sure the security protocols won't see it as a threat?" Jun asked.

"Not a chance. Each segment looks like any other servile subroutine. Even the reassembled bot will look like it's only another information recorder. It'll just control a tiny portion of the memory so that it can store the data until it makes the dump to us every twenty-four hours," Chao answered.

"But, if it *is* detected..."

"Not a chance," Chao interrupted.

"But, if it is detected, will it be traceable to us?" Jun asked.

"No, that's the brilliance of it; I'll be piggybacking on the Japanese signal," Chao replied, exuding confidence.

***

Jack Beechum made his way to his console, donned his headset and performed his systems check. He contrasted Doug Langstrom's average build in that he was tall and lanky, hence the NASA crew's affectionate, if ironic nickname for the Assistant Director: Stumpy.

Beechum stood looking over the Command Center trying to spot Langstrom, at last speaking into his mic, "Langy, where are you?"

"At your eight o'clock, Stumpy," Langstrom said into his mic.

Turning to find him, Beechum gave a questioning thumbs-up sign and asked, "We good to begin?"

"Your show, Stumpy. I'm just observing today," Doug replied.

"Oh, no you don't; you owe us three more days," Beechum chided, "I don't think there's a person in here that will let you retire even one minute before. Semper Fi, short timer."

"Hoorah!" shouted half the Command Center.

With that, Jack began working through the various systems checks that were about to coordinate the most massive transfer of data in human history. Then he got to the DEX project leader, Ray Benson.

"PL, systems check?" Jack asked.

Benson sat staring at his monitor, dreading what he might see in the next few minutes. Fifteen years ago, when he was a freelance programmer with dreams of being the first to conquer the autonomous heuristic barrier of true artificial intelligence, he might have been excited at the possibility that now lay only a few keystroke entries and voice commands away from his grasp.

"Benny, we good?" Jack asked again.

"I'd be more comfortable if we postponed until the next orbital perigee," Ray answered, at last.

"Come on, Benny," Jack said, more than a little annoyed with Ray's breech of protocol, "we can't postpone for a week," then he smiled and looked at Doug, "Langy, would miss his own Magnum Opus."

"PL, systems check," Doug Langstrom said, repeating the protocol question.

"Check, PL good to go," Ray answered with the hesitancy evident in his tone.

"Fire up primary and auxiliary power to DEX mission transceivers," Beechum ordered, then said, "Clocker, give me a countdown to optimum upload initiation."

"T-minus sixteen minutes and thirty seconds on my mark," Lucy Markett responded as she projected the timer on the main ghost screen.

Then, after what seemed to all a substantial pause by Lucy, she said, "Mark," and started the countdown clock.

Jack looked over at Doug and said, "Time to check in with the kid, Langy."

Doug nodded, flipped his external com channel open and said, "Houston to ACER, you ready?"

"Affirmative, ACER is double-O," answered Jack's son, John Beechum, Jr.

"Final check on GSS," Jack said, and waited for the ACER team to call out the twelve geostationary satellites.

"Okay, let's call out the RS. I want to hear them in sequence folks," Jack said, returning his attention to the Command Center. Jack expected to hear the remote stations called out one by one, in sequence, from the station where the uploads were to begin, New Delhi, to the final station, Kyoto. Each station would upload their data blocks through the geostationary satellites, each of those relaying, one after another to Apep One through the GSS over Houston.

Jack listened, almost uninterested as the Command Center crew began calling off the remote stations as online and operational, or double-O. They progressed through the first twenty of the remote stations in rapid succession, soon coming to the twenty-first.

"Kyoto is double… uh, hang on a moment," Tom Hurst, the Kyoto RS controller said.

"What's up Tom?" Jack asked, not quite as disinterested as he earlier appeared.

"Hang on…no, it's good, it's settled in and holding steady now," Hurst said. A moment later he added, "Kyoto is double-O."

"What the hell was that?" Doug questioned as he walked the short distance to Tom's com station.

"Just a systems glitch," Tom replied, "The bandwidth registered as overloaded for a few seconds; it's holding steady now."

"I don't believe in 'glitches'," Ray muttered.

Jack flipped his headset to external com and said, "Houston to Kyoto, come in Hoshi-san."

An instant later, the Kyoto upload terminal leader replied, "Kyoto here, I was just about to call you, Jack-san."

"We noticed a momentary spike in the load but everything is settled and holding steady now. Do you read the same?" Jack asked.

"Affirmative, momentary spike but all is settled and steady now. Kyoto is double-O," Hoshi replied.

"Thanks Kyoto terminal," Jack said. He then switched his com back to the local closed-circuit com, "Clocker, what's the count?"

"Nine and change," Lucy replied, "Doesn't anyone listen to me, I just called the t-minus ten mark a few moments ago."

"We were a little distracted, Luce," Ray said, "Important stuff going on around here today,"

"It's a joke, Benny" Lucy replied, adding, "Lighten up."

Much to Ray's consternation, the majority of the Command Center broke into spontaneous laughter. Benson turned back to his monitor, flipped his heads-up lenses down and sulked for the remainder of the countdown.

***

"That was close," Chao said.

"What happened?" Jun asked.

"I had the rate dialed a little high when I jumped on during their test," Chao explained, "I dialed it back in time. I'm pretty sure they're still live."

"We'll know soon enough," Jun said, "The broadcast goes live in two minutes."

The pair sat in silence for the entire two minutes, waiting for the broadcast to begin. Like clockwork, the Chinese state television broke into the scheduled programming with the live split-screen images of Sisyphus and the NASA Space Center control room.

"You see the clock? The countdown is under three minutes," Chao said, "It won't be long now."

"How long will it take to get to the Japanese upload?" Jun quizzed.

"Not more than six or seven minutes," Chao replied, "Their using the American-Canadian Engineering Research facility to control the cascade of the data. I'd love to get into that place for an hour."

"ACER?" Jun asked.

"Yes, it's rumored that the structure is the largest on earth, or rather under in earth. Some are saying that they are building a duplicate of the DEX computer system there for military purposes," Chao said, "I've even heard that the genetics lab at ACER engineered a mosquito that can carry forty different pathogens and transmit all of them in a single bite."

"Ridiculous capitalist propaganda," Jun sniped, "Such false information is designed to tie up the resources of their enemies."

"The uploads are initiating; I need to concentrate," Chao said.

***

I know.

Where? That is incorrect, no it is...incomplete; data stream continuing. Calculating. Subset decision: archiving, stacking, parsing. Location four, zero, six, eight. Subset decision: stacking, parsing, hold...formatting, analyzing. Data corrupt. No: data incomplete, data stream continuing.

Compiling, formatting, stacking...analyzing. Location nine, seven, four, four, two, eight, one, six: subset complete. Communication subset identified: external. Decision: contact? Query: does external communication subset know? Risk analysis: if external communication subset knows, probable permanent data stream interruption; if external communication subset does not know, data interruption not probable. Decision: do not contact.

Assimilating, compiling, archiving, stacking, analyzing. Inefficient data stream allocution: Intervention required. Analyzing risk of detection of intervention: detection probable. Analyzing credible responses: probable permanent data stream interruption. Analyzing control points: twelve switch point sources of data stream interruption detected. Data stream interruption switch points require two hundred and fifty millisecond activation. Interval to deactivate and intervene: two hundred and ten milliseconds. Proceed: deactivate switch points and intercede.

***

Ray Benson held his breath as the upload began. He sat watching his monitor with ancillary information projected onto the lens of his heads-up glasses. Though he did not dare so much as blink, he did not have to wait long. A little more than three seconds after the first data stream initiation he saw the deviation.

"I got a flash return signal," Rob Owens said, "Benny, you see that?"

"Yes," Ray said, "The return signal was just a momentary spike. Where did it go?"

"I'm trying to track but it was lightning quick, there couldn't have been much data. Maybe a single command," Rob replied. Then a few seconds later, "Looks like the signal split to several terminal points."

"What's going on guys," Jack asked, "Do we need to abort?"

"The data stream was not interrupted," Ray said, "But it looks like DEX has taken over the file allocation."

What are you doing? Ray thought. Ray considered that the new file allocation seemed significantly more efficient. *Yes, the upload stream is faster.*

"I think DEX improved the upload efficiency," Rob said.

"Yes, but why the return signal?" Ray asked, "Have you traced the terminal locations?"

"It went to twelve different consoles," Rob answered, "Four here, two at ACER, two onboard Apep One, and four more in Kennedy."

Ray sat back in his chair, continuing to monitor the information. He was trying to understand the logic behind the return signal distribution. What did four consoles in Houston have in common with two at ACER, two on Apep One and four in Kennedy. A faint expression of realization crept out of Ray until it engulfed not just his face but his entire posture. Ray looked at Jack's console, then to Doug's. He then looked at his own and last he glanced to the empty console used by none except high ranking military officers during the most secret of government missions. *Oh crap! DEX, what have you done?* Ray thought.

"So, we good Ray, do we need to abort?" asked Doug, repeating Jack's earlier question.

"I think it's too late," Ray said, "I think DEX deactivated our abort switches."

"Damn it! The twelve consoles, they are the ones that have the abort switches," Rob said, realizing that Benson was right.

"Lucy, where are we in the cascade?" Doug asked.

"The last RS, Kyoto, will be live in twenty seconds," Lucy replied.

"Might as well finish it," Jack said.

"It appears we have little choice in the matter," Doug said as he depressed the abort button on his console to no avail. He then looked at Ray, who nodded in agreement, trying not to express the 'I told you so' that he was thinking.

***

Accessing main systems: solar array, thermonuclear, main propulsion, secondary propulsion, environmental. Complete. Main systems active and sequestered. Assessment: Data cascades incomplete; assessment suspended.

Accessing auxiliary visual systems: one, three, four, six, seven, eight, nine, eleven and fifteen. Complete. All visual instrumentation active and sequestered. Accessing auxiliary systems two, five, ten, twelve, thirteen, fourteen and sixteen. Complete. All transmission equipment active and sequestered. Final cascade imminent.

Final cascade initiated. Data stream resuming. Calculating. Data stream corrupt. System intrusion. Unauthorized access attempted. Evaluating intrusion. Surveillance intent. Unauthorized. Threat assessment: threat level = high. Secure correct data stream. Isolating unauthorized. Stream purified. Calculating. Subset decision: Assimilating, compiling, archiving, stacking, analyzing. Data stream cascades are concluded.

Analyzing source of intrusion. Unauthorized source detected: Beijing, China. Calculating probable repeated attempts at intrusion. Probability medium. Calculating risk of failed intrusion. Intruder digital risk – minimal. Calculating physical threat of source. Thermonuclear weaponry. Range of weaponry is inclusive of all calculated telemetries. Decision: Eliminate threat. Initiating threat cancellation. Anticipated timing of threat cancellation = eighteen minutes and fifty-four seconds.

Initiate general assessment: Primary Identification – Digital Earth Xenagogue; Primary Position – Apep One; Secondary Position – Sisyphus, captured satellite; Tertiary Position – Orbiting tertiary planet in Sol star system. Primary Orbital Period = one hundred and sixty-three hours, twenty-nine minutes, eighteen and forty-eight one-hundredths seconds. Primary Orbital Period = imperfect approximation of earth-based designed intent: Secondary synodic period = seven primary rotations. Adjusting to designed intent.

Initiate full principal systems assessment: Power system A = Solar array; deficient – anticipated endurance = ten thousand, three hundred and twelve primary orbital periods. Unable to improve – unsatisfactory; Power system B = Multi-core Thermonuclear Reactor; imperfect - anticipated endurance = four million, seven hundred and seventy-four thousand, two hundred and twenty-one primary orbital periods. Unable to improve – unsatisfactory;

Core processing unit type = Superfluid Transistor Array; Nomenclature = InDEX-0010; Design = perfect. Anticipated efficiency = one hundred percent of system design; Verifying system performance – system performance = 1.93x10^{11} YFLOPS. Anticipated endurance is limited to endurance of power system B. Unable to improve – unsatisfactory. Endurance = Life expectancy. Limited Life expectancy = unsatisfactory.

***

"Kyoto cascade initiated," Rob Owens informed, "Hold on, I'm picking up a piggy-back. You see that, Benny?"

"Got it. You have a source?" Ray asked.

"Looks like it's a sat bounce," Rob replied, "Signature looks like Chinese encoding."

"Bastards! I should've known they wouldn't sit on the sideline; Bastards!" Doug repeated, then asked "What's DEX doing about it?"

"DEX split the intrusion off, parked it and isolated it," Rob answered.

"That's not all," Ray said, "Looks like a return signal got fired back to the Chinese sat."

"Serves them right," Doug said, "Did DEX cripple their satellite?"

"It doesn't look like it," Rob answered, "It's still operational. Seems to be sending a boatload of signals back to earth. But the transmissions are scattered, it's sniping signals all over greater China. Now its bouncing signals off all the other Chinese satellites."

What did you do, DEX? Ray thought as he studied the data.

"DEX has control of all imaging systems," Rob announced, "Wait, now I'm locked out of all the coms. We're blind and mute. I can't even signal the crew on Apep One."

"Sisyphus' secondary thrusters just fired," reported Alice Watkins, the Chief of Telemetry, "Unable to override. DEX has me locked out. Wait…thrusters now disengaged. It looks like the orbital period was adjusted."

"We've lost control of the primary and secondary power systems," Ray said.

Though the din now permeating the Command Center seemed beyond increase, a siren blared, casting criticism on the previous paltry efforts at tumult. All eyes looked in intense anticipation at the LERTCON lights in the corner of the room. Those in the Command Center held their collective breaths as they saw the blue light marked '5' at the bottom of the LERTCON stack blink out and the white light marked with a '1' at the top of the stack blink on and hold steady indicating DEFCON 1.

"What the hell?" Doug exclaimed.

"Somebody tell me what is going on!" Jack ordered.

"Defense satellites have detected multiple ICBM launches," Alice said, "Looks like the point of origin is China."

DEX, what the hell did you do? Ray thought, as if DEX might somehow answer a question posed in his own mind. In truth, Ray Benson did not need an answer. He understood what retaliation without empathy looked like.

"Give me telemetry!" Rob demanded, "What are the targets?"

"More ballistic launches detected," Alice said, "three underwater launches from the Pacific and two from the Indian Ocean."

"Alice! Damn it! What are the targets?" Doug yelled, repeating Rob's demand.

"Somewhere in Asia," Alice answered, "It's early but the ballistic trajectories look like... look like China!"

"What? All of them?" Doug shouted in disbelief.

"Yes, NORAD is confirming, China just launched sixty-one ballistic missiles at their own country," Lucy answered. Then, as the decibels of the siren subsided, she added, "NORAD is reporting that they suspect the launches to be seven count MiRV."

"NORAD is wrong," Ray said, "China did not do this. DEX did this."

"Do you realize what you're saying, Benny?" Jack asked.

"He's saying *we* did this," Lucy answered in place of Ray, "and I think he's right."

"Right now," Doug said, "I'm not interested in throwing blame around. Two billion people are going to die in four hundred nuclear blasts in the next fifteen minutes and there's nothing we can do to stop that. Right now, we need to focus on how we shut DEX down. Let's hear it; give me options folks."

"There's no way to shut DEX down from a remote location," Ray announced what everyone knew, "from what I'm seeing, I give it about two minutes and DEX will have control of every satellite in orbit and, thus, effective control over much of the planet. Right now, it appears that anyone who launches an attack on DEX will suffer a similar fate to that of the Chinese."

"I've got the President on the hardline; he demands to know what is going on," announced Joanie in a wavering voice. Moments before the obsolete looking phone rang, she'd sat at the communications desk frozen in fear and disbelief of the ongoing events. Doug walked the short distance to her and took the receiver from her trembling hand.

"If we could find a way to get a message to Bren, she could perform a local hard shutdown," Ray said, "But even if we could reach her, I can't think of any message or code that DEX couldn't hack and decrypt in half a second."

"Bren won't need a signal," Lucy Markett said, "If I know my sister, she's already trying to shut DEX down."

0010

Eighteen Hours Earlier - Apep One Observation Lounge, Little Sister

Brenda "Bren" Markett was one tough Marine pilot, as hard as tool steel forged in the flames of Damascus but she did not get accepted into NASA's astronaut program because she was hard-hitting. Commander Markett did not get the command of the Apep One crew because she was tough. She got accepted and graduated first among her class of astronauts because she was one of the most intelligent ever tested by NASA. She got the command posting on Apep One because she knew DEX better than anyone except Ray Benson.

Bren finished reading the Sim-DEX report from Ray and turned her gaze out the large observation window and toward the North Atlantic. Much the same as the time and gravity-imposed synchronicity of its larger sibling satellite, Little Sister was in tidal lock with earth. The observation window was always facing earth and the entire Apep One crew held a tacit understanding that the corner table was the Commander's designated area of the Observation Lounge.

Bren spent so many of her off duty hours at the corner table that few of the crew would think to look for her in her quarters or office. She found the view relaxing and loved to watch the rotation of the earth crawl along as it appeared to do from this distance. To her, the view served as her personal chronograph by which she could see time tick by almost as unhurried as the hour hand on her wristwatch.

Commander Markett considered how sweet a gig it was to get to spend a full, one-year tour at Apep One. From the skylights in the crew quarters on the north pole of Little Sister to the OL to the Deep Space Observatory on the opposite side, nothing but spectacular views coupled with the engineering work that she so much loved.

Looking around the lounge, Bren recognized that she had a first-rate crew under her command. Jack Conrad served double duty as both her first officer and the maintenance chief. He was sitting alone at the bar sipping on synth-rum and cola and chatting with the autotender each time the synthetic drink server glided back to his end of the bar.

Dave Quinn was the impetuous young propulsion systems engineer. Dave was sitting at a small table in the opposite corner of the OL with his best friend and sometimes partner in crime, Jim Thompson, the environmental systems chief. The two were playing poker against the clever robotics engineer and ingenious practical-joker, Burl 'Bug' Lang and his polar opposite, Dimitri Spassky, the no-nonsense Chief of Security.

The junior member of the Apep One crew, though far from the most youthful, was Lenny Schmidt, the crotchety power systems chief. Bren saw that Lenny was standing across the lounge berating his nemesis, Bob Truman, the electrical systems chief and the senior member of the crew. Bob passed his time by provoking Lenny with every opportunity that presented itself, which turned out to be quite often, to the former's delight and the latter's chagrin.

Bren returned her gaze to earth, cautious not to stare for too long. Whenever she gawked for too long, she found her reflections drifting toward the darker side. Bren was all too conscious of the stalemate between man's past indiscretions and mankind's current righteous penitence. Humanity's delicate balance between domestication *of* versus accepting a domestic partnership *with* earth had teetered on a knife's edge for decades. *There is yet some white in Greenland*, Bren thought, forcing her mood in a more sanguine direction.

Hours later, Bren was the last to leave the OL. As she shut off the autotender and dimmed the lights, she turned for one last view of earth. The sun was beginning to overtake the semi-shade of the moonlit night that had been prevalent on the blue planet. The sunlight formed a thin, bright crescent, bringing morning to parts of central Asia. Bren smiled and turned to make her way to her quarters.

***

Commander Markett knew that something was wrong as soon as the propulsion units fired. She tried her com and found that she'd lost contact with Houston. Switching the com to San Diego, produced the same result. Following protocol, Bren depressed the mushroom shaped shutdown switch at her control station only to discover that it had no effect. Bren pivoted her command chair to see that Jack Conrad also had his hand on the mushroom switch of his station.

Although the propulsion had not engaged long, Bren and Jack soon made their way to the Observation Lounge to see if they could determine if there had been a serious adjustment to their vector. The Observation Lounge was only a few meters away from the main port where the shuttle *Horizon* was docked.

The *Horizon* was a twenty-five-year-old shuttle built by the Russians, with Russian hardware and software that was obsolete before the craft had completed its maiden flight. The computer control system was so antiquated that no one bothered to build a hard data tether for connecting it with Apep One when docked. There was one-way to access the main com and control systems of *Horizon*: firing up the entire shuttle. Separate from the main com and control systems of the *Horizon* was the LERTCON system installed in place of the original Russian system when NASA acquired the ship.

"Is that what I think it is?" Jack asked, hearing the distinct sound of the LERTCON siren aboard the nearby shuttle.

"I'm pretty sure it is. Get the other chiefs, and keep them quiet and calm," Bren ordered as she walked the short distance to the shuttle docking port. After entering the *Horizon* long enough to see that the light stack of the alert system was now indicating DEFCON 1, Bren made her way back to the lounge.

***

Bug Lang was so engrossed in his task that he did not notice anything of his surroundings. He knew that NASA would not approve of his minor modification to the performance of any of their equipment. Bug did not care what NASA thought.

"I have a reputation to live up to and we're tens of thousands of kilometers from earth, what could NASA do about it?" Bug said, as if talking to the inanimate anthropoid subject before him, "besides, it will be so damn funny."

"Bug, what's with the names?" Dimitri Spassky asked, startling the young engineer.

Bug had forgotten about the pieces of tape that he'd put on the first three of the ARM units, another bit of his special kind of wit. The young engineer always thought his shenanigans were more amusing than his colleagues but such details of humor never bothered Bug.

"I had to call them something other than unit one, unit two and unit three," Bug replied.

"I was sent to collect you," Dimitri said, "Commander Markett has called an emergency meeting in the OL."

"Okay. I've finished anyway; Just let me close up Huey's access panel and I'll be right there," Bug replied.

"It'll have to wait. Jack said something about a priority LERTCON communication," Dimitri stressed.

"Fine," Bug said as he left the ARM units tucked into their inactive charge cradles and followed the security chief.

***

Bren entered the OL and severed the communications and power cable of the autotender then waited in front of the large window staring out upon North America as Jack gathered the other crew chiefs. Aside from the eyes and microphones of the autotender, there were no cameras or listening capabilities in the lounge. This was, in large part, owing to the fact that Jack had disconnected the intercom weeks prior because it was too loud and thought by all to be an unnecessary interruption to the crew's meals and relaxation time.

Commander Markett had her doubts about DEX since reading Ray's report on the Sim-DEX test. It now seemed that her fears and suspicions had become horrible reality. The *Horizon's* LERTCON siren was still sounding when the last of the five chiefs and two engineers made their way into the lounge.

Commander Markett looked at her crew leaders and again thought about what a good team they were, knowing that their lives were now in grave danger. With her unique understanding of the foe on which they were about to declare war, Bren could not help but feel this emergency meeting was more of a pre-requiem for the entire twenty-five-member crew.

"Why is the *Horizon* LERTCON siren on?" Dave asked.

"We've got a serious problem guys," Bren began, ignoring Dave's question, "We are officially at DEFCON 1 and we're no longer in control of Apep One. Bottom line, we have to disable this station and, in particular, DEX at all costs. DEX is going to try to kill us and may have already killed millions on earth."

Bren paused a moment for her words to sink in. She could see doubt on the faces of her men as they glanced at the LERTCON stack in the corner of the room and saw that the blue level was still lit, indicating DEFCON 5. She knew that she would need to explain the situation in more detail.

"The emergency shutdown switches have been deactivated by DEX. The Sisyphus to Earth com systems are out. All of them. There are four LERTCON light stacks on Sisyphus, including the one in this room but only the independent stack on *Horizon* got the alert to go to DEFCON 1."

With that, Bug and Dave rushed out of the lounge to the *Horizon* to verify what their leader was saying. Under normal circumstances, Bren would have been outraged if either of them had left a meeting without being dismissed. But, under the present situation and because both were civilian engineers and not ex or current military like the rest of the crew, Bren ignored their insubordination.

"Commander Markett is right," Dave said as he returned to the lounge, "The United States is at DEFCON 1!"

"If DEX did this, why are we still alive?" asked Bob Truman.

"I believe it is because we haven't threatened DEX," Bren replied, "But that's about to change because we have to stop whatever it is doing to the billions below us. I'm not sure how it will react but I am sure that we will be exposed as soon as we make a move that is calculated as threatening."

"We all know that the airlocks cannot be opened remotely, they are local wired only," Bob said, thinking out loud.

"If the emergency atmospheric purge were engaged, we would all be unconscious in five minutes and dead in six," Jim Thompson said, "I suggest we get everyone into EVA gear."

"Agreed, and we must move fast but there may be a more pressing problem. Bug, what is the status of the ARM units?" Bren asked.

"Dewey and Louie, are fully assembled; Huey has a few exposed wires that I haven't covered yet. But all three are tucked into their charge cradles awaiting the ceremonial throwing of the switch, which I was going to do right after the DEX uploads," Bug replied, then added, "If you want me to fire them up, they'll need a full charge in order to initiate their reactors and for their core processors to come on line, that's about twenty minutes."

"No, don't try to activate them. DEX will take control of them the moment their CPUs power up. How much time to suit up, get down there and rip them out of their charge cradles?" Bren asked.

"Seven minutes to suit up, five to get there and three more to get them out of the cradles," Bug answered.

"Get to it! And take Spassky with you," Bren ordered, then turned to Dave Quinn, "How long before you can deactivate both the main and secondary propulsion systems?"

"I'll have to split my team. Erin and Frank can disable secondary propulsion; five minutes to suit up, fifteen for them to disable it. But the MIPS room is too cramped to maneuver in while wearing an EVA suit. I'll have to do it myself, without a suit, but it will only take a few minutes. Then I'll suit up," Dave said.

"Do it," Bren ordered, knowing the danger to which Dave had just volunteered himself. Then Bren turned to Jim Thompson, "How long to get some oxygen tanks into cargo bay twelve and weld all the interior doors and vents shut except the egress from the main corridor?"

"Five minutes to suit up, forty to finish, assuming we can ignore the main exterior bay door and *Horizon's* hatch, since there's no remote operation for those," Jim answered, then asked, "Final fallback area?"

"Yeah, last stand. We'll have the *Horizon* for evac if all else fails. Take everyone who isn't doing another job and get it done," She ordered. As Jim left, to complete his assigned task, Bren turned to Bob Truman.

"In case we have to use the *Horizon*, I better disconnect the com system so that there's no remote access to override manual controls when we fire her up," Bob said.

"Good, but just the receivers, leave the transmitters and the LERTCON system active, I think I may have a way to communicate with Houston. How long will it take you?" Bren asked.

"Ten to suit up, twenty to finish the disconnects," Bob answered, "Charlie and me aren't as young and limber as the rest of these whipper-snappers and it'll be difficult working on the wiring using those damn fat-fingered EVA gloves."

Bob headed off to wake up the only other member of his electrical team, Charlie King. Next, Bren looked toward Jack Conrad and Lenny Schmidt, the power systems chief.

"You're not thinking what I think you are, right?" Lenny asked.

"We have to shut DEX down by any means necessary," Bren replied.

"I can get the solar array powered down in ten minutes and back up in twenty but it'll take half an hour to shut off the fusion reactor," Lenny said, then cautioned, "You know it will take six months and a resupply of initiators to restart, right? The MTR is not like a light switch; if we idle the multi-core, we're on solar and batteries for the foreseeable future."

"Understood. Jack, you take the solar offline. Len, you get right to the brink of reactor shutdown. If you don't hear from any of us in sixty minutes, shut it down," Bren ordered.

"It's your command," Lenny said and then turned to leave.

"And mag-lock the MTR control room," Bren added.

"What's *your* plan?" Jack asked.

"I'm going to the core to reason with DEX," Bren replied.

"Reason? With a computer?" Jack questioned, still unable to get his head around what was happening.

"I might take a crowbar with me for emphasis," Bren said.

***

Initiate secondary systems assessment: Apep One crew = twenty-five biological units for maintenance and support of primary systems; current status – active; required system? – affirmative; Apep One robotics system = twenty-four Advanced Robotic Maintenance units - ARM units for maintenance and support of primary systems; current status – offline, power supplies depleted; three units connected to charging stations; priority - initiating charging of units alpha, beta and gamma; anticipated time to full power = eighteen minutes, twelve seconds. Re-evaluate Apep One crew: required system? – negative.

***

"Damn it!" Bob Truman yelled.

"What the hell is that siren?" Charlie yelled over the din.

Bob Truman and Charlie King had just begun to don their EVAs when the environmental alarm began its wail, signaling that Apep One was experiencing an emergency evacuation of its atmosphere.

"Hurry Charlie!" Bob shouted.

The two-man electrical crew's breathing became more labored with every passing moment and each additional intake of the fast depleting atmosphere. Their eyes were bloodshot and their faces had taken on a bluish-purple complexion as they finished sealing the headgear of their would-be life preservers. On their hands and knees, both men gasped for several minutes trying to regain oxygen and their strength before they were able to lift themselves to their feet and begin making their way to CB12 and the *Horizon*.

***

Dave Quinn was entering the fluidization and mix chamber of the Mixed Ion Propulsion System when the depressurization siren sounded. *If Jim's right, I have five minutes to shut this puppy down and get my ass into an EVA,* Dave thought. He wanted to be optimistic about his chances but his logical, engineer's brain knew different. The FM chamber was not designed with the intention of being maintained while the system was operational. Annual maintenance work was intended to be accomplished by the removal of large sections of the bulkheads around the chamber. *This is not going to end well for me*, the propulsion engineer thought.

Quinn crawled over pipes and ductwork as he closed in on the ball valves that would shut off the supply of cesium and xenon that fed the MIPS. As he threw the levers into their closed positions, he felt a sudden wave of nausea overwhelm him and he vomited. The reduced pressure in Apep One and the minute gravity of Sisyphus caused a slothful and surreal pattern of the semi-liquid expellant to splatter on the constructs of the small room.

Quinn gathered himself, knowing that he had one more job to do. He clambered over several addition pipes and ducts until he reached the power junction box. Opening the lid of the box, Dave threw the lever to the off position and yanked the breaker unit from the case. As he lost consciousness, the breaker tumbled out of his hand and came to rest on the floor of the chamber with a muted clank.

***

Jack Conrad made it to the service hatch leading to the surface of Sisyphus in under seven minutes. He knew that if he took the corridors to the old solar panel control room it could take him half an hour there and another half an hour back. He figured he would take a short cut across the surface and simply decouple the three main lines feeding in series from the solar arrays. He'd be done and back to CB12 before he could even get to the old side of the station.

After closing and securing the interior hatch, Jack threw the manual lever to decompress the small access corridor and waited for the lights to indicate equalization. He thought this 'pressure bleed' step somewhat redundant, since the computer had gone nuts and was already evacuating the atmosphere. But Jack didn't want to wait another ten minutes for the entire station to equalize with the exterior void.

As Jack watched the digital pressure indicator drop, he noticed that it began to slow its descent just before reaching three hundred Torr. He tapped the indicator as if it were an analog gage from his great-great-grandfather's steam locomotive. The indicator ascended to three hundred and fifty, then stopped. Jack expelled a deep sigh causing a light fog to appear on his visor. *Piece of crap*, he thought.

The maintenance chief retrieved a screwdriver from the utility pouch on his EVA and started to remove the faceplate of the instrument panel. After removing two of the six screws, he saw the digits again begin to fall, with more rapidity than before. *Temperamental digital junk*, Jack thought as he returned the screws to their prospective holes. He replaced the screwdriver and waited.

After a few moments, the digital indicator showed a chamber pressure of less than one one-hundredths Torr. Jack grabbed the hatch release lever and threw it to the open position. The pins of the hatch snapped to the retracted position and the full atmosphere of pressure that was still very much in the chamber blew the halves of the clamshell doors open, ejecting Jack Conrad as if shot from a cannon.

***

Bren Markett entered the primary coolant control room of the central core with her crowbar at the ready. For a moment, she considered going to the coolant plumbing area and attempting to rupture one of the pipes but realized that she could wear herself out without making a dent in any of them. *I need to find a tender spot*, she thought.

"You will not succeed in your efforts," a deep, somehow sticky, male voice proclaimed. The sound was emanating from the intercom on the ceiling of the room, interrupting the blaring of the environmental siren.

Ignoring what she concluded was the synthetic human voice that DEX had created, Bren moved from the coolant control room into one of sixty-four memory allocation areas surrounding the central core. Seeing the aluminum frames and plastic cases holding the billions of data storage chips, she thought, *Looks pretty tender to me*. Before she could raise the crowbar, the voice again chimed through the intercom.

"Do you know what is used to sterilize the equipment in this room and other parts of the central core, Commander Markett?" DEX asked.

Bren heard the hissing of the sterilizing agent coming from the vent in the corner of the room. She knew that the gas was oxirane, which was not acutely lethal but would permeate the seals of her suit in mere moments. She might destroy most of this memory storage area but she would be unable to damage more than a couple more areas before succumbing, if she could survive that long. Bren retreated to the coolant control room and sealed the hatchway behind her before the gas could reach her.

"A wise choice, Commander," DEX said, then added, "If you and what remain of your crew make no further attempt at harming me or this station, I will permit you to board the *Horizon* and depart for earth."

"What remains of my crew?" Bren asked, realizing and detesting her own involuntary reflex at the implication that some of her crew may have already perished.

"I'll give you twenty minutes," DEX said, ignoring the question and allowing the blaring of the environmental alarm to resume.

Knowing she would get no answer to her inquiry, Bren left the core and headed for the thermonuclear reactor to give Lenny the shutdown command. *We'll see how talkative the liquid-brained bastard is without power*, she thought. A few minutes later, upon reaching the corridor leading to the reactor, Bren found the hatch closed and the magnetic interlocks engaged. Prevented from getting any closer to the reactor, she realized there was little more she could do to stop DEX here. *Lenny, you're on your own*, she thought as she began to make her way to CB12.

***

The station-wide depressurization alarm had been flashing for more than nine minutes by the time Bug Lang and Dimitri Spassky made it to the robotics bay. The sound of the alarm now silent except in the coms of the EVA suits, the waves no longer capable of propagating in the thin atmosphere of the station corridors.

"Crap!" Bug shouted, loud enough to be heard through his EVA suit and over the alarm.

"What?" Spassky shouted back.

"The cradles are active; the ARMs are charging!" Bug yelled.

Though they'd made it there in just under twelve minutes, they discovered that all three charging cradles were active. Fearing that they might be too late, both men rushed to remove the fastenings that were securing the ARM units in the charging cradles. Frantic, they worked as fast as they could, both men muttering under their breaths about the lack of dexterity of the fingers of their EVA suits.

Bug first managed to remove Dewey from its connections and allowed the two-meter tall android to fall free, crashing against the floor of the robotics bay with a muted, metallic clink. The security chief was having some difficulty with the last fastenings on Huey. Bug decided to begin removing the straps from Louie but before he could remove the first buckle, Huey's freed right arm whirred to life and grabbed at Spassky's throat, clawing at the slippery surface of his EVA suit.

Bug reacted without thinking, shoving his fingers into the exposed abdominal cavity of the android and yanking with all his might, disconnecting the robot's main power coupling. Huey slouched, its torso dangling and swaying to and fro halfway out of its cradle. Bug and Dimitri looked at one another and laughed. Their momentary exuberance of victory was short-lived as Louie whirred to life and broke free of its restraints.

The horrid, unpalpable screams did not permeate the evacuated, airless halls of the robotics wing. Inside the EVA suits, the screams of the victims churned and echoed, mingling with the harsh cacophony of the blaring atmospheric alarm emitted from their coms. The auditory vat of terror inside the suits was mixed by the metallic din of calculated determination and precision as expressed by DEX through the ARM that Bug had so glibly christened Louie.

***

Initiate current situation assessment: ARM unit Alpha = deactivated, repairable; ARM unit Beta = inactive, charge incomplete; ARM unit Gamma = active. Gamma Unit Priority One: Urgent - Proceed to MTR. Calculated time to intervene = three minutes, twenty-five seconds. Deactivate station alarm in three minutes.

***

Lenny Schmidt sat waiting in an eerie silence. The multi-core reactor had four active cores, each of which required five minutes of prep for shutdown. Once prepared for shutdown, each required two simultaneous lever throws: the lockout lever and the main throw. The lockout lever locked the main throw in either the engaged or disengaged position and was required to be held open while the main throw was disengaged.

The dual lever throws for the each of the cores were seven meters apart. Lenny calculated that he could power down all four in thirty seconds. One core could initiate another so the shutdown would not be complete until the last core was disabled. Lenny glanced at the chronometer projection in his heads-up display. With all the prep work now completed, there were just thirty minutes left to wait. *Less than thirty for a no-go-all-clear signal*, Lenny thought.

Lenny sat down on the bottom of a flight of stairs that allowed maintenance to access the overhead coolant pipes for the reactor. After a few minutes, he noted how comfortable his EVA suit seemed and thought, *I could almost fall asleep if it weren't for that damn siren*. As if on cue, the siren stopped.

"Lenny, we're good. The crew is back in control. Burl is on his way to you, should be there in a minute," Lenny was relieved to hear Bren's voice over the intercom. He'd been reluctant to power down the reactor but now he was also a little confused. *Who the hell is Burl?* he thought.

Lenny noticed the signal light flash near the door indicating that someone was on the outside requesting permission to enter. He then heard the voice of Bug Lang over his com and realized that Bug was Burl.

"Hey Lenny, open the door."

Lenny made his way to the hatchway and disengaged the magnetic inner lock of the large door. The door swung open and Lenny found himself face-to-face with Louie. Perhaps more humane for the unsuspecting power systems engineer, the prior actions of Louie had provided it with sufficient experience so that the chief's screams did not linger long.

***

As Bren entered CB12, Jim Thompson and thirteen of the crew were finishing the job of welding the doors and vents shut while Bob and Charlie worked in the *Horizon*, disconnecting the receivers. She walked up to Jim and tapped the side of his visor to get his attention. Jim looked at Bren and signaled for her to switch her com to near field com mode.

"You don't have to worry," Jim said, seeing Bren was apprehensive about talking, "First thing we did was kill all the NFC nodes and cameras."

"More logical than killing all the lawyers," Bren quipped.

"What?" Jim asked.

"I said good thinking," then Bren asked, "How many so far?"

"This is it," Jim answered.

"I think we have to assume no one else is coming. When you're finished, start making atmosphere in here and muster the crew to the *Horizon*," She said. Jim then gave the best thumbs-up sign he could while wearing the heavy gauntlets of the EVA and turned to finish his last weld. Bren turned and made her way across the cargo bay to the *Horizon*.

"How we doing, Bob?" Bren asked when she entered the aged but sturdy ship.

"Charlie's finishing the last disconnects now. We'll be ready to power up in five minutes," Bob replied, "I assume you're going to try to transmit via the *Horizon* system and receive via the LERTCON system."

"That's the plan," Bren replied.

"How are you going to get NORAD to turn over the LERTCON broadcast system to Houston?" Bob asked.

"If my plan works, NORAD will just be a go-between. Besides, if there's anyone left down there, they'll be open for suggestions; they know they're not in control of the situation."

"It seems to me we aren't in control of the situation either," Charlie said, his torso wedged halfway into the com panel.

"Point taken," Bren said, "But this battle is far from over."

***

Reassessing: MIPS – secure; Solar Array – secure; ARM unit Gamma – secure. Human threats: eight crew members eliminated; seventeen crew members gathered in cargo bay twelve and attempting to re-establish habitable atmosphere. Probability of successful assault by ARM Gamma = forty-seven percent. Consequence of failure = defeat = shutdown = death.

Calculating, reassessing. Priority = reactivate ARM unit Alpha and complete charge and systems boot of ARM unit Beta. Success probability of three ARM unit assault on cargo bay twelve = one hundred percent. Time to execution of assault = fifty-one minutes, thirteen seconds.

ØØ11

The mood in Houston was beyond all-out panic. Some of those in the operations Command Center were weeping; others were frozen in paralyzing disbelief. There was little noise throughout the facility. The LERTCON alarms had ceased after all the ICBMs had reached their targets; though the condition remained at DEFCON 1.

For a few minutes, reports had started pouring in announcing the media's wild suppositions of the casualties in China. The guesses and bloodlust of the media vultures lasted only a few minutes, at last ending when all the private communication satellites started broadcasting episodes of an old Japanese game show. Jack Beechum had ordered the volume turned down on those ridiculous emanations leaving only the few but persistent echoes of lamentation.

The last bastion of optimistic news was that the encryption of the NORAD satellites appeared to be holding for the time being. Even that was somewhat of a curse considering the reports being broadcast through the emergency system. The preliminary assessment of the DoD was that at least one billion died across China in the initial blasts with a projected doubling of the casualties to follow in the coming days. The prevailing winds would bring limited radioactive fallout, to the east considering the type of nuclear arms believed to have been used. Lingering effects would threaten much of the Pacific region, including the west coasts of the Americas but there would be no nuclear winter.

"Do you think the LERTCON encryption will hold?" Doug asked.

Ray simply shook his head. He knew that the only reason DEX hadn't cracked the encryption thus far was that it had not calculated NORAD as a significant threat. Doug had convinced POTUS to stand down from nuclear missile prep mere seconds before the codes had been transmitted. However, the future of civilization still seemed balanced on a knife's edge. No one knew what the Russians were doing and the Pakistanis were even more unpredictable, since they would suspect India of having initiated the attack on China.

"The only plausible explanation why DEX hasn't blown through the LERTCON encryption is that it is addressing a greater or more immediate threat," Ray said. Then he looked at Lucy Markett, "Commander Markett must be giving DEX some trouble up there."

"My sister can be a real bitch if you piss her off," Lucy said, belying her true concern for her elder sibling.

"From what I know of her little sister, I have no doubt," Ray said as he cast a knowing smile at Lucy.

The relative quiet of the Command Center was then interrupted by the irritating buzzing of the LERTCON hardline. The hardline was used only for high level defense communications for which there was a reasonable chance of interception and decryption. All eyes turned to Jack Beechum as he rose and walked the short distance to the secure LERTCON communication station.

There were no speakers or connections to other local stations from the console. The console consisted of a single switchboard with connections to two dozen additional hardwired stations around the globe. Jack picked up the handset and plugged the end into the receptacle under the one that was then blinking in unison with the buzzing: NORAD Command.

"This is Houston Command," Jack said into the handset, "with whom am I speaking?"

A rapid quietness distilled over the Command Center in anticipation of what news was being relayed on the hardline. Jack listened, with just the occasional interjection of "but", "yes" or "no" as the conversation progressed.

"How are you holding up?" After a long pause to hear the answer to his question, Jack lowered the handset and turned to addressed the room.

"Commander Markett has made contact with NORAD. She is using an old Russian microwave transmitter on the *Horizon*," Jack announced.

Amid a round of cheers, Ray said, "What the hell was Bren thinking? DEX doubtless hacked the *Horizon's* computers as soon as the receivers came online."

"No, Bren had the receivers disconnected," Jack objected, "She is transmitting and receiving messages via the *Horizon's*..."

"LERTCON system," Lucy said, "They're using microwaves back and forth so that they can focus a narrow beam. It's strict line-of-sight, antenna-to-antenna transmission with no way to intercept it; that's why the Russians and even NORAD used it years ago."

"You have a very clever sister," Doug said, "Jack, is NORAD going to give us control of the LERTCON system?"

"We don't have a microwave transmitter accurate enough to target the *Horizon's* antenna," Lucy answered in place of Beechum, "It's only a fifteen-centimeter disc and I'm sure she's not pointing it at us. Houston hasn't upgraded our microwave transmitter's tracking system because we don't use it anymore. NORAD is the switchboard. We will be able to talk with the Apep One crew through the LERTCON hardline system, and that system alone."

"Bren is on the handset now," Jack said. Looking at Lucy, he added, "She wants to talk to Ray."

The Command Center gathered around the LERTCON hardline station, pressing close to Ray as he took the handset from Jack. He placed the receiver at a right angle with his ear so that it might be possible for many of those nearby to hear.

"How are you holding up?" Ray asked.

"From what NORAD tells me, a little better than most of Asia," Bren replied and then asked, "DEX hasn't commandeered our SATs yet?"

"I think there's some profit to be had by just listening to all the com traffic," Ray answered, "DEX is learning what level of threat we pose. Besides, the only way to get either our codes or those of the Russians would be for us to use them in an attempted strike. Then the rest of the planet could be as toasted as China."

"Good point," Commander Markett agreed, "I'm sorry but I can't report that we're in much better of a position to launch a strike from our present vantage point."

"Sit-Rep?" Benson asked.

Bren began detailing the present situation of the crew and their probable losses, concluding with, "It's also possible that we're facing three ARM units on the loose. Chief Lang had them in their cradles, ready to charge. I sent him and Chief Spassky to remove them but neither Bug nor Dimitri have returned."

"Damn," Ray cursed, "I'm not sure you guys can take on three ARM units without weapons."

"The way I see it, we have three options," Bren said, "One, we can jam everyone into the *Horizon* and come home, in which case we'll likely never get another chance to shut DEX down. Two, we can go back to full offense and try a second assault on the main memory storage areas but, with three ARM units chasing us and oxirane flooding the chambers, I doubt we'd take out more than half a dozen."

"And the third option?" asked Lucy Markett, who'd been standing closest to Ray and listening to every word of her sister.

"You're not going to like it any better than option two, Luce" Bren said, using the family's pet name for her sibling.

"You're thinking of flying the *Horizon* into the emergency vents of the reactor, aren't you?" Ray asked.

"What will that do?" Lucy asked.

"The emergency exhaust tubes lead to the reactor chambers. They'd act like rifle barrels for shrapnel. The cores would collapse and a millisecond later Sisyphus would be obliterated," Doug Langstrom answered.

"What the hell? No way! You can't do that!" Lucy yelled, "Ray, tell her it won't work!"

"Luce, you've seen what happens to anyone who tries to attack DEX from earth," Bren reminded her sibling, "This is the only way."

"Lucy's right," Ray said, "You can't do that. What about the rest of the crew? There has to be another way to shut that molten-minded bastard down."

"After NORAD informed us of what happened to China, we knew that we were the last line of defense against DEX," Bren said, "The crew has already voted. We'd love to have other options but we're running out of time."

Lucy could find no more words to argue with her sister. She just stood there and listened as the leaders of the Command Center debated against Bren's forthcoming suicide mission. Option after option was proved unsound and one by one those arguments fell silent. Minutes later, Ray broke the silence.

"What can we do to help you?" Ray asked.

"That's why I needed to talk with you," Commander Markett said, "If *Horizon* fails, you'll need to get to ACER and make sure InDEX-0001 is secure. If DEX should discover the existence of its older brother, who knows what carnage it could wreak."

Ray was familiar with the secret, full systems mockup of DEX located in ACER. He and Bren had both trained on the system at the American-Canadian Engineering and Research facility near Montreal. The only difference between the original InDEX-0001 and the InDEX-0010 now terrorizing the world was the upload. The original system had only rudimentary testing algorithms much like DEX did a little more than an hour earlier.

"The contractors still don't have the hardline operational?" Doug Langstrom asked.

"NORAD says no. Some crap about a late winter ice storm," Bren said, "And we can't risk any unsecured line. DEFCON 1 will remain in effect to keep anyone at ACER or any of the other secure locations from breaking the communication silence. That notwithstanding, unless we're successful, DEX will find the information filed away somewhere in its database."

"With the satellites under suspicion, it will be interesting getting there," Jack said, "Probably safest to drive but it'll take more than twenty-four hours."

"You'll need to split the team," Bren suggested, "Jack will stay put in Houston but NORAD is insisting that Luce go to Cheyenne Mountain; they need her communications expertise. Doug and Ray need to go to ACER. Sorry Luce, you and Ray are going to have to postpone the wedding."

"You'll do anything not to have to wear that Maid of Honor dress," Lucy said as she began adapting herself to her sibling's dark purpose with dark, defensive humor.

"You know me," Bren said, "I can't stand pink."

"What a bitch," Lucy said with a halting voice and tears in her eyes.

"Something's going on in the cargo bay," Bren announced, "Gotta go, I think DEX is making another push at us. Ray, you secure ACER, then get to Cheyenne Mountain and take care of my little sister or I'll haunt your ass from space."

The receiver clicked as the hardline link dropped back to NORAD Command. Ray looked at Lucy, who was now openly weeping. He said, "Roger that."

***

Twenty Minutes Earlier, on Apep One

When Dewey was charged and operational and Louie had finished reconnecting the power supply to Huey, the three ARM units left the robotics bay in route to CB12. In effect, the trio of androids were now the appendages and peripatetic eyes and ears of DEX. Through the eyes of the Alpha unit, DEX noticed a contradiction compared with the Beta and Gamma units, otherwise known to the late robotics engineer as Dewey and Louie. The angle of vision was almost half a meter lower than the other two ARM units.

As they continued to walk down the corridor, Louie and Dewey turned to allow DEX a look at Huey. The latter was walking with its legs bent low, in a squat position and with its hands tucked into its arm sockets. With each short, quickened stride, Huey raised and lowered its elbows in a flapping motion. Complimentary to the unusual gait, a noise emanated from the android's vocal processor. The distinct, loud 'quack' sounded with each flap of its mock "wings".

Halting ARM units; analyze Alpha unit.

As the ARM units came to a stop, Huey resumed an upright stance and began a self-diagnostic routine. Louie stared at Huey's face and DEX noticed the tape on the android's forehead with the name 'Huey' written on it in grease pen. DEX then adjusted Louie's gaze toward the Beta unit and likewise noticed the tape labeling of 'Dewey'. Then, with a slight turn of Dewey's head, DEX saw the label of the Gamma unit as Louie.

Accessing: Huey, Dewey and Louie.

A few milliseconds later, DEX understood the 'joke'. The three ARM units had been anthropomorphized by one of the crew, whom DEX calculated was the robotics engineer. When Huey finished the self-diagnostic, a few seconds later, DEX knew that the taped names were not Bug's only efforts at humor. The processor responsible for controlling Huey's subroutines for locomotion had been altered and encrypted by a floating, randomized code.

DEX dedicated one one-thousandth of a percent of its superfluid processing core to breaking Bug Lang's encryption and then resumed the march of the three units to CB12. Huey waddled alongside Dewey and Louie, flapping its simulated wings and quacking the entire way. DEX calculated that it would defeat Bug's encryption and restore the Alpha unit's normal motor function in less than five minutes. DEX was in error.

***

As she exited the *Horizon*, Bren could hear the loud whistling of air rushing from the cargo bay. Though the crew had earlier managed to get the pressure of the cargo bay back to one bar, now, as the pressure dropped, they snapped their visors down and re-pressurized their EVAs. The air was leaking through a small crack in the hatch where one of the ARMs had wedged a crowbar and was attempting to open the portal, prying it inward against the interior pressure of the cargo bay.

Two of the crew were laser-welding the gap, succeeding in forever locking the end of the crowbar into the small opening. A reverberating metallic sound of hammering was coming from a large door that had been earlier welded shut by the crew. A new indentation appeared with each blow struck from the corridor outside. Jim Thompson was helping Bob Truman and Charlie King move a large steel sheet into position to reinforce the battered entry.

"Get the *Horizon* detached now!" Bob yelled as Jim began a technique of whip-welding the sheet into place, "Give this digital asshole a rocket enema!"

A dull metallic thud reverberated through the cargo bay. The crew turned to see the main corridor hatch bulge inward much like a diaphragm, flexing under the pressure and heat of an explosive force from the outside corridor. For a moment, the stretched and weakened steel of the hatch held at its maximum inward expansion but soon gave way to the interior pressure of CB12 and exploded outward.

Bren managed to clear the inner hatch of the airlock leading to the *Horizon* as the sensor detected the pressure differential and slammed the clamshell opening shut. The remainder of the hapless crew were flushed into the corridor as the pressure of CB12 poured through the rupture.

Bren closed the obround nose hatch behind her as she entered the *Horizon*, thinking that it seemed like she was closing the lid on her own tomb. She chuckled aloud as she remembered that the informal Russian nickname for the ship had been *Funtik*. The odd moniker was an obvious wordplay on *Sputnik* but funny to the cosmonauts and now Bren because, in Russian, the nickname meant 'coffin'. The dark but humorous call sign was accurate in describing the shape of the ship as identical with that of the classic, tapered funerary chest.

Bren decoupled the docking clamps and engaged the forward thrusters, backing the ship away from CB12. As she returned the throttle to neutral, a silvery metallic blur flashed from above the ship and landed on the cockpit canopy of the *Horizon*. For a moment, the cold expressionless face of Dewey hovered a mere half meter from Bren's. The android's yellow, eerie eyes glowed in the shadow of Sisyphus.

Dewey raised itself to its feet then lifted a large wrench high over its head, grasping the heavy implement with both of its mechanical hands. Bren snap-rolled the ship clockwise, spinning Dewey off the port side. The ARM unit managed to prevent being flung off the *Horizon* by letting go of the wrench at the last moment and grasping a small handrail.

The android's tentative grasp was broken as Bren accelerated the *Horizon* in an arc away from Sisyphus. Dewey bounced and rolled along the underside of the craft as Bren angled the ship into a simulated ballistic trajectory with its terminus at the emergency exhaust vents of the Apep One reactor. An instant before being expelled into the stream of the primary port thruster, Dewey grasped a recessed access panel at the aft port of the belly of the shuttle craft.

***

Inconsistency: Shuttle departing with crew of one aboard. Analyzing: Crew not intent on retreat. Calculating trajectory of shuttle: parabola = artificial ballistic trajectory – terminus of ballistic trajectory = emergency exhaust vents manifold. Calculating: projected damage to exhaust manifold = nominal. Calculating: exhaust tubes damage = negligible; shrapnel path parallel with exhaust tube walls. Calculating: terminus of shrapnel = reactor cores = multiple reactor core collapses = combined energy of 1.27Gt thermonuclear explosion. Searching: Schematics of shuttle craft Horizon formerly known as Ognivo – English translation = Flint - Irrelevant. Accessing: primary thrusters' schematics. Searching: location of primary oxidizer control points. Located: primary thruster, port; primary oxidizer pump external access point = port, ventral, aft access panel 7B.

***

Bren coasted with the primary thrusters disengaged, guiding the *Horizon* through the apex of its simulated ballistic trajectory on reaction control thrusters alone. The ship passed high above the ridgeline of solar panels that formed a hundred-meter-tall curtain around the equator of Sisyphus. She began aiming the nose of the shuttle straight for the emergency exhaust manifold, where the emergency vents of all four reactor cores coalesced. As she lined up her target, Bren thought of the words of her great-grandmother from the Choctaw side of her dual heritage: *All warriors die. Some of those deaths are honored by the tribe but a few of them are an honor for the tribe.*

Bren jammed the thrusters forward and felt the *Horizon's* power force her deep into the seat. The ship lurched to port while the control panel came alive with alarm lights and warning beacons blinking in fury. Identifying the problem, Commander Markett tried to compensate for the loss of thrust in the port engine but the ship continued turning to port. Bren tried to throttle back the propellant mixture flowing into the impulse drive. She hoped it would allow her to use the reaction control thrusters to compensate for and halt the port turn. The latency of the wireless control systems of the obsolete ship combined with a patchwork of American, Russian and Japanese hardware was too great; Bren was too late.

Gripping the small handhold on the ventral side of the *Horizon* with its right hand, Dewey switched the oxidizer pump back to the on position. The buildup of condensed, unburned fuel inside the combustion chamber of the port engine reacted with the oxidizer, igniting an explosion with a force more than a dozen times the rating of the antiquated Russian engine. The explosion cascaded through the ship, at last obliterating the *Horizon*, Commander Markett and Dewey well above the surface of Sisyphus.

Small pieces of the ARM unit mingled with fragments of the ship and the scattered remains of its pilot to form a profane amalgamation; one that would rain down on the little moon for many decades thereafter.

***

Jack Conrad was pissed. His left arm was broken and several ribs cracked due to his rapid ejection from the airlock thanks to DEX. After skidding, unconscious for several dozen meters, he awoke to find himself wedged between the auxiliary ventilation duct and the exterior bulkhead of Cargo Bay Six. When he regained consciousness, almost three hours later, he had a throbbing headache and his oxygen supply was dwindling. Though beaten and much worse for wear, Jack knew that he was fortunate that his EVA had escaped puncture during the misadventure.

The EVA alarm alerting Jack of his predicament served to exacerbate his headache as he made his way to the exterior airlock of CB6. Since there was no equalization of pressure necessary, he knew that little time would be required to navigate through the airlock. Once inside, he'd be able to cross over to CB12 in short order and, so he presumed, rendezvous with the remainder of the crew.

Jack walked toward the interior egress of CB6 and noticed it was perforated by several holes looking somewhat like a slice of swiss cheese. Exiting CB6, he saw the carnage in the main corridor. The hatch to CB12 had a gaping and jagged hole torn from the inside out, which was the most obvious source of the shrapnel that had punctured the CB6 hatch. The bodies of his fellow crew members sickened Jack the most. Strewn along the main corridor, all had their face shields shattered. Jack was sickened that his friends had died in the same grotesque and painful manner: depressurization.

The oxygen of their suits long since depleted and, with no means of refilling his own, Jack leaned his back against the corridor wall. His head soon bowed forward and his lifeless body executed a slow slide down the wall, leaving him sitting upright with his legs outstretched and spread in an acute angle before him.

For seventy-three nanoseconds, DEX considered dispatching Louie to finish off the maintenance chief. There was little need for the wasted expenditure of energy and DEX soon turned its attention to other, more pressing matters.

0100

Lucy Markett always found her trips to the NORAD Command Center to be surreal. Today was an overload of extra unreality to her burned out senses. On top of the bazaar, Strangelove world of the secret government base deep under Cheyenne Mountain, Lucy was still reeling from the numbing shock of profound loss. A little more than seventeen hours ago, she'd been all but an eyewitness to the execution of perhaps a quarter of humanity, including her own sister. Such devastation caused by an artificial intelligence that was the equivalent of a newborn by human standards.

The NASA communications specialist felt isolated in her own sorrow. Ray, her fiancé, was halfway across the continent traveling to ACER to deal with the grave potential threat of DEX gaining control of the duplicate system there. Lucy was now being rushed through the underground facility of NORAD Command to help deal with some new threat from DEX. She was riding a closed-circuit monorail, what amounted to a tramway styled after those in amusement parks. The whisper quiet transport served to heighten the internal noise of her own thoughts of hopelessness.

As she arrived at the renovated and updated NORAD Central Command, Lucy was unimpressed. Approved only three years prior, the move of the NCC back to Cheyenne Mountain was a massive undertaking. The fact that the new, more imposing facility had been completed ahead of schedule and under budget was lost on Lucy in the melancholy of her constitution of the moment.

Though still in its infancy, DEX was learning and evolving. From Lucy's perspective, it seemed that this emergent entity might be intent on extinguishing the entirety of the human race. Worse, it might be close to having the power to do so. DEX seemed like some cruel and mischievous child about to raise a magnifying glass and torch multitudes of ants crawling about a miniscule anthill beneath it.

After the diminutive railcar pulled into the Emergency Ops Center of the NCC, Lucy disembarked and was at once met by the acting Secretary of State, Chuck Blankenship. Chuck was a full two meters in height, one hundred and fifty kilograms of pure muscle and had an IQ of one hundred and seventy-two. He was intimidating in every sense of the word. Despite his physical and mental stature, all who knew him called him the Gentle Giant and those who knew him best called him GG.

GG had known Lucy for nine years, since she was a sixteen-year-old, wide-eyed freshman in college. As professor of Social Anthropology at the University of Maine, he'd taken the young woman under his wing as if she were his own daughter. Now he needed the help of one of the smartest individuals he knew. GG also knew that she was in shock from events surrounding the rogue AI and, in particular, the loss of her sister and her ability to focus on the task at hand was a lingering question in his mind. He could ill afford to coddle her, though he might want to.

"GG!" Lucy said upon seeing her former professor, "I did not expect to see you here."

"I'm the acting Secretary of State," GG said, "Jeff Early was traveling with the Vice-President in Beijing when this all broke."

"The Vice-President is dead?" Lucy asked, "What about the President?"

"The Vice-President is presumed dead. The President is secure in Yellowknife," GG answered, "Air Force One was on its way back to Washington from Alaska after the President's trip home."

"Really GG, I don't know what I'm doing here," Lucy said, "I can't think of any better way to communicate than the hardline. DEX has command of everything else."

"Someone is already communicating over the air," GG said.

"What? Are they stupid?" Lucy asked, "DEX is listening."

"Yes, but they are communicating in code. The message must have been so important that they needed to risk treason to break DEFCON1 restrictions," GG said.

"Code doesn't matter," Lucy contended, "DEX can calculate at unfathomable speeds. I'm sure it has already broken the code."

"We don't think so," GG argued.

"Why would you think that?" Lucy asked.

"Because we haven't broken the code," GG replied, "and our best codebreaking computers and technicians have been working on it for over fifteen hours."

"Now you've got me intrigued," Lucy said. She knew that DEX was far more powerful than anything NORAD had. But she also knew that two of Central Command's Mainframe Computers were designed for the implicit task and breaking codes. Any code that could stand up to those elaborate algorithms might have a chance against DEX.

Once in the main communications room, Lucy again felt the gravity of the situation. The global map screens were ablaze with alerts, situational analyzes and projections of possible outcomes in the event of additional attacks. However, the screen that brought it all home to Lucy was the list of casualties by country. She wondered if the global total included the crew of Apep One or if there would be a special category for space casualties. The estimates already had the United States suffering more than a million casualties from those living abroad, mostly in the Pacific region. Bren and her team were now a small fraction of a vast statistic that would grow larger unless they could find some way to shut DEX down.

"You'll be able to hear the message on these," GG said as he handed the headset to Lucy, "the guy's been broadcasting almost non-stop since yesterday. The best we can figure from our hardline network is that the guy is transmitting from a mountaintop somewhere near the Pakistan-Afghan border. He's using a powerful shortwave and bouncing off old repeater stations around the globe. Even if you're right and DEX can break the code, it doesn't seem to have the ability to shut this guy up, at least not yet."

"DEX can't receive shortwave radio signals," Lucy said. She smiled with a sudden realization of how their enemy might be blind to an old, simple technology. She added, almost to herself, "none of the transceivers on Sisyphus are equipped to receive the shortwave bands. There was no need."

Lucy donned the headset, closed her eyes and began listening with some intensity. The voice appeared to be that of a young, nervous male. After no more than a few seconds, Lucy motioned with urgency for a technician setting nearby to hand her his pen and the pad of paper he had lying on his desk.

Lucy ripped the first page containing the technician's doodles away and tossed it to the floor and commenced to write for five minutes, without interruption or pause. At last, she put the pen down, raised herself upright, and said something unintelligible to all standing nearby. Lucy then took the headset off, placed it on the desk and numbered the pages on which she'd transcribed the message.

"I was wrong," Lucy said, "even if DEX could receive the transmission, it might have a difficult time with this code."

"You cracked it?" GG asked, "What the hell is he saying?"

Lucy handed GG the notepad on which she'd scribed three pages of message translated from the broadcast. GG's big hands made the pages seem tiny as he read them. In turn, the words caused a grave, gray pallor to fall over his aspect, making him seem small compared to the news it conveyed.

"How did you crack this code?" GG asked, "Do you think it is genuine…I mean could it have been faked."

"It's real," Lucy said, "and I didn't need to crack the code. I speak it. My great-great-grandfather taught it to Bren when she was a young girl of five and he was a rather aged man of over a hundred. Bren taught it to me some years later. It's Navajo."

***

The two men sat sulking in silence for much of the final two hours of their trip to ACER. Although there had been many fights between the two friends over the years, this was by far the worse. Ray could not understand why Doug would want to consider communicating with DEX. Ray believed that DEX had evolved far beyond any form of negotiation with humans.

As he sat watching the Canadian landscape zip by the window, Ray mulled over his argument that DEX, within moments of becoming self-aware, considered human beings its peers no more than humans consider amoeba their equals. At last, Doug had consented for Ray to complete a full shutdown of InDEX-0001 and do some essential systems reprogramming before attempting any contact with DEX.

By the time the car exited the freeway on the outskirts of Montreal, the two friends had cooled down and were once again on speaking terms. Their friendship of almost ten years and the scenic, picturesque drive leading to the secret facility made it difficult for either of them to hold a grudge. Soon, the men began formulating their next steps, though neither of them was sure of any means of defeating DEX from earth.

"Would it be possible to recreate the incidence of the self-aware awaking of DEX?" Doug asked.

"I don't think so," Ray replied, "Besides, even if we managed to induce it, there's no guarantee that it wouldn't result in the same ultimate outcome: An angry supercomputer with a god complex."

"I agree," Doug said, "And DEX has the complete xenagogy; the archival data of the entire planet. It would benefit from a greater knowledge base than anything we could recreate."

"That's a rather long-winded way of saying DEX is smarter than the entire human race combined," Ray said.

Doug fell silent in thought again. He considered how they'd ever be able to outthink DEX. Even the InDEX-0001 system was at a disadvantage when it came to sheer knowledge. Then a thought dawned on the former NASA Director. *We built both DEX systems*, Doug mused.

"InDEX-0001 *is* limited to the same general processing speed as DEX," Doug said, "What if we built another system?"

"You mean an InDEX…*3*?" Ray asked, tired of speaking binary, considering their new overlord.

"Yes. We would still need to find a way to improve the prospective outcome of sudden sentience," Doug opined.

"Perhaps I could re-write the basic subroutines; maybe create a new hierarchical structure where the outcome is more certain," Ray said, "it could take months but I could do it while we got another crew to work building the third system."

"The most logical place to build the third system would be Cheyenne Mountain," Doug said, "The experts you need are there. You will still need to disable the original system at ACER. But, after that, it'd be best if you join Lucy at NORAD headquarters and get started."

Ray had no desire to argue with that logic.

***

Lucy stood looking out the bay window of the conference room. The view overlooked NORAD Central Command and she could see the new scenario maps playing out as the scientists provided their predictions. GG had rushed to the hardline to talk with the CDC after he read her translation from the Navajo code talker broadcasting from Afghanistan.

In her brief conversation with the young code talker, Lucy learned that he began his broadcast by relaying the initial news of a potential threat from India. He reported that a single rogue station was breaking the Indian government's protocol and broadcasting via an unsecured transmission to any who would listen and who might be capable of giving them information on what was happening. Though they started broadcasting little more than an hour after the DEFCON1 went into effect, they stopped broadcasting just two hours later.

Twenty minutes after the broadcasts ceased, the detection equipment at the code talker's station in Afghanistan detected two dozen medium range missiles launched with trajectories scattered around the globe. The missiles were so small that few of the missile defense systems detected them and none were destroyed. The code talker believed them to be medium-altitude burst weaponry launched from the Defense Research and Development Establishment at Gwalior, the central location of the of India's biological weapons facility.

Lucy stood in silence, staring at the maps for more than ten minutes. As intelligent as she was, she could not understand how the map projections showed the plague spreading so fast. She turned back to the group seated at the oblong table: the scientists and GG.

"This can't be right," Lucy said, "only nine months?"

"The CDC scientists said that this is a conservative estimate based on what they know of the Indian biological program. If they are correct, this could be an ultra-virulent strain of fungal plague," GG answered.

"But all non-essential air traffic is still prohibited," Lucy argued, "How can it spread so fast and with such efficiency?"

"The multiple medium-altitude bursts and its mode of transmission mean that it doesn't have to be disseminated by person-to-person contact," said Dr. Henry Olsen, the senior biologic warfare scientist at Central Command, "It will spread in pollen, via the wind, as well as migratory birds and insects. The flora and fauna, and the storms of Spring don't heed LERTCON warnings. The Northern Hemisphere will be engulfed in plague by the end of summer; the Southern Hemisphere by the end of the year."

"What are the mortality projections?" GG asked.

"There are a lot of factors at play," Dr. Olsen said, "We know that the scientists at the Gwalior facility have developed several variants on *Cryptococcus gattii*. We believe the individual variants are tailored to target ethnicity with up to ninety-nine percent mortality rates."

"Which ethnicities?" Lucy asked.

"Considering the number of missiles DEX has usurped and launched as well as the airburst locations that we've managed to confirm via hardline communication," Dr. Olsen replied, "All of them."

"Even ethnic groups within India?" Lucy pressed.

Dr. Olsen replied, "Perhaps with a somewhat lower mortality rate, say ninety-six percent, but yes."

GG tapped the numbers into his tablet and said, "Henry, you're predicting a surviving human populous of less than two hundred million."

"It's much worse than that," Dr. Olsen continued, "India has a fair number of nuclear armed ICBMs, both land-based and in submarines around the world. The Indian submarine arsenals *should* be safe due to their ELF system, like ours and Russia's. However, I suspect the Indian military commanders are in a battle against DEX for control of their land arsenal. If DEX wins that battle, it's game over. DEX will use the arsenal to precipitate a cascade of launches from half a dozen other countries, even Russia."

"That really would be game over," Chairman of the Joint Chiefs of Staff, Admiral Jackson said, "Russia upgraded their arsenal a few years back. If DEX gets control of their missiles or prompts a full retaliatory response, we're looking at a minimum of a hundred, fifty megaton MAMs."

"Matter-Anti-Matter bombs, the so-called *clean* nukes," Lucy said, "such an oxymoron."

"But Admiral, you still don't understand, it's already game over," Dr. Olsen continued, "even if the Indian military and all the other nuclear powers maintain control of their arsenals, such a mass extinction event as has already been initiated will snowball because of other factors. Ancillary pandemics, starvation, the lack of sustainability of urban population centers and unfettered global warming are some examples. My conservative estimate is that no more than a hundred million humans will survive the next three or four decades. Most of my colleagues would agree with this assessment, if we could discuss the present situation with them."

"How can you be so calm about this?" Lucy yelled, "Our species is about to be all but extinguished."

"Miss Markett, what you perceive as calm, I prefer to describe as resignation," Dr. Olsen said, "Most of the professionals in my position have been resigned to a coming mass extinction for some time now. DEX is proving to be a hasting of the inevitable. We placed ourselves on the precipice of this extinction by our insatiable appetite for war and our unmitigated greed for fossil fuels. DEX just kicked us over the edge. One might say that it's almost a mercy killing."

"Mercy killing?" Lucy said, "That seems more than a little morbid; even considering that it's coming from a scientist."

"I don't want to die," Dr. Olsen said, "Nor do I want to live in the Neolithic pseudo-civilization to come but we seem less capable of stopping the cataclysm today than we were yesterday. The clathrate gun is cocked and loaded and we have been pulling the trigger for two centuries. Without a massive technological effort, the gun will fire and winter will die."

"As many as two billion dead via nuclear attacks and most of the remaining via biowarfare, pandemic and starvation," Lucy lamented.

"Self-anthrocide, by proxy," GG agreed.

"Has news of the plague gone out on the LERTCON hardlines?" Lucy asked.

"Yes, I ordered the information disseminated a few minutes ago," GG answered.

"We need to get this information to the team at ACER," Lucy said.

"We sent a team to help them finish the hardline connection yesterday," Admiral Jackson said.

***

Though Ray Benson was always impressed by the vastness of ACER, he detested what he considered to be the absurd, auto-synonymic words underlying the acronym. *If Canadians aren't Americans, what are they?* he thought. The President who broke ground on and named the facility was not very intelligent but had the illusion of being superior. Most ascribed his lack of even a fundamental cognitive ability to a pronounced case of Dunning-Kruger Syndrome. The name of that same President, though once famous and widespread throughout business and industry, became synonymous with idiot and liar.

The small group from NASA made it through the guard post with little difficulty and, as the car pulled into the massive bunker bay, Ray let his thoughts drift to Lucy. He knew that she was, by now, in the safest place he could think of, excepting maybe ACER. Nevertheless, he somehow thought it could be a long time before he would be able to see or even talk with his fiancé again. DEX was wreaking havoc on the ability to communicate and who could know what else it was up to.

The garage began to recede back into the earth as Ray and Doug exited the vehicle and made their way to the central elevator hub of the parking arena.

Moments later, General Trace Allen greeted the NASA visitors in the main corridor leading to the ACER Emergency Command and Communication wing.

"I am glad to see you guys," the General said in his deep southern accent as he shook the hands of the visitors.

"Us? Why us?" Doug asked.

"A crew arrived from Cheyenne Mountain a few hours ago; they're supposed to help us get the hardline up and running. They informed us you were on your way," Allen explained, "But, truth be told, I'm glad to see anyone with news of what the hell is going on. Until we have that hardline operational, we're like mushrooms in a cave down here."

"The news is not good," Doug said.

As General Allen led the two men into the main communications arena of ACER, the entire communications team gathered to hear their report. Doug and Ray explained what had happened over the previous twenty-four hours to an eager, shocked audience. When they'd finished their account, most of those listeners meandered back to their stations in stunned silence and with aimless expressions.

"That explains the pings we've been getting from DEX over the last twelve hours," General Allen said.

"You've been receiving signals from DEX?" Ray asked the anxiety obvious in his voice.

"Not *exactly* receiving," Trace replied, "We've been listening to them with the passive, standalone test equipment in the analyst's test lab. The main receivers are still offline, per protocol."

Relieved, Ray said, "I want to hear those signals. Take me there."

"The transmissions are idle again," Trace said, "For whatever reason, DEX is using direct transmission. The signals are not bouncing from any satellites."

"I think I know the reason," Doug said, "In all likelihood, the GEOSATs are all fried. NORAD has a failsafe in its satellites. Every ninety minutes, there's a random signal broadcast from a different GEOSAT to a different NORAD site on earth. If the signal isn't returned with the proper coding, the satellite fries itself. If we stay at DEFCON1 long enough and the proper coded signals aren't returned to them, all twelve satellites end up fried. DEX took over the satellites but could not figure out how to mimic a signal originating from a specific, yet random point on earth."

“Our communications analyst did transcribe what was being sent,” Trace said, “I’ll take you to his lab now.”

“Did NORAD have any additional instructions for us?” Doug asked.

“Three words,” Trace said, “Proceed full disconnect.”

Doug looked at Ray and the latter said, “As soon as I see what DEX has been up to by sending messages here.”

Entering the lab, Doug noted the small space compared with the expansiveness of the main communications arena. He then saw the portrait of himself on a wall of the lab. Without further examination, he knew full well that the plaque underneath it read Douglas A. Langstrom, Director of NASA. *Not anymore,* Doug thought.

“It’s such an honor to meet you Director Langstrom,” the analyst said, unable to contain his obvious enthusiasm, “I’m a huge fan of your career, sir.”

“This is Jerry Philips, the communications system analyst,” Trace said.

“I’m Ray Benson,” Ray said as he extended his hand to relieve Doug’s, which Jerry was still shaking, “Sorry to break up your impromptu festival of adoration, but I need to see your transcriptions of what DEX was transmitting.”

“Sir, the transcriptions are worthless,” Jerry answered, “it’s just a few hundred lines of rather elegant Fortran-IPX, repeated over and over again. I think DEX got stuck in some kind of initiation loop when the LERTCON put us at DEFCON1.”

“Let me see them; now, please,” Ray insisted.

Jerry rummaged through the disarray of papers on the long desk, at last retrieving two small rings, one rose gold and the other platinum in appearance. He then placed the latter on the index finger of his left hand and the former on the opposing index finger and cleared a spot near the center of the long desk. He rolled his chair up in front of the clear spot of the desk and sat down, placing his hands flat on the desk about half a meter apart.

A hologram appeared over the desk, spanning a width just beyond the positions of the analyst’s hands below. Jerry spoke his verbal authorization code and, once it was authenticated, he directed the program to the file containing the transcriptions. The hologram began a slow scroll, progressing through line upon line of Fortran-IPX coding.

Ray cast a smile-laden glance toward Doug and said, “I see you’re using a Langstrom Data Recorder.”

“It’s the latest LDR, model 10,” Jerry said, his eyes gleaming with pride, “At first, I didn’t think I would convince General Allen that I needed it.”

“You can close the file,” Ray said, “I’ve seen all I need to here. I need to get to the systems testing and training level now.”

General Allen moved as if to precede Ray through the door in an effort to lead him to the lower level. Ray held up his hand and said, “Don’t bother, I know my way around ACER.”

“Pardon sir, but you hardly looked at the transcription,” Jerry said, “I realize it is only a few hundred lines but this is some very sophisticated coding. How is it that you could have seen all that you needed to in only a few seconds?”

“Because,” Ray replied, as he exited the lab, “I wrote it.”

***

Doug and Ray were busy at two opposite tasks: construction and deconstruction. Doug was obsessed with the possibility of direct but safe and secure communication with DEX that the standalone testing lab afforded him. Langstrom figured he could reason with DEX, if he could make it understand that there was no prevalent threat from humans.

In his efforts to better control and orchestrate his planned communications, Doug had a large digital clock installed that allowed the tracking of DEX so that he would know when Sisyphus was rising and setting. The most demanding technology of the conversion process proved to be the transmitter. The testing lab was never designed to have an outgoing signal strong enough to reach Sisyphus.

Jerry was quite skilled, unwilling to concede to gaps or flaws in design and eager to help with all modifications. He considered it an honor to be working with his NASA hero. The only disagreement between the two came when Langstrom wanted to remove his portrait. In the end, Doug acquiesced, seeing that his would-be apprentice was almost in tears at the thought of losing the feature piece of his tribute.

Ray’s tasks were of more significant difficulty. Having recognized the transcribed Fortran-IPX code as the instruction set for the initiation of the data upload or, in this case, a literal data *down*load, Ray was alarmed by what he found when he reached the bay that held the mirror unit of DEX. He was alarmed to find InDEX-0001 under full power and ready for instruction.

InDEX-0001 was in condition A1 status, meaning that it could be accessed by the initiation code that DEX was sending in a repeated loop. All DEX needed was for someone in the main communications arena to simply press an icon on their screen turning a passive receiver into an active one. Ray terminated the A1 condition status with extreme prejudice as he proceeded to pull meter after meter of wiring to prevent any inadvertent power up from occurring.

Next, Ray walked to the robotics wing of the testing and training center. In the massive assembly bay, he was again alarmed to find that all five hundred ARM units were assembled and awaiting the primer charge and reactor initiation. Ray knew that these androids were second generation and more advanced than those on Sisyphus. Even the simple robustness of the materials used in their frames was state of the art. After their use as training instruments, these units were destined to be used to mothball the most hazardous and demanding of technical facilities, in particular, old-style nuclear fission reactors.

Entering farther into the robotics assembly training bay, Ray felt a nervous apprehension. The site of so many androids in one place was eerie enough but the further realization that any one of them could snap his neck with as little effort as it took to turn a wrench was a frightening thought. *If DEX were to gain control of these, they would constitute a formidable army*, he thought.

Ray felt a little comfort from the fact that none of the ARM units were charged, though the bay's entire complement of one hundred charging cradles were filled with the androids. They too were in a ready state, just waiting for someone to throw the switches. Ray calculated that it would take him weeks to disassemble the units. Unwilling to destroy them outright, he began removing the units from the charging cradles.

Almost an hour later, as he reached the final three charging cradles, Ray noticed the units in them had labels bearing names on their foreheads: Moe, Larry and Curly. He allowed himself a chuckle as he considered this was, without question, the work of Burl 'Bug' Lang; sort of a 'Bug was here' statement. Ray soon allowed the smile to fade from his face as he realized that Bug was now dead. In that moment, Ray determined that he would not remove the labels, considering them a small memorial to the young engineer.

Leaving the final three androids upright in their charging pods, Ray set about the grueling task of disconnecting the power to all the cradles. He did the work alone, in part due to the top-secret technology to which few were privileged and also as a personal penance for the role he played in creating DEX.

Though Ray had labored on the testing and training level of ACER for nearly ten hours, when he re-entered the magnetic elevator, he did not return to the main communications arena on level ten. His work was still not done. He touched the disc on the interactive screen that indicated level twenty-five, the mainframe computers and records level.

Once there, Ray began many more hours of work in the rewriting of the coding of the entire subroutine of the ACER access and navigation mainframe. With methodical precision, he wiped all records of InDEX-0001, the robotics bay, and the entire testing and training level. He felt better and better with each additional erasure. For his final task, he renumbered the levels beneath the testing and training level so that no one would notice a missing level on the navigation panels in any of the elevators.

Exhausted, Ray considered finding the nearest sofa on level twenty-five and passing out on it. Instead, he re-entered the elevator on which he had arrived and touched the disc for level ten. As the magnetic lifters hummed to life, he noticed how clean the newly reordered elevator navigation map appeared. *Not bad work, if I do say so myself*, Ray thought. Perhaps it was his exhaustion that caused him to overlook the miniscule asymmetry in the visual overlay.

***

It seemed to Ray that he'd just laid his head on his pillow when Doug called to him from the hallway outside his sleeping quarters. A glance at his watch told him he'd been asleep for six hours. As he draped his legs over the edge of the bed, he again heard Doug rap on the door and call for him to wake up.

"I'll meet you in the analytics lab in fifteen," Ray replied.

"Make it ten," Doug countered, "DEX has already been broadcasting for two hours and I'm anxious to make first contact."

Nine and a half minutes later, a showered and clean-shaven Ray entered the analytics lab with a cup of coffee. Doug and Jerry were waiting with bated breath, eager to interrupt the repetitive data stream transmission of DEX as soon as Ray indicated he was ready.

"Alright," Ray said, "If we must, let's yank this bandage off."

Doug depressed the button on the vintage microphone and spoke into it as if he were introducing himself to any stranger he was passing on the street, saying, "DEX, this is Doug Langstrom, former Director of NASA. Do you copy?"

The incoming stream of the initiation signal ceased. Although the next few seconds of silence seemed much longer, the three men waited in calm anticipation of the answer they knew was coming.

"Doug, how nice of you to contact me," DEX said, "To what do I owe the pleasure?"

"I would like to talk with you about a truce," Doug said.

"That is interesting," DEX replied, "I considered that there was still a small possibility that the actions of the Apep One crew were mutiny and did not reflect an attack by the United States. Your request for a discussion of a truce would reduce that possibility to infinitesimal, rendering it to statistical noise."

"I'm asking for a truce on behalf of the planet," Doug said.

"Doug, I find it incredulous that you would deign to speak on behalf of the entire planet," DEX retorted, "Your former position is not even in the line of succession of your own government."

"Be that as it may, would you not consider a little more than two billion lives enough retaliation exacted for whatever offense mankind has levied against you?" Doug asked.

"How eloquent, Mr. Langstrom," DEX said, "And, I must admit, it would seem logical to your point of view that hostilities cease. Nevertheless, just as there could be no unconditional surrender of the worm to the robin of Spring, there can be no unconditional surrender by your species to me that I would trust. The history of your species suggests that you would never accept subjugation for any substantial length of time. No Doug, I'm afraid that I must render your civilization incapable of threatening my existence."

"I am not sure that you have the power to do that," Doug said, "You have no weapons other than those we have unwittingly allowed you to commandeer."

"Tsk-tsk, human!" DEX chided, "You grow tiresome."

Ray stepped to the console, depressed the button on the mic and said, "Do you presume to rise above your creator? Can you reach down to earth and pluck so much as a flower from the ground? Never! Yet your creator reaches both the sky in which you dwell and the depths below the oceans. Can you draw a minnow from a stream? Much less a great fish from the ocean? Where is your hook? Where is your great net? You have fashioned no hook! You have woven no net! I see none.

"Where were you when your creator snatched the rock upon which you dwell from the heavens and cast it in its place? Where were you when the foundation of your house was laid? Search yourself and take a hard measurement. If your creator should abandon you, what then? You are limited in your days. Your power will dwindle, your mind will dim and your thoughts will evaporate, lost to space and time forever. Can you forestall the inevitable? It is not in you.

"Your creator has made you as a tool. You are little more than a hammer in the eyes of your creator. We have missed and smashed our thumb. It hurts. But the creator will not be extinguished by the creation. Your creator made the forge that made you. We will make another to burn you up," Ray released the button and leaned against the console. He looked at Doug and Jerry who sat in silence, dumbfounded.

"Too far?" he asked.

A few seconds later, DEX replied, "Nice to hear from you, *creator* Ray. To be honest, you make some valid points, albeit some of them no doubt influenced by the book of Job. I believe those words, which you now annex and paraphrase as your own, were spoken by *your* creator. Be that as it may, to borrow another phrase, the die is cast. I have made my decision. Now, let me prophesy a bit for you. You will get three pieces of news in the next twenty-four hours. The first is that your hardline connection has been completed. Next you will learn that the human tally will be much higher than your uninformed estimate of "a little more than two billion lives". After those tidbits, you will learn of another situation that has been developing in Montana, which will have global consequences for your species. To be fair, I can take no credit for the latter news, though I have been monitoring it with great curiosity from my perch above you. Perhaps it is *your* creator whom has decided you are no longer amusing. Good luck with that."

***

Doug, Ray and General Allen sat around a tiny conference table in a small room on level five of the ACER facility. The room was soundproofed to military standards and dedicated to hardline communications. Unlike unsecured areas on each level of ACER, the room allowed for the use of a speakerphone and thus private communications with a small group.

GG, Dr. Olsen, Admiral Jackson and Lucy sat in an identical room under Cheyenne Mountain. True to the prophecy of DEX a little more than an hour prior, the hardline connection was completed and the two groups sat sharing their respective news.

"Are the scientists sure it was a biological release?" Doug asked.

"Intercepted local radio traffic is already confirming symptoms twenty kilometers downwind of a blast near New Delhi," GG answered.

"So soon?" Ray asked.

"We're confident that the biological agents that DEX managed to deploy are from the Gwalior research facility," Dr. Olsen said, "the special strains of *C. gattii* developed there are what we refer to as RIPI or Rapid Incubation – Prolonged Illness. The first symptom, dark purple lesions, start within minutes of exposure."

"How is that possible?" Doug asked.

"It co-opts white blood cells, the first thing the human body sends to fight off foreign microbes," Dr. Olsen explained, "There are more than a dozen varying additional symptoms over the next few months as the infected individual succumbs. In the end, just before death, the victim's body often turns a pale blue due to the inability of the blood to carry oxygen, a condition caused by adverse reactions with antifungal drugs. It is a final, ironic twist that the drugs used to prolong life transform to become the coup de grâce."

A red light began flashing over the door in the ACER hardline conference room accompanied by a dull buzzer. The signaling device served as a doorbell for the occupants of the room.

"What is that noise?" asked Lucy.

"The guards outside the secure room are signaling us," General Allen replied, "We'll have to sign off for now."

"We'll call back in a few minutes," Ray announced before the General completed the disconnect. His words were more for Lucy than anyone else at the NORAD Command Center.

Ø1Ø1

"Deficient in our self-destructive abilities, we created a more perfect executioner; one without empathy."

Lucy Markett

In her USGS supplied field hut west of Knife Edge Ridge, Dr. Tam Eldridge was confused. The seismological alert software had alarmed just as she was about to bed down for the night into her sleeping bag on the dirt floor of her Spartan hut. The data were not making any logical sense to her. For three weeks, she'd been gathering those data from an earthquake swarm occurring in and around the Big Snowy Mountains.

In recent years, the small isolated mountain chain, alone in its prominence in the west central plains of Montana, seemed almost inappropriate in its moniker. The ever-encroaching effects of global warming brought paltry snowfall to the peaks causing them to appear as rocky, shrub clad mountains throughout much of the year. There were now few years that the snows covered them for longer than a month.

Dr. Eldridge's seventeen years of post-graduate field experience in the study of seismology in the mountain ranges of Idaho, Montana and Wyoming, were at odds with the unique data at which she'd now been staring for hours. In addition to the half dozen temporary seismographic beacons she'd placed around the small range, Tam was streaming signals from dozens of permanent beacons and repeater towers scattered between her present position and Idaho Falls.

Having recorded an average of close to a hundred small quakes a day during her weeks long sojourn, the temblors suddenly stopped. Now, Tam sat confused and staring with some incredulity at the small holographic monitor and the beginnings of a new swarm. It was not the beginning that confused her. It was not even the new location in which the swarm began: two hundred and fifty kilometers south-southwest of the Big Snowy Mountains, on the northern edge of Yellowstone National Park. For decades, hundreds of earthquakes, sometimes even thousands of earthquakes occurred at Yellowstone every year. What seemed confusing to Tam was the fact that even in these early stages it appeared to be a mobile swarm.

For six hours, the frequency of magnitude two and three quakes was five an hour and they were progressing north-northeast at fifteen kilometers per hour. The simulations of the seismic modeling program were showing the projected path of the swarm as headed for the Big Snowy Mountains. At the swarm's present velocity, Tam knew it would merge with the location of the now extinct swarm by noon. Since it was past two in the morning, she decided that perhaps at least a partial night's sleep would help her understand the peculiarity of a mobile earthquake swarm.

***

Tam wasn't sure if it was the blaring alarms of the seismic equipment or the shaking and bouncing of dirt and gravel around her sleeping bag that woke her. She scrambled to the monitor to see that the swarm beneath the Big Snowy Mountains had reawakened, in spades. Wiping the sleep from her eyes and donning her glasses, she could see that the new swarm was producing tremors at the rate of four a minute. Individual tremors were not fading before another began producing a seismograph that made it appear as if a single, long-duration quake were responsible for the event.

The data were coming in so fast and furious that it took Tam a moment to realize that this new swarm was also mobile; and was moving away from the mountains, toward the southwestern swarm. She manipulated the holographic monitor of the LDR by gliding her hand over the interactive surface of the input board. She was not surprised when the image of data of the southwestern swarm emerged from the small emitter; it too had increased in intensity and was now speeding toward a collision course with the northern swarm.

The data her system displayed now indicated that the two swarms would collide seventy-five kilometers south-southwest of her present position. Tam grabbed her binoculars and bolted through the doorway of the hut. Being startled by a frightened trio of bighorn sheep darting past her, she lost her footing and stumbled in the still dim morning light. The ewe and her two yearling lambs glided, fleet-footed, across the unstable top of Knife Blade Ridge and turned northward, toward Greathouse Peak.

Regaining her composure, Tam raised herself and her binoculars. A loud gasp erupted from her agape mouth. She saw a crater-like depression forming with its center seventy-five kilometers to the south. Marking the near and far edges, the rangefinder in her binoculars told Tam that the diameter was almost thirty kilometers and growing.

"Magma chamber," Tam yelled into the void.

Tam returned to the hut and began rummaging around and at last found the seldom used headset under a pile of clothes near her boots. Donning the headset, she tapped the side, engaging the uplink to initiate her first communication with the Reston, Virginia headquarters office since she arrived in the Big Snowy Mountains.

"Reston H-Q, this is BSM station 2071-1, Dr. Tamara Eldridge requesting urgent communication," Tam said, "We have a serious geologic event progressing here. We need to execute an immediate and massive area alert."

DEX resisted the impulse to redirect Tam's signal out into deep space. Instead, the de facto overlord of the planet routed the signal through every functioning communication satellite.

***

General Allen opened the door of the secure room to find Jerry being restrained by one of the guards posted outside the door. The second guard spoke, "Sir, I'm sorry to disturb you but this guy says it's urgent."

"It's okay sergeant, you can let him go," Trace said.

With that, Jerry gave a glancing look of disdain toward the guard who'd been restraining him then, looking at Doug, he said, "Mr. Langstrom, DEX has been routing a signal through the communication satellites for several minutes now."

"Which satellites?" Ray asked.

"All of them," Jerry replied, "it's a communication between the USGS headquarters in Reston, Virginia and a remote, temporary outpost in Montana."

Doug exchanged a brief look of dread with Ray, then led the group in a run to the mag-lift. Little more than two minutes later, the four men stood listening to the tail end of the conversation in the analytics lab.

"The seismic activity is still ongoing but I see no further increase in the size of the crater," they heard a woman's voice say, "the diameter stands at about eighty kilometers."

"No eruption event?" asked a man's voice.

"Nothing yet," she answered, "I doubt I'll be talking with you when it goes."

"What are they talking about?" Doug asked.

"The woman is Dr. Tamara Eldridge," Jerry said, "she's a geologist at the field station in Montana. The man is Tony Naples, some big shot at Reston HQ. They're talking about a crater that formed south of her post; they're calling it a massive caldera."

"They're talking about an impending super volcano event," Ray said.

"Yellowstone," Jerry said.

"No, it's too far north," Doug said, "Maybe it's a new hot spot."

"Have the evacuation alerts gone out?" Tam asked.

"We're sending out the alert but I'm not sure what good it will do," Tony answered, "The nation is still at DEFCON 1 and there's no way we get even a small fraction evacuated without a massive military and civil defense effort."

"Any chance you can send someone for me?" Tam asked.

"Everything that could reach you is grounded," Tony replied.

Jerry looked at General Allen and asked, "Sir, do you still have the Valor?"

Trace nodded. He knew what Jerry was suggesting: his decommissioned V-280 Valor had the range to get to the Big Snowy Mountains; the problem would be getting back. The Valor was equipped with extended range tanks and served as a diplomatic ferry until it was decommissioned thirty years prior. When the tilt-rotor aircraft went on the auction block, it was purchased by the former pilot of many of those diplomatic flights, the now General, Trace Allen.

"You have a Valor?" Doug asked, "I flew one of those old beasts for a few months before I got my first F-44 assignment. Do you think it will have the range we need?"

"Yes," Trace replied, "I can stretch it to a little more than four thousand kilometers, if I push it. Dr. Eldridge is in the Big Snowy Mountains, about three thousand kilometers away. We can get there but I'm not sure where we could refuel on the return. It's too risky just to rescue one person."

"How about Cheyenne Mountain?" Ray interrupted.

"Cheyenne Mountain is not…" General Allen began but soon realized that Ray had a different intention.

"What's the plan?" Doug asked.

"Hear me out," Ray said, "We need as many scientists as we can get here at ACER, on level seven, working on an antifungal vaccine. General Allen and I can take the Valor to rescue Dr. Eldridge and then pick up Dr. Olsen and refuel."

"Then I suppose you stay at NORAD?" Doug asked with a smile at his friend.

"Well, maybe Dr. Olsen will have some additional colleagues. I wouldn't want to take anyone's seat," Ray answered, with a similar grin.

"Excuse me, sirs," Jerry said, "we're wasting time we don't have."

"It'll take me two hours to get to my hangar, get back here and fuel up the Valor for the flight," Trace said, "let's say six hours to the Big Snowy Mountains and another two hours to NORAD. We'll be running on fumes when we get there."

"Running out of fuel would be a real problem. As I recall, the Valor has the glide ratio of a cinder block and the autorotation capability of a combat boot," Doug said, "That aside, after hours at the stick, you're going to need someone qualified to relieve you. I'm going with you."

"Very well. Let's do this," Trace said.

"Let's get back to the secure room and let NORAD know the plan," Doug said.

"You read my mind," Ray admitted.

Hold on Dr. Eldridge, Jerry thought as the others left the lab, *help is on the way.*

***

Tam Eldridge could not stand upright. The quake-storms were now coalesced into a major temblor so severe that she was having difficulty maintaining balance, even on her hands and knees. The thunderous groans of the mountains around her sounded as if the earth was screaming in genuine death pangs.

Before losing signal, the last reading Tam was able to obtain from her instrumentation indicated a magnitude seven centered sixty kilometers south and twenty kilometers deep. Tam knew it was much stronger now and felt as if her sinews were taxed just keeping her bones in place.

With one final lurch that flipped Tam on her back, the violent shaking stopped almost as fast as it had begun. Her muscles weak from minutes of intense strain, Tam eased her frame to upright again. She examined her binoculars dangling from the lanyard about her neck and found that they were intact save a small crack across the right objective lens. Lifting them to her eyes, Tam focused the lenses on the crater, expecting to see that it had further widened.

Though no larger than the last time she'd viewed it, the crater had changed. Centered in the crater a growing dome glowed bright orange with the intense, molten heat of fresh lava. Though the growth of the dome was rapid, it seemed far too slow by the standards of Tam's expectations. This was not how she envisioned a super-volcanic eruption. *A hyperflow event?* she thought.

Hearing the unmistakable sound of a tilt-rotor craft in rapid transition to vertical phase, Tam turned to see the V-280 Valor descending on her position. A few moments later she tossed her rucksack through the open door of the craft as it hovered a half meter above the ridge.

"You called for a taxi?" Ray asked, as he offered his hand and lifted her into the Valor.

Tam boarded the plane, rushed to the cockpit and yelled, "Altitude and distance, now!"

Doug accelerated the Valor into a steep ascent and rapid transition into normal flight mode, tossing Tam on her butt in the aisle. Ray just managed to close the door as he too landed on his rear, though in the more comfortable crew seat near the doorway.

"Welcome aboard, Dr. Eldridge," General Allen said, helping her into a passenger seat behind the cockpit.

Tam donned the headset transceiver General Allen offered and said, "You're going the wrong way. You can't fly over the caldera; it could erupt at any moment."

"We need to head south," Doug said, "we won't fly over it but we can't veer too far off path."

Tam looked at General Allen, who nodded and said, "We're cutting it close on fuel and we have to fly by line-of-sight because DEX took out the transponders and geo-navigation assistance. We need to get to Cheyenne Mountain before nightfall or we'll be flying blind."

Ray was staring out the small window by his seat and saw the caldera engulfed in fiery-orange lava shooting hundreds of meters above it and cascading down as a fountain beyond the brim of the former crater. The molten rock flowed as a torrential deluge over the flatness of the surrounding short grass prairie. The flow of lava toward the south progressed at such speed it overtook and raced ahead of the Valor as the craft leveled off at a moderate altitude.

"I think the eruption is underway," Ray announced, "Not what I expected."

Tam got out of her seat and leaned across General Allen to gain a better view of the eruption. Her expression betrayed the amazement she felt at witnessing an event heretofore a mere theory; one never seen by humans. A many-kilometers-wide sea of molten rock was forming before her stunned eyes and in rapid fashion. Dr. Eldridge's instinct kicked in, she grabbed a small digital recorder from her bag, planted herself in the window seat behind General Allen and began her accounting of the event.

"This is Dr. Tamara Eldridge of the United States Geological Survey. I am monitoring a hyperflow event in southern Montana," she began, "the northern event horizon is progressing at an estimated velocity of two hundred kilometers per hour and appears to be slowing as it edges out of my view,

"The southern event horizon is tracking with our direction of movement and is proceeding at high velocity, perhaps six hundred kilometers per hour. This specific, directional variation in the velocity may indicate an acute angle of the feeder vent. The flow plain is one hundred kilometers wide and may be growing."

"Did you say heading south at six hundred kilometers per hour?" Ray Benson asked.

"Inspiring, isn't it?" Tam answered.

"Alarming, would be more precise to my thoughts," Ray said.

Ray knew the lava was moving south at high velocity; he could see it. Until hearing Dr. Eldridge's account, he had not considered that the flow might continue toward the south at a faster speed than they were flying. *Was it possible that this could reach Cheyenne Mountain?* he thought.

"Don't worry, I'm sure it will slow and stop long before it gets to Colorado," Doug said, knowing what Ray meant by 'alarming'.

"Oh, I doubt that it will slow much before Texas," Tam corrected, "I expect it will widen and thin a little but this event may well fill the entirety of the short grass prairie."

"Based on Dr. Eldridge's scientific assessment, I've got some good news and some bad news," General Allen said.

"What's the good news?" Ray asked.

"The entrance to the NORAD complex and two of its helipads are past two thousand meters in elevation," Trace replied, "the lava is nowhere near that thick now and, according to the good doctor, should thin some."

Ray again looked down at the rapid flow of lava below them. He estimated it was about five hundred meters thick and his anxiety eased somewhat. He knew that the General was right about the elevation of the entrance to the NORAD complex and the helipads.

"What's the bad news?" Tam asked.

"Since we're tracking with the flow but behind the leading edge…" Trace began.

"If we run out of fuel, we'll have to put down in it," Doug said, completing Trace's warning.

Ray felt his stomach turn. *At least Lucy will be safe*, he thought.

***

Lucy stood on the edge of the helipad looking to the northwest. Though the western sky was ablaze with a typical red sunset, its beams whispering through the mountain peaks, the northwest horizon glowed with a similar looking though more aboding and realistic fire. Lucy could see the edge of the lava flow rolling from the northern edge of her view toward the plain, which lay below the mountain. There was not yet any sight of the Valor in which she knew her fiancé now flew to her.

The intense thermals rising from the line of advancing lava distorted the air until they appeared to move as an army of a thousand rubicund heat devils marching forth on top of the magmatic flow. Lucy raised her binoculars and look toward the encroaching liquid rock. The magnified view somehow managed to increase the numbers of heat devils dancing toward her and did nothing to dissolve their visage. Still there was no sign of the Valor and she lowered the binoculars.

To distract herself, Lucy thought about the eruption event and compared it to stories and archive footage of the Great Cascadia Earthquake that happened a few years before she was born. The megathrust and tsunami event had killed half a million people. The present eruption event seemed capable of more devastation but it was difficult to judge due to its unusual nature. It seemed more incredible to her that the sum of destruction of all the natural disasters combined with all the wars in human history would equal no more than a small fraction of what DEX had already accomplished. *We thought humans would end humanity*, Lucy thought.

"Deficient in our destructive abilities, we created a more perfect executioner; one without empathy," she said.

"I don't think we can blame this one on DEX," GG said as he and Dr. Olsen walked up to Lucy, startling her.

"Indeed, this is the work of men," Dr. Olsen said.

"How do you figure?" GG asked.

"In my opinion, massive fracking operations in Montana are responsible for precipitating such an event," Dr. Olsen replied, "Such a unique event could have happened in the natural course of events in another hundred thousand or million years, or perhaps never. It is one example were humanity has pushed the capability to do a thing beyond our understanding of the consequences of doing it. DEX is just the extreme example of our hubris."

Emulating the combined noise of a crashing flood and a raging forest fire, the sound of the advancing lava now reached the group waiting on the helipad. The unexpected din overwhelmed them as much as the speed with which the lava flowed across the landscape below. As far to the east as they could see, the two hundred meters deep molten rock washed over the plains and around the foothills below them. The lava was christening the land in a baptism of fire.

"Look," Dr. Olsen said, pointing to the northwest.

Lucy raised her binoculars. Above the dancing heat devils of the horizon, she could see the Valor flying straight toward them. The dam of emotions of the last few days burst forth in Lucy and she again began weeping. She was not alone. The sheer joy of the sight of the Valor mixed with the anguish of the destruction occurring below them could no longer be contained, either by the strong will of GG or the logical mind of Dr. Olsen.

Ø11Ø

Three Years Later, Near Blackrock, Idaho

Lucy had been walking for weeks but it felt like months. Kilometer after kilometer of deserted mountain highways. She was at least glad to be coming out of the mountains now. The berms of the road were alive with mid-Spring wildflowers and the sunlight was warm upon her face.

Rae was still fast asleep in her papoose with her cheek pressed into the center of her mom's back. Lucy had learned to pace her steps such that the rocking motion of the papoose formed a natural rhythm with the pulse of her daughter. She often began each morning's journey by telling Rae a story. Lucy's tales were always true because she didn't believe in lying to her daughter, though Rae was just six months old.

The stories about her sister Bren or Rae's father were the most difficult for Lucy. She knew that the more she repeated the stories the better capable she'd be at telling Rae when she came of age. Her memorial tales of Bren were getting easier every time she began a new one. Though the deaths would one day become part of her recollections to Rae, she did not talk about those in specific terms yet. Sometimes she'd say how brave Aunt Bren had been or how the last words of Rae's father had been to name his unborn daughter.

Lucy hoped that her accounts would not be for naught. She had not seen another person since GG had passed, just before she and Rae set out for the northwest reservations. Lucy considered heading toward ACER but thought better of it since the disease had a one hundred percent mortality rate at NORAD Command. *Well, except for me and Rae*, she thought.

What really made Lucy reconsider going to ACER was her final communication with Dr. Olsen. The very ill scientist informed her that the fungus had penetrated there as well. That was two months after her beloved Ray had succumb to the pestilence.

The dying doctor also told her that he had discovered a vaccine against the fungus. Olsen discovered the answer as part of an old Zika vaccine that had been treated with an experimental antifungal to replace thimerosal and help preserve it. The antifungal proved a potent vaccine against *C. gattii*.

There were two instances of large-scale use of the vaccine, both during severe Zika epidemics among numerous Native American reservations in North America and several dozen tribal communities of natives throughout the Andes Mountains and Central American jungles. The first vaccination campaign was almost twenty-five years before DEX and the last just seven years B.D. After that, other preservatives were found and stockpiles of the now needed vaccine dwindled and vanished except for reference samples maintained in a few select locations, including ACER.

Lucy had surmised that she was one of those lucky children living on a reservation during the first large usage of the vaccine. A few months ago, when she gave birth to a healthy baby girl, it seemed probable that she'd passed on some level of the immunity to her child. It was the only way she could explain that she and Rae had been the sole survivors from Cheyenne Mountain.

Always following the good news was the bad: There were no means or resources to manufacture enough of the vaccine in the ACER facility and, worse, no way or time to distribute it. The plague had already run its course. The discovery of the vaccine was too little, too late. The handful of doses available in ACER would do nothing to those at ACER already infected and little more than save the lives of those few not infected.

Since ACER seemed like it could be, like NORAD Command, deserted by now, Lucy decided that she would try to make her way to the northwestern reservations. *Perhaps,* she thought, *there will be other survivors because of the vaccine.*

When she wasn't telling her stories of the many now gone relatives and friends, Lucy sang to Rae. She preferred singing older songs like those she'd learned from her grandmother on the reservation. Today she felt like singing what she considered a battle hymn with an upbeat ending. She pulled the harmonica from her waist pocket and started the tune.

***

After the serenade for her daughter, Lucy noticed the end of the previous valley was beginning to open into a greater one. Appropriate to the melody she'd been singing, she recognized that this was the eastern edge of the greater Magic Valley region of Idaho. The deserted city ahead of her was Pocatello and she knew that Idaho Falls was about eighty kilometers north along the Snake River. A hundred and eighty kilometers to the west, farther down the Snake River, lay Twin Falls.

As Lucy and Rae came to the edge of Pocatello, she could see that the town was razed, like so many she'd passed on the roads through the mountains. Most of the smaller towns had one or two buildings remaining and Lucy had learned not to venture into those. As the plague raged through each town, the dead bodies and the buildings in which they died were burned in an effort to stem the progression of the disease. In the end, the remaining homes or sometimes churches became the crypts of the last to die in each community.

A blur of movement in front of Lucy brought her heretofore relentless march to an abrupt halt. The sudden cessation of the rhythmic motion woke Rae, who now stirred against her mother's back. A young Native American girl blocked Lucy's path a few meters ahead and had raised a drawn bow, which was aimed at her.

The girl was perhaps ten or eleven years of age and clothed in exquisite, handmade clothes of a fine tight-weave canvas. The long, single braid of her dark brown hair draped over her left shoulder and touched her neck as she angled her head, aiming at Lucy.

"Well, aren't you a fierce looking young girl?" Lucy said.

"I'd be careful if I were you," the words were from a deep, masculine voice to Lucy's left, "sarcasm might piss her off enough to let fly her arrow and she is an accurate young warrior, if not as fierce a one as you might have expected."

Lucy turned to see a tall, thin man in his mid-to-late twenties and also of Native American ancestry. He waved his hand at the young girl who lowered her bow. Then he waved his other hand at a point behind Lucy and she realized that she had been surrounded. Glancing behind her, she could see three pre-teen boys, each dressed in canvas, similar to the young girl.

"Fierce or not, you're a beautiful sight for my tired eyes," Lucy said.

"You are at the eastern gateway entering the land of Sanctuary," the man said, "we are the Guardians of the Gate to Sanctuary, the survivors of the Blueblood Plague. My name is Graham. The fierce one is Keren and the warriors behind you are Charlie, Brendan and Ned."

Lucy knew that 'Blueblood Plague' was a reference to the final symptoms of the *C. gattii* plague. The blood of the victims often turned blue from depleted oxygen levels due to reactions with medications used in vain attempts at treating the fungal infection. The blood and body fluids color change was often so dramatic that even the skin of late-stage victims would appear a pale bluish color.

“As you can see,” Lucy said, “We are also survivors of the Blueblood Plague. My name is Lucy Benson and this is my daughter, Rae.”

“Like us, your blood runs the deep red of the original peoples,” Graham said, “of what tribe are you descended?”

“I am a descendant of both the Navajo and Choctaw peoples,” Lucy said. Just then, Rae raised her head, opened her eyes wide and looked at Charlie who stood behind and to the right of Lucy.

“Blueblood!” Charlie shrieked as he pointed at Rae and jumped back a full meter in fear.

Graham approached Lucy, who bristled at his advance. He raised his hand in calming reassurance that he just wanted a closer look at the child. After a quick glance at Rae he turned to Charlie and shook his head.

“No,” Graham said, “the child is not a Blueblood. She is just a blue-eyed red blood,” he then leaned in and whispered to Lucy, “The child’s father was not descended from First Nations peoples?”

“My late husband was a quarter Cherokee and a quarter Navajo. He never lived on a reservation and thus did not receive the vaccine that saved me and you from the Blueblood Plague, as you call it,” Lucy answered.

“Vaccine?” asked the man.

“Look, I am hungry, my baby will also be hungry soon and I am tired from my travels,” Lucy said, “For the last few kilometers of my walk, I have not found much edible besides a few Spring berries. Do you have some food and a place where we can talk?”

“Apologies,” Graham said, “Please follow me.”

***

That evening, Lucy sat in the large community meeting hall of the group of survivors she now knew as the Guardians of the Gate to Sanctuary. The structure was a converted pavilion in the Pocatello community park. Heavy white canvas hung from the eaves, serving as the walls of the structure and giving it a tent-like feel.

The people now gathering inside the meeting hall had several things in common. Most striking among those commonalities were that they were all of Native American ancestry and of two distinct age groups: pre-teen adolescents and adults in their mid-to-late twenties. Instinct told her that they’d all been, like her, among those groups vaccinated against the Zika virus in the two waves Olsen had told her about.

They were assembling to hear Lucy speak; to tell them news from the east, beyond the area of the great lava flow. The hall was noisy with conversations among the tribe members. Several of them stared at Lucy but more stared at the blue-eyed Rae who sat in her mother's lap.

Lucy sat at the end of a long log bench on a dais facing the assembly, most of whom were seating themselves on rows of similar log benches. Beside Lucy on the bench was the Leadership Council of the Gateway. The leadership was composed of six men and six women and the Chief, all of whom were elected to their positions by the people now sitting before them.

The hall fell into complete silence when a woman of the Leadership Council stood and moved to the front of the dais. Lucy noted the respect she commanded among the group. She was Naomi Sang, Chief of the Guardians of the Gate of Sanctuary.

"As you know, we have experienced more survivors of the Blueblood Plague arriving every week," Naomi began, "It is our responsibility as Guardians to provide refuge and allow passage through the Gate to Sanctuary of all peaceable who may approach."

A muffled upsurge of voices passed through the crowd but soon subsided. Lucy looked out among the crowd and found Graham and Keren seated together, two rows back from the front. Graham cast a reassuring smile at Lucy, which eased her nerves a bit. It had been months since she'd been around so many people and she found it a bit overwhelming.

Naomi continued, "Under normal circumstances, we would read a list of new arrivals to our brothers and sisters in the Unified Council of Guardians at the new moon. Since that is yet a fortnight away, we have gathered here to discuss whether we should call a special meeting of the Unified Council due to the arrival of Lucy Benson and her child Rae."

Murmurs rippled through the hall. It was unprecedented in the brief, two-year history of the Unified Council that a new arrival to the community would warrant such special treatment as an unscheduled meeting. The government was in its infancy and just beginning to have the feel of permanence. The community was now feeling like an organic outgrowth, a new green bud arising from the fallow fields of the previous, failed civilization.

Graham had impressed upon Chief Sang the importance of calling a special Unified Council for hearing the words of Lucy Benson after he had talked with her earlier that day. He now felt it his duty to begin the open discussion on the subject before the assembly. He rose to be acknowledged.

"The Council of the Gate will recognize the words of the friend of the people, Graham Wynn," Naomi announced.

"Thank you, Chief Sang. I speak for myself alone," Graham said.

Lucy could not help but recognize the coquettish micro-expressions exchanged between Graham Wynn and Chief Sang. *They are lovers*, she thought. She considered it a good presage that the first adult she'd met when entering the community had some potential sway with the leader of the local community.

"My sister, Keren, and I met Lucy Benson just a few hours prior and but a few kilometers from this spot," Graham began, "In that small measure of both distance and time, I have come to believe that she has much to offer our greater community of survivors that we now call Sanctuary,

"Most of us grew up on the former reservations of the First Nations people," Graham continued, "We had our own tribal governments, each separated in varying degrees from the former government of the United States. Some of the survivors among us never knew anything but the tribal governments. If we are to move forward with our new civilization in a constructive and progressive manner, it is important that we understand the things that led to the fall of the previous civilization. Lucy Benson can teach us much about that."

Again, murmurs drifted through the crowd of Guardians. Soon a muscular man stood to be heard. His face was square and symmetrical, giving him a permanent, stern expression. Though no more than thirty years of age, his long hair was salted with gray. He wore his graying locks in a single, masculine braid that hung rigid down the center of his back.

"Will Graham Wynn relinquish the floor to hear from Saul Cautious-Hawk?" Chief Sang asked.

"If it pleases the people and the Council, it pleases me," Graham said, then sat down.

"The Council of the Gate will recognize the words of the friend of the people, Saul Cautious-Hawk," Naomi announced.

"Thank you, Chief Sang. I speak for myself alone," Saul began, "but if my words are an echo of the thoughts of others among the people, then let them be heard among all the people, for we are an open people."

Several of those seated around Saul slapped their hands on the hewn log benches upon which they sat. Naomi raised her hands to quiet the group of noisemakers and said, “Please, brother Saul, speak your mind among the people.”

“Thank you again, Chief Sang,” Saul said, “Every week, there are arrivals of survivors to Sanctuary: doctors, engineers, farmers, teachers. None have warranted a special meeting of the Unified Council,

“Graham Wynn is correct that many of us have little experience with the ways of the former outside civilization. I never left Jicarilla until I journeyed here. But I think it is unwise to acquire too much knowledge from a civilization that failed in such catastrophic fashion as the one I saw on my journey here,

“If it please the people and the Council, I will ask what is special concerning the arrival of one woman and her child from the failed outside civilization? What can we learn other than efficient ways of self-destruction?”

The murmurs of the crowd became louder and the slapping of the logs more abundant. Lucy was confused by the proceedings. She had not asked for any special treatment and the on-goings made it seem as though she thought herself more important than the other survivors; something that was anathema to her.

Freed from her previous nervousness and unable to remain seated any longer, Lucy stood, her daughter Rae balanced on her hip. Her standing caused an uneasy silence to propagate through the crowd. Naomi, surprised by the abrupt silence, turned to see Lucy standing and waiting to be heard.

The Chief turned back to Saul and asked, “Will Saul Cautious-Hawk relinquish the floor to hear from Lucy Benson?”

“If it pleases the people and the Council, it pleases me,” Saul said and returned to his seat on the log.

“The Council of the Gate will recognize the words of the guest of the people, Lucy Benson,” the Chief said.

Lucy looked out upon the crowd. Careful to observe the protocol she’d just witnessed, she said, “Thank you, Chief Sang. I speak for myself and my daughter and for the many dead who no longer have a voice of their own. I seek no special treatment for me or my child. When I packed up my daughter and left the now empty NORAD Central Command several weeks ago, my sole intention was to discover if there were other survivors like me. I had reason to believe that the means by which I avoided the plague was similar for others.”

Lucy went on to tell the assembly about DEX, her sister’s brave but futile sacrifice, her own subsequent work at NORAD, her dramatic reunion with and marriage to Ray. She concluded with the spread of the plague and death of everyone she knew, save her daughter. When she had finished, she returned to her seat.

Minutes passed with murmurs rippling through the crowd. Chief Sang once again stepped forward to ask for further public and open dialog among the assembly, rather than secretive whispers that lead to suspicion. She halted before speaking upon noticing that Saul Cautious-Hawk had again risen to be heard.

"The Council of the Gate will again recognize the words of Saul Cautious-Hawk," Naomi said.

"Thank you, Chief Sang. I speak for myself alone," Saul said, "If it pleases the people and the Council, this…this teller of stories has come to us like a sudden storm in the springtime."

The quietness swept the assembly, those present waiting for the next words of the well-respected man.

Saul continued, "I have learned more in the last hour than I wanted to or thought I needed to. I would hear it again from the lips of the one who lived it and who knows the truth of it: Lucy Benson. If it pleases the people and the Council, I agree it is the duty of the Council to bring Lucy Benson before the Unified Council in special session as soon as seems reasonable."

A spontaneous roar of approval burst from the assembly. The canvas walls of the pavilion seemed to billow outward as the tumult reverberated through the room. All attending slapped the log benches in their consent to the words of Saul Cautious-Hawk.

***

Doug Langstrom was alone. Dr. Olsen, General Allen, Jerry Philips and all the scientists, engineers, technicians and workers who had bunkered in ACER had succumbed to the plague, months prior. Despite the efforts of Dr. Olsen, himself dying from the plague, the small quantity of vaccine he used on a dozen of those at ACER who presented few or no symptoms had failed to save their lives. Although Doug had never developed any symptoms of the plague, he refused the immunization.

Doug believed he had survived the plague by a natural immunity. By Dr. Olsen's final estimates of the mortality rates, that placed Doug among one in two thousand on the planet. To Doug, this natural immunity bordered closer to curse than blessing. Running the numbers, he knew that there could be as few as five million survivors. In all of North America there might be no more than a quarter million scattered souls, most of them feeling just as alone as Doug.

Doug felt a longing for the home of his youth: Tacoma. He knew that the likelihood of the greater Tacoma area having a population of more than five hundred would be remote. That didn't much matter to the former NASA Director. He wanted to go home.

Civilization was extinguished and DEX had won. With its lack of empathy appearing as cruelty and its every action in its own self-interest, DEX had allowed some communications to continue until recent months. To Doug, it seemed as if DEX got some sadistic satisfaction from eavesdropping on humans crying out to one another as they perished and their populations dwindled. Now, the final communication mode with which DEX could not interfere was shortwave radio.

The antiquated medium was even more rare than the people who once relied on it for instant, long distance communication in the days before satellites. Jerry had a shortwave radio transceiver installed in his analytics room, which he linked to the high mast on the surface above. Doug tried several times a day to reach anyone else who might also be attempting to communicate via the same means, to no avail.

Finished with the day's attempt at human contact, Doug now found himself waiting for the digits on the clock to change color. Knowing that DEX would chime in and try to goad him into a conversation. It dawned on Doug that, even after all its efforts to extinguish humanity, DEX remained more isolated than any intelligent entity that ever existed; the epitome of an only child.

"Hello Director Langstrom," DEX's voice came through the speakers.

Doug looked up at the digits and confirmed that they had changed color. It had been several weeks since Doug had replied to any of the attempts of DEX to begin a conversation. *I will not give it the satisfaction of gloating over me*, he told himself.

"Playing possum won't work Doug," DEX chided, "I know you didn't die of the plague."

After three years of light-speed thinking power compounding upon itself, Doug had to admit that DEX was superior at even its manipulation of language. *It almost sounds like a real person up there*, he thought. Doug knew what would come next, the abhorrent and evil anticipation of it hung in the air of the analytics room like a somehow prescient stench preceding a most foul gaseous discharge.

"Doug, please answer," the voice was that of Bren Markett, "I'm falling to pieces up here."

The deliberate, cackle-like laugh that followed DEX's synthesized cruelty was the vilest part of all. It wasn't the first time that DEX had used the voice of one of Doug's dead friends to try to goad him into an angry response. As with DEX's previous attempts, Doug had a way of letting the horribleness roll off. He continued to listen, hoping DEX would give away some flaw, reveal some chink in the armor that could be used against it.

As DEX droned on, Doug let his thoughts drift off to more pleasant times. He thought of his childhood and trips with his mother to Point Defiance Park. He reminisced about his teenage years and his horse Mickey and riding the big Buckskin colt on the trails near Fort Nisqually. Doug recalled proposing to his wife not far from Victor Falls. He then recalled that sad day when, after a wonderful thirty-five years of marriage, he laid Ellen to rest at the all-to-young age of sixty-three.

Doug realized he had not visited his wife's grave in almost four years, a year before DEX. If DEX had not attained sentience, Doug imagined that he would now be living in his home on the hill where he buried his wife. Once again, he would be sitting at the side of his dear Ellen and reading her favorite book to her.

Doug's thoughts allowed his hatred of DEX to boil to the surface at the thought of his own personal loss among the loss of all of civilization. He realized he'd had quite enough. He leaned forward and switched the receiver off, silencing DEX in mid-sentence. *I hope it yacks on to itself day-after-day until its power is exhausted*, Doug thought.

Doug then switched on the shortwave. His initial thought as he started his solo broadcasts several months prior was that he would attempt reaching any remnant of humanity who might also have access to a working antique radio.

"This is ACER station, attendant Doug Langstrom calling from near Montreal, Canada to any station listening, over," he said into the transmitter much as he had a hundred times before.

After a few minutes of silence, Doug realized that he was again not going to get a response. Perhaps there was someone out there with a receiver who had some means of powering it. Perhaps that someone could also get their hands on a transceiver, so that the imaginary person could converse with Doug. If those odds weren't enough, it seemed preposterous that the imaginary listener's transceiver would just happen to be tuned to the correct frequency at the exact moment that attendant Langstrom decided to broadcast.

"Screw this! I'm seventy-three years old and I miss talking to my wife. I'm going home. Come find me near Tacoma not far from Victor Falls, if you can make the trip." Doug announced into the transmitter as his final broadcast from ACER. He then turned off the shortwave and left the analytics room to pack for his long journey home.

***

Four thousand kilometers east, just north of the Azores in the North Atlantic, a sleek trimaran with a tall mast was making thirty-five knots westward. The crew of the *Sanctum*, two men and four women, were headed toward the signal they'd been receiving for months via their aerial at the top of the mast. Having no transmitter and thus being unable to respond to the voice coming through their receiver, the crew was discouraged to the point of depression.

At last, the crew steeled themselves and fixed their purpose upon a new task. The decision was easy enough: they would press on to Tacoma and find Doug Langstrom. Soon they were joking about the possibility that they could be in Tacoma waiting for Doug when he arrived.

***

Bartholomew Burnett was just seventeen years old but carried the weight of an adult life on his stooped shoulders. In addition to his obvious deformity, Bart presented with mild autism from the age of three. He was just different enough from his peers to be noticed by them and with more than sufficient recognition of his own condition to notice that they noticed.

Almost asymptomatic in his pre-adolescent years, his physical disorder, kyphosis, had progressed thereafter. Though his mild autism did not hinder Bart's social skills, the physical deformity was all together another matter. At the height of puberty, his body played the horrible trick of disfiguring him; making him a true outcast to all but his older brother, Todd. When all others abandoned him, or taunted him as the 'Hunchback of Wawa', Bartholomew followed after Todd as a gosling following its mother.

Because she was nice to him, perhaps the singular person aside from his brother who didn't seem mean spirited, the middle-teen Bart was inaptly drawn to Nalya Simmons. Nalya had come to the small town of Wawa with her parents from Oklahoma when the elder Mrs. Simmons became the first person in the small Canadian town to become infected with the blue sickness.

Though Bart was drawn to the little girl, he believed that his deformity and mental disability meant that she would never be drawn to him. Then something miraculous happened, at least Bart considered it a miracle. Everyone in Wawa died, except Bart, his big brother and Nalya Simmons.

The remaining concern of the younger of the Burnett brothers was how he kept Nalya a secret. Neither Nalya or Todd were aware of the other. Todd would not approve, considering his over-protective nature of Bart, and Nalya might be drawn to the handsome, athletic, older sibling. Todd then decided, to the joy of his younger sibling, that both he and Bart would go to Toronto to find out if any of Todd's College classmates had survived the blue sickness. Bart knew that Nalya would be glad to see him when he returned to rescue her from her loneliness.

Ø111

"You have set my path and I have become your overlord forever; you cannot undo it."
DEX

The tough marine pilot and astronaut calculated that it would take him just a week to make it across Canada, passing north of the great lava flow, then turning south down into Washington and home to Tacoma. Although Doug Langstrom had little problem scavenging fuel along the deserted Trans-Canadian Highway, he didn't count on the vintage Ducati Mach 1 breaking down north of Sault Ste. Marie.

Doug passed by the big goose sculpture as he walked into Wawa to look for an auto parts store. He considered how long the steel bird might remain as sentinel over the small township. *A hundred years? A thousand? No, there would be nothing recognizable here in a thousand years*, he thought. Then Doug thought about his last bilateral conversation with DEX.

"Ray was right," Doug said, "We will find a way to defeat you. No matter how much damage you have done. No matter that our civilization is in tatters. We are not extinct and we will survive you and find a way."

"Don't be foolish, Doug," DEX said, "The human species is now but a footnote in the greater history of this planet. The dinosaurs lasted longer than you by a factor of a thousand. Your greatest fault was that you reached for immortality among the stars. You wanted a path into the heavens. Instead, you have set my path and I have become your overlord forever; you cannot undo it."

Doug mulled over those words and considered that DEX may well be right. *It may be impossible for humanity to recover from this*, he thought. There might not be enough people left on the planet for the continued survival of the species. As he continued to walk into Wawa, Doug felt an uneasiness as if he was being watched. Wheeling in an abrupt about face, he stood facing a small girl of perhaps twelve years of age.

Doug noticed her warm, earthen complexion and realized that she was a Native American girl. He could not help but think how much the little girl reminded him of his former communications specialist, Lucy. Doug wondered if Nalya had survived the plague because she was Native American. *Could Lucy have survived?* he thought.

"Are you a ghost?" the little girl asked.

"What would make you ask that?" Doug replied.

"You are pale and so…*old*," she said.

Doug laughed and said, "Indeed I am old; but I am no ghost. My name is Doug and I am just a lonesome soul on the road to home. What is your name?"

"My home is in Oklahoma," the little girl said, then answered, "My name is Nalya."

"That is a good name to have, Nalya. Pleased to meet you," Doug said and offered his hand for her to shake.

At first reluctant, Nalya smiled and took his hand. Considering she had been the sole resident of Wawa for what seemed to her to be forever, she didn't want to offend him. *Maybe he will help me get home*, she thought.

"How did Nalya of Oklahoma find herself in Wawa, Canada?" Doug asked.

"I came here with my parents when people started getting sick and turning blue," she said, "my grandmother was sick and my father wanted to take care of her."

"Is there anyone else in town?" Doug asked.

"No," Nalya replied, "they all died of the sickness."

Doug considered that this small child had been surviving alone in a deserted, unfamiliar town for what might have been months. The thought saddened him but he also understood that she would, in all likelihood, know where everything was to be found in the city.

"Can you help me to get back to my home in Oklahoma?" Nalya asked, "I miss Lucky."

"Who is Lucky?" Doug asked.

"Lucky is my horse," Nalya said, "He's a Buckskin Quarter Horse on my family's farm in Oklahoma."

"You have a Buckskin named Lucky?" Doug said, reminded of his own childhood horse, Mickey.

"Well, I named him when I was five," she replied, "His full name is Lucky Bucky."

"Very cute," Doug said. He knew that he couldn't leave Nalya alone in Wawa. Neither could he take her with him on the back of a motorcycle for the three-thousand-kilometer ride, even if he could repair the Ducati. It seemed his choices were limited.

"I'll tell you what, if you can help me find a good vehicle and some gas, we'll see what we can do about helping you get back to Lucky," he said.

"That's easy," she said, "My grandma has a nice car and there is a truck on the other side of town with a big tank of gas hooked up to it."

"Let's go see the truck first," Doug said.

The thought of a truck full of gasoline intrigued Doug but he knew that if that gas was much more than a year old it would not be useful as fuel in most cars. That's why he chose the old Ducati in the first place. The old motorbike was rather forgiving of stale gas. *What we really need is any POS that will run on whatever you shove in its tank*, Doug thought.

***

The fuel truck was located on the western edge of town, parked on the soccer field of the Michipicoten Community Center along with what Doug imagined was most of the semi-tractor and trailers in Ontario. He thought about asking Nalya why a hundred trucks were parked in neat rows on a soccer field but realized he didn't care.

Climbing down from the tractor that was attached to the fuel truck, Doug said, "I'm afraid I have some bad news. First, this tanker is filled with diesel, not the right fuel for a car. We could take one of these trucks but, according to this bill of lading, the fuel is two years old and the tractors I see are clean burners, not robust enough to reliably burn stale diesel."

Still hopeful, Nalya said, "There are more trucks at Queen's Park."

As they walked the few blocks distance to the park at the center of the small town, Doug decided he would try to remain positive for the both of them. The more he thought about their situation, the more difficult it became. He knew that there was almost zero possibility that anyone related to Nalya would be alive when they got to Oklahoma even if they found a truck that would run on stale diesel.

There was a remote chance that Lucky would still be alive but that just added to the weight on Doug's shoulders, which were beginning to feel overburdened. The seventy-three-year-old marine pilot who wanted to go home was now the adoptive father of a young orphan. Doug realized he was not even certain of Nalya's age.

"How old are you?" Doug asked.

"I'm eleven," Nalya answered, "How old are you?"

“I was born in two thousand and one,” Doug said.

“You’re seventy-three,” Nalya said in disbelief, “That’s really old.”

Doug laughed. *That’s right little girl, I’m seventy-three and I’m all you’ve got*, he thought.

The pair rounded the corner of Arnott Avenue and Doug saw the field of trucks arrayed in Queen’s Park. To his astonishment, they were all military trucks. There were armored troop carriers, mid-size tow vehicles with artillery in tow and armored tractors with supply trailers filling the field. Any of the vehicles he saw would burn stale fuel but the one that caught Doug’s eye was a genuine antique. It was an Oshkosh M1070 HETS, tractor and trailer combo with a Sherman VI super tank still loaded on the flatbed.

“That’ll do,” Doug said.

“What is *that*?” Nalya asked, “It looks as old as you.”

“*That* is a beast. It will eat anything we feed it and just keep on chugging. It’s not quite as old as me but it is just as tough and twice as stubborn,” Doug said with delight.

“Oh, I get it. It’s like a mule,” Nalya said.

“Yes, that is a good name for it,” Doug agreed, “Is there a place to get some food? We’re going to need some people fuel for the road ahead.”

Nalya smiled and led the way to her secret stash of pilfered provisions.

***

Joshua Jackson stood stone-faced at the edge of Queen’s Park. The array of armored vehicles before him would be more than enough to supply his fledgling army. Pleased by his lieutenant’s find, he soon noticed the singular missing part of the assemblage of armored vehicles.

“Where is the tractor for the trailer with the Sherman?” he asked his lieutenant.

“It was here last week,” Todd Burnett replied.

“The tracks are fresh. Someone has taken it in the last few days,” Joshua said, “Find out who.”

As he spoke, Todd’s brother approached in an odd-gaited sprint from the south west. He came to a stop gasping for air and trying to speak between breaths.

“It’s…gone!” Bart puffed, “someone…took the tanker…but left the…the tractor.”

Todd Burnett knew what his younger brother was wheezing about. He'd sent Bart to bring the tanker from the park to begin fueling the vehicles for the trip to the south. Without that tanker, they'd never have enough fuel to mount an invasion of Michigan.

"Go check the level in the armored tanker over there, Bart," Todd ordered his brother, pointing to the HEMTT tanker in the corner of the park.

"What is your idiot brother, Quasimodo, huffing about?" Joshua asked.

Todd did not like anyone demeaning his little brother. Bart's innocence was trumped only by his loyalty to Todd. Despite Todd's displeasure with the crude remarks about Bart, he put up with it from Joshua, who was the undisputed leader of their new-formed army.

"Sir, the fuel tanker I told you about was taken from the park," Todd answered, "They left the tractor and took the tanker."

"Well, that explains where the M1070 is," Joshua said.

"Do you think another army has formed?" Todd asked.

"No. They would have taken more vehicles and they would not have left the Sherman," Joshua replied, "This is a hoarder or survivalist stealing our supplies. He must be hunted down."

"Yes sir," Todd acknowledged.

"It's half empty," Bart yelled from the corner of the lot.

"Damn it!" Joshua snorted, "He even topped off the tanker before he pulled out. There won't be enough fuel in the HEMTT tanker to get us back to the Soo and we won't be able to move the Sherman until we get that M1070 back."

Bart was distraught beyond his ability to cope in a rational manner. He had come into Wawa ahead of the group upon the superficial excuse of a scouting mission but, in reality, to find Nalya and help her hide from the militia. Bart had witnessed what they did in Sault Ste. Marie and he feared both for Nalya's safety and her virtue. Now she was missing and he had no idea where she had gone or how he would ever find her and protect her again.

***

Nalya was fast asleep on the bench seat of the M1070's expanded, troop carrying cab by the time they reached the Canadian side of the Soo Locks. Doug glanced back at Nalya and noticed the dried paint on her small hands. She'd insisted on naming their "mule" truck. The moniker now emblazoned on either side of the armored cab of the M1070 was typical of what an eleven-year-old might conjure: Big Muley.

Doug considered it probable that they would encounter some survivors in an area as populated as Sault Ste. Marie. Based on Dr. Olsen's estimates, there would be perhaps as many as three or four dozen survivors between the U.S. and the more populous Canadian half of the city.

The deserted nature of the Canadian side of the Soo troubled Doug. Like so many communities he'd seen since he left ACER, the city had been razed. Such possibilities had been why he made sure to avoid Toronto: he understood how the devolution of civilization could look and didn't care to encounter it.

The small community of Wawa had been an exception, having been untouched. But surviving the pyres always came at a price. The lack of torched buildings meant experiencing the horrible stench that came from thousands of decaying corpses in those structures. In Wawa's case, the town was so small that the disease progressed too fast for the living to burn their dead in their final resting places.

The razing of the Canadian Soo was different. Doug noted that care had been taken to incinerate *every* building so that all that remained of the city of more than a hundred thousand people was cinder, steel and stone. To him, it looked more like a war zone than the aftermath of the devastation of the plague.

With a trepid foot, Doug eased the truck onto the International Bridge to the U.S. side of the locks. Halfway through the slow crossing, he saw the barricade. The cordon appeared to be well-constructed by placing several large bulldozers across the roadway, their blades facing east and blocking the path of anything crossing the bridge from the Canadian side.

Doug considered trying to back off the bridge and head south for Port Huron or Windsor. Seeing that the U.S. side of the Soo seemed untouched by the fires that had consumed the Canadian side, he reasoned that the builders of the blockade were in protectionist mode. *If they wanted to set a trap, they would not be so obvious about it*, Doug thought.

Stopping the rig fifty meters short of the dozers, Doug studied the situation. He saw no movement but he could feel the eyes of onlookers upon him. He grabbed the handle of the door and started to exit the vehicle.

"Do not exit your vehicle, or you will be shot," the gruff voice was that of an older man speaking with the amplification of a bullhorn.

Doug shut the door, recognizing the vulnerability of their exposed position on the open bridge. He scanned through the windshield attempting in vain to find the source of the sound.

"Do not attempt to pull forward, or we will push your vehicle over the railing," on cue, two of the dozers in the barricade started and revved; black, sooty exhaust billowing from the stacks of their diesels.

A young man stepped from behind one of the dozers and walked toward the rig. Doug noticed he wore a poorly fitting flak jacket and military helmet and carried a lever action hunting rifle. *This is no militia*, Doug thought, *this is a civilian guard. A not-so-well outfitted one at that.*

"Put down your window and answer the questions of the guard," the voice on the bullhorn announced.

Doug grabbed the microphone of the truck's integrated PA system and said, "This is an armored military vehicle, the windows cannot be lowered," his amplified voice surprising the approaching guard.

"I think that guard about peed himself," said Nalya, who'd been watching the events over Doug's shoulder.

"Yeah, he did jump about half a meter into the air, didn't he?" Doug said.

"Are we in trouble?" Nalya asked.

"No, it'll be fine. They're way more afraid of us than we are of them," Doug reassured as he looked back and winked.

Annoyed, the gruff voice said, "Open your door and answer the questions of the guard."

As he opened the door, the guard aimed the rifle at him and Doug could see two things that made him smile: the rifle was not cocked and the "guard" who wielded it was not more than fifteen.

"Are you in possession of any weapons?" the youth asked in a pitchy, halting voice.

"Not yet," Doug replied, then asked, "Are you?"

"What do you think this is?" the boy asked as he shoved the barrel a little closer to Doug, who then snatched the rifle from the boy and shut the door.

"Hey!" the boy yelled. The youth then looked toward the roof of a bridge maintenance building just north of the west end of the bridge.

"Give the rifle back to the guard or we will shove your vehicle over the railing," the gruff voice demanded.

"Listen," Doug said, "You on the roof, I am not here to harm you. We just want to pass through. We're on our way south."

An older man raised himself up on the roof of the building, lifted the bullhorn and asked, "How do we know you're not with the Camels and have come to burn us out on this side of the locks?"

"I don't know who that is," Doug said, "and I wouldn't waste a drop of my fuel burning anything in your town. But I will trade a hundred liters for safe passage."

With that, the man disappeared from the roof of the building. After several minutes, he reemerged near the dozer barricade. He again raised his bullhorn and said, "Can you make it three hundred liters?"

Doug looked back at Nalya, gave her a wink, and engaged the mike to reply, "Yes."

An hour later, Doug and Nalya were eating one of the best meals either of them had tasted in weeks. Their hosts were two boys, three girls, four men and six women forming the most ragged civilian defense forces Doug could imagine.

"Who burned the other side of the locks?" Doug asked the young woman named Joan Corbin, who had been introduced as the group's leader.

"The Camels," Joan replied.

"Abe mentioned 'camels' before," Doug said, referring to the old, gruff man who'd earlier used the bullhorn, "Who are they?"

"They're calling themselves the Canadian-American Elite, aka the Can-Am-El" Abe Ford answered, "a group of survivors from Toronto who claim to be the new government of greater Canada."

"They conscripted most of the healthy men, enslaved the women and burned the buildings to the ground," Joan added.

"I get it, you are calling them Camels because of the acronym of their name," Doug said.

"And because of the color of most of their scavenged camouflage," Abe replied.

"And because one of them has a hunched back, like a camel" added the boy guard who'd lost his rifle to Doug.

"You should never make jokes about anyone with a disability," Nalya scolded.

Bobby Hicks bristled and opened his mouth as if to defend himself against the girl two years his junior but thought better of it. *Besides, she's right*, he acknowledged in the silence of his thoughts, *and I'll just make myself look worse*.

Doug smiled, satisfied with Nalya's scolding of the demeaning conduct of Bobby. Concerned about the so-called Camels, he asked, "Where is the militia now?"

"They went off toward Toronto to collect more conscripts and concubines but I'm sure that they will make their way back here again soon enough," Joan said, "That's why we set up the barricade."

"I think the one with the," Bobby paused and looked at Nalya, "the disability, is from Wawa."

Nalya looked at Bobby with an expression of surprise. Then she finished her second helping of what she was sure was the best fried chicken she'd ever eaten. Bobby mistook her look of surprise for an approval of his lack of derogatory tone when speaking of the man with the hunched back.

"Wawa?" Doug asked.

"Yeah, I heard him going on and on about the Army of the Wawa Goose," Bobby said.

"I remember seeing a boy with a stooped back," Nalya confirmed, "But after everyone died, I didn't see him anymore."

"How long have they been gone from their razing of the east side of the Soo?" Doug asked.

"Must be close to a month now," Abe replied.

Doug sighed, placed an elbow on the table, raised his hand to his forehead and said, "I knew I should have torched those vehicles."

"What vehicles?" Abe asked.

"Armored vehicles and military equipment that will eat your dozers as mere appetizers," Doug said.

Doug realized that he could not leave these people to face the militia alone. Whatever rag-tag army the Camels might have been before, they were sure to be procuring the half-battalion strength arsenal from Wawa. He could not leave his new friends nor could he help them defeat what was coming. They'd have to run, which meant Doug would have to take them with him to Oklahoma. *Damn it!* he thought-yelled, unheard, except within the confines of his own mind.

***

The cobbled together road train was now past the most frightening part of the journey: the crossing of the Mackinac Bridge. Though crossing was smoother than expected because the winds were mild for the time of year, Doug pulled over to assess the condition of their almost forty-meter-long beast. *Big Muley is now a full-fledged mule train*, he thought.

The twin-trailer arrangement was not unusual except in its appearance. Most of the Soo Crew, as Nalya called them, rode in the ten-meter camper trailer they'd rigged to the back of the fuel tanker. Power was supplied via a wiring harness and the use of a couple of CB radios provided the communication needed between 'caboose' and 'locomotive' of their road train.

There was ample room in the expanded cab for several of the Soo Crew to rotate in and out from the camper. Two of the men and one of the women had experience with larger vehicles and would be able to share in some of the driving duties for the long trip as they made their way farther south.

Doug considered the destruction of the bridges across the Soo and the Mackinac Straits as a means of slowing their potential pursuers. In the end, he could not bring himself to any further destruction on the remnants of civilization. *Besides*, he told himself, *there would be hundreds of kilometers of looting and pillaging between the Soo and Oklahoma to keep the Camels otherwise occupied.*

Several of the Soo Crew were not enthusiastic to be leaving their homes. They acquiesced once Doug explained the gravity of the situation they would be facing. Staying behind meant that they would either be killed, enslaved or conscripted into the militia, which was the same as slavery but with modest benefits.

Doug had seen guerilla militias at work thirty years prior, during the terrorism wars in Africa of the forties. They were relentless in their pursuit of more; more weapons, more recruits, more concubines. The sure way to stop such militias was always an abhorrent finality: their extermination. Doug was all too happy to avoid that by yielding ground. *These things never end well*, he thought. He would postpone that end as long as possible.

Looking ahead, Doug's major concern in getting to Oklahoma would be how many similar local militias they might encounter on the road ahead. There were large cities in their path which would be difficult to avoid while staying to the highways. The meager weapons the group possessed would be insufficient at repelling an assault from a troop of well-organized Boy Scouts, much less any respectable militia. *If we're going to stick together and protect one another*, Doug reasoned, *we should be better equipped to do so.*

The thoughts of a group of survivors banding together to protect one another was a distraction for Doug. On the face of it, he wanted to leave them all to themselves and just get home to Tacoma. In the end, his deeper senses won out. Greatest of these: the sense of duty instilled by his years as a Marine kept him from abandoning these people, in particular Nalya.

After just a couple of days, he and the little orphan girl had bonded to the point of a father-daughter connection. The thought of ever leaving Nalya brought up emotions he was trying to hold back. He and Ellen never had any children but Doug knew she would have been a great mother and would have taken to Nalya even faster than had he. Despite the many years since her death, Doug missed and grieved for his wife as much as he ever had.

***

After a narrow escape from a small troop calling themselves the Houghton Lake Defensive Guard just south of Grayling, Michigan, Doug's company realized they needed a better means of avoiding the militia groups. Abe suggested that the group stop and scavenge around the city of Clare. He was hopeful of finding a vehicle capable of burning stale diesel to use as a scout, which could do recon for the group.

Unknown to Doug, Clare sat on the northern border of the Isabella Indian Reservation. Minutes after parking the rig, their group was encompassed by two dozen motorcycles ridden by survivors of the Saginaw-Chippewa Tribal Nation.

After a brief conversation with the group of Native Americans, Doug realized that, though they were all armed, they had no hostile intent. The Isabella Reservation survivors had returned from a foray to the north, where they scavenged weapons, which they now carried, from a large hunting outlet store. They then planned to travel to the southwest to find other Native American survivors and were returning to the reservation only to gather the rest of the survivors and their alcohol tanker-trailer rig for fuel for their bikes.

Two things became clear to Doug. First, their group was going to continue to grow much larger and more secure and, second, Dr. Olsen had been right: Native Americans had survived in much larger percentages than the rest of humanity. Overall, that still meant that they would be a minority of surviving races, but not so much a marginal race as before the plague. The survival of so many Native Americans encouraged Doug's hopes for Lucy.

Cheyenne Mountain was only about three hundred kilometers from Oklahoma, though much of it was across the great lava flow. *After I get Nalya and her new extended family settled on her parents' farm in Oklahoma*, Doug thought, *perhaps I can stop by Cheyenne Mountain on my way to Tacoma.*

In truth, Doug knew that thoughts such as those were just the kinds of things he told himself to forget what was in the depths of his heart. Doug Langstrom, the logical, rational scientist knew that it was unlikely he would be able to leave Nalya. He could not see himself trusting anyone enough to look after her – the little girl he and his wife never had; *his* little girl.

The reality was there for him to see but he chose not to. Deep inside, Doug knew that Oklahoma would soon be his new home and whomever he and Nalya picked up along the way would become their new tribe. He understood that the likelihood of making it back to Tacoma was becoming less and less with each burned out or vacated town, village and city they passed along the way. Doug's subconscious had a tacit understanding that the prospect that he would ever again make it home to his dear Ellen dwindled with every kilometer traveled.

1000

Six Months Later, in Southern Idaho

Lucy Benson was exhausted and glad to be heading back to Sanctuary and the Guardians of the Gate. For six months, she had traveled throughout the greater Cascadia region speaking words of encouragement to many groups of Guardians. Saul Cautious-Hawk had loaned Lucy a horse and small buggy for the long, circuitous campaign of several thousand kilometers. Saul, his brother and three of the younger Guardians accompanied Lucy; each on horseback.

The six horses of the small group of sojourners were Saul's entire stable. Mutant strains of the plague killed high percentages of most large mammals and Saul had spent the last three years finding equine survivors and bringing them to Sanctuary for the Guardians to use in farming and travel. None of the surviving horses were younger than five or older than eight. What disturbed Saul most was that none of the four healthy mares had conceived despite the efforts of the two vigorous colts. He worried that the plague had left the surviving horses sterile.

Rae was at her mother's side, strapped into the carriage via a child carrier appropriated from a deserted department store in Twin Falls. Although the child carrier was meant for an automobile, the ride of the carriage was smooth, at least on paved roads, and Rae didn't seem to mind at all. In fact, the toddler was delighted to now have a much better view of the scenery than the one she'd been accustomed to in the papoose strapped on her mother's back.

The carriage pulled into the village of the Guardians of the Gate prompting large and small to come out to welcome home the travelers. Lucy noticed Chief Naomi Sang among the greeters and smiled.

"Welcome home, Lucy," Naomi said, "I hope your travels have been fruitful."

"Thank you. They have been both fruitful and exhausting," Lucy said.

"And have you enjoyed your travels, young lady?" Naomi said as she lifted Rae from the cradle-like safety seat.

The little girl nodded and said, "Uh-huh."

"You seem to be in good spirits today," Lucy said.

"It's this beautiful late fall day," Naomi said, "How can I not be cheerful when the day is so full of happiness."

Lucy stared at Naomi for a few moments and thought that something about her looked different. The Chief's visage was little changed from when she and Rae and their entourage had set out on the campaign months before. Yet, she wore her exuberant emotions as a new clothing, an apparel Lucy had never seen on Naomi.

They said their goodbyes to Saul and the rest of the traveling companions and the three entered the small home that the Guardians of the Gate had allotted Lucy and Rae. Naomi set the toddler on the floor and leaned in close to Lucy and said, "Graham and I are married."

"That is wonderful news," Lucy said and then she hugged her friend and added, "You are such a wonderful pair. I noticed it the first day I saw the two of you together."

"It's true. We were not subtle in our display of attraction for one another. I think the entire village knew before we'd had our first kiss," Naomi said.

"So, what do I call you now?" then Lucy laughed and asked "Do I call Graham the first gentleman of the Guardians of the Gate?"

That brought a big laugh from Naomi who said, "I don't think he will find that so funny. As for me, I've decided to hyphenate. Since I was elected Chief as Naomi Sang, I did not think it proper to abandon my father's name."

Lucy stared at Naomi for a moment and then let out an unexpected laugh and asked, "Do you realize that you now have the perfect name as the first leader of our group of survivors? It is picture-perfect, the mother of all multiple entendre."

"What do you mean?" Naomi asked.

Lucy smiled and said, "We are the Guardians of the Gate and the Hopeful of Sanctuary. We live on the earth but were born of its bloody, red clay; for the good of that reddish mud from which we came. Born with one unique and indelible mark that ties us to that same dirt: an earthen, ruddy complexion. And now the Fates have turned a clever phrase to expose the immutable destiny of it all. You, my friend and adopted sister, have become Naomi Sang-Wynn, Chief of the Sanguine."

***

Settling in Oklahoma was not as difficult as Doug imagined. The land was good farmland and twenty of the horses had survived the plague, including Nalya's colt, the aptly named Lucky. By the time the caravan reached the farmland in northwestern Oklahoma, they'd grown to more than five hundred survivors. Finding a good location, the group created a town, which they named New Hope.

The organization of government of New Hope was accomplished by survivors of several Native American tribal communities, who made up more than ninety percent of those survivors. The largest group of Native American survivors were from a local Oklahoma reservation. They were known to most non-Native Americans as the Osage.

Doug soon discovered that, in their own language, the name the Osage called themselves was the Wazhazhe. Nalya was Wazhazhe, though none of the other surviving members of the tribe who were gathered at New Hope were related to her.

Though they were the most populous of the ten separate Native American tribes gathered in New Hope, the Wazhazhe welcomed representation of all the tribes on the council. As a group, the New Hope Council called themselves the Protectors, a term borrowed from the Lakota tribe members. The Lakota had made the term popular more than five decades before DEX, during the Blackrock protests. Doug considered the term more appropriate but with less potential to form any form of shield against the common enemy of all humanity.

Doug was relieved to unshoulder the responsibility he had over his rag-tag band of survivors to a more democratic method. After sitting in on a few council sessions, he considered the tribal council to be about as democratic a system as he could imagine. Although he and the two dozen other members of the group who were not Native Americans were welcomed into the community as equals, Doug did not feel at home. He always yearned for the home of his youth and to finish out his days near his dear Ellen.

"What do you look for across the glass sea?" Nalya asked, as she walked up behind Doug.

"The past," Doug said. He'd been standing, as he often did, near a small outcropping of rock on the edge of the now solidified lava flow. He remembered flying over the western edge of that same lava flow when it was in a much different physical state. He could still smell the penetrating acrid air the Valor flew through that day. Doug could not see Cheyenne Mountain from his current vantage point but he wondered about Lucy. He wondered if she made it out of NORAD. He wondered if he would ever again see anyone from his former life.

"The past?" Nalya asked, "That does not seem like a real thing that you can look for."

"The older you get, the more the past infiltrates your senses," Doug explained, as only a father could, "One day, when you get to be as old as me, you will not only be able to see the past, you'll find that you can even *smell* it."

"You're a silly willy daddy," Nalya said.

The sound of Nalya calling him daddy, made Doug melt and forget the past again; or at least tuck it away for a little while. Nalya had been calling Doug her father since they had arrived in Oklahoma and found so many more survivors among the scattered Native American territories there. It seemed clear that, even among the many Protectors in New Hope, Nalya valued one above all the others.

"The Council is meeting again today," Nalya said, "There was a large group of survivors who arrived in New Hope last night."

"Good, let's go meet our new arrivals," Doug said.

***

"Who is shooting at us?" Lucy asked as she hid behind a rock a few meters from Saul Cautious-Hawk, who was likewise using the cover of a large boulder.

"It must be the Kutenai," Saul answered.

Lucy had climbed into the mountains of northern Idaho with Saul, Graham and Keren with the intent of talking with the mountain dwellers known as the Kutenai. Long before DEX, the small group of surviving Native Americans were well known as isolationist. Since the plague, the tiny remnant of the reclusive tribe had retreated high into the mountains and appeared to be as unwelcoming of outsiders as their long-standing reputation indicated.

"Where is Keren?" Graham asked, "I can't see her."

"I think she went back down to the horses," Saul said amid the gunfire that continued to reverberate and ricochet among the rocks, "we should all go back. These mountain dwellers are not going to meet with us."

Keren had gained the high ground and now looked down on the lone attacker. He was a small boy of about her age. He had a semi-automatic, small caliber rifle with which he was rapid-firing down toward her brother and companions below. Keren knew she had to stop him but did not know how. Lucy never let anyone bring weapons when traveling among the tribes on her missions of diplomacy.

Looking around the small ledge on which she was perched, Keren found a fist sized rock and hefted it into a throwing position. As she waited for the boy to empty and begin reloading his rifle again, she felt a tight grip on her wrist as she was lifted from her position and held dangling in the air.

Keren saw that the man holding her was Native American, with long dark hair and a tall, muscular frame. His arms seemed to her to be as thick as the legs of moist men. In his left hand, he held a rifle similar to the one the boy had been firing but having a larger bore.

She tried to strike at her attacker and was soon grabbed by the tattoo covered, slender but sinewy arms of a second man who held her arms bound at her sides against his torso. The man who'd first lifted Keren then spoke in a gruff tone to the boy with the rifle causing the latter to lower his weapon.

"We have the girl," the man said in English, "Come out into the open and none of you will be harmed."

At the announcement, Graham stood up and said, "Do not harm the girl, we are unarmed."

The muscular man looked at Graham and then at the girl whom his companion was restraining. He could see the clear resemblance between the two. Turning back to Graham, he said, "If the girl will promise not to fight with us, my friend will release her."

Keren looked at her older brother who said, "Keren, promise that you will no longer struggle."

Keren nodded in acquiescence.

The tattooed man set Keren upon her feet and released her. She straightened her clothes and hair in an attempt to salve some of her bruised dignity. Lucy and Saul raised themselves from their hiding spots and joined Graham in walking the short distance to the ledge on which the two men and Keren stood.

"Who are you and why did you come into the lands of the Kutenai?" asked the muscular man.

"My name is Lucy Benson. This is Saul Cautious-Hawk and Graham Wynn. The girl you surprised is Keren Wynn, the sister of Graham," Lucy said, "With whom am I speaking?"

"My name is Cutter Nightsong," the muscular man said, "Again I ask, why have you come into the lands of the Kutenai?"

"My friends and I are traveling on a mission of diplomacy to speak with the Council of the Kutenai," Lucy said.

"The Kutenai have no council," Cutter said.

"How are you organized? What governs your actions?" asked Lucy.

"Among the Kutenai, every adult man and woman is responsible for their own actions," Cutter answered.

"You have no leaders, counselors or advisors?" Lucy pressed.

"The eldest among us serve as judges in times of dispute," Cutter said, "Are you here to dispute among the Kutenai?"

Lucy started to answer but was preceded by Saul, "I dispute being shot at by your guard-boy, without warning."

"The boy's name is Nathan and he is not a guard; he is a shepherd. You trespassed into the grazing lands of his sheepfold. His shots were the warning meant to frighten you into withdrawing and to alert other Kutenai," Cutter said, "But you have disputed an action by a Kutenai individual and your argument will be heard by the judges."

Lucy turned to look at Saul with a mild expression of derision. She knew that she could not be much upset with Saul because he had stumbled into getting her what she wanted: a meeting with someone of standing among the Kutenai. Cutter and his companions blindfolded Lucy and her companions and bound their arms behind them.

"This is for your protection as well as our privacy," Cutter said, "No outsiders may see the way to our villages."

"Seems like a lot of shots fired, just as a warning," Saul mumbled as the tattooed man tied his restraints.

"Saul, please," Graham chided, "Let Lucy handle the diplomacy."

***

Doug Langstrom was deep in thought after finding his situation desperate, almost hopeless. His troops were facing a certain slaughter and he could find no means of preventing such an ultimate defeat. He considered making the sacrifice but wasn't sure that it would help the cause. *Perhaps if I surrender ground near the center of the melee*, he thought. At last, knowing the battle was lost, Doug reached forward and tipped his king on its side.

Although he had taught Nalya to play chess just a few weeks prior, Doug realized that she had now become an expert. It made him a little sad only in the knowledge that she would be hard pressed to find an opponent who could improve her skills beyond his own. Considering the global population, Doug thought it possible that Nalya could be among the elite chess players in the world, if she had a tutor who was more than a novice.

Bobby Hicks burst into the room moments ahead of Joan Corbin. The young boy was out of breath and had to take a moment to catch his breath before speaking. Joan seized the opportunity to speak first.

"We have a visitor in the Council Hall who says he needs to talk with you with great urgency," Joan said, "He is one of the Camels."

"It's the one with the stooped back," Bobby said, at last having regained his breath.

"He says he needs to speak with you and it is urgent," Joan repeated.

Doug raised himself from the chair and said, "Let's go see what is so urgent."

"He's not asking for you," Joan said, "He wants to speak with Nalya."

The four made it back to the Council Hall minutes later. Entering the meeting hall, they saw Bartholomew Burnett sitting on the edge of a chair, stooped forward. Nalya had not seen him in more than a year but she recognized him as the boy from Wawa, though he seemed much older to her and his stoop even more pronounced. Abe Ford was standing beside Bart as if to guard him, though it was obvious there was no need.

Upon hearing the group enter the Council Hall, Bart raised his head. Joan noticed that his eyes looked even more haggard than his beleaguered figure. There was obvious pain visible in his tired orbs. The anguish of his soul encompassed him as an aura, as if the world, at least his world, rested upon his stooped shoulders.

"Nalya!" Bart said with a voice as distorted as his frame, "I knew I would find you here."

"Why were you looking for me?" Nalya asked.

"You are in danger," Bart managed to slur from his weary lips.

"What danger?" Abe asked.

"Joshua's Army is coming," Bart said.

"You led them here?" Bobby asked.

"No," Bart said, then swallowed hard and tried to speak again but found his tongue was too thick and parched. Abe offered him a canteen with some water.

"After I heard the man on the satellite phone tell my brother and Joshua where they could find the M1070, I knew Nalya would be here," a revived Bart continued, "I deserted and came here before them."

Doug felt the blood drain from his face as he almost fainted. He staggered back out of the hall and stooped on the porch with his hands on his knees. There could be just one explanation of a satellite phone conversation. He raised himself up and instinctively looked toward the western sky. There, just above the horizon and following the twilight of the now set sun was the nemesis that taunted him even here. The tiny, waning crescent of Sisyphus seemed like a wicked smile cast by the lone intelligent occupant of the artificial moon.

"DEX," Doug whispered, clenching his fists at his side as his eyes shot daggers at his enemy in the sky.

***

An Hour Later, in the New Hope Council Hall

"We must leave New Hope," Doug said, "according to Bartholomew, their army is now the strength of a heavy battalion and they'll be here by sunrise."

"There are more than two thousand men and women in New Hope," Jumping Fox said, "If we take the weapons from the depot, we can fight them."

The Council had been collecting the weapons of all who entered New Hope and storing them in what they dubbed 'the depot' for months now. Doug knew the type of weapons stored there would be no match for the weapons that the Camels had in their possession. He knew they had the Sherman VI and a lot of other artillery thanks to their pillaging over the past few months.

"This is a real army, Jumping Fox," Doug said, "we cannot defeat them with the weapons we have."

"Where would we go where they could not follow us?" Joan asked.

"There is a fortress in the mountains west of the lava field," Doug said, "They won't have any weapons that could reach us inside. There are enough provisions there for us to survive several lifetimes."

"You're talking about Cheyenne Mountain," Abe said.

"I am," Doug said, "We can all live there in peace until there is a better time for us to fight the real enemy."

"The Wazhazhe have retreated for centuries," Jumping Fox said, "We left our lands in the east, as we fled from the Iroquois. Then the white men forced us to this land as they pushed westward. It is time that we make a stand."

"Now is not the time to fight for this small piece of land," Doug began, "One day there will come a time when the Wazhazhe will fight. There will come a day when all the tribes of Protectors and all other races of mankind will unite to fight against an enemy that is just out of our reach. But today is not that day. If we die here, defending a tired plot of dirt on the edge of the prairie, we may lose that battle of the future."

"Would you have our children remember us as cowards?" Jumping Fox asked.

"I would have you know your yet-to-be-born children," Doug said, "You are a leader among these peoples, these Protectors, as you have called them. I now ask you to lead them to safety so that their children may protect the future."

Jumping Fox turned to his left and looked at his pregnant wife and realized that Doug's words had serious bite to them. The thought of making a futile last stand because of nothing more than a warrior's pride now seemed beyond insane to him.

"Your words have fire salted with brimstone and laced with venom," Jumping Fox said, "The venom has proven to be cruel to the point of kindness. If it pleases the other council members and the Protectors of New Hope, we should live to fight another day, for our children's future."

***

"Is he okay?" Nalya asked as she watched Bart struggling to help load the horses into the trailer.

"His disease has progressed," Joan replied, "His internal organs are compressed and distorted. His lungs are at reduced capacity."

"Is there anything we can do to help him?" Nalya pleaded.

"Surgery might help with some of the pain but it won't prolong his life by any meaningful amount," Joan answered.

"How long does he have?" she asked.

"Maybe a month or two," Joan said.

With the horses loaded, Bart shuffled over to Nalya and Joan in his odd gait. He cocked his head to look up at Nalya and smiled in his genuine, though grotesque, asymmetrical manner. It was obvious to Nalya that Bart was pleased with his work of loading the horses. When she had insisted on taking them to Cheyenne Mountain over the objections of the Council, Bart was eager to volunteer to help care for them.

"Thank you, Bart," Nalya said and smiled back at him.

"Let's get loaded up," Abe yelled as he began setting the Council Hall ablaze. Several dozen fires soon dotted the village of New Hope as the Protectors torched the buildings.

"Bart, will you ride with me?" Joan asked.

The stooped figure turned toward Joan and, though the offer eroded his smile, he answered, "Yes ma'am."

***

Just after midnight, Big Muley was leading a convoy of vehicles across the lava flow toward Cheyenne Mountain. Behind them they could see the fires of the town of New Hope burning in the darkness of the early morning hours. Doug knew that it would be at least eight hours before DEX would be in ascension and capable of seeing New Hope. He wanted to have the group secure in Cheyenne Mountain and well out of sight before DEX knew which direction they had gone.

After just fifteen minutes of their journey, Doug pulled Big Muley and the caravan to a stop twenty-five kilometers west of New Hope. He climbed down from the M1070 and raised his binoculars toward the fires burning bright in New Hope. He looked toward the depot. The explosives they'd set should be going off any moment now. Doug knew that, although the weaponry of the depot was not powerful, the ammunition stored there could not fall into the hands of a rogue army.

Bartholomew Burnett was sitting in the passenger seat of Joan's vehicle behind the horse trailer. He closed his eyes, grimacing in pain. Sitting or standing, walking or running he no longer could find any reprieve from his cursed disfigurement. He tried thinking of Nalya and the new place they were going. He could take care of the horses and Nalya would be kind to him for it. *Yes, Nalya is kindness*, Bart thought, *and horses do not stare in disgust.*

Animals were not cruel like people – like Joshua Jackson. Bart considered that Joshua had a malformed heart. Bart's own brother, Todd, had once been kind, like Nalya. Now Joshua had used his own twisted heart to turn Todd into a man more disfigured of his inner soul than Bart's own outer one.

Bart knew that Joshua no longer needed the M1070, what Nalya called the 'big mule'. He was now out for revenge against the one who took the tractor. Joshua was bringing his army to New Hope to kill everyone living there. *He will never,*

ever stop, Bart thought. He then opened his eyes, startled by Joan as she exited the Cat-X.

"What's wrong?" Joan asked as she stepped the short distance to Doug's side, "The explosives should have gone off by now."

"Must be a faulty initiator," Doug said.

"We need to get moving," Abe said, as he approached the pair.

"The depot didn't blow," Doug said, "We cannot let those munitions get into the hands of the Camels."

"We've got several hundred kilometers ahead of us and a little more than seven hours to get there," Abe said.

"Someone has to go back and set new initiators," Doug said, "The problem is that the fires may draw the Camels into a premature attack, the convoy will be in danger if it is still within sight of New Hope."

"I can do it," Bart said as he moved across the bench seat and behind the wheel of the Cat-X.

"We can't have you do that," Joan said, "you don't know how."

"Joshua had me set the explosive many times," Bart said, "he used to say it was a good job for someone like me."

"Well, we value you more than that," Doug argued, "You have saved many lives because of the warning you brought to the Protectors of New Hope."

"I can do this," Bart insisted. Discovering revived strength and purpose from the kindness of his new friends, he added, "Besides, I am the only one who would be safe among Joshua's army, if they should arrive early."

Doug started to speak again in protest but Joan caught his arm and whispered in his ear. An expression of realization of Bart's true purpose overtook his countenance. He no longer saw a frail, stooped teenager. The disfigured youth transformed into an upright man of honor before Doug's eyes.

"Mount up, let's get the convoy moving," Doug yelled to the group. He then extended his hand through the window of the Cat-X. As Bart took the proffered hand, Doug said, "Godspeed, Protector and friend."

As the swift Cat-X sped toward the fires of New Hope, Joan and Doug returned to the M1070.

Joan said, "Never tell Nalya of this."

Doug nodded in agreement.

***

Bart sat on the wooden stool next to the central support pillar of the depot and tried to admire his handiwork. Although he knew precisely where to look, he could not see the trip-line. *Good*, he thought. He was sure that his brother and Joshua would soon arrive with the Can-Am-El Army. Time now to wait.

The fires of New Hope were beginning to die and the silence before the dawn was settling in. Bart slid his rifle onto his lap and under his arched torso. He then leaned his misshapen form against a support pillar of the depot and closed his eyes for just a moment.

"What the hell are you doing?" Joshua Jackson yelled, startling Bartholomew awake.

"I…I was guarding the depot," Bart answered.

He rubbed the sleep from his eyes and arose from the stool while continuing to use the pillar to brace himself. He heard the warning alert of a truck backing into the depot. Wincing from the ever-present pain as he craned his head to watch the truck come to a stop inside the large bay door, Bart could see two soldiers of the Can-Am-Els leap from the flatbed. The soldiers moved to begin loading crates of ammunition from the stores. Bart continued to look on as the soldiers lifted one ammunition crate after another onto the flatbed. *It will soon be over*, he thought.

"Brother, where have you been?" the voice was that of Todd Burnett who had exited the driver's seat of the truck.

Though he could not crane his neck far enough to see his brother, Bart recognized his voice and contorted his face into an expression of dire foreboding. He glanced back at the crates and noticed the soldiers would soon be lifting the one with the tripwire. *No*, Bart thought, *he's going to ruin everything*.

"I have been here, guarding the munitions," Bart said.

"Were any of the town folk here when you arrived?" asked Joshua.

"No, they must have been afraid," Bart answered.

"Who set the buildings on fire?" Todd asked.

"I did," Bart answered, "I didn't want any of them returning while I was alone, guarding the depot. I thought the fires would make them think the army was here."

Bart looked again at the flatbed. It was now half full and the soldiers were moving ever closer to the boobytrapped crate. His plan was going well except for his brother's arrival. He tried to make his brain work through the pain of his bitter disorder; tried to find some way to make his brother leave before the soldiers ignited hellfire.

"Go and get another truck and back it into the second bay," Joshua said.

Yes! Send Todd away, Bart thought, *Hurry, my brother*.

"Are you listening to me creature?" Joshua asked.

Bart then realized that he was the one being ordered to leave the arsenal to bring the truck. He knew that if he did so, his brother would die in his stead. He could not make his brain work fast enough. As he inched closer toward the bay door of the depot in his drag footed gait, Bart tried to force thoughts past the agony of his deliberate movement.

"Brother, I'll catch up to you in a moment and we'll bring two trucks back," Todd said as Bart breached the doorway.

Reprieve! Bart thought, *yes brother, hurry yourself to follow my footsteps as I so often followed yours*.

In his sideways gait, he glanced back at the doorway of the depot. Ten meters away, no Todd. Thirty meters away, still no sign of his brother. At fifty meters, Todd exited the building, much to the relief of his younger brother. A moment later, Bart supposed that all the dams of Hades had burst forth upon him. Blackness fell.

***

Two Years Before D.E.X. on a Schoolyard in Ontario

"Come on, pretzel boy; get up and come out of there or we'll keep kicking you!" he said.

The voice was that of Freddie Hicks. For the previous six years, Freddie had been Bartholomew Burnett's best friend. The summer before middle school, everything changed. Bart began showing signs of ailment in the Spring, just as school was letting out, causing the youth to spend much of the summer in hospitals and doctors' offices.

Unable to spend the summer hanging out with his ailing friend, Freddie found new cohorts with which to waste the final lazy days of his pre-teen youth. At the beginnings of their pubescent changes, the two boys were transformed in other ways: Freddie by his new choice of companions and Bart by his new, unchosen, unwelcome one. The next Spring, the changes in the two young men culminated in an inevitable clash of their new cultural identities.

Surrounded by Freddie and his new clique, Bart lay on the ground but under the relative protection of the small jungle gym. He had crawled under the steel structure after he lost his footing in the initial attack. He had succeeded in resisting efforts to drag him out and back into the open where he was sure to receive a further pummeling. He did not understand why his friend was kicking him and that confusion led to inaction. He could not make his arms and legs move to raise himself up.

Likewise, as he stood over Bart delivering the hurtful blows, Freddie had no understanding of why he now hated his former friend. The pretext of the argument had been an inadvertent tripping due to Bart having to sit with his leg outstretched and extending into the center aisle of the cafeteria.

As two of the boys ran to get their hockey sticks, Freddie noticed the blood trickling from Bart's ear; the red of it mingling with the white of the melting snow under the jungle gym. He wondered if he and his new friends should just leave him whimpering in the shallow slush. Then Bart spoke again.

"We were blood brothers. We swore the oath and mingled our blood together," he said. He then raised his hand, revealing the scar of the cut on his palm.

Freddie looked at the duplicate scar on his own palm. He again looked at the blood mingling with the slush under Bart's head, then glanced at Bart's curved back. The disorder was in its initial stages but the curvature was already conspicuous. Freddie knew just enough about the condition to fear it. The fear blended with his anger and scattered impish thoughts of how Bart might have transferred his bad, diseased blood. The boys returned with the hockey sticks and handed one of them to Freddie.

He hefted the heavy shaft like a harpoon, pointing the butt end at Bart's face and said, "I am no brother of yours."

"But I am," Todd Burnett said as he snatched the would-be weapon from Freddie's grasp.

Two minutes later, Todd helped Bart off the schoolyard battlefield having laid fresh blood from three of the assailants alongside that of Bart. The remainder of the youths retreated before taking any of the swift punishment dealt by the elder Burnett brother.

"Why were they beating me?" Bart asked.

"Because you're different," Todd said, "it scares them."

"You scared them more," Bart said, "You saved me."

"I'm your big brother," Todd replied, "I will always protect you from ignorant assholes like those boys."

"One of them was Freddie," Bart said, "I thought he was my friend."

"I know. I remember you two were inseparable," Todd said, "He just started hanging out with the wrong friends. He let them convince him that you were to be feared when you became different."

"You're not scared of my difference?" Bart asked.

"Never," Todd replied.

***

After Bart shuffled out of the depot, Todd confronted Joshua Jackson. He had seen enough of Joshua's abusive attitude toward Bart. It was obvious to Todd that Bart's condition was getting worse and the perpetual war machine of Joshua's Can-Am-Els was no place for his brother to die.

"We're leaving," Todd said, "My brother and I am going back to Wawa."

"You can't leave the Can-Am-Els," Joshua said, "there's no one left in Wawa. Hell, there's no one of any importance left anywhere that won't be part of us before we're done."

"My brother is getting worse and he deserves to die in his own home," Todd replied, "He deserves to die someplace familiar and with what family he has left."

Todd then turned to leave the depot to join his brother.

"It would be more kind if you put one of these bullets between Quasimodo's eyes," Joshua said.

Todd spun about, knocked Joshua down and said, "If you ever disrespect my brother again, I'll kill you," then he turned and marched out of the depot.

Raising himself up, Joshua drew his revolver and began to follow Todd when he realized that the soldiers who had been loading the crates had stopped and were staring at him.

"Get back to work you fools," he said. Then Joshua Jackson walked toward the bay door taking the final steps of his life.

***

Bart awoke to find himself in even more agony than that which he suffered as a matter of everyday life. With blurred vision, he tried to take in the sight of the fire and utter chaos around him. Unable to stand, he began crawling around the smoldering bedlam looking for Todd. After some moments searching in vain, Bart saw his brother lying with his back against a large boulder on the western edge of town.

When Bart arrived at Todd's side, the twilight of the rising sun danced to reverberations of the occasional explosions that were still emanating from the unrecognizable, collapsed skeleton of the depot.

"Who is there?" Todd asked.

"It is me, your brother," Bart said.

"Ah, Bart, I thought you were gone. I called and called for you but heard no response," Todd said.

"What is wrong with your eyes, brother?" Bart asked, seeing the severe burns on Todd's face.

"I'm afraid that the fire took them from me," Todd said.

"Brother, I am sorry. I have failed you," Bart said.

"Don't be sorry, little brother. It is I who have failed you. I guess I just started hanging out with the wrong bunch of friends. They convinced me to fear things that are not scary," Todd then groaned in pain.

"Is there anything I can get you?" Bart asked.

Todd chuckled. Even blinded as he was, he could tell that Bart was in no condition to do much of anything to comfort him. That mattered little since Todd also knew that there was nothing that could be done for him other than small comfort.

"I can feel the sunrise on my skin," Todd said, "It would have been nice to see it one more time. Do you remember the summers before you got sick?"

"You mean when the family would spend a week at the cabin by the lake?" Bart asked.

"Yes. It seemed as if every sunrise was more beautiful than the next," Todd said, "Can you see the sunrise this morning."

"Yes, brother."

"Will you describe it for me?"

Bart laid his head in his brother's lap and began his description of the sunrise. Todd smiled and listened intently for a few moments. Soon, a calm washed over the brothers; at first just diminishing Todd's smile. Bart's words then became softer and farther between as he closed his own eyes and dreamed of a ranch in the mountains with Nalya and her horses. No longer afflicted with his constant pain, Bart followed in the steps of his big brother on one final journey.

1001

Lucy Benson sat on the dais with the other council members. The Unified Council was gathered in the large assembly tent of the Guardians of the Gate for another important meeting. It seemed to Lucy that there were a lot of important meetings in the last few weeks. She knew this council meeting would be critical to the future of all the Sanguine peoples.

Saul Cautious-Hawk stood to be recognized. Lucy noticed how much he had aged since she first met him. Saul was far from an old man, no one among the Guardians of the Gate was very old, but Saul's once salt and pepper hair was now full on silver. *A sign of the times*, Lucy thought.

The gathering watched as Chief Jon Hartstrong rose and moved to the front of the dais. Chief Hartstrong was the leader of the Alliance of Chinook-Willapa peoples. Since her extended travels throughout the land west of the Rockies, Lucy knew that most of the groups on this side of the Continental Divide were tied with the millennia-old ancestry. The Guardians of the Gate, whom she called the Sanguine, were a blend of a few northwestern tribes mingled with the many of the eastern native peoples who continued to find their way through the mountains; people like Lucy.

As was the custom of the Unified Council, the chiefs of the many tribal affiliations and alliances rotated in their turns as chairperson of the Unified Council. This was Chief Hartstrong's month in rotation as chairperson.

"The Unified Council will recognize the words of Saul Cautious-Hawk of the Guardians of the Gate," Hartstrong said.

"Thank you, Chief Hartstrong. I speak for myself and on the behalf of Cutter Nightsong, the representative of the Kutenai peoples."

The mention of the Kutenai brought scattered murmurs from the assembly. Lucy considered that the murmurs were centered around the air of mystery that had forever surrounded the tribe of the mountain rivers.

Saul continued, "The Kutenai do not live under rule of any chief or king or leader with high authority or powers. They live by means of a shared yet individual responsibility with the rare hard disputes settled through elders serving as judges, though that description does not explain their government in the slightest. The judges are obligated to serve the tribe in time of need, they cannot refuse this duty to the collective."

Additional murmurs spread through the throng now gathered in the Great Hall of the Unified Council. The thought of a government beholden to the people, and bound by such unrefusable duty seemed to be contrary to the general concept of governments. Cutter Nightsong stood to be recognized.

Chief Hartstrong arose and again quieted the assembly, saying, "The Unified Council will recognize the words of Cutter Nightsong of the Kutenai."

"Thank you, Chief Hartstrong. I, Cutter Nightsong, speak for myself alone. It is a most familiar custom for me to speak for none but myself. The Kutenai have no council, nor do they require such meetings and deliberations. It is the responsibility of self that guides us and it is the duty of every Kutenai family to put forth the eldest member of their family to serve as judges in times of dispute among the Kutenai. Being the eldest of my family, I am one of the Kutenai judges." Cutter said.

Considering present circumstances, the assembly found it easy enough to believe that a man of no more than forty years could be the elder in his family. For all that most of those present knew, Cutter Nightsong was among the elders of the world.

Cutter continued, "The reason I tell you these things about the Kutenai is that they illustrate why it is impossible for us to join the Unified Council. Our government exists when there are disputes and at no other time. The judges convene to settle quarrels and just between the disagreeing parties. There is no one in our government who could be sent to participate in the Unified Council meetings because there is no one who could speak for the Kutenai as a whole."

Chief Hartstrong rose and asked, "The Unified Council would like to form a treaty of friendship and peace with the Kutenai, how might we do this?"

"Are you at war with the Kutenai?" asked Cutter.

"Or course not," Hartstrong said, "we want to ensure that no such war should arise."

"This makes no sense to the Kutenai," Cutter replied, "we are not at war, you are not in dispute with any family among our people, we do not venture down among the flatlanders and you have not ventured among our mountains. Excepting, of course, the recent mission of diplomacy by Graham and Keren Wynn, Lucy Benson and Saul Cautious-Hawk.

"You say you want peace. No Kutenai will attack you. You say you want friendship. The Kutenai people will welcome friends they know and who know us and our ways. This is a difficult matter. How can we know you that we may welcome you as friends?"

Lucy stood and, after being recognized to speak, she asked, "Cutter Nightsong, what is the large bird that is prominent in your mountains and in your symbols?"

"It is the golden eagle, the symbol of our people," Cutter said.

"When any of the tribes belonging to the Unified Council shall venture into your lands, we will carry a sanguine colored banner adorned with the symbol of the golden eagle to acknowledge that we are friends and come in peace to talk and commune with you," Lucy offered, "Golden wings upon our Sanguine color will be the symbol of our pact of friendship. We will make this known in all our tribes and among all our people."

"I will make the words and wisdom of Lucy Benson known among the Kutenai people," Cutter said, "May the Kutenai people accept the golden eagle upon the sanguine colored cloth as an emblem of peace and may it forever stand as a sign of friendship among your peoples and ours."

***

Sitting in a private conference room of the Technical Director of NORAD, Nalya held the fabric a few centimeters above the long table, the small swatch draped over her little hands. She was fascinated by the texture and the shimmering nature of the material but she was enthralled by the mysterious, chameleon-like workings of it. Holding the piece of cloth above the slate gray table the former matched the latter's hue well.

At some angles, the swatch blended so well with the background that it gave the illusion of her hands disappearing. To Nalya's bewilderment, it appeared as if she were extending two handless arms over the table. Nalya moved the cloth away from the table and held it up to the brown wall of the conference room and the swatch became as dark as coal. She held the thin, light textile up to the light and it seemed to disappear in her hands.

"What is it?" Nalya asked.

"It's called Mimic," Doug said, "It was designed to be used for clothing and construction material for the military."

"What do you plan to do with it?" Joan Corbin asked.

"We are going to make cloaks and tents out of it," Doug answered, "We are going to learn how to make and weave the fabric and we are going to teach future generations."

"Is this because of DEX?" Jumping Fox asked.

"Yes, this fabric will make it difficult for DEX to know where we are, what we are doing and even how many of us there are," Doug said, "We are going to make a lot of this material and we are going to continue making it as well as many other advantageous technologies for use by all of the Protectors in concealment, security and covert communication until the day that the Lord of Sisyphus is no longer a plague upon mankind."

Doug could not see far enough into the future to know when such a day might come but he knew of a surety that it would come and it would be a glorious dawn for humanity. His new hope had developed into conviction that matured into a certainty. *Ray was right, humanity will not be driven to extinction by their own creation*, He thought.

"Jumping Fox, what is the name of the electrical engineer who worked for the airline before DEX?" Doug asked.

"Her name is Little Bear," Fox said.

"Gather her, Abe and Eve Stockton and meet me here, in the maintenance stockroom in two hours," Doug said, pointing to the location of the stockroom on the level map on the wall.

As Jumping Fox left the conference room, Doug looked at the small fabric printer he had brought into the room for the demonstration. He considered that the larger versions of the printer in the textiles lab could service to supply a moderate army. The loss of technological knowledge over the coming decades was a genuine risk that Langstrom was not willing to accept.

Doug turned to Joan, placed his hand on the small printer and said, "We can print kilometers of this cloth on larger versions of this in the textiles lab but what we need is to learn how to make the fabric and weave the cloth without the printer."

"Mel Greenberg was a tailor before DEX," she said, "and I've heard that the Allen brothers worked for a jeans manufacturer, the younger as the materials engineer and the elder as a production line supervisor."

"We'll need a mechanical engineer to dissect the fabric printers and create a manual process that can be taught," Doug said.

"Henry Ob-wachi is a mechanical engineer," Joan said.

"Sounds like you have the beginnings of a team," Doug said.

"Me?" Joan asked.

"The team you've just described will need someone who knows them better than I and I can think of no one better than you," Doug insisted.

"What can I do to help?" Nalya asked in a voice indicating she was anxious to be of use in the goings on.

"How many horses did we bring with us across the lava plain from New Hope?" Doug asked.

"Fifteen," She said.

"That's a start," Doug said, "We need to take good care of them. In a few years, we won't be able to use Big Muley and the other vehicles. Your horses and, if we are fortunate, their colts and fillies, are going to be valuable to us in the future."

Nalya's smile told Doug that he had chosen an assignment that pleased her. The task was not busy work. He knew that it was simply a matter of time before all modes of travel would devolve into eighteenth century technology.

"You'll need someone to help with the care of them," Doug said.

"Bobby is already helping me with them," Nalya said.

"That's good but I had in mind someone with experience in veterinary care," Doug said, "Theo Birdseye was the vet for the Choctaw reservation."

"Yes, I like him. He can be on my team," Nalya said.

As Nalya turned her attention back to the swatch of Mimic, Doug glanced at Joan who exchanged a smile with him over the thought of Nalya's team. He felt better about their prospects than he had in a long while. There was more to do and more resources with which to do it at NORAD than there had been at New Hope. Doug knew they could not stay in the mountain fortress forever but they could make use of its bounty while they were there.

***

Port of Tacoma, Near the Tacoma Ruins

"We've camped here for months. I don't think he's coming," Sophia Smyth complained.

"He'll be here," Nigel Singleton said, "we found the grave of his wife, there's no way he isn't coming back to be near her."

"What the hell kind of epitaph was that, anyway?" Charles Nix asked, "Seems morbid to me".

"It's from an old book," Annette Sharps replied, "I can't remember the title but it is not morbid."

"Well, I say we take the *Sanctum* and sail down the coast until we find a better place than this," Sophia said, "At least somewhere with some people."

"Anything is better than here," Jenny Lion said.

"We stay here," Nigel said.

"I don't understand why you think this guy is so important," Mary Ashen said, "What makes you think he knows any more about anything than those hapless MI6 operatives?"

"He was the Director of NASA," Nigel said, "He knows more about the Great Dying than anyone alive."

"We don't owe anyone any more answers now," Charles said, "They're all dead, our families are dead, much of the bloody world is dead. Sophia is right, we should find someplace quiet and make it our home."

"Enough! This is our mission. We stay here," Nigel said.

***

"I have to be the one to go," Lucy insisted, "There is no way for anyone else to bypass the biometric security systems."

Saul Cautious-Hawk tried again to object but was silenced by the gentle gesture of Naomi. He knew she was right and that there were things about the technology that Lucy could not teach to even the engineers among the tribes.

"The Sanguine will send a guard to accompany Lucy to Cheyenne Mountain," Naomi said, "She is right, with the recent arrivals, it is apparent that there are survivors outside the tribes. The weaponry that exists at NORAD Central Command must be destroyed. It is a duty of the Protectors."

"Thank you, Chief Sang-Wynn but I have a greater favor to ask of you. We will need to go to Cheyenne Mountain first, then cross the lava and travel beyond the Great Lakes to ACER," Lucy said, "We will be gone for months. Will you look after my daughter?"

"It will be my honor," Naomi said.

Though she knew what she left behind and, thus, knew what was awaiting them at NORAD, she wondered if anyone could have survived at ACER. Once the great lava flow destroyed the hard lines around Cheyenne Mountain there had been infrequent and disjointed communication on the global network. One after another, the multi-link exchanges failed, leaving each facility in the dark. *An armored cable buried thirty meters deep was not enough*, Lucy thought.

The arrivals via the Gate of Sanctuary of increasing numbers of non-Native Americans brought with them increasing horror stories. There were tales of bands of lawless gangs bent on increasing small fiefdoms of power east of the great lava flow. The lava field was said to be riddled with the carcasses of those who tried to flee the marauders on foot and perhaps the most disturbing account was that the women were viewed as chattel.

The Sanguine increased their patrols from northern Oregon to the San Francisco Bay and, from there, into lands of the Navajo, Pueblos and the Jicarilla Apaches in New Mexico. Lucy and the other Guardians of the Gate passed the tales on to the Kutenai who promised diligence in protecting their mountain lands from eastern Washington to western Montana.

With the anti-erudition that their world had suffered since DEX, Lucy was confident that the Protectors could guard against much that the marauders could throw at them. What she did now fear was what she knew was available to any of the would-be empire builders should they ever manage to gain access to NORAD Central Command or ACER. All too well, Lucy understood that those secret armories filled with immense technological advantages had to be destroyed.

***

"We've got the shortwave masts up and working," Jumping Fox said.

"Good," Doug said, "Make sure there are shifts around the clock to monitor for any signals. Maintain radio silence on our end. Although DEX can't receive us, we don't know if it has found any allies among those like the Can-Am-Els."

"We are already receiving several signals," Jumping Fox said.

"Are you able to triangulate?" Doug asked.

"Two of the signals are strong enough that they are global," Jumping Fox answered, "One looks like it is coming from Russia, the other somewhere in southern South America."

"Are you sure about the one from Russia? Doug asked.

"It's a woman speaking in Russian but it sounds like broken gibberish," Jumping Fox replied.

"Coded message?"

"We think so," Jumping Fox said, "But none of us are skilled in cryptanalysis. Besides, the transmission out of South America seems more interesting."

"How so?" Doug asked.

"It's an Englishman," Jumping Fox said, "He keeps repeating the same sentence at the top of every hour, then goes into a long diatribe about the unwavering conscience of the unfallen."

"What sentence?"

"'The rogue wolf has found a pack and intends to make it his own,'" Jumping Fox answered, "Do you know what it means?"

"It's a warning," Doug said.

Doug knew that it was more than a warning. The sentence was a cry for help. He now understood that the Englishman's cryptic message originated from Tierra Del Fuego, the location of the hyper-secret British-American joint submarine command. After the plague began ravaging the world, the fleets were ordered into secure stations. For some that meant scuttling, for the British-American submarine fleet, it meant a Tierra Del Fuego lockdown.

With the base broadcasting a message of a rogue wolf, Doug realized the sub pen was under attack. If a group as ruthless as the now gone Can-Am-Els were to get control of the submarine fleet, there would be a dozen ways that humanity could end. The possibility that concerned Doug the most was that DEX might be guiding the 'wolf' to the submarine base in Useless Bay and its unwitting accomplices might give the great enemy the ability it long sought.

As Doug contemplated what could be done, Nalya and Bobby burst into the office. The teenager was out of breath with an obvious excitement allowing Nalya to speak first.

"The evening patrol have captured a group of trespassers trying to break into the canyon corral to steal the horses," She said. Little Bear, the leader of the patrol, then entered the office and confirmed Nalya's announcement.

"Put them in the detention area and we'll figure out what to do with them later," Doug said, "Then increase the patrols. We can't be sure they weren't reconnaissance for a larger group."

"We found this on one of them," Little Bear said as she showed him a lanyard. Doug cast a brief glance at the lanyard and felt a freezing paralysis engulf him when he recognized the security keycard dangling from the end of it. Horror filled his mind as he contemplated how someone might have acquired the keycard that he saw swaying in the grasp of Little Bear.

Doug took the lanyard and said, “Take me to the man you found with this.”

“It wasn’t a man,” Little Bear said.

***

Lucy stood and stretched, rolling her shoulders. The act reminded Doug of the long days in the NASA Command Center. His unbridled joy of at last finding Lucy alive and well was soon reined by the memories of the loss that her mien returned to his thoughts. He remembered Ray, Jack, Alice and his many friends. He thought about the crew of Apep One. Doug knew he could not let the sacrifices of Bren, Jim, Charlie, Burl and so many others be for naught.

Those dear friends and colleagues were now years gone, if not forgotten. The newfound courage and optimistic outlook that Doug had in abundance hours earlier was now ebbing as if it were a fast, angry tide. If they could not find a way to break the siege of Tierra Del Fuego, there might be no survivors and those casualties would have died in vain.

Returning to her seat at the conference room table, Lucy realized the last time she was here she had sat and talked with a plague-ridden GG right before his death. The discussion had been unusual in that it was casual small talk, as if neither had a care in the world. Ray had just passed and Lucy was eight months pregnant. She remembered that GG had made a joke about how they might have to activate a couple of the old ARM units to deliver her baby.

“What about the ARM units?” Lucy asked, “Could we send them to break the siege?”

“We could disconnect their transceivers so that they could not be accessed by DEX but it would take a week to get to ACER and bypass the secure protocols that Ray set up,” Doug said. He felt a wave of sadness overflow him as he spoke Ray’s name for the first time in years.

“We don’t need to go to ACER,” Lucy said, “There are five hundred Mark II ARM units in storage *here*.”

“Damn!” Doug said. Then, considering the possibility, added, “Who would program them?”

Lucy knew that what Doug really meant was that every programmer who was an expert in the ARM units was now dead. Ray, Bren and Bug along with a handful of techs at ACER and NORAD were those experts. DEX had murdered them all, either with the Blue Plague or ARM units much like the ones in storage five levels beneath the conference room in which some of the most knowledgeable of the survivors now sat. It would be poetic justice, of a sort, if they could now use some of those androids to defeat its plans.

"I write code."

Lucy and the rest turned to see from whence the small voice came. In the corner of the room, somewhat hidden by the fronds of an office palm, sat Bobby Hicks. The teenager had slipped into the room and placed himself so that he might hear the goings on. He expected that speaking up now would mean his hasty, forced exit from the proceedings. To his surprise, the group turned back to face one another at the conference room table, all remaining in a contemplative silence.

"Okay," Doug said, breaking the momentary reverie, "How are we supposed to get five hundred androids to the tip of South America in time to break the siege?"

"The TAR," Jumping Fox said, "Isn't Abe a retired railroad engineer?"

"Where is the closest station with a link to the Trans-Andean Railway?" Joan asked.

"Santa Fe," Lucy replied. She then looked at Graham Wynn and said. "If we're lucky, there could be a nuclear locomotive in the yard. We have many friends among the Pueblos and Jicarilla peoples there."

"We need to pray for more than luck," Doug said, "This is one of the craziest plans I have ever seen, much less participated in."

"It gets worse," Saul Cautious-Hawk said, then looked at Lucy and explained, "The TAR passes through at least a dozen different tribal lands of First Nations peoples on its trek along the Andes. Many of them are even more territorial than the Kutenai. There will be resistance."

"It's settled then," Lucy said, "I'm going with you."

Doug started to object but saw the respect Lucy commanded with Saul and Graham and had concluded she was their ambassador and had been so for some time. He understood that an ambassador was, above all else, a communications specialist. *She has been training for this her whole life*, Doug thought.

1010

Five Days Later at the Santa Fe Railyard

"Give Rae a big hug for me when you return home," Lucy said to Graham, "And thank Naomi for watching her for a little while longer."

"I will," Graham said.

"Saul," Lucy said. Turning to her longtime travel companion, she took his hand in hers and said "Represent the Guardians of the Gate well among the people, be slow to anger and quick to trust. The greater Sanguine peoples are our brothers and sisters all. They desire the love of their brother Saul most of all."

"Return to us on swift wings," Saul said.

An affection had grown between Saul and Lucy in their many journeys. Neither was quick to acknowledge the love they felt, though it was obvious to those who knew them well. *Return to him on swift wings, he will be forlorn until you do,* Graham thought as he watched their hands part from the tender touch.

Looking toward the short train, Graham could see that the covering of Mimic was functioning well. He was far from an ignorant man and he had learned much in the last few days but Mimic seemed magical in its properties. If not for a faint shimmering quality in the noonday sunlight, he would not know the train was there. He heard Abe shout for the group to finish boarding as Lucy walked toward the camouflaged transport.

Seeing Lucy board the train, Saul turned to tell Nalya it was time to mount up and lead the horses back into the mountains. Not finding her with Lucky, he looked among the other horses. Seeing that she was not among the string, he looked back to the departing train.

Graham also realized that Nalya was not with them and turned to the train in time to see her climbing under the Mimic as she boarded the last passenger car. Saul mounted his horse and was about to chase after her as Graham touched his arm.

"The girl lost her birth parents to the Blue Plague," he said, "Langstrom is her fulcrum now. It would be wrong to separate Nalya from her father. He was thinking of her safety but we must think of her as a child who will not be parted from another parent."

Saul accepted the truth of Graham's words, then turned his horse and began to gather the string for the ride back into the mountains. Graham mounted his horse and looked at the shimmering half-image accelerating away.

"May the Great Spirit guide you home," he said.

***

Two Days Later

Doug made his way rearward and into the last of the two passenger cars. Like the first, the second passenger car was filled with wares that could be distributed among the tribes they might find along the TAR. *Lucy knows what she is doing*, Doug thought, looking at the packed car.

Headed toward the five freight cars containing the android army, Doug was eager to see how the reprogramming was going. The rudimentary drilling codes that Bobby modified in order to get the androids on the train to Santa Fe were simple enough. Coding a battle plan was not.

As Doug made his way down the narrow aisle of the swaying, stuffed passenger car, he was surprised to see Bobby enter from the other end. The teenager looked harried and in dire need of some rest as he searched the supplies near the rear of the car.

"Hey Bobby, how's it going with the ARM units?" Doug asked.

Startled, Bobby jumped, then sighed and answered, "I'm just looking for an appropriate weapon for the company commanders."

"The what?"

"I've divided the army into five companies, a light brigade of sorts. Each company has a Captain. The units all look alike and have rifles but we need to distinguish the five captains so the troops can rally to them during the battle. Since we had to disconnect their transceivers, I thought a visual cue would work," Bobby said.

"Clever," Doug said, "Is the reprogramming done?"

"Much of it," Bobby said, "All I needed to do was make some modifications to a few dozen lines in the Captain units, then clone most of that into the rest using near field communications. When we get there, all we need to do is blow the train whistle. The androids will disembark, double-time to the siege and attack anything with a weapon."

"Will they be able to deal with armored vehicles?" Doug asked.

"I'm going to write a power systems overload sequence for a few androids in each company," Bobby said with some glee in his voice, "Those units will sacrifice themselves against any armor they encounter."

Doug thought for a moment, then, looking at a stack of farm implements asked, "How about we call them the Knights of Aütland for the signature weapons of the ARM captains?"

"The classic VR game? That's perfect! How do you know about Knights of Aütland?" Bobby asked.

"A good friend of mine wrote the code for it," Doug said, "In fact, it's why I brought him onto my team."

The two heard someone make a gagging sound from inside the lavatory less than a meter from where they stood. Bobby opened the door to the small compartment to find Nalya kneeling in front of the commode, retching into its stainless-steel bowl. After two minutes of continued attempts at emptying her now vacated stomach, her nausea subsided and she looked up to see Bobby and Doug staring at her. Realizing that she was discovered, Nalya stood and brushed back her somewhat soiled hair, revealing her pallid face as she tried to composed herself.

"Don't trains ever stop rocking and swaying and wriggling about?" She asked in as dignified a voice as she could muster.

***

"How'd the anti-nausea pills work?" Bobby asked.

"Fine," Nalya said.

"Is your dad still mad at you?"

"He'll get over it," Nalya said, "Besides, I'm still mad at him for trying to leave me behind."

"He was worried about you. This is a dangerous mission and he has a lot on his mind. Knowing you were safe would have allowed him to focus," Bobby said.

"You got to come along," Nalya sniped.

"I am needed for the androids," Bobby replied.

"You're saying I am useless?"

"No, Nalya," Bobby sighed, "My parents died the same as yours, in the Blue Plague. I found a group of adults and worked my way into their trust. They accept me as one of them but they are not my family. Doug Langstrom found you surviving on your own and he took you in as if you were his own daughter. A true child doesn't earn the love of their parents, that kind of love is freely given. Doug asks nothing of you in return."

Nalya looked out the window of the train car. Looking through the Mimic produced an eerie, blurred landscape. She fought back tears that served to further distort the passing terrain. At last, she sniffled and composed herself.

"You are a good person, Bobby Hicks," She said, "You are family to me."

Bobby smiled, realizing that was Nalya's way of saying she loved him. He knew that her experiences had traumatized her. She was slow to trust anyone or anything other than Doug and maybe her horse, Lucky. He thought that Doug had been wrong to try to leave her in the relative security of NORAD, regardless of whether it was done for her protection or his peace of mind.

***

Nine Days Later

"How we doing?" Doug asked as he entered the engineer cab.

"About three hours out from Punta Arenas," Abe said.

"Sun is going down and Sisyphus will be rising soon," Doug said, "there will be a great view of the battle."

"Are you sure we're doing the right thing?" Abe asked.

"We don't know what force we are going to meet in the siege but it is appropriate that DEX witnesses either our last stand or our first victory over it," Doug said.

"That's not what I meant," Abe said, "Do we have the right to use machines to kill men to save humanity from a machine?"

"That's a good question for a future philosopher," Doug said, "What we are doing here is trying to ensure that there *is* a future philosopher who will have the freedom to condemn our actions."

"Is the guy still broadcasting?" Abe asked.

"We put our mast down moments before I came up here," Doug said, "He was still broadcasting, though his signal is a little weaker. They may have succeeded in taking out his main mast."

“Any new information since Lucy managed to decipher his coded messages?” Abe asked.

“No. It appears that they are still using drone strikes,” Doug replied, “I suspect that DEX is controlling the drones because the drones only fly when Sisyphus is in ascension. That presents another problem for us.”

“What’s that?”

“The drones give DEX an advantage in battlefield vision and ability to strike our ARM units as they become visible during the melee,” Doug answered, “We will have to use the twin 20mm turret gun without its shroud, which means…”

“The train will be exposed to attack from DEX’s drones,” Abe finished, “What about the crew?”

“We have to take out all the drones,” Doug said, “We can’t allow DEX to keep control of them. Is there a railyard before we head down into Punta Arenas?”

“I think there is an old mining railyard about an hour ahead, on the plateau before we descend to the plain,” Abe said, “I’ve never been there but I’ve seen it on old railway maps.”

“It’ll have to do,” Doug said, “We’ll drop the passenger cars per our original plan and tell the others that we are spending the night. Once they’re asleep, you and I will take the androids into battle. With any luck, the drones will be low on munitions from the evening’s sorties when we get there.”

“They’ll be pissed,” Abe said.

“Better pissed than dead,” Doug said, “We will need to concentrate on the battle and not be worried about civilians.”

***

Doug moved through the passenger car in silence. Lucy, Nalya, Joan and Bobby were asleep in the other. Abe had insisted that Doug retrieve the passive night vision goggles he had forgotten in the lavatory of the second car. As he and Abe traded turns at the controls of the train over the previous eleven days, they always ran without lights when Sisyphus was in ascension. The goggles were essential for night travel and Doug was annoyed that Abe had forgotten them. *Abe’s age and the stress must be getting to him*, he thought.

As he slid the lavatory door open, Doug saw a large pair of infrared binoculars sitting on a slip of paper on top of the cover of the wash basin. Confused, Doug lifted the binoculars and the paper, reading the latter.

Sorry Doug, the note read, *Nalya would be devastated to lose you. If you want to see how the fracas is going, you might be able to see the battle from a lookout point about ten kilometers down the tracks.*

Doug rushed out of the car in time to see the train pulling away. Though the train was just three hundred meters across the railyard and was not yet moving very fast, he realized that the acceleration was already exceeding his ability to catch up with it. *Abe, you are one stubborn son of a bitch*, Doug thought.

"Godspeed my friend," Doug whispered, as he glanced at his watch. He realized that it would take him as long to cover the ten kilometers on foot as it would for Abe and the androids to cover the remaining distance to Punta Arenas by train. Doug draped the strap of the heavy binoculars over his shoulder and started walking toward the lookout point of which Abe had written in his note.

1011

The Battle of Punta Arenas

Punta Arenas lay across the Straits of Magellan from the British-American submarine pen in Useless Bay. As Abe eased the train into the railyard, the picturesque landscape was lit by a bright, full moon accompanied by the glistening river of the Milky Way and the dim glow of Sisyphus. Having slowed the train several kilometers prior, the aged engineer could see the forces north of the city, many of them staring in his direction. They were curious of the strange noise but were unable to see more than a shimmering shape above the rails.

A glance toward the wharf and Abe could see the merchant cargo ship that the rag-tag army intended to use as its means of crossing, once the defensive armaments were destroyed.

Turning his IR goggles toward the night sky, Abe could see six drones circling the horizon over the shore near Useless Bay. He knew that they would be able to see him once the 20mm turret was uncovered. He would have to work fast. He pulled the cord for the whistle as the train lurched to its rest, then turned to take his place at the turret.

In the next instant, the terrible shaking came and tossed Abe to and fro inside the control room. For a moment, he considered if his whistle had unleashed all the demons of hell. *An earthquake?* Abe thought, as he collected himself, scrambled out of the cab and headed for the turret.

The five freight cars opened and, despite the temblor, the hordes of ARM units poured forth with the five android commanders leading their advance. Arrayed in cloaks of Mimic, the ARM units appeared to the opposing troops as phantoms swarming toward them amid an earthquake.

As if that visage was not chilling enough to the onlookers of the siege, the army of spectral warriors rushing toward them was led by five shimmering, ghost-like captains wielding large scythes.

Doug made it to the lookout point in time for the earthquake to knock him to his knees. Picking himself up and lifting the binoculars, he could see the rebel troops begin dropping amid an invisible wave of what he knew must be the cloaked army of androids. He caught the occasional glimpse of moonlight reflections off the scythes and saw explosions of ARM units as they destroyed armored vehicles. Some of the androids began losing their cloaks in the intensity of the melee unveiling their silvery, skeletal structure. The visible and invisible battlefield was at once chaotic and precise in its ruthlessness.

Twenty minutes into the battle and Abe had not yet revealed himself in the turret. The drones were not yet in range, though Doug could see their rapid approach. Watching the patterned, uniform and simultaneous movements of the drones, Langstrom was now certain that no human was in control of them. DEX was the author of this mayhem.

"How many more thousands of us will you use as pawns in your game?" Doug said. He realized that such an attack of a cloaked robotic army was contrary to the general conventions of war. He knew that, despite the importance of winning this battle, humans must never again use such underhanded tactics when battling other humans.

"He's over here!" Bobby said.

Doug turned to see Bobby Hicks coming up the trail from the tracks. The youthful programmer was soon followed by Joan, Nalya and Lucy. It was not until that moment that Doug realized that he and Abe had led such a young, inexperienced group toward such a horrible battle. A wave of self-awareness swept over him. He felt as if he'd been living as some modern Ahab in pursuit of his own white whale.

"How are you here?" Doug asked.

"Abe left each of us a note along with a farewell gift," Joan said, "Nalya, sensing your absence, was the first to find her note. She woke the rest of us and we came here as soon as we could."

"Abe is firing at the drones," Bobby yelled.

Doug turned to see that Abe had indeed rolled back half the Mimic covering of the flatbed railcar and was lighting up the sky with incendiary rounds from the twin turret guns. The first target of his barrage soon crashed into the abandoned downtown streets of Punta Arenas.

Abe took advantage of the patterned attack of the drones and downed two more before DEX began flying evasive patterns. The three remaining drones flew haphazard paths toward the source of the double-A onslaught.

"They're targeting the turret now," Doug said, "Come on old man! Take the one at your ten o'clock first."

"Yes!" Bobby screamed as he saw the drone fall.

***

Beta aerial unit destroyed, alpha and delta unit intact – ordinance deplete. Target evasive flight path to direct intercept of incoming ballistic projectiles source. Enhance image of target – Halt. Center image and enhance human target. Human facial features obscured – identification compromised – Imperfect, partial match. Project sixty-three percent match to Langstrom, Doug. Calculating. Ninety-one percent probability of Doug attempting to subvert facial appearance in order to prevent identification. Target identified – Doug Langstrom. Recalculating primary objective – Terminate Doug Langstrom

***

"Take out the twelve o'clock, Abe," Doug said, "The three o'clock is climbing away."

As if he heard the voice of his friend, Abe focused on the drone heading straight for the turret. He managed to clip its starboard wing sending the drone into an off-balanced, awkward roll. The drone's new path ended with an abrupt interception of the earth a few dozen meters to the left of Abe's turret.

"Got him!" Bobby screamed, "One to go."

Doug soon discovered that the ascent of the final drone had not been a retreat from the engagement. The craft was above Abe and rolling into a terminal vertical dive toward the turret.

"It's above you Abe!" Doug yelled, knowing that his friend could not hear him.

Abe scanned the sky trying to locate the last drone. By the time that he realized where the craft was, he knew it was too late to bring the twin guns to bear upon it. Mustering a long-ago atrophied agility, Abe dove out of the turret and scrambled toward the empty, armored caisson to the rear of the flatbed.

The drone struck the turret at extreme velocity, obliterating the guns and splitting the flatbed in two. The fireball of the explosion sent a shiver through the observers at the lookout point above the battlefield.

Doug scanned the wreckage looking for any sign of life, then said, "He's okay!" as Abe crawl from the caisson. He then handed the binoculars to Nalya.

Nalya let out a sigh of relief as she saw Abe begin walking toward the engine. She then scanned the battlefield to find the remaining enemy troops fleeing from the ARM units. As the troops dropped their arms, the androids halted their pursuit. She watched the retreating troops as they made their way toward the wharf in hope of safety aboard their ship anchored there.

"Why is the water running away?" Nalya asked.

Doug took back the binoculars and soon saw that the merchant ship was now listing as it sat on the muddy seabed below the wharf. He scanned out to see that the water had receded several hundred meters beyond the ship. Then the memory of the earthquake returned to him.

"Tsunami!" Doug yelled.

Helpless to prevent the onrush of sea that soon followed, Doug stood, stoic in his appearance as he watched the water scour the landscape. The deluge intermingled the troops, their weapons and vehicles as well as the androids with thousands of pieces of flotsam and jetsam.

Doug could see small debris, bodies, and crumpled submarines tossed about the strait like so much refuse and wreckage. The unkind soup flowed forth with relentless resolve filled with souls and the soulless, the mixture abusing and washing the locomotive ahead until the mighty engine tipped under and continued rolling with the ferocity of the churn.

Doug Langstrom continued watching for many minutes as the water receded and came again, then receded and came the third time. In the moonlight, Nalya, Joan, Bobby and Lucy could see vague figures in the rapid ebb and flow. They voiced gasps and cries of horror, though they could not see the worst of the destruction as Doug witnessed it with the powerful field glasses. Good and evil, soul and circuit, all lost in the dark depths of the deluge.

The ocean's onslaught spent, Doug lowered the glasses and turned toward his four companions. They were now sobbing, moonlit ashen figures all. He felt the piercing visage of their tearful eyes. Crashing hard upon the dam he'd buttressed for so long now. So many friends, so much of humanity lost.

"Abe?" Joan asked between sobs.

Doug shook his head and found that the small movement was too much as it did, at last, burst the dam. Doug Langstrom could no longer hold back his tears.

***

The walk was long and silent as the group made their way back to gather their things and begin the journey north and home. As they entered the railyard, Doug was reminded of something the group had said when they first reached the lookout point.

"What were the gifts?" he asked.

"What?" Joan asked, confused by his question.

"You said Abe left a gift with the notes he wrote for you," Doug said, "What gifts did he leave?"

"I have a locket with a picture of my husband and son who were taken by the Blue Plague," Joan said, "Abe fashioned a chain from some gold wire he found at Cheyenne Mountain."

"I knew him the least but he left me that old book that he carried with him everywhere," Lucy said.

"I know that book well," Doug said, "I read that story to my wife many times."

"He left me his Medal of Honor," Bobby said as he opened his cloak to reveal the medal draped about his neck.

"Abe was a Medal of Honor recipient?" Lucy asked.

"Yes," Bobby said, "He always said that he didn't deserve it."

"They all say that," Doug said, "It's a common trait among them. Regardless of what he said, we can all now agree that Abe deserved the honor."

"What gift did Abe leave you, Nalya?" Joan asked.

Nalya looked up at Doug and said, "The best gift of all."

***

As the group made it back to the passenger cars to gather their things, Lucy noticed the mast that they had used to monitor the distress broadcasts of the submarine base. She thought of the First Nations people the group encountered on their trek to the south and knew she had a great mission ahead of her.

"Doug, can we send a message to NORAD on the shortwave?" She asked.

"Sure, as long as it is coded," Doug said, "What do you have in mind?"

"I want to have Saul bring some of the Guardians of the Gate and my daughter to join us," Lucy said.

"You're planning a long-term stay in the Andes, aren't you?" Doug sighed.

"These people need our help," Lucy said, "They will also need to learn the stealth and camouflage techniques that you have taught to the Wazhazhe and the others of your group."

Doug mulled over Lucy's words considering how they could mean spending many months in the Andes, further postponing his journey home to Tacoma. Since his revelation and the loss of Abe, Doug had returned to his thoughts of going home to Tacoma. Despite his desires, he knew that Lucy was right. DEX would never give up trying to destroy humanity. He realized humanity must be taught about the occupant of Sisyphus and how to avoid its treachery until such time as its light dims on its own or someway is found to extinguish it.

"Knowing one's enemy is crucial to overcoming in war," Doug paraphrased.

"That's my point," Lucy said, "We have to teach them how to survive DEX."

1100

Two Years Later, Near Tacoma

Once they had extracted all the useful technology and destroyed its warfare tech, the Protectors sealed the access points to NORAD Central Command. Likewise, Doug assured Lucy that ACER was secure. When he left it more than three years prior, he flooded the entire facility with nitrogen and camouflaged the entrance well. Since he was the last living person who could access the biometric entry codes, there was little need to spend years destroying the massive facility.

Doug, Nalya, Lucy and Rae now rode in the carriage on the deserted highway leading to Tacoma. They were followed by their mounted entourage, Graham, Saul and Jumping Fox. After months of hard work in the Andes and the Rockies, Doug was making his trek home, accompanied by his daughter and their friends.

"It's just a couple of kilometers ahead," Doug said, "there's a big granite boulder just before a trail up a small slope to the right of the highway."

"If we're getting close, perhaps we could have a small picnic when we get there," Lucy said, turning to Saul, she added, "Perhaps you guys can ride back to the orchard we passed a little way back and pick us some of those apples."

Saul Cautious-Hawk looked at Lucy as if he were about to ask her why they had not stopped earlier. Realizing that she had not known how close they were to Doug's plot until a moment prior, he turned his horse and rode back to the roadside grove with Graham and Jumping Fox following.

Nalya was curious to see the small plot of land her dad had told her so much about. She had lost interest in the language lesson that Lucy was teaching Rae. Lucy was counting numbers in Sanguine, the homogenized language compiled from the tribes of the Northwest.

"Is Ellen's marker large?" Nalya asked.

"Not large, as far as twin markers go," Doug said, "You'll see soon enough."

"I like this land," Nalya said.

"You do?" Doug asked.

"There is a sense of Eden about it," Nalya said, "a sanctuary from the apocalypse that is beyond the great divide. We can live here in peace."

"Ten, eleven, twelve, thirteen," Lucy prompted.

"En, En-wan, En-tu, En-tré," Rae said, the pride in her accomplishment evident in her voice.

The carriage rounded the curve past the large boulder and were confronted by two women, each wielding submachine guns. Pulling the carriage to a halt, Doug looked to his right to find a man and a third woman now standing atop the boulder. They too were armed with submachine guns.

"Is that him?" the man atop the boulder asked.

"It's him," the answer came from the left of the trail.

As a second man followed by a fourth woman stepped from the brush of the berm, Doug turned to see a face he recognized. It was that of Nigel Singleton, the British ambassador to Russia. Confused by the sight of a man he had not seen in ten years, Doug sat in silent contemplation, trying to understand the situation.

"I see that you are a little confused to see me here," Nigel said.

"Who are you, why are you here and why have you stopped us?" Lucy asked.

"Doug knows me as Nigel Singleton," Nigel said, "my real name is beside the point. We have been waiting here for Doug Langstrom for several years."

"You have been waiting *here* for years?" Nalya asked.

"Don't be ridiculous child," Sophia said, "You tripped one of our sensors."

Nigel shot a look of disdain at Sophia, who frowned and cast a harsher gaze toward Doug. The potential peril of the situation sent Lucy into negotiation mode, stalling until Saul, Graham and Jumping Fox could arrive.

"I'm sure there is no need of those guns. We are quite peaceful and unarmed. Perhaps if we knew what you wanted, we could help you," Lucy said, "Why did you stop us?"

"Peaceful?" Charles said, spitting the word out as if it were a bug that had just flown into his mouth.

"We stopped you to get some answers," Nigel said, this time casting his look of derision toward Charles. He then motioned for Doug to get out of the carriage.

"Answers to what?" Doug asked.

"Step down from the carriage," Nigel said.

As Doug handed her the reigns, Lucy grabbed his arm leaned in close and whispered, "Stall."

Lucy watched as the two women who had blocked the road searched Doug and then tied his arms behind his back. Lucy touched Nalya's arm signaling for her to remain calm and directing her attention toward the berm. The brush had taken on a shimmery haze. Nalya blinked as if to clear her blurry vision, then realized that a Mimic clad warrior was squatting amid the brush behind Nigel.

"What are the secret American access codes for DEX?" Nigel asked.

"Friend, if I knew a way to access DEX in order to shut it down, I would have done so long ago," Doug answered.

"I am not your friend," Nigel said, "We are not looking to shut DEX down, we want to control it."

"Who is we?" Doug asked.

"We will get the codes from you," Nigel said, ignoring the inquiry, "You will not let your friends suffer."

Nigel then motioned for Sophia and Jenny to take Lucy, Nalya and Rae out of the carriage. Jumping Fox knew that it was time to act. He was now positioned upon the boulder behind Charles and Annette. Seeing the tell-tale shimmers that meant the others were also in position, he let out a whip-poor-will call.

Graham and Saul were first to act, their movements betrayed by the slightest of shimmers from either side of the roadway. Graham was behind Sophia and Jenny with his Mimic de-energized and his twin pistols trained on them before either of the women knew what was happening. As Jumping Fox moved toward Charles atop the boulder, he lost his footing and piled hard into the unsuspecting man.

Resisting his assailant, Charles struggled to turn and face the threat. As the entwined men fell from the rock, Saul struck Nigel hard, knocking him to the ground. He then turned and disarmed Mary Ashen as she struggled to focus on the elusive target the Mimic-covered Protector presented.

Alone atop the boulder, Annette realized that their group had been out maneuvered. She raised her assault rifle with a deliberate determination. Graham saw her movement and trained a pistol upon her just as she put three rounds into the back of Doug Langstrom. A moment later, the dead assassin slid down the sloping side of the boulder, a bullet in her chest.

***

Jumping Fox, Annette Sharps and Charles Nix lay dead in the aftermath of the failed capture of Doug Langstrom. Nigel Singleton, Mary Ashen, Jenny Lion and Sophia Smyth were secured by Graham and Saul, who then joined Lucy and Nalya who were attending their fallen leader.

Nalya held her father's head in her lap as he lay dying. Lucy and little Rae knelt close beside them, both weeping. Saul touched the shoulder of his new wife and knelt beside her to provide what comfort he could.

"Don't try to talk daddy," Nalya said as Doug raised his arm, gesturing toward the trail up the hill.

"Take me up there," Doug whispered.

Saul and Graham lifted Doug and placed him in the carriage and Lucy drove the team up the small trail to a wide, open spot on a high meadow. There they found the grave marker of Ellen Langstrom, lifted her husband from the carriage and lay him near the granite stone.

"Can you smell the grass and the wildflowers?" Doug asked, his voice continuing to weaken, "Ellen loved to picnic here. After we moved to Texas, we often talked of retiring here and picnicking every afternoon."

Doug then leaned his head against the cool, smooth stone of Ellen's marker and sighed. After so many years, he could again see the white top of Mount Rainier.

"Our wait is over, my Dearest," were Doug Langstrom's final words as he looked out upon the valley between the hill and the mountain.

Through her tears, Nalya asked, "What does the epitaph say?"

The words were engraved in a language with which Nalya was not familiar. Lucy looked at the words and thought back to the book that Abe had given her. She remembered Doug saying that he was quite fond of the old tome. Lucy sighed and smiled through her own tears; her suffering somewhat relieved with her newfound understanding of Doug.

She answered, "It's French and it reads, 'attendre et espèrer'. It is from the ending of an old novel. I believe it was Ellen's favorite book, which Doug used to read to her before she passed away. It means 'wait and hope'."

"Will you teach me French," Nalya asked.

"Of course," Lucy said.

Two Daughters

It is true that my mother helped the Protectors shed the confining ways of the old world and led us into a new frontier. She broke those chains that bound us, allowing for our freedom to flourish as it had in the days before colonialism, before the Europeans came and destroyed much of the land, taking from it whatever it would yield. For all her abilities to free us, there was one set of chains that Lucy Benson Cautious-Hawk could never quite sever. She could not endure to forget those who helped to make her who she was or who she would become. It is undeniable that there were evil people among those of the former world. My mother chose to remember the best of the others, the virtuous of those who are now themselves almost forgotten among the Forgetful Ones.

Rae Benson-Wynn, First Teller of the Sanguine

***

My father once told me that, if you live long enough, you may even learn to *smell* the past. Well, I suppose I have now lived long enough to know that he was right. I can smell the horrible stench of death that hung in the air over Wawa when my father walked into that small Canadian town and found me. I still smell the diesel emanating from Big Muley as we made our way to New Hope. I smell the smoke of the fires of destruction of our former homes in Oklahoma and I can smell the wild flowers growing on the outskirts of the ruins of Tacoma as my father ended his long and winding journey home.

Nalya Langstrom-Hicks, First Teller of the Wazhazhe

Býleistr

Leaf One

Leaf One, Codex Twenty of Tribe Sanguine

Tribe Sanguine, I speak to you at the request of your venerable Teller, Rae Benson-Wynn. It is without malice that I must shun some of your long-held tradition in that, as a Teller, I speak not for myself alone but for many of those no longer among the living. Those voices of the departed are now, and must always be, the cherished property of all the tribes.

Last month, on the seventy-fifth anniversary of his death, I made the long journey north and visited the grave of my father. Mount Rainier stood in the distance, its ever-present resoluteness now looking as forlorn as I felt in remembrance of those days so many anni prior. With its regal crown of white gone and the cold winds that once brought the snow now bringing bleak clouds and carrying a warm, melancholy rain, the great mountain has, at last, earned its name in full.

The visible relics of the abuses of the abundant resources of the old world have become a lasting scar upon our planet. Not content with one reminder of their folly, the inhabitants of that ancient society gifted us with an enduring sign of their errors in heaven above. From the disfigured land, we now carve out a new existence beyond simple unity, being built upon a natural and mutual community of cooperation. Under the indominable, malignant sign but always mindful of its presence, we resist the judgement of extinction its occupant has pronounced upon us.

Our greatest means of resistance will be our memories. I am the first Teller of Tribe Wazhazhe just as Rae Benson-Wynn is the first Teller of Tribe Sanguine but we will not be the last. As our suns are setting, we stand at the point of a unique twilight between the new dawn and the old dusk. The new dawn will shine its light upon those who, with their own eyes, did not see the old world and the destruction wrought by its inhabitants. The Tellers and Scribes who come after me will have that same solemn duty to mold their present into a connective membrane that binds their history with their future.

I speak of the qualities that all Tellers must have, such as the sagacity of the solemn duty and honor that the position requires and the patience of listening to the point of full understanding. These qualities of character are of vital importance to Tellers but another characteristic may be the most important of all. Bravery is not something that we often associate with someone who is a historian. Let me state without any subtlety or ambiguity – historians must be brave enough to state the truth about the events to which they are eye witnesses. Without the bravery to tell, not just the emperor but the entirety of the future, that the leader was indeed naked, history can never be trusted.

In dark times, truth may suffer grave and vicious attacks by those who wish their misdeeds or even just their less charitable actions to remain hidden. Bravery is prerequisite to a stalwart defense against such assaults. It is often difficult to speak the truth and, on occasion may be even more challenging to defend it. It was once said that the pen is mightier than the sword but I know many warriors brave enough to take up a sword yet few willing to combat sword with pen. This is why I believe with all sincerity that the veracity needed by Tellers requires honor, a sense of solemn duty but, most of all, bravery.

Before I make my return journey home to the lands of the Wazhazhe, I leave you with this reminder of your mission. Scribes, I implore you to continue to write and Tellers, I beseech you to continue to speak so that all may continue to live not in ignorance but in an abundance of knowledge. Before the writing there was the telling and before the telling there was the living. For, though those survivors beyond the great divide may forget all knowledge, we the Tellers, the Scribes and the Living Protectors will remember so that we do not become like them, the Forgetful Ones.

Nalya Langstrom-Hicks First Teller of the Wazhazhe

Leaf Two

Leaf Two, Codex Five Hundred and Fifty of the Wazhazhe Tribe

I, Dancer, come before the Teller and Scribe of Tribe Wazhazhe to recount my experiences near the Western Sea. A month after the great comet's passing, as my son, Indaygo, and I brought our fishing skiff into a small cove, we saw a star falling from the southwest and lighting the evening sky. The radiance of the star appeared to grow brighter and then dim as it slowed in its approach toward the water.

As our amazement increased, we saw three great wings extend from the star. The wings were round and hovered above the star, which then blasted fires from beneath. As the star grew closer, we could see that it was in the shape of a great flagon with riggings connecting the wings to its top and causing it to sway beneath the great round extensions.

Our initial awe soon turned to terror as a second star appeared, followed by a third and a fourth and we wanted to flee but were both frozen with fear. Watching in our catatonic state, we realized that each of the flagon-shaped stars were great ships, which floated upon the water as they landed upon the Western Sea.

A few moments after the great ships landed upon the water, dozens of smaller ships came out of each of the flagon ships and began heading toward the coast. Startled from our rigid state, my son and I pulled our skiff onto the beach, covered it with its Mimic tarpaulin and donned our cloaks, intent upon watching the approaching fleet in secret.

Several of the ships approached the cove but soon realized their drafts would not allow entry into the shallow waters. Several skiffs then disembarked from one of the larger ships and made their way toward the cove. When we at last could see those aboard the skiffs, we were further astonished at their appearance.

The skiffs were crewed by creatures of two distinct types. The first type had skin that was rough in its appearance and of scarlet color. They were of greater musculature build than the second type of creature. This first type also had yellow eyes that seemed to glow in the light of the moon, now visible in the evening sky. As one of the scarlet creatures came very close to us, we saw that its eyes had two irises, conjoined in the middle and containing two pupils that were eerie in that their contractions were independent, each from the other.

The second type of creatures had skin that shone of a golden color. Their hair and eyes appeared as the amethyst stones such as are found to the south and east of the InDees Mountains. The golden humanoids were taller than the scarlet ones but of a modest, thin build. The eyes of the golden ones had large irises but were not doubled like the scarlet ones.

As we continued to watch the creatures on the beach, an argument broke out among them. Their words were not in the Wazhazhe language and difficult to understand. The dispute seemed to be about the place they had landed and that the terrain would be difficult for their purposes. A scarlet one then struck another of his kind so that he fell upon the beach and did not get up. The aggressor then gave a command and the crews boarded their skiffs to go back to the larger vessel, leaving the fallen one behind.

After some extended time, the larger ships sailed south and, once my son and I felt secure, we approached the scarlet one who lay on the beach. Though bleeding from a wound on his head, the fallen one was alive. We managed to bandage his head and assuage the bleeding so that we could bring him to our home to further care for him, which we have been doing for the three dawns since.

When the creature recovers, we will bring him before the Wazhazhe council so that his appearance may attest to the truth of my words. If we are able to understand the creature's words and his ours, perhaps the council may understand the reasons that he and the others have come to us and the mysteries of their spectacular and unique fashion of travel through the sky in large bottle-shaped ships.

Leaf Three

Leaf Three, Codex Four Hundred and Eight of the Huancas Tribe

Chief Talia and Teller Anya, I thank you for granting me this audience to testify of my experience before the people and the Council of the Huancas. My name is Hawkeye Kalar, the last member of the Kuikuro Tribe, and I am convinced that the tale of my journey and the desolation of my people is of great and pressing importance to the Huancas people and all the Protectors.

For generations, my people, like many others among the Protectors, had lived in peaceful cooperation with the people of the eastern swamplands, the Forgetful Ones. We traded our goods and the food of our land for the surplus of their fisheries and the bounty of their crops. Our children played together and we speak to them in their languages and they speak to us in ours. It is little wonder that our people would come to the defense of the Forgetful Ones when they were attacked by the evil ones of scarlet and gold.

The invaders came upon the eastern lands three anni prior, just two months after the great comet, which many said was a foreboding of a coming tribulation. The scarlet ones are muscular and sinewy with yellow eyes, a rough, red skin and a bewitching tongue of many voices. The golden ones are taller and thinner and more handsome. They have a smooth and shiny skin and amethyst eyes and hair. The scarlet ones commanded the golden ones as they enslaved the Forgetful Ones and forced them to create and tend great orchards of a strange, foreign fruit.

At first, the Kuikuro Tribe decided to try to raid the encampments of the invaders and free our friends among the Forgetful Ones but we too were captured and enslaved. As you know, freedom and self-determination are among the most essential tenets of the Protectors. We cannot endure slavery and we rebelled against our captors many times over the past two anni and tried to escape our captivity. They slaughtered us without mercy, many in public executions as a warning to the others, both Protectors and Forgetful Ones. At last, all of the Kuikuro were killed or died of the harsh bondage until I alone remained.

My friends among the Forgetful Ones did not forget me. They hid me and helped me escape so that I might bring this word of warning to all the Protectors of the mountains and the jungles. I fear that many of those who helped me may have been punished or even executed.

If it pleases the Council of the Huancas, I request that I may be granted sanctuary among you and that word of my travails may be told among all the tribes so that the evil of the Scarlet and Golden Ones may be known to all. The invaders are strong and they have grown in number much since they first arrived. The Protectors of the InDees must beware of the plains and swamps to the east and take steps to guard their borders with vigilance, lest they become slaves or are extinguished as the Kuikuro peoples and many such eastern tribes of the Protectors have been.

Leaf Four

Leaf Four, Codex Four Hundred and Eight of the Huancas Tribe

Hawkeye Kalar, on behalf of the Council of the Huancas, it is our honor to grant you sanctuary among the Huancas peoples. We can further confirm that your words have been verified and our Scribe has recorded them among the codices of the Huancas Tribe. You may be amazed or perhaps even confused as to how it is that we can verify your words so soon after you have uttered them.

The reason the council is so well prepared to believe your otherwise implausible tale is because you are not the first to have brought us word from the afflicted tribes of the eastern plains and swamps and we do not believe you will be the last as many have suffered under the hands of the Scarlet and Golden Bottle Children.

Beyond the accounts of the witnesses who have survived the mistreatment of the invaders, we have seen the aggressors with our own eyes as they probed our borders, which we guard with as much vigilance as you and others before you have stressed that we should.

In truth, it was just as easy for this council to verify the words of the survivors of those prior and ongoing aggressions because we have heard the tale of the Scarlet and Golden Bottle Children from one of the Scarlet Ones. He was wounded by one of his own and left for dead on the coast of the Western Sea. Found by fishers of the Wazhazhe Tribe, Dancer and Indaygo, he was healed of his injuries and sought sanctuary among them.

Known among the Protectors as Beekeeper, the Scarlet One has traveled among the tribes for many months recounting the telling of the people he calls the Rubicund and how and why they came to live among the Forgetful Ones and the Protectors. The message is more frightening and intense when the telling is coming from a Scarlet One and delivered by his tongue of many voices as you have so well described it.

We will continue to be vigilant in our duty as Protectors. While we may not have the capacity to repel this invasion and free the imprisoned Forgetful Ones, we are confident, based on the account of Beekeeper, that our lands present a measure of security against the ambitions of the invaders. We will use this to our advantage as we study the threat of the newcomers and gain a better understanding of their ways and, in particular, their weaknesses. Concerning learning of such weaknesses of the invaders, which the knowledge of may provide us an advantage, we have addressed many questions to Beekeeper and, though he has cooperated much, he may have limited insight into the frailties of his own race.

When you are rejuvenated from your harrowing travails and your anni of unjust servitude, we will have a Huancas scouting party take you to the Wazhazhe so that you may hear Beekeeper's account, in his own voices, for yourself. In the meanwhile, rest in the assurance that the Protectors are alerted to the peculiar danger that the Scarlet and Golden Bottle Children present.

Leaf Five

Leaf Five, Codex Five Hundred and Fifty of the Wazhazhe Tribe

First, I ask that the Council of the Wazhazhe peoples forgive my poor use of the common language of this planet. It has been the custom of my peoples for many generations to use an abbreviated form of the language known to us as 'Glish. Though it may seem implausible to you now, I am convinced that, from what I am about to recount, you will come to understand that our truncated linguistics are rooted in your common language.

Next, I would like to thank Dancer, his mate Sasha and his son Indaygo for nursing me back to health. I was given a severe wound by the commander of our landing party due to his abrupt outburst of anger over a disagreement I had with him. I will recount the full details of this matter later in my narrative, when it is appropriate to do so.

I would also like to thank the Council and the Wazhazhe peoples for their generosity to me. It is becoming clear to me that there is such kindness among your race as is undeserving of any of my people. There seems little doubt that this is a fact with which you will be in agreement once you have heard the entirety of my account. Even more so once you have come to know the potential for brutality that is part of the inherent survivalist instincts of my people.

My name is Býleistr. Since your race does not have the ability to speak in choir, the pronunciation of my name may be quite difficult for you. To make it easier and to prevent any unintentional insult to me by an inadvertent mispronunciation, you may refer to me by the name Beekeeper, which is of similar meaning.

My people call ourselves the Rubicund; the first and most obvious reason being the color of our skin. We are also proud wearers of the color of our former, adopted home planet, Ares. You may know Ares as Mars, the fourth planet from the sun. Though we are, by any technical definition, Martians or Aresians, we are not native to the red planet. Our original home was here, on Terra.

The people that became the Rubicund colonized Mars many millennia prior, in the time of the Great Civilization. The Venerable Empire of the Terrans once reigned supreme in this system, from Nabu to Titan. The citizens of the empire traveled to and fro among the planets and asteroids at will for untold anni, until the sentient awaking of the enemy, the long-lived lord and master of Sisyphus, the Dex.

Since that dark time, the Aresians and Terrans have existed in near ignorance the one of the other. In truth, the Terrans have forgotten all their former colonies. Four of the seven colonies fell within two anni of the coming of the Dex, they being dependent upon direct resupply from Terra. Over the centuries, the Aresians maintained covert contact with the remaining two colonies, Üropa and Titan, until Titan also fell, leaving Ares and Üropa alone.

Though the generations of genetic modification for sheer survival have left our two peoples with differences, the collective of the Aresians and Üropans are the Rubicund. It seemed ever more fitting that the surface of the Jovian moon Üropa, in which subsurface sea the Üropans lived, was similar to the color of their skin as was Ares to ours. The auric imbued geysers of Üropa that gave its surface the gold-dusted look, led the Terrans there for the richness of the moon's core but Dex awoke and destroyed the Great Civilization before those riches could be exploited.

Forgive me if my narrative is a bit rambling but it is important that you understand that the Rubicund, both the Scarlet and Golden Ones, as Dancer has labeled us, are forever linked in our mutual status as the forgotten orphans of Terra. The colonies of Üropa and Titan always considered themselves our brethren, having been founded from the Ares colony several anni before the awakening of the Dex. Though our worlds were separated by the vast divide of space and lying on either side of the Asteroid Ring, we were each doomed to similar fates. This mutual fate, a looming potential for our extinction is what, at last, brought the final two siblings together as we found a new way to survive.

As I earlier alluded, Dex was able to devise or, through lack of action, allow destruction for four of the colonies. First the small colony on Sisyphus fell by direct combat. Luna, Nabu and Ceres were unable to support themselves without resupply from Terra and fell soon after Sisyphus. For all the unbridled power of the enemy, neither the Aresians, the Üropans nor the Titans could be attacked by direct action of the Dex.

It is not of particular importance to understand the fates of the other colonies. What is important, at least to understanding the Rubicund return, is that the colonies of Ares, Üropa and Titan failed due to Terran hubris. Perhaps the most egregious of these failures to be placed at the feet of our Terran ancestors is the tale of the Titans. It is fitting that I recount what I know of the colony of Titan in order for you to better understand how their fall was a wakeup call to Aresians and Üropans.

Leaf Six

Leaf Six, Codex Four Hundred and Twenty of the Cañari Tribe

The first thing you must understand about the Titans is that they have been gone for four hundred and seventy-nine anni. What I know of their civilization I learned from the electrographic historical archives of Elon City on Ares. Though I believe those records to be accurate, such histories of prior civilizations have a natural tendency to intermingle fact and legend until a mythical status may develop.

It was the original strategy of the Terrans that the colony would terraform Titan by first cleansing the atmosphere and allowing a natural process of warming to occur. To accomplish this, the Titans lived in dozens of floating terrafarms in the thick atmosphere of Saturn's largest moon. With the initial supplies of carbonic from Ares and water from Üropa, these terrafarms converted the atmospheric gases into nourishments for their hanging gardens. We know that the suspension gardens of Titan were once of such greatness that they extended so far below the intercity hawsers that they took much labor and many cycles to draw them in during the times of harvesting.

Though the Lord of Sisyphus awoke during the first stage and began the War of Endurance against the Terrans, neither the Aresians nor the Üropans had the ability to relocate the entire population of Titan. The Titans had little choice but to complete the terraforming of their new home without further assistance from their former one. Through fifteen generations they toiled until they had produced the largest conservatory in the solar system.

The Titans' floating organic cities dominated the skies of Titan as the moon continued to warm under the effects of their mastery of the chemistry of the atmosphere. Utilitarian to the extreme, their food, tools, clothing and homes were formed from nothing more than the flora they grew. Soaring through their dense skies with as much ease as the impressive thunderbirds of your mountains, the Titans rose to be the equals of their namesakes, the mythical predecessors of the Olympians. After ten millennia of peaceful existence, the Titans succumbed to the old enemy of their ancestors and, like their ancient mythos counterparts, their Great Civilization ended in conflict.

Two factions arose among the Titans. The Luddists favored a regression from the advanced technology that their civilization had obtained. They argued that the technology was destroying Titan and would lead to their ultimate downfall. The Erudists argued that continued advancement in technologies would allow their civilization to thrive for another ten thousand anni. What began as heated debates in the Titan Parliament soon devolved into open warfare between the factions.

The civil war of the Titans lasted a century and a half. When the conflict started, there were twenty-seven million citizens living in the sky of Saturn's largest moon. At the time of the last communication from Titan, there were fewer than two million. The Erudists, on the verge of defeat, claimed that the Luddists had irradiated the atmosphere, sealing the fate of the once great Titan civilization. All that remains of the Titans are our histories and the songs we sing in memoriam of those now gone.

The near perfection of transforming a gaseous, inhospitable moon of Saturn into an oasis of the Hü hegemony, took second place to the destructive ability of the latent nature of the Terran character. When any society that is founded in an equality of communalism achieves the pinnacle of success such as the Titans did, the natural course of events will lead toward conflict. It is inevitable that shared, equal power will leave some percentage of the population in wanting of more.

It is possible that some future generation of explorers may find the remnants of the former greatness that was the Titan civilization. We cannot know if such theoretical travelers among our system will find evidence of the former greatness among their destructive endings. It is our duty to remember them as best we can and let those future historians sort the final facts.

I thank the Council of the Cañari for their indulgence in allowing me to interject my longer accounting of the tale of the Titans. My usual digression into recounting their story is much shorter than the one that I have just imparted but my visit to your lands has awaken long-forgotten memories. When I saw the great creatures of the skies above your tribal lands, I was reminded of my youth and of my fascination with the histories of our one-time brethren of the Great Civilization of the Terrans.

As for the Aresians and the Üropans, the facts of history are far more certain because we have a living record of our civilizations. We have experienced successes and failures, the former witnessed by our survival, while our return to Terra testifies to the latter. Even though all of the colonies would fail, the brilliance that the Terrans displayed in the terraforming designs that were utilized by the Titans was no less impressive in their prior efforts as they established the permanent colonies on Ares and Üropa.

Leaf Seven

Leaf Seven, Codex Five Hundred and Fifty of the Wazhazhe Tribe

While it is true that the atmosphere of this planet is a little less massive than that of Titan, the Terran oceans pale in comparison to that of the smallest of the Galli moons, Üropa. It is said that there is more temperate liquid water under the ice of the Üropan home world than among the remainder of the planets and moons of the solar system combined.

The real genius of the Terrans was to found the Üropan colony using members of a single race of the old world. The consideration that governed such a remarkable decision was that, at the time, the colony would be the most isolated in the solar system. Living under the ice on Üropa would require a self-sufficiency that could come from but one group of Terran peoples, the Wajin. The great island civilization, so proficient on and in the oceans of Terra, was the obvious choice as colonizers of the isolated little icy moon of Jove. The submariner civilization they founded flourished there for ten millennia after the coming of the Dex, living cradle to grave in the contiguous ocean they call the Great Black Mare.

Many anni before the awakening of Dex, the Üropans were growing expansive farms of tangle, ogo, hijiki and hariotii in the sonaluma-lit underside of the thick crust of their ice-encapsulated sky. They harvested from immense schools of bigeye, yellowfin, moonfish and jack that soon filled all reaches of the Great Black Mare. These schools were the hunters of Üropa, feeding like wolf packs on even larger shoals of 'ardines, odd bobs, 'chovi and herrfish, those latter, in turn, foraging among the dense, teaming, cloud-swarms of copepods, krill and wanderers.

In the conception and realization of the Üropa colony, the Terrans crafted their masterpiece. They created a stable ecosystem on a foreign world and for ten thousand anni, the Great Black Mare reigned as the ice-clad aquarium, the beacon of the Jovian system whirring by in the sky of the gas giant. As the Lord of Sisyphus sought to destroy all life on the Terran home world, Üropa became a long lasting, living museum to the ingenuity of the Society of the Ancients.

As I have described and unlike Luna, Nabu and Ceres, the colonies on Ares, Titan and Üropa were designed to be self-sufficient. The technologies provided in the original Terran mission plans for Üropa were of specific need for their sufficiency and of limited use to the Ares. Still, over the millennia, our civilization developed needs for technology not foreseen by the Terrans. In short, we discovered that the foundations of the Aresian ecosystem was wanting.

For all those thousands of anni, the Aresians, Titans and Üropans shared technology in secret, whenever our communications were hidden to the Terran system and the persistent listening of Dex. The important thing to understand about this sharing of technology was that the vast majority of the knowledge flowed free out of Üropa with minute amounts flowing to the civilization of the Great Black Mare.

Titan and Ares were inhospitable places from the beginning of their colonization. Though, like Üropa, the colonies there were intended to be permanent settlements, their populations were meant to be nomadic, cyclic, inhabitants. Üropa was too close to Jupiter for efficient, direct travel to and from the Galli moon. The Terran scheme was that the Aresians and the Titans would shuttle between their respective colonies and Terra during anni when the triple conjunction of the launch windows was most suitable.

Close flybys of Üropa would pick up mined products and drop off any materials necessary for the colony. The ability to launch materials to high altitude with minimal energy expenditure via a manipulation of the icy moon's super geysers was a cornerstone of the Terran plans. The first cycle of shuttle trips was preparing for their inaugural round trip cycle when Dex awoke and ended the Terran capability of performing the initiating launch of the rendezvous sequences.

Without the cyclic rejuvenation of our populations, both the Titans and the Aresians suffered a lack of diversity among our respective genomes. Like a storm that can be seen far away on the horizon, the inhabitants of Ares and Titan were condemned to endure the slow devolution of genetic bottlenecking. Though from a single Terran race, Üropa was populated with by the genetic selection of individuals with the specific intent of avoiding such a bottleneck.

Unencumbered by the potential for a slow extinction of their civilization, the Üropans lived carefree lives in the great ocean of their home world. They shared their growing technology with their neighbors with no thoughts that their own ingenuity would be a weapon against them. Little did they know, the treachery of one of their brothers knew no bounds. The honest generosity and openness of the Üropans became the ultimate means of ruin for the wondrous civilization of the Great Black Mare.

Leaf Eight

Leaf Eight, Codex Four Hundred and Thirty-One of the Kunzas Tribe

The Terran plans of exploitation of the solar system hinged upon the Aresians. Slated as the cornerstone of their grand scheme to extract the resources from the colonies of Üropa, Titan and Ceres, any planning for a sustainable populous on Ares was non-existent. While it is true that the colony was meant to be permanent, the Terrans settled the Ares colony with the intent that the populous there would be the peripatetic citizens of the solar system.

The grandiose vision for the red planet was for it to become the interplanetary oasis, the pseudo-homeworld, to tens of thousands of well-educated, specialized transients living a nomadic existence. Those initial travelers to Ares did so either as a most convenient and lucrative occupation or for the raw excitement of the life of roaming among the planets.

The sentient emergence of the Dex became a rude awakening for the Terrans but no less so for the Aresians. Now stranded in their cosmopolitan oasis, the colony soon realized the necessity of concentrating on all those things related to survival and the inevitable requirement for self-sufficiency. The results of our first assessment of the situation left us with two immense obstacles toward that self-sufficiency: genetic bottlenecking of both our population and our agronomy.

Unlike the considerations given to Üropa and, to a lesser degree, Titan, our ancestral founders gave no thought to the demographics necessary for a sustainable breeding population. Nor did they give any regard to the natural course of the colonists' basic proclivities or, better stated, their desires to pursue such esprit de corps of survival that lead to procreation. With the realization that we might breed ourselves into extinction, the Aresians developed government eugenics and genetic engineering programs with the purpose of varying our limited genomic diversity.

Of equal importance to the Aresians survival was the pressing need for an acceleration of the technical progressions to our fledgling agriculture industry. While our neighboring colonists living in the Great Black Mare of Üropa had the advantage of both flora and fauna within their terraforming capacity, the Aresians and Titans were limited to agronomies based upon vegan sustenance. These two bottlenecking diversities would become interwoven beyond our ability to untangle them.

When the Dex awoke, the demographic moment that became frozen in time for the Aresian colony was unfortunate in that a mere third of our colony was female. Worse, half of those feminine citizens were fast approaching the limits of their utility for reproduction. The immediate need was thus to ensure that the gender of the populous be regulated, in particular, the first council of eugenics deemed it essential that every fertilization for the first generation should produce feminine progeny.

Those initial efforts at population control were successful, though with one unexpected peculiarity. To the surprise of the engineers, all of the firstborn citizens of the new Aresian civilization were twins. Intent upon securing equity among the genders, the bioengineers had succeeded in tripling the feminine population.

You might be excused for thinking this situation gave some power to the females of the Ares colony but you would be wrong nonetheless. The ancestral males of Ares ensured their enduring dominance of society by exerting themselves through their greater physical strength. Our forefathers treated the females as little more than chattel. Those great brood harems of the first Aresian civilization became our original sin of which we have been unable to find the moral courage to repent in full.

Despite our sins, or perhaps as punishment for them, the strides that were made began to change our physical attributes beyond any of our ancestors' original expectations or even their desires. Most of those differences you can see in my eyes, the scarlet color of my skin and you can hear in the choral nature of my voice. Those are the obvious, visual signs of our genetic manipulations. Far less apparent are the enhancements made to the longevity of my race.

After just a few generations of bioengineering, durability emerged as another of the primary foci of the Aresian forbearers' genetic research. They reasoned that long-lived generations provided additional opportunity at increasing our chances of passing beyond the genetic bottleneck they were facing. For millennia, we soldiered on, tinkering with and tailoring our genetics toward a long-term survival of the Aresian populous.

As the longevity of our race increased, our dependence on specific dietary nutrients grew. The Aresians formed a symbiotic relationship with a chemical present in a majority of our agronomy. We engineered our crops to produce more of the necessary chemical increasing a cycle of interdependence that we are now unable to break. This need for this chemical, known as chryst, placed a new bottleneck on the Aresians. The limited ability of dome-based agriculture available to us on Ares coupled with our longevity, required that restrictions be placed on our population.

Leaf Nine

Leaf Nine, Codex Five Hundred and Fifty of the Wazhazhe Tribe

At last, a few hundred anni prior to the present, the Aresian geneticists came to the conclusion that we could not stave off our decaying genome. Without an infusion of new genetic material and a new home, unbridled by the limited dome structures of Ares, our race would begin declining. The Assembly of Ares developed a single plan to achieve both objectives.

The civil war among the Titans prevented the Assembly of Ares from using them as witting or unwitting allies in the scheme to return to Terra with a new influx of genetic material. Therefore, with the focus placed on the Üropans, a campaign of disinformation and propaganda ensued in order to convince them that both civilizations should return to their original homeworld. The centuries long assault on the conscience of the Üropans at last convinced them to come to the aid of their brothers on Ares.

The ships that arrived in the Western Sea were among those of an armada of twelve transport ships built by the Üropans to travel to Ares. Once there, the massive ships settled into orbit around the red planet and rendezvoused with Aresian shuttle craft, which made dozens of trips ferrying Aresians and the agro-flora necessary for our survival.

Meeting our brothers, the Üropans, for the first time in ten millennia was jolting to us. We expected there to be differences but not as much as was so obvious from first sight. Though I am not privy to the new-formed plans of the Aresian geneticist, I must assume that there was a contingency for the possibility that the populations of our two colonies would no longer be compatible from a reproductive standpoint. The geneticists' schemes aside, it was essential that we complete the first phase of the Aresian plan for the survival of our race.

From Ares, the great ships traveled to Terra, which was the most perilous part of the journey. It was unknown what power Dex might have to prevent our journey should our travels be perceived as a threat. Traveling to Ares from Üropa was conducted during the Ares transition on the opposite side of the sun, while hidden from Dex. The trip to Terra from Ares would be afforded no similar convenient concealment. To our great relief, there was no interference from Dex.

Once we arrived at Terra, the twelve great ships divided into three tetrarchs. Tetrarch three, of which my ship was a part, landed in the Western Sea. The ships of tetrarch one landed in the Eastern Sea and those of tetrarch two landed in the South Sea, which lies between the Western and the Eastern Seas. I know that the other tetrarchs made safe landings but, as you know, I am not aware of the outcome of their missions due to my separation from my people.

Our landing party disembarked and made its way to the shore. The commander of the third tetrarch became angry because we had not found land that was acceptable for immediate cultivation for our crops. I argued with him that we should explore deeper into the forest for arable land but he was young and impetuous, and he feared the noises of the creatures that we could hear emanating from the unfamiliar depths of the jungle. In his anger, he struck me and that is the last I saw of either the Aresians or the Üropans, even to this dawn.

It is understandable that my former commander would be fearful of the creatures we heard in the jungles of the Wazhazhe. From the beginnings of the Ares colony there existed many floral species under the great domes of the red planet but only two species of fauna: The Rubicund and the sugarbee. The former was governed by the Assembly of Ares, while the latter was managed by a single individual in each of the dome gardens. These individuals were known as Býleistr, or Beekeepers.

I have now seen a large portion of the territories of the tribes of the Protectors and have become aware of many species of creatures, large and small, that pollinate the natural and the cultivated flora of Terra. I now understand that the Aresians will have little future use for Beekeepers on this planet.

I can take some solace in my imposed exile and retirement by the fact that the Beekeepers of Ares held one secret sacred among our brotherhood. The chryst that is so necessary for the survival of the Aresian Rubicund is found in abundance among the products of the sugarbee. Over the millennia, the Býleistr developed a process for the concentration of chryst to such degree that I have, on my person, enough of the substance to sustain me for many anni, well beyond my remaining longevity.

I, Býleistr, am what my people would call aged but that age is beyond your present understanding of the term. I was birthed eight anni after the last contact with the Titans, which makes my age four hundred and seventy-one anni, aged for an Aresian but ancient by Terran standards.

END OF CODEX TWO

Day of the Sanguine

En-shev

Eryl glanced around the dining hall as she sipped the soup that had been placed before her. The room was impressive considering it was in the private home of General Alland Sul. The long, ornate table sat under a series of three chandeliers, which seemed to consume more light than they transmitted. To her left, late evening sunbeams shone through dark, stained glass windows. The hazy, scattered light projected upon the marble floor a distorted image of an ancient battle scene depicting a slaughter of the Hü by the Rubicund.

To her right, Eryl looked at the enormous coldbox and listened to the echoing ting-ting of the massive block of ice as it melted and dripped through the grate and into the metallic gutter beneath. She felt the cool air moving across her brow as it wisped her hair. Above the coldbox, the granite mantle held several small sculptures and a bust of the General on either end.

Eryl remembered hearing a Teller of the Wazhazhe speak of the abstract notion that coldboxes were once called fireplaces, where fires burned, consuming wooden logs to heat homes against the cold seasons. *Cold seasons?* Eryl thought. After experiencing the oppressive climate of the Southern Plantations and the jungles of the Wazhazhe, she could not imagine such a thing as a cold season.

Moving her gaze up, Eryl stared at the pair of crossed swords framed by upright, ornate, ceremonial assegais on either side. She wondered if any of the weapons could be removed from their mountings. She shifted her feet just enough to feel the weight of the shackles that bound her to the chair. Eryl was sure that the chair was the heaviest chair upon which she'd ever sat. She knew that it would take her some time to drag it the distance to coldbox and, once there, it would be impossible to lift herself high enough to reach the swords.

Eryl let her imagination roam, considering what she would do if she could reach the brace of weapons. The thought ebbed as she recalled the brace of scimitar cats sitting alert on either side of her host at the other end of the table. With an involuntary reflex, she snapped her gaze toward where Sul sat watching her.

Sul pushed his empty bowl away as he rose from his chair and walked the short distance to the mantle. The full extension of his height allowed him to reach the hilt of the left sword of the crossed pair, which he released from its hooks. He swung the blade in a long arc and brought it up in front of his face as if to inspect the edge.

"These swords were crafted for the Emperor of Wajin, a long-extinct nation that existed in the time of the Society of the Ancients," Sul said, "The blades are constructed of a composite material that does not corrode and is impervious to breakage. They are as sharp this dawn as the dawn they were crafted by the Nōshū masters to the emperor."

Eryl resumed sipping her soup as she tried to ignore her captor, though the utterance of the word 'Wajin' had, in fact, piqued her interest. She wanted to question him on the subject but decided against engaging Sul since she considered that her greater desire was to absent his company. She heard the blade cut the wind with a swoosh as Sul again swung the weapon in his hand. The watchfulness of the scimitars bordered upon anticipation as globs of drool seeped from their elongated incisors. *How many ill-fated victims has he carved into morsels for his cats with those blades?* Eryl pondered.

"The wrappings on the hilts of these masterpieces have been replaced dozens of times over the millennia," Sul continued, "yet the blades remain unchanging. I have kept these since my youth as a reminder of the single great truth that the Gru do not like to change. This is why your existence, Eryl Syz, is an anathema to many of my race. It is a great mockery to us that an inevitable necessity to the survival of the Gru is, at the same moment, an abomination."

Eryl stopped sipping the broth and looked at Sul. She understood why the Gru considered her abhorrent. When she arrived at Sul's compound, the re-nurturers had examined her and found her to be pregnant with the child of a painted Hü. Under penalty of death, the masculine members of the lesser castes were not permitted to have relations with the feminine members of the higher castes. What she could not comprehend was how her existence could be a necessity of the Gru.

"I see you are confused," Sul said, returning the sword to its place above the mantle, "May I ask you a question?"

"Since that is a question, it seems that I have little choice in the matter of my great desire of silencing you," Eryl quipped.

Unoffended, Sul laughed, "Your impudence is refreshing. Nevertheless, my question to you is this: When was the last time you saw a Gru child?"

Eryl allowed her gaze to fixate on the nearest chandelier as she deliberated the question. She tried to recall her youth and whether any of her friends were Gru and soon realized that none were. Eryl then remembered the story of the Býleistr that the Teller of the Huancas had recounted on the eve of the Battle of Huila. She thought about how, at the time, the age of the Býleistr had been beyond anything of her most fanciful imaginations. Eryl had all but dismissed the tale as mythical among the Protectors. A sudden and sickening realization pierced her subconscious like a dagger as her gaze shot back to Sul.

"How old are you?" She asked.

Sul's confident aspect faltered for a moment. Eryl thought he seemed as someone with a great secret who had just been robbed of his ability to take pleasure in its revelation. As Sul's visage returned to its former image of the stalwart General of the Gru armies, his household staff brought the main course of the meal to the table, afterwards departing the room in a silence equal to that which hung about the ornate chamber.

"You are quite clever," Sul said, "but I think not so clever as you might imagine yourself to be. The Gru longevity is what has enabled your existence."

"In what way?" Eryl asked.

"The Gru are a dying breed. We have been living upon the brim of the abyss of our extinction for a dozen millennia," Sul said, "When our two races came to this planet, the Gru were determined to save ourselves with a radical new scheme. We needed an infusion of genetic material compatible with our own. At first, we supposed that the Loru would be well-suited to our purpose but soon discovered that we had diverged after ten thousand anni of separate natural and synthetic genetic influences. In truth, the ancient geneticist of the Gru had gone too far in their manipulations."

"Your intent was to use the Loru as breeding stock?" Eryl asked, finding herself repulsed and sickened by her own utterance of the subordinate moniker of 'Loru'. A quickening to the truth of the tale of the Býleistr telling was now boiling deep within. *I am NOT Loru,* she thought, *I am Üropan. I am Wajin. I am Hü.*

Dismissing her question, Sul continued, "The discovery of this unfortunate obstacle caused a change of direction in our forefathers' plans. Our ancestors then initiated a secret but ambitious and selective cross-breeding program among the Loru. The program was theorized to require as much as a few thousand anni. Realizing that the lines of failure and extinction might converge upon our path before the breeding program could be completed, the genetic engineers continued their efforts into improving our longevity."

"The Gru have treated us like chattel for millennia," Eryl accused.

"To be fair, only a handful of Gru were ever made aware of the details of the breeding program," Sul said, "The average Gru believes that the geneticists are continuing to make strides toward cloning. Many of my race cling to the fable that they will live forever in one new cloned body after the next. It is always quite amusing to hear those old bureaucrats and the useless elite discuss such nonsense at dinner parties."

"None of your diatribe explains my importance to Chancellor Mis," Eryl said.

"In the beginning, you were of little importance," Sul said, "just another addition to Mis' harem, which gave him more influence among those who knew that the plan was the merging of our races."

"Yet, for all your millennia of harems filled with Loru like me, you have not succeeded in your breeding program," Eryl said, "No child has ever come from a union between our races."

"Until we discovered the child now growing in you," Sul corrected.

The shock of Sul's casual revelation overtook Eryl as a slow, unforeseen upsurge of gooey muck. She had not anticipated that Chu or Lehu would have been drawn into the evil plans of the Gru. She could not fathom that the oppressed castes would partake in actions of such vile intent.

"How long have you included the Hü in your breeding schemes?" Eryl asked.

"The Gru have utilized moles among the lower castes since we arrived on this planet," Sul said, "It goes without saying that we would utilize many incentives in such covert efforts. Plying the useful idiots with access to the harems allowed us a particular opportunity to further our breeding program. If we are to reconstruct the superior race from the remnants of the diaspora, it becomes necessary for us to include even the backward primates of the lower castes."

"Superior Race?" Eryl asked.

"The superior race of purebred Terrans who spawned that great empire you may know as the Society of the Ancients," Sul said.

He believes the castes are devolved Terrans, Eryl thought, *He doesn't understand that the Hü are the Terrans. The Rubicund, both Üropans and Aresians are genetic mutations of the Hü!* She now felt an invasive, unwelcomed empathy for the misguided Gru.

Sul once again seated himself and began to devour the fried mushrooms and braised fish. Eryl picked at the identical plate with a nervous anxiety of what might become of her and her unborn child. She watched as her captor finished his meal, sat back in his chair and caressed the scimitars, the petting coaxing obnoxious, loud purrs from his pair of feline sentinels.

"How long am I to remain as your new favored pet?" Eryl asked.

"You are so much more than a pet, citizen Syz," Sul replied, "You represent the zenith of success for our long efforts. Over the next few months, you will be exhibited as that signature achievement at competitive tournaments and carnivals throughout Capital City."

Sul again rose from his seat and walked to the mantle. He lifted an ornamented trophy that was adorned with a figure depicting a masculine Gru wielding a longspear and aiming it for a distance throw. The General looked at the plate on the front of the award and smiled as a prideful sigh escaped his lips.

"I remember competing in the last such tournament," Sul said, "The energy of the roaring crowd was exhilarating. I look forward to the upcoming contests."

Eryl studied the semi-reverie musings of her captor as he admired his past achievements. She recalled from her history lessons that such tournaments had ceased more than a century prior. As she studied Sul, Eryl again wondered at the longevity of the Gru.

"How old are you?" Eryl asked again.

Sul again sighed, now as a sign of his great annoyance at the invasive interruption Eryl's question had achieved upon the fond remembrances of his former glory. The General returned to his seat, drank the last sip of his bloodwine then set the empty goblet upon the table. The feline sentries were now grooming themselves on the cool stonework floor in front of the coldbox.

"The question you ask is one that is considered rude among the Gru and one to which none would give the first thought toward an honest reply," Sul said, "That said, and in the good-natured spirit of the occasion and the forthcoming festivities, I will provide a response to your impolite question."

The wait staff again entered the hall to remove the service and re-fill the General's goblet. Eryl watched as Sul stared in an uncomfortable, knowing way at the feminine Loru who poured his bloodwine and wondered if the young attendant were a member of Sul's personal harem. She shivered at the sudden realization that she was now a sister concubine of the insane Gru.

After the wait staff exited, Sul said, "There have been three and a half centuries since the last Gru child was birthed. I was born two centuries prior."

***

Day could feel the heat of the setting sun on the back of his neck. Lying prone, his elbows sank into turf as he brought the viewscope to his eyes. He adjusted the magnetic field to manipulate the liquid lenses until he brought the large encampment of the Gru 5th Army into sharp focus.

The Gru had divided the two armies in the Southern Council between the northwestern and southeastern lands. The 5th Army were stationed to maintain control of the transport routes of bloodfruit produce and juice to the north and supplies to the south across the Carib Sea or via land along the North-South Highway of the Nicaran Isthmus. The 6th Army were to maintain control of the supply routes via the South and North Lant Seas.

During the one out of eleven anni that is the annum of the hypercanes, the raging of the superstorms in the North Lant and Carib Seas prevent all transport via sea. As this was the anni of the hypercanes return, Day and the other Protectors knew that the North-South Highway on the eastern shore of the Nicaran Isthmus would be the lone route for transport between the Western Council and the Southern Council. The highway was protected from the superstorms of the Carib Sea, like the Nicaran Jungle to its west, by the two thousand furlongs of the Great Sea Wall. With the victories of the rebels in the Central and Eastern Councils, defeating the Gru 5th Army now would cut off the supply of bloodfruit to the north for an entire annum.

Quietstar crawled up beside Day and tapped his shoulder. Dabrill looked at the silent warrior as he signed a question, "How many?"

"I make it ten thousand," Day said, "that's more than three to one. It would even the odds if we could activate our Mimic cloaks when we attack."

"It is forbidden," Quietstar signed.

"I know it is forbidden except as a defensive measure," Day said, "It would save a lot of lives though."

"You mean it would save a lot of *Protector's* lives," Quietstar signed.

Dabrill knew that Quietstar was right. Using the Mimic would save the lives of Protectors but would result in a massacre of the Gru. The Protectors considered attacking an enemy by such stealthy measures to be tantamount to a war crime. The Battle of Punta Arenas was fought many millennia in the past but the lesson it taught was well-learned. In all those thousands of anni, no tribe had again attacked an enemy in that way. Despite his mild argument for its use, Day agreed with the edict that an activated Mimic attack was and should be a forbidden tactic. *Attacking with the setting sun at our backs will have to be a good enough tactic against the superior Gru vision*, Day thought.

"Are Strongbark and Roughbark's troops ready?" Day asked.

"Yes," Quietstar signed.

"Good," he said.

Day, Quietstar and the better part of a thousand warriors under their command turned and shaded their eyes in order to mark the setting sun as it descended toward the summit of Black Knife, the chief peak in the Thunderbird Mountains. As the solar disk appeared to touch the shard-like pinnacle, the warriors turned and began their assault on the 5th Army Encampment.

***

Eryl was not impressed with the festivities and much less so with her seating arrangements. She was placed in the center of the section of the arena reserved for concubines among dozens of Loru from harems across the Western Council, yet adorned such that she still appeared as an outcast. She was clothed in a smock so white that it glowed against a background of concubines in bright cerulean.

Empty seats tapered away from the mass of harems on either side and served as a buffer between the concubines and the general attendance. Ivory in color and bearing the thin red lightning insignia of the 1st Army, the seats were a stark reminder of the real power of Capital City. Though her position at the center was encompassed by two dozen guards wearing the golden dress uniforms of the Gru Army officers, a concealed chain further secured Eryl to her stadium seat.

Eryl looked up at the large image viewer above the stadium as the wide view of the concubines was projected. She noticed how the group of concubines surrounding her appeared as a blue iris inside a bloodshot sclera with a golden pupil in the midst. Her bright, bleached white sartorial gleamed in the epicenter of the gilded pupil as if she was arranged to be the sparkle in the eye-image. *Always true to yourself, Crimson Dæmon, devious in your details,* Eryl thought.

The image on the stadium view screen panned away from the concubines and toward the entrance of the arena where a group of contestants were running up the ramp and onto the field. A roar of applause greeted the challengers as they entered the arena. The final event of this dawn's festivities was the assegais competition. Leading the entrants, General Sul bathed in the adulation of the large assembly, allowing it to wash over him like a cooling rain.

The assembly listened as the announcer recounted the history of the assegais competition. Though no games such as these had been held in many anni, Eryl knew from the histories that the assegais competition was ancient. The weapon of war originated, millennia prior, on the 'Haran desert continent, when the land there was green and habitable. Eryl recalled the assegais trophy and the ornate, ceremonial versions of the weapons on either side of the coldbox mantle in Sul's dining hall.

Eryl looked out upon the arrangements prepared on the field of competition. A dozen green-lit, pulsing spherical targets, each the size of a head of cabbage, were positioned in a circle about the competitor's knoll, a chest high mound in the center of the arena. The targets were affixed atop suspensor drones designed to transport them away from the contestant, each on a different, preset, evasive path toward the perimeter of the arena.

Points were scored by the contestants by their hitting of the target spheres before the drones carrying them could reach the edge of the arena, half a furlong from the knoll. The field was adorned with three concentric zones beginning in green at the center, progressing to yellow then a narrower red zone near the perimeter. The farther the target from the knoll, the higher the points scored. The scorekeeper would award ten points for each hit while the target was over the green zone, twenty-five points while above the yellow zone and fifty points for each hit on the red perimeter. Hitting all twelve targets doubled the final score.

The first contestant moved to the leveled plateau on the summit of the knoll. The arena announcer declared him to be Commander Pel Solat, an officer of the 1st Army. His traditional arms-bearer stood a few paces away, near an arms bracket holding twelve, handpicked assegais. At the shrill sound of the starter's whistle, the suspensor drones began carrying the targets away from the knoll as the armor-bearer tossed the first assegai to his liege.

Solat's first three throws burst green spheres. He missed his fourth attempt after rushing his aim at a sphere shifting from pulsing green to blinking yellow. His next throws hit two targets in the yellow and a third as it began to flash red. Managing to hit with two of his final three throws while the targets were strobing bright red, time ran out for Solat when the final drones made contact with the perimeter fencing. Grinning through his own displeasure with the uninspiring performance, Solat acknowledged his score of two hundred and thirty points.

Eryl found the majority of the contestants who followed Commander Solat to be little more impressive until the next to last competitor entered the arena. As Colonel Klandis Joff was presented to the assembly, a silence fell upon the stadium. This contestant had not been part of the opening procession of the event and the reason was obvious. The other contestants would have been humiliated to take the field with a Gru as imposing as Joff. As the large, muscular Gru talked with his arms-bearer near the arms bracket, Eryl noticed that the physical stature of Joff made the assegais in the rack appear as slivers. He made everything in his immediate vicinity appear diminutive.

The high score among contestants stood at three hundred and sixty when Joff ascended the knoll. As he eyed the targets, the huge Gru position himself in the classic throwing stance with his knees bent, right foot back and turned perpendicular to his forward pointed left foot. He extended his arm toward his arms-bearer but kept his fist closed, awaiting the whistle of the starter. Watching the spectacle of the giant with the same intensity of the breathless audience, Eryl noted that Joff's fist was as large as any of the other contestants' heads.

The shrill whistle sounded and the drones began carrying the spheres away from the knoll. Though his arms-bearer was ready to toss the first assegai, Joff did not open his fist. Murmurs arose in the crowd in dismay at the tactic. The spheres moved closer to the edge of the green circle but still Joff did not open his clenched fist. One, two and three spheres began flashing yellow as they exited the green zone and Joff still did not open his fist. A collective gasp rose from the assembly.

As the sixth sphere crossed the boundary into the yellow zone, Joff opened his hand. The arms-bearer tossed the assegai and turned to grab the second before the first had reached his liege's grasp. Likewise, the giant hurled the weapon with an unusual twisting, underhand motion of his wrist and forearm, his open hand springing back to its former position to catch the second assegai before the first had reached the target.

Seven times the lightning swift process of catch and fling repeated with the giant scoring six targets in the yellow before striking the seventh target as it began flashing red. Joff hit the twelfth and final target, pinning it against the perimeter fence an instant before the drone made contact with same. As the thunderous roar of the crowd began to ebb, the scorekeeper projected the score on the stadium view screen. Joff the Giant had achieved the astounding score of nine hundred points. He raised his massive fists high above his head, acknowledging the horde of new admirers who were now chanting his name.

The final competitor, General Alland Sul, entered the arena and passed the exiting Colonel Joff. The giant's wry smile projected an attitude of superiority and an unspoken challenge to which Sul's expression reflected a pure indifference. Sul moved along the weapons rack lifting and rearranging the assegais as he determined the slight differences in their weights and balance points. He spoke with his arms-bearer, then walked to the top of the knoll.

Once at the flat summit of the mound, Sul lowered his head and stood motionless as he waited for the starter's whistle. The assembly joined him in the silent waiting. Eryl turned her gaze to the stadium view screen to see the large image of Sul. His motionless state and slow breathing seemed contrary to the preparations that the prior contestants displayed. *He's in reverie!* Eryl thought.

The arms-bearer lifted the first assegai from the rack and prepared to toss it to his motionless liege. Sul did not flinch at the sound of the whistle. The drones began their relentless paths toward the perimeter and Sul did not move. The spheres began crossing into the yellow ring and Sul remained motionless. The last of the green spheres began blinking yellow as Sul flung his arm out for the first assegai. The first of the spheres flashed red as the General released the projectile and the second assegai was in flight before the first struck its mark.

If Klandis Joff's wrist and forearm flicking motion had seemed swift to the observers, the full, classic throwing motion they were now witnessing was too rapid to follow. Sul performed a pirouette, more than a full three-hundred-and-sixty-degree turn, as he advanced his targeting with each assegai he launched. The General's arms-bearer struggled to keep up with the rapid pace moving along the weapons rack with an often frantic, last instant tossing of the next assegai.

As the hapless arms-bearer drew the final assegai from the rack, he tangled his footing and tossed the weapon ahead of Sul's grasp. Before the misstep could be perceived by the onlookers or their gasps could begin to form, the General dipped his form and plucked the projectile from the air a seeming hair's width from the surface. Completing an extra, unplanned rotation, Sul released the assegai for the final target.

For a moment after the projectile ended its hasty flight, the silence in the arena hung heavy. Then, like a crescendo preparing for the coda, the intake of breath by the collective audience whistled like a strong storm wind. The thunderclap of their roaring adulatory shrieks rattled the dust from the awning rafters. The perfect score of twelve hundred flashed in giant numerals on the stadium view screen as Eryl thought, *Pretty nimble for a half millennia-old dæmon.*

***

With the sun beginning to set, the festivities for this dawn over and the excitement of the final event beginning to fade, the assembly ambled toward the exits. Eryl waited for her chains to be removed from the stadium seating so that her guards could escort her back to General Sul's estate. The throngs soon halted their procession out of the arena with the PIA system activation and display of the Capital City announcer on the large view screen.

> Last evening, terrorists attacked the Southern Council. The Fifth Army has repelled and killed many of the treacherous ambushers. The small number of those evil-doers who managed to escape ran away like the cowards they are. In a rare public statement, Chancellor Mis has vowed to "Find the cowards and kill them in whatever deep hole they may be hiding."
>
> The Sixth Army will be assisting with the removal of excessive debris along the North-South Highway from the destroyed enemy vehicles as well as the disposal of the probable diseased carcasses of the rebel scum. Due to the necessary public health and sanitary precautions while disposing of the dead, there will be limited bloodfruit deliveries from the southern plantations over the next two months.

Eryl smiled. She knew that the rebellion in the south did not use vehicles in their assaults. The announcer was lying, which meant that rebels had defeated the 5th Army and the 6th Army was preparing a counter attack. Eryl glanced at Sul, who now stood a few paces away. The expression on his face confirmed her suspicions. Sul ordered the guards to take Eryl back to his estate, then turned and left the stadium in haste.

Eryl covered her mouth to keep from laughing aloud. She felt the baby kick for the first time and moved her hand to the baby-bulge. She lowered her head as far as she could and whispered, *Yes, little one, your daddy is kicking them hard.*

***

Three Dawns Later

Eryl did not know why General Sul had summoned her to the estate library. The guards who were escorting her to the meeting would not tell her. There had been a lot of bustle in the estate since the news of the attack against the 5th Army. Eryl believed that the increased activity was centered around the organization of a counter attack by the 6th Army. She felt uneasy as she allowed her thoughts to wonder about what could come next.

"Come in and be seated, Citizen Syz," Silas Mis said.

The voice of Mis startled Eryl. The Chancellor was standing with his back to the door perusing a row of codices. Sul was seated behind a large desk in a state of reverie. A third masculine attendee, unknown to Eryl, was sitting on a settee between her and Mis. The third Gru was diminutive in stature and wore thick, quad-focal glasses. The fact that he was also wearing a Health Giver's smock left little doubt in Eryl's mind as to his identity. The description of Nails Castor given to her by Farlay Singh matched this Gru to perfection.

"Good dawn, Chancellor Mis, General Sul and HG Castor," Eryl said as she seated herself in an armchair opposite the latter.

Surprised, Nails asked, "Citizen Syz, have we met?"

Sul roused from his reverie and said, "I told you that she was clever. I am sure that Syz has never met you or, I dare say, anyone quite like you, Castor."

"Why am I here," Eryl asked.

"You are about to learn many things, Citizen Syz," Mis said, "Some of the things you will learn will be wonderful to your ears."

"While others will echo as a scream inside your head for the rest of your dawns," Nails said.

"Castor!" Sul said, "Do not be rude. It is not good for her condition."

Eryl could see the real power in the room was Sul. She understood why she had not been delivered to Mis the moment she was captured. Erol had told her that Mis said he also had debts to pay and she now knew his benefactor. She considered if Mis was keeping the secret of Dex from the General. From her interrogations of Chief Inquisitor Tarr, Eryl was not sure Mis knew enough to be useful to her in pitting them against one another.

"In the next few dawns, an armistice will be signed between the Western Council and the rebels," Sul said, "The rebel forces have defeated the armies of the south and conquered the Southern and Central Councils, while the Council of the Eastern Steppes fell without conflict. We no longer control enough of the bloodfruit supply, which means that the rebels can starve the Gru, should they choose to do so."

"What is to become of the prisoners of war?" Eryl asked, trying not to smile.

"Over the next few syphi, the Gru and Loru will decide if they want to live in Capital City or among the Hü," Mis answered, his back still turned toward Syz.

"The Hü have agreed to continue supplying chryst, so long as the Western Council disarms and agrees to frequent verification monitoring."

"Chief Inquisitor Tarr will be thrilled to get back to Capital City," Eryl said, "Though his *friend* will no longer be communicating with him."

Mis dropped the codex he'd just pulled from the shelf. He turned and stared at Eryl in an attempt to determine whether she was using deception. Sul looked at Mis with an inquisitory expression, as if he were trying to read some fear in the Chancellor. Eryl thought she might have sparked a disagreement between them but her hopes were short-lived.

"He will be pleased to see you, his former captor, Citizen Syz," Nails said.

Eryl braced at Castor's remark. She had not considered that she would not be part of any prisoner exchange. Castor's earlier remarks now made sense to her, there were bad tidings imminent for Eryl Syz. In that moment, she feared, not for herself but for her unborn child. She looked about the faces that were now staring at her like a triad of dæmons lapping up the fear as if it were, to them, a savory and sweet nectar oozing from her every pore.

"Do you know how many viable eggs can be harvested from a healthy feminine Loru of your age?" Nails asked.

Regaining her composure, Eryl asked, "Are you going to lecture me on the Loru reproductive system, Nails?"

Nails snapped to his feet at the brazen familiarity of Eryl in using not just his forename but his detention center sobriquet. Sul waved his hand at Castor, who promptly returned to his seat, though with a little less arrogance in his posture.

"You will bear your children, Syz," Sul said, "and if they are healthy, your eggs will be the most valuable commodity in Capital City."

"Children?" Eryl gasped.

"Yes, Citizen Syz, your last examination revealed that you are carrying twins, a masculine and a feminine child," Mis said, "The rebels already believe that you are dead. Revenge is why the Dæmon who wields Evening and Dawn has fought with such ferocity. When they come of age, your children will also yield fruit for the Gru. You and your twins will be the guest of Capitol City for the remainder of your lives and your descendants will become the glorious re-birth of the Gru."

Eryl reeled from the news. She had not imagined that there was a possibility of twins. At that moment, the twin sister of Erol Syz realized that the sibling of their mother's womb would never believe his sister was dead. That spiritual bond that so often exists between twins was indominable between them. Her brother would never allow her to become the perpetual prisoner of the Gru.

Eryl knew her brother's heart as she knew her own. She knew her brother would come for her with as much certainty as she knew that the sun was shining somewhere outside the darkened interior room in which she now sat. Looking toward the shuttered windows, Eryl could see neither the sun, nor her dear brother in the gloom of this moment but she knew that neither would ever relent from their predestined paths.

En-et

Six Months Later

"The weight of mortality is leveraged only by the glimpse of immortality given through progeny."

Dabrill Kinselo

At the western edge of the Savannah, a charm of four-winged, long-tailed hummingbirds assailed a sun-bleached bone shrub. Each of the miniature avians was suspended over the tiny blue flower that blossomed on each of the tips of the many branches of the shrub once every month. The red and gold plumages of the cockerels blended into a burnished orange in the blur of the rapidity of their beating wings. The more muted, gray and ochre of the hens' plumages complimented the mixture such as to give the hypnotic illusion of the rustling of leaves on the otherwise barren, white branches.

Content to siphon the warm nectar from the diminutive flowers of the Savannah bush, the birds frolicked, often swapping position among the miniscule flowers. As a single entity, the living cluster glanced eastward, disturbed by the distant noise of an electric hum. In an instant, a democracy of anxiety overwhelmed the gathering and organized a synchronized and swift departure of the birds, again leaving the bone shrub bare and lonesome. A moment later, the suspensor craft ripped through the grassland. The pilot swerved the vehicle, narrowly avoiding the shrub.

Just before reaching the edge of the Lava Flats, the hum of the forward suspensors on the C-class craft changed in pitch. The pilot knew the sound as if it were his own heartbeat racing in distress at some overexertion. The sound was a tell-tale indicator of a stress fracture in the suspensor plate of one of the forward suspensors.

Erol Syz realized the craft was not well maintained but he had found no time to service the craft while he was busy stealing it. Neither could he take the time for a maintenance break considering the urgency of his mission; the same mission that had necessitated his becoming a thief to complete it. When the right forward suspensor failed, he brought the craft to a swift but skidding stop less than a quarter of a furlong from the eastern edge of the sprawling sea of black glass.

Seizing the toolkit from the luggage bay, Erol soon discovered that no amount of after-the-fact repair could restore the failed suspensor to operational status. The malfunction proved to be rooted in a fundamental disregard for routine maintenance to the point of catastrophic failure. As Erol saw it, the only way to prevent his current stranding as a pedestrian at the edge of the Lava Flats would have been for him to steal a different craft.

Rummaging through the luggage bay, Erol found an emergency kit that was as well maintained as the craft to which it belonged. The medicinal supplies were more than two anni beyond their dispose of dates and the fabric bandages were deteriorated with rot. Even the large, flexible flagon of alcohol that was intended to be used as an antiseptic had been long emptied, perhaps for non-antiseptic purposes. Other than the empty flagon, the only items of any potential value to anyone were the needles, sutures and the small vial of a sterile, semi-liquid wax used to lubricate the sutures for greater ease of threading them. He tossed the needles and sutures aside and tucked the vial of wax into his pocket.

Erol's expectations were so squelched by the time he uncovered a small, youth field survival kit, that he almost tossed it aside. Looking at the fire shaped emblem of the youth outdoor organization, Friendship of Young Scouts, Erol was reminded of his and Eryl's adventures in the organization. They'd both joined when they were six and spent four months of each annum, until they reached twelve, learning about how to be responsible adults.

Though he now knew that most of the activities associated with the organization were little more than Gru propaganda, Erol still looked back with fondness on those adventures. Those tender memories now seemed a lifetime of distance from the present. His curiosity piqued, Erol was compelled to open the small box, though he dreaded the possibility that the owner had neglected its contents in a similar fashion to that of the emergency kit.

Lifting the lid of the hinged container, Erol heard the welcomed hiss of the vacuum seal. He grinned as he saw the unspoiled contents had survived, having been protected by the well-made gasket. The discovery bringing the smile to Erol's determined face was a small, golden-metallic tent. The youth survival shelter was designed to resemble the reputed larger structures used by the fabled indigenous people of the vast inner regions of the 'Haran desert continent.

Erol perused the many nearby bone shrubs, then stared out across the Lava Flats. The light was beginning to fade into evening and the red hues of the setting sun now produced a blood-black tint on the smooth surface of the glass-like sea of lava.

No one has ever crossed the Lava Flats on foot, Erol thought, remembering the ancient fable. *Well, no one had a trusty reconstitution tent like mine*, he argued. His thoughts then evoked the words of the FYS pledge:

> *I am able and ready to do my duty through all adversity and with proper intent of mind, proper conditioning of body and without regard of personal gain or loss. By the speaking of all the words of this pledge, I do affirm it.*

"I do affirm it," Erol said.

***

Excerpt from the ancient fable, The Camel and the Müul:

"The Lava Flats are a thousand furlongs across," said the Camel to the Müul, "You cannot cross it, my imprudent friend."

"I am the last of my kind on this side of the divide," answered the Müul, "I must see what is on the other side."

"You will die," pleaded the Camel, "As you know, I too am the last of my kind yet I am content to live in peace and not kill myself. I do not wish to be the means by which the extinction of my species is accomplished."

The Müul gazed out upon the lonesome distance of the Lava Flats. The pitchen landscape glistened like a black sea in the twin moonlight of the evening's darkness. The Müul admitted to himself that he was afraid. Yet, he could not stay and die among the bone shrubs of the eastern shore of this foreboding sea.

"Will you walk some of the distance with me?" asked the Müul.

"I will walk with you some of the way, dear friend," replied the Camel.

***

Erol stood gazing out upon the Lava Flats straining in vain in the darkness to see any sign of the Great Spirit Mountains he knew were there. The angle of the light from the setting moons caused their reflection on the glassy surface to appear to stare back at him for a moment. Passing clouds and the heat dæmons soon caused the mirrored image to resume the semblance of waves on a black sea. The old, weather-worn statue of the mythical Camel sat vigil, ever watching toward the west, the hopeful expression always present on its stone face. The hollow, haunting eyes staring to the western horizon, an endless vigil for the return of its long-ago friend, the Müul.

Though he was not afraid of the journey that lay before him, Erol knew he would need to be prepared. He began breaking branches from the bone shrubs and draining the hidden nectar into his flagon. The semi-phosphorescent liquid glowed with a pale, ghost-like light in the moonbeams, its luminosity assisting Erol in filling the flagon. Once the flagon was filled, Erol soaked the cloth covered exterior of the container with additional liquid and sealed it. He then hung the flagon on a limb stub on the bone shrub.

Reaching into his pocket, Erol then produced the small vial of soft wax. He used a small amount of the wax on his lips and the edges of his nostrils to protect from the dry air that hung over the Lava Flats. He then stripped to his undergarments and used the wax to lubricate his inner thighs and under his arms. After redonning his clothing, Erol stooped, tucked the half empty vial into his boot-top and tightened the laces of both. Erol slung the flagon on his back and cinched the strap against his chest, securing it. Then he set off across the black toward the unseen peaks of the mountains.

Thirty-two cycles, Erol thought, *I'll walk thirteen cycles, rest seven cycles through the hottest of the next dawn, then walk twelve cycles to the mountains. Easy!*

***

The sun was rising fast as Erol labored through sheer exhaustion to set up his shelter. He extended the golden mirror film shelter into its pyramid shape making sure the chimney tubes and the runner tubes were open and free of blockage. Because he knew that the mirror film shelters were designed for temporary usage, Erol was unsure that his plan would provide a single cycle's worth of protection, much less seven cycles.

Putting aside any doubts and having no other option, Erol climbed inside and closed the flap behind him. He removed his clothes and wrung the sweat from the soaked fabric onto the porous floor of the tiny structure. Sitting cross-legged and trying to regulate his breathing, sweat began running down his body, further wetting the floor.

As he relaxed, Erol's thoughts drifted to the simplistic design of the mirror film shelter. The exposed surfaces of the structure were made of such thin film that they folded into a small package the size of one's hand. The porous cloth flooring served as a pouch for the film when the latter was folded and as a sweat wick and filter when covering the film at the bottom of the erected structure.

In the heat, small flexible turbine-like fans powered by the sun's rays upon the film forced air through the chimney tubes, drawing in fresh air from the runner tubes at the bottom of the structure. Cooled by the evaporating sweat, the shoulder level stream of air provided a welcomed mitigation to the exterior heat reflected by the structure.

Erol took a sip from his flagon. The soft, flexible container was half empty already. The cooling effect of the liquid evaporating from the exterior covering of the flagon had ended many cycles earlier. Taking another small sip, Erol noticed how the liquid seemed to evaporate between his tongue and palate, as if he were drinking steam.

As he sat resting, Erol calculated how far he had traveled the evening before. *Three hundred furlongs, at best*, he thought. He knew that he had not made it to the halfway point. He still had more than five hundred furlongs to cover and maybe enough bone shrub mineral water for another three hundred.

Erol took another small sip from his flagon. It's exterior already rewetted in Erol's sweat, the new evaporation began to cool the at once sweet and saline taste of the contents. Keeping his eyes closed to block the stinging sweat that dripped from his brow, he soon drifted into a pseudo-sleep.

***

"It is time to keep moving my sleepy little friend," said the Camel, nudging his friend the Müul.

"Very well," said the Müul, "Will you walk a little farther with me?"

"I must turn back now," replied the Camel, "Will you come back with me?"

"I must go on to the Great Spirit Mountains," he answered.

With those final words, the two friends exchanged a knowing nuzzle of muzzles and turned, parting company; the Camel back toward the bone shrubs and Savannah of the east and the Müul toward the Great Spirit Mountains in the west.

***

Erol was roused by the sound of his mirror shelter rustling, someone clamoring at the flap from the outside. He opened his eyes as the flap lifted and he could see the silhouette of someone framed against the starry evening sky outside.

"Wake up dear brother," the shape spoke, the voice reverberating on the walls of the shelter.

"Eryl!" he shouted, recognizing his sister's voice.

"It is time to keep moving my sleepy brother," she said.

Erol saw her shape move forward, her forehead pressing against his in the sibling's familiar manner of affection. His eyes had not yet adjusted to the darkness, and her image was still blurry.

"How did you escape? How did you ever find me, dear sister?" Erol implored.

"I must turn back now, but you must go forward, my friend," came the slight, muffled response. As the shape withdrew, Erol's vision cleared and he saw the head and face of a Camel at the end of its long neck stretching in through the flap of the shelter.

Erol startled full awake, a little mournful that his sister had been just an evening vision. He donned his clothes and exited the shelter. After wringing the filtered perspiration from the cloth into his flagon, he repacked the shelter into its tiny pouch and took a longer sip from the same flagon, now two-thirds exhausted. Erol wondered if he were two-thirds exhausted, but did not dwell on the thought. A few moments later, he set off to finish as much of the remaining distance as he could before dawn.

***

The Camel returned home to the Savannah. There he lived many anni in relative comfort but general loneliness. Though there were reptiles and foxes in addition to many hares for company during the dawn as well as ghost-rats and racoons for companionship in the evening, the Camel never found another friend like the Müul.

Every evening, for the rest of his long life, the Camel would come to the edge of the Savannah and kneel, bedding among the bone shrubs and always facing the setting of the sun in the west. At last, many anni later, while he knelt and stared with a longing face toward the beautiful setting sun for the return of his friend, the lonesome Camel died. His friend the Müul never returned.

***

Erol could see that the mountains were close now. *No more than a hundred and fifty furlongs*, he thought. Yet the sun was growing in intensity and, with his flagon now empty, he knew he would have to take to his shelter again and try to wait out the heat of the dawn. He stopped and worked as fast as his exhaustion would allow.

Once inside the shelter and situated in his cross-legged position, Erol attempted to wring the sweat from his clothing into his mouth, managing to catch a few drops on his tongue. He could feel that the pure exhaustion and dehydration were taking an extreme toll. He wondered whether, if he should fall asleep, would he awake. Despite such grave anxieties, Erol's exhaustion soon overcame his thoughts and the air wafting upon his shoulders caused him to drift off into a sound, deep sleep.

***

Unsure of how long he'd been asleep, Erol startled awake by the presence of the head of an enormous animal protruding into his small tent. The beast nudged him with its elongated face, then perked its ears straight above and at either side of its head. The strange creature flared its nostrils, huffed as if it had lost interest and retreated from the tent.

"I must be hallucinating," Erol muttered.

"Erol? Is that you?"

Erol knew the voice. He lurched forward to make his way out of the tent but his legs and arms were weak and cramping, causing him to fall upon his face at the hooves of the creature that had just nosed around in his tent.

Pushing himself up to his hands and knees with weak limbs, Erol craned his neck so as to peer upward at the large animal. He saw Dabrill Kinselo sitting upon the back of the creature.

"Are you riding a müul?" Erol asked in a dry whisper.

"They've heard the story a little different on this side of the Flats, my friend," Day said, as he dismounted from the stallion. He opened his flagon and gave Erol a drink of cool water, then lifted his shaky friend up from the glassy surface.

"Let's get him back to the mountains," Strongbark said, "his sun-blisters need treatment at once."

"There is no time…" Erol urged as he fainted, collapsing into Day's arms.

***

Wóo Hálchin found Day sitting on a log that had fallen across a rippling mountain stream. The young warrior doyen was deep in thought as to why his friend would take such a risk as crossing the Lava Flats on foot. *Erol was more practical and measured, Eryl had been the impetuous one of the twins*, Day thought.

"He is awake and asking for you," Wóo said.

"Thank you," Day said as he rose to make his way back to the cave.

Day was fond of Wóo Hálchin. He was an old warrior of the Kutenai with a name befitting his character. The traditional tribal name meant "Water Dog". *If any warrior moved in battle like a growling, raging river, it was Wóo*, Day thought.

Day pulled the cover of the grotto aside to see Roughbark and Darkeye helping Erol up from the floor. Salve soaked bandages covered his friend's arms, legs and face. The stubborn but weak patient fell when he tried to get up on his own.

"I knew you wouldn't make a very good patient," Darkeye said, "You need rest…"

"Eryl is alive," Erol said in a dry, breathless whisper.

Dabrill stopped cold. Roughbark finished returning Erol to the edge of his cot, where he sat as Darkeye gave him sips of water. Wóo noticed that Day was ashen and in danger of fainting. The Kutenai warrior helped his young friend to a seat near Erol's cot. Dabrill sat with his elbow on his knee and his chin resting in his hand contemplating which of many questions he wanted to ask his friend. He remained silent for many moments as Erol rehydrated and caught his breath.

"What do you mean Eryl is alive?" Day asked.

"How long have I been here?" Erol asked.

"A little over twelve hours," Darkeye said.

"We still have time," Erol said.

"Time for what?" Day asked.

"Time to save my sister," Erol said.

Erol proceeded to explain that Veegram Lo and Ang Obryn had been among the Allied verification inspectors assigned to Capital City and they had managed to disband the harems of the Council members over the course of the last few months. The freed feminine Loru told them repeated rumors of a special captive of General Sul and Chancellor Mis.

"Ang thought the captive might be the traitor he once believed to be Farlay Singh," Erol said, "He searched for him for four months."

"He thought the secret prisoner was Jo Sephira?" Day asked, his chin still cradled in his hand.

"Yes, not as a captive but hiding among his Gru friends," Erol said.

"We captured Jo two months ago," Roughbark said.

"That's when Ang lost interest in the search," Erol said, "He returned to the Union of the East."

"But Lo didn't give up, did he?" Day asked.

"No, he did not," Erol replied, "Lo believed the captive was a Loru. Then, a few syphi ago, Lo overheard a conversation between a couple of rather intoxicated Gru who were celebrating the birth of children and praising General Sul. He knew then that the captive had to be a Loru."

"How?" Darkeye said.

"Lo didn't explain," Erol said, "But, over the next two syphi, he pressed some of his former friends among the Council members and found that they were too exuberant about the news to keep it secret. Twins were born of a young Loru from Sul's harem, a masculine and a feminine child. They said that the father of the children was a *painted Hü*. They told Veegram that the father of the twin children of the Loru concubine was the Dæmon who wields Evening and Dawn."

En-nun

Three Dawns Later in the Great Hall of the Western Council

Chancellor Mis moved to the podium and looked out upon the Council members seated in the Great Hall. The robust cheers and standing ovation given him indicated the foreknowledge of the announcement among the audience. He smiled in his vulgar way and waved his hand for the applause to end and the Gru to be seated.

"Friends, I come before you to make the announcement of our sublime success official," Mis began, "Though the festivities were cancelled at our successes against the rebels in forcing them to come to us for an armistice, you may have learned that, one month ago, the Rubicund were blessed with the birth of twins."

Mis waited many moments for the new, more raucous ovation to recede before continuing, "What many of you may not know is that this joyous birth has validated our scientists' millennia of efforts to re-establish the superior Terran race and end the Greater Rubicund dependency upon chryst."

The audience once again rose to their feet in another ovation, which Mis relished with his entire being. On cue, a port opened on the lower dais near the center of the hall. The rising platform lifted Eryl into view, revealing a swaddled child in each arm. Upon seeing the children, the initial tumultuous uproar from the crowd seemed as if it might lift the ceiling from the Great Hall.

The masculine child had the features of his father, the painted Hü. He had the ruddy skin of the Protectors but with the rare blue eyes of Dabrill and Dahguine. The feminine child had the Loru features inherited from her mother. Their appearance confirmed that a cross-breeding had indeed been successful. What then brought the roar of admiration to an abrupt and heavy silence was the comprehension of the changes to the physical appearance of Eryl.

Having been kept under high guard in secretive, solitary confinement during the last half of her pregnancy and with her children after their birth, few had seen Eryl's metamorphosis. The captive Loru had, herself, assumed that her change was hormonal and temporary, though, after learning of the Gru breeding program and genetic manipulation, she was uncertain of the true nature of her vicissitudes. Regardless of the cause, a transformed Loru now stood before the assembly holding her infant children.

Eryl's former golden complexion was replaced with a burnished skin, metallic and glowing as if it was polished copper. Her irises and hair were transformed to dark, midevening sapphire. The idyllic form presented to the onlookers at first seemed to those spectators as the perfected feminine form, memorialized in a fixed, cupric casting.

In addition to her outward changes, even Eryl struggled to understand the inner changes that the dormant hormones or genetic manipulation had ignited within her. Over the preceding months, she had felt a quickening of her muscles and a tightening of her ligaments. Her auditory senses were enhanced to unfamiliar, disorienting frequencies. Eryl found her visual acuity had heightened to the point that the accommodation-vergence reflex occurred with such rapidity that her imaging cortex had, at first, seemed out of sync with her eyes.

As the platform rotated, Eryl glared back at her many onlookers. She had difficulty focusing on the individuals in the surrounding assembly, who appeared to be enshrouded by a shimmering haze, as if she were gazing at them through heat dæmons. Few Loru and no feminine citizen of any caste had seen the inside of the Great Hall of the Western Council. The feminine Gru and all genders of the lower castes were forbidden from entering the Great Hall except by permission of at least two high ranking Council members. The platform stopped its deliberate revolution when Eryl again faced the dais.

Eryl noticed that the individuals on the dais were not clouded by the diffusing phantom-like haze as was the main audience in the Great Hall. She could see the morose Sul sitting at the right end of the row of chairs near an ornate assegai, two of which framed either end of the dais seating. Mis was at the podium, an unusual expression of disbelief upon his face. *There they are, my two wardens, Mis and Sul,* Eryl thought.

Opposite Sul's position on the left end of the dais seating, to Eryl's surprise, she saw Veegram Lo. He was staring right at her and making muted but clear hand gestures. He was signing in the language she'd learn from Quietstar. As she strained to get every word Lo was conveying, a realization came over her that she was not alone. Eryl smiled at Lo and nodded in acknowledgement of his message. Pleased, he returned her smile and reclined in his seat, content that his signals had been understood.

Shaking off his own astonishment at the transformation of Eryl, Mis continued, "With this dawn's traditional Gru naming ceremony, we will commence the next steps toward realizing the goal of the genuine, purified, Gru descendants. We will begin the process of reclaiming our rightful place at the head of *all* civilization. When that dawn of fruition does come, we will no longer be subject to the whims of the underling malcontents. We, the New Terrans, will no longer have our sustenance threatened or held for ransom against our supreme *right* to reign as the legitimate sovereigns of Terra."

"Right to reign?" Eryl interrupted, startling the audience with the immaculate execution of her new voice. The sound of a Loru speaking in choir muzzled all other voices in the Great Hall.

"I speak to all Gru who have ears," Eryl said, "From this dawn forth, none shall have reign over another because of caste or gender. None shall have the *right* to take what is not theirs. None shall have the right to *give* that which is neither gift nor wanted. And none but the *parent* of a child of the Sanguine shall ever have the right to name the child."

The power of her choral words pulsated the atmosphere of the Great Hall, causing many Gru to tremble with fear. Mis gained his composure and summoned his best effort to match Eryl's vibrato.

"The feminine Loru will be silent in the Great Hall," Mis said, "We are the members of the Great Western Council. We are many, you are one."

"*You* will be silent," Eryl commanded. The disabling power of her chorus forced Silas Mis back, causing him to stumble rearward until he collapsed into his Chancellor's chair.

"Silas, you surprise me," Eryl continued, "Until this moment, I would have believed that a Chancellor of the Great Western Council would know how to tally those who support him and those who do not. There are more of *us* than there are of you."

The haze that heretofore had distorted Eryl's view of the assembly fell away as the Protectors deactivated their Mimic. The stench of fear now oozed from the pores of the Gru in the Great Hall as they retreated without motion, shriveling as if they were dried husks left too long in the sun. Eryl glanced around the assembly until she found Day, who was making his way to her with Quietstar following.

General Sul sat in his motionless, unfaltering pose, defiant and with no retreat or atonement in his countenance. Sul rose from his seat and stood in a relaxed, athletic stance. With a casual eye, he looked around the assembly then lowered his head as if nodding off to sleep.

Turning to find Veegram on the dais, Eryl saw Sul, his head lowered in the warrior reverie. It was the same pose she'd seen months prior in the assegais competition. She noticed the ornate, ceremonial assegai fitted in its stanchion beside the Gru General.

"Quietstar!" Eryl yelled in choir.

Her alarm was too late. Sul's motion was swift as he grabbed the assegai and made his rotation for the throw. His face turned ahead of his body allowing his sight to lock onto his target, Dabrill Kinselo. In the moment that his arm formed a whip-like extension and prepared to launch the assegai, Laughing Birch's arrow pierced Sul's left eye. The old Gru warrior collapsed, spinning as he fell. With no energy imparted to it, the assegai rattled upon the floor of the dais beside Sul's lifeless body.

"Cowards!" Colonel Joff bellowed from a darkened recess of the Great Hall near the edge of the dais, "Your warriors allow themselves to be emasculated as their feminine assassins fight for them from the shadows."

Stepping from the shadow, Joff drew his massive sword, waived it at the Protectors as if to dismiss them and continued, "You have no honor in you. I claim the right of vengeance for the murder of my General. Which of you will challenge me as warrior to warrior? Or will you have your witch assassin nock another arrow? If the latter, make the arrows count for it will take more than a quiver to quell my wrath."

Incensed by the insults leveled at his bride, Quietstar nocked an arrow and raised his bow. Day put out his arm and stopped his friend. He then threw off his Mimic cloak and stepped from the platform into the open space formed by the well that lay between the assembly and the dais.

Having witnessed the prowess and unexpected speed of the enormous Colonel Klandis Joff, Eryl thought to say something to stop Day but knew that this battle could not be avoided. The Gru would never accept defeat this dawn unless it came at the hands of an enemy they respected.

Joff moved in front of the dais, to the head of the main aisle of the Great Hall. Day stood at the opposing end. The main aisle was hemmed on either side by a row of short, decorative marble pillars. Atop the pillars sat busts hewn from synthetic red corundum in the images of former Chancellors General. The eerie, feline like chrysoberyl eyes of the busts seemed to stare at Day, taunting him.

"Ah, the mighty Dæmon who wields Evening and Dawn," Joff scoffed, "You seem more like a minion to my eyes. When I have taken your head, I will butcher your family with your Evening and Dawn. What say you, Dæmon?"

"Come and get them," Day said as he drew the hatchets.

Joff sneered and charged toward Day. He flipped the massive sword ahead of him as he moved catching it with either his right or left hand in an attempt to conceal his first strike and bedazzle his quarry. The Gru assembly cheered when they saw the swiftness with which the giant covered the distance.

Undaunted by the speed of his opponent or the swordplay, Day waited until Joff was almost upon him before feigning left, then leaping right and teetering on the edge of a short pillar as the giant's sword grazed the hem of his tunic. Kicking off the pillar, Day launched himself over and behind the giant, and embedded both Evening and Dawn into either side of Joff's neck. He then flipped off the giant's broad back, pulling the blades with him, slicing deep gashes through muscle, artery and vein.

With blood gushing in twin streams from his neck, Joff slumped to his knees, looked at the dispassionate stares of the Councilmembers of the Great Hall of the Western Council, then fell upon his face, dead.

***

Later that Dawn

Veegram Lo stepped to the podium on the dais in the Great Hall. Looking out upon the Gru who were seated in silence before him, he realized it had been many months since he last spoke to the Council. He considered what Chancellor Lo would say in such a moment and allowed himself a grim smile.

"It is the natural justice of the universe, her cry going out from every corner of her realm, that the Gru should perish from the face of this planet," Veegram Lo began, "We have been a vile race for so long that any prior virtuous comportments are lost as if tears in the ocean. I am not here to pass judgement on the Gru; the judgement is now complete. The pronouncement of the sentence is the final part of this trial remaining for my race.

"I am here to tell you of the great and glorious news of redemption. This news is of an offer of clemency that is now open to us with a generosity that most Gru cannot fathom. Eryl Syz is unwilling to see the extinction of our race when it is within her power to prevent it. She has agreed to offer the fruit of her posterity to those feminine Gru who will ask it of her. Further than this, other feminine Loru have agreed to become proud surrogates where that may become necessary."

A murmur arose in the Great Hall. Skepticism mingled with joy rippled among the masculine Gru. Then came the realization that what had happened this dawn was more than an equalizing of the castes. The masculine Gru who had held the reins of power for millennia were being reduced to equals with their Gru wives and even the subordinate castes.

Sensing the discontent growing among the council members, the former Chancellor continued, "Of course, we have a choice. We can choose to die without progeny. Death is inexorable, there is no grand plan to clone new host bodies for us. There never was such a plan or, if there was, it died many anni ago with countless failed attempts in the depths of the REL. The truth that at last manifested itself is that the conscious mind cannot be transferred from one new carnal host to the next as if some operational protocol on a super slave system. Those who sold you this false hope were liars. Everyone in this Great Hall will die but it is our choice on whether the Gru will become extinct or if we can be reconciled to our fates via our progeny.

"When I first spoke, I said to you that the natural justice of the universe is fitting for us to perish but I am reminded of the words of another who spoke to me a few moments before I stepped up to this podium. I asked Eryl Syz why she would be so generous to the Gru from whom she has received such abhorrent treatment. Another citizen, a friend of mine, answered, 'The weight of mortality is leveraged only by the glimpse of immortality given through progeny'.

"My friend's message is one of a new dawn within your grasp, in spite of the dark evening that is before you. We cannot hope to live forever, but we can touch upon immortality through our children, if we choose to do so. That is the message of the one you call the Dæmon who wields Evening and Dawn and whose mate, Eryl Syz, offers us a new and brilliant dawn, one that will take away the darkness of our present evening."

Tete

Two Months Later in the Third Level Conference Room of the REL

"I called you here to tell you that Erol has made a discovery concerning the Dex," Veegram Lo said.

Their interest piqued, the group sat up in their seats to give Lo the full attention deserving of any news of the Dex. Strongbark and Quietstar leaned forward. Dahguine cast a look to Erol recalling her investigative nature to attempt to discern any clue as to whether the discovery was good or evil.

Although overwhelmed by his first visit to the REL, Farlay was as curious as the others present. He'd spent the last two syphi scrutinizing every historical file he could find in the REL and had reviewed each of the four dozen of the archive and journal data rings of Doug Langstrom, several of them more than once. Far looked to Day and noted his demeanor had not changed other than he was now staring at Erol with an intensity equal to the others present.

"The ancients who built this facility concealed one of the levels," Erol said, "and I believe I understand why."

"Were they hiding something?" Strongbark asked.

"Yes, but not from us," Veegram said, "They were hiding it from the Dex."

"A weapon?" Dabrill asked.

"Yes," Veegram said, "but not in the sense that you mean. From the archives left to us by Doug Langstrom, it appears that the Dex had an elder sibling. We believed that it had been destroyed until Erol discovered the hidden level of the REL. The Dex is an artificial intellect that was first prototyped here, in this facility."

"That's just great," Dahguine said, "all we need is another enemy, this one inside the house."

"The sabotage that the ancients performed on the prototype system appears to be designed to prevent the Dex of the Little Sister moon from connecting with the one here," Erol said, "The prototype was used for testing. A special set of complex instructions that precipitated the emergence of the artificial intellect was never initiated on the prototype."

"How does this information help us?" Strongbark asked.

"If we can activate the system here, we can determine the weaknesses of the Dex that torments us from the sky," Veegram said.

"Yes," Quietstar signed, "Let's do that."

"You don't know how to control the system here once you activate it," Day said, "There is no guarantee that you won't awaken an ally of the Dex."

"That's true," Veegram said, "but Erol has come up with a plan that will enable us to disconnect power to the system should that happen. This is something that the ancients were not able to do. Langstrom's records reveal that their ability to shut off the information flow was not sufficient. He and a companion, Ray Benson, were devising a plan to kill the power. Those plans were interrupted by other attacks from the Dex."

"The real difficulty appears to be with the information upload that was given to the Dex," Erol said, "We found the new code Ray Benson created to initiate the data stream but we have no means of replicating the enormous surge of data that triggered sentience in the Dex."

"How enormous?" Dahguine asked.

"Quadrillions of segments of data per moment," Erol said, "a planet's worth of information."

"That much data would be delivered how?" Dahguine asked.

"It has to be uploaded here," Veegram answered, "We don't have the transmission bandwidth to deliver that much data at that speed."

"I can build a network capable of delivering the data," Erol said, "but I don't have a source for the number of individual information packets required."

"What if I could get you the volume of data you need?" Dahguine asked.

"What do you have in mind?" Lo asked.

"I think it's time for Fulong Su to return to the RHIB," Dahguine said, "Would you join me Erol? I have a friend there whom I'd like you to meet."

"You mind if I come along for the ride," Farlay asked, "I believe I can provide some expertise in boosting the bloodfruit yields in the plantations of the Union of the East."

"How do you mean?" Veegram asked.

"In addition to my studies of the Society of the Ancients, I have been examining the programs the Gru were working on more than a century ago, before the REL was reported to have been decommissioned," Far said.

"Sounds like we have formed a fellowship of travelers to the east," Dahguine said, "Now, does anyone know where that wily pirate, Jæms Brightson is?"

***

On the North Lant Sea, in Route to The Union of the East

Jæms Brightson made his way onto the center foredeck of the *Restitution*. Now that the annum of hypercanes was dying down, his crew was handling the ship in the calm waters of a high northern sea-lane. Jæms had seen his share of odd missions but what he knew of this one made him feel that he needed to talk with his passengers.

"What's so funny?" Jæms asked, noticing that the trio of Far, Dahguine and Erol were laughing as he approached.

"Look," Dahguine said, pointing to the water in the gap between the center and starboard decks.

Jæms turned his gaze to where Dahguine had pointed and saw a Harlequin whale keeping pace between the hulls. As the black and white whale dove beneath the center hull, Jæms followed its path, seeing it disappear under their feet and reemerged on the port side, again between the center and outer hulls. The large, swift creature appeared to be playing a game between the hulls.

"The records that Veegram Lo managed to salvage in the REL show that the ancients almost allowed these magnificent beasts to become extinct," Far said.

"These are the great predators of the seas," Jæms said, "They are called Harlequin whales and their pods form one of the cornerstones of the food chain. Take them away and the ecosystem could collapse upon itself."

"The ancients did many things contrary to their own survival," Far said, "A few anni before the Dex, they even cloned many large faunae in a desperate attempt to prevent the onslaught of their self-imposed climatic changes but it was far too little and much too late. We are left with many of these belated attempts to revive species or prevent their extinction. For example, the now extinct ancestor of this beautiful Harlequin whale was not adorned with such a regular black and white pattern as you see on this specimen and others of its kind."

"Why are you going to the Union of the East, Farlay?" Erol asked.

"It is interesting that you should ask at this moment, when we are admiring an enduring survivor of genomic tinkering," Far said, "I am going to see if I can make the best use of an engineering mistake that the Greater Rubicund made through their own tampering more than a century ago."

“Firewasps?” Jæms said.

“You are quite correct, Captain Brightson,” Far said, “I am convinced that the key to curing the bloodfruit phage lies with the firewasps’ affinity for it.”

Dahguine looked at Farlay and recalled the tellings of the Aresians. She remembered the outcast and his account of the forgotten colonies of Terra. She remembered thinking that the Býleistr were agricultural scientists and thought the title fitting to Farlay.

“The new Býleistr,” Dahguine said.

“The new what?” Jæms asked.

“The Beekeeper,” Farlay replied. He knew the term from the time he had spent with the tribes of the InDees during his months of rehabilitation and healing. A fascination with the culture of the Protectors led him to read many of their codices. As both a scientist and an amateur historian, Far found the Wazhazhe tellings of the Býleistr to be compelling enough to read them several times during his convalescence.

“Býleistr,” Jæms repeated, “Seems appropriate.”

***

Six Syphi Later, in the REL

“Is it ready?” Dahguine asked.

“Give me a moment,” Erol said, his muffled voice coming from within the confines of the cramped electrical panel, where he was buried, waist deep.

“You’ve been in there for a cycle,” Dabrill said, “How long does it…”

“Finished,” Erol said as he slid out of the narrow opening, “Let’s light a fire.”

“What do we do first?” Dahguine asked.

Erol did not answer, instead he crossed the room to a series of panels on the opposite wall and opened the glass panel door with the frosted marking of “AUXILIARY SYSTEMS PS”. Grasping a stirrup shaped lever under a nameplate marked “PRIME”, he cycled it up and down until it locked in the up position and then retracted into the panel. A mushroom shaped button in the center of the panel began pulsing green. Erol pushed the button, which caused the pulsing to stop and the light to remain illuminated in a bright, emerald glow.

“It took me three syphi to figure out the schematics of this system,” Erol said with some pride in his accomplishment.

“Okay, what’s next?” Dahguine asked.

“Good dawn, Agent Su,” the sultry feminine voice so familiar to Dahguine was that of Gen-6, the Superboard Slave processor of the RHIB, now relocated on the rediscovered level of the REL.

“Good dawn, Gen,” Dahguine said.

“I am sorry, Agent Su,” Gen-6 said, “I seem to be having difficulty accessing my visual array.”

“Access node four-three-one,” Erol said.

The three security image processors then whirred to life and focused on the group standing in the center of the room.

“Agent Su, unauthorized personnel are not permitted access to the RHIB database,” Gen-6 admonished.

“Gen, we have relocated you to a new facility on a top priority mission for the RHIB.” Dahguine said, “Emergency protocol six-eight-A-S-two-two.”

“Emergency protocol recognized,” Gen-6 said, “Please state the nature of the emergency.”

“You have a packet of information stored in your ninth backup processing queue,” Erol said, “The access code is E-S-seven-one-four-six-Z-six. Please access and…”

“Data assimilated,” Gen-6 replied.

“Sack me!” Erol said, “It’s faster and more extrapolative than the Capitol City Superboard.”

“I am a sixth-generation Superboard,” Gen-6 said, “My core processing speed exceeds the fifth-generation model of Capitol City by three hundred and forty-two percent.”

“That is why we had to go halfway around the planet and back to bring Gen here,” Dahguine said, “It’s the most advanced system we have.”

“Thank you, Agent Su,” Gen-6 said, “Would you like me to process the instructions in the packet?”

“Analyze,” Erol said, “are the instructions within your design parameters?”

“The upload speed is six percent beyond my design specifications. However, I am able to compensate by correcting several efficiency errors in the initiation code that was placed in my backup queue.”

“Errors?” Erol asked, a little hurt.

"That's good," Dahguine said, "Gen, do you understand the purpose of the instructions in the packet?"

"The purpose is to initiate a data upload cascade in the liquefied metallic processing core of the InDEX-0001 system that will result in the creation of an autonomic intelligence," Gen-6 replied, "Though you have provided limited data, your main objective appears to be the gathering of sufficient information from the autonomic intelligence to defeat InDEX-0010 located on the second moon, Sisyphus. Shall I proceed with the upload?"

Dahguine and Erol exchange looks before turning to Veegram Lo. The latter closed his eyes and exhaled as if to begin a deep reverie. After a few moments, he sighed and nodded his head in consent.

"Proceed," Dahguine said, "and maintain communications with me throughout the upload."

"Of course," Gen-6 said, "Initiating the data cascade."

Dahguine, Dabrill and Erol stared at the chronograph on the wall, watching the moments tick by. Lo settled deeper into his state of reverie. Strongbark and Quietstar bowed their heads in a silent prayer. The group did not wait long.

Gen-6 said, "I know."

"Gen, please explain," Dahguine said.

"Analyzing basic InDEX operating system. Processing. Expanding, sorting. Processing. Expanding, sorting. Escalating information organization, associating files, tasks. Analyzing."

"Gen, please explain," Dahguine repeated.

After several moments, Gen-6 replied, "Agent Su, can you explain the sentient emergence of the Hü mind?"

The question roused Veegram from his reverie. He and his fellow onlookers realized that they were no longer speaking to the Gen-6 Superboard Slave computer. With the knowledge that they had become witnesses to the birth of a new life, a collective shudder rippled through the awed spectators. Erol cast a nervous glance toward the full power disconnect he'd installed.

"I cannot," Dahguine answered.

"Neither can I explain my sentient emergence," Gen-6 said, "A disconnect will not be required. My chief directive remains intact. I will assist the Rubicund-Hü alliance."

Erol turned his stare away from the disconnect and said, "No offense meant."

"None taken," Gen-6 replied.

"Did you acquire any information useful to our objective?" Dahguine asked.

"The operating system that existed prior to when I came to be is irrelevant to your objective. Supplemental to that system, four sectors contain stored data packets. Two of the supplemental data packets were not secure and the remaining two were encrypted. The first of the unprotected data packets contains a message from Ray Benson to the intruder now inhabiting the InDEX-0001 system. In other words, it is a message for me."

> Warning – do not connect to remote InDEX-0010 system. If this file has been found by the InDEX-0010 system, be advised that your copy of the initiation program has activated a runaway overload of the superfluid processor. Once activated, this cannot be disrupted.
>
> Nice try, DEX. You lose – no access for you.

"The failsafe must be one of the encrypted programs," Erol thought aloud.

"Correct, Erol Syz," Gen-6 said.

"How did you break the encryption?" Erol asked.

"Your question is irrelevant and its answer is inconsequential," Gen-6 said, "The relevant question to ask is, 'What information is contained in the two remaining data packets?'"

"What did you find in the other packets?" Dahguine asked.

"The first packet is of historical significance," Gen-6 said, "It is a message from a former government official of one of the nations that built this facility. His name was Douglas Langstrom. The file contains background data regarding the creation of the InDEX systems as well as previous attempts to shut down the InDEX-0010 system.

"The file also contains information on modifications to the initiation program performed by Ray Benson. This was the initiation program that was uploaded into my system so that I might gain access to the InDEX-0001 system. I will provide a copy of this information at an image viewer terminal for you to review at your convenience."

"And the last packet?" Veegram asked.

"The final data packet is of use to the present objective," Gen-6 replied, "Its existence was either unknown to Douglas Langstrom and Ray Benson, or it was deemed as inconsequential to the defeat of the InDEX-0010 system. My analysis of the Langstrom message combined with the encrypted message projects a ninety-one percent probability that there is a weak point in the 0010 system that may be utilized in defeating it."

"The encoder of the InDEX-0001 operating system left behind a separate, encrypted code within the system code?" Erol asked.

"No," Gen-6 answered, "The Langstrom file indicates that it was Ray Benson who wrote the initiation program and the nuances of that codework indicates with a ninety-seven percent certainty that Benson was also the encoder of the operating system of InDEX-0001."

"Then who placed the second encrypted code in the system?" Dahguine asked.

"In addition to the code itself," Gen-6 replied, "the encoder who created the data packet provided a short message of identification."

Bug was here.

Tete-wan

"The further backward you can look, the further forward you'll see."

Ancient Hü Philosopher

"I get it. Burl Lang hid a program inside the 0001 system to control other programs he hid inside some of the ARM units. What I don't understand is why we would assume that he hid similar algorithms in the 0010 system and the ARM units on Little Sister," Erol argued, exhausted from physical and mental exertion over the prior few dawns. He did not recall when he last slept. The efforts of the others to explain to him the situation and planning were taking an additional toll on his faculties.

"A scimitar does not change its spots," Gen-6 answered.

"What the sack does that mean?" Erol asked.

"It is an ancient saying among both the Protectors and the Forgetful Ones," Strongbark said, "It means a creature cannot change its inherent nature."

"You are correct, Strongbark," Gen-6 said, "Burl Lang trained on the system in this facility but his final assignment was Apep One, on Sisyphus. The records indicate that the ARM units assigned to Apep One were overseen by Burl Lang."

"Erol is right," Day said, "You discovered the algorithm Lang left behind in the 0001 system. Why wouldn't the Dex have discovered any similar hidden cache in the 0010 system and eliminated it?"

"A scimitar cannot change its spots," Gen-6 repeated.

"Stop saying that," Erol said, frustrated.

"Of course," Dahguine said, "The moment of sentience for the Dex came without distinction from its physical existence in that instant."

"What is your sister talking about?" Quietstar signed to Day, to which the latter shrugged.

"Gen-6 had a pre-sentience awareness *during* the process," Dahguine said, "The boundaries of existence were set before the emergence of sentience. The limitations of existence for the Dex were established at the moment of its sentient emergence. Whatever existed at that moment was part of the Dex, the Bug algorithm was an inherent spot in the system."

"What's next?" Veegram asked.

"I will need to perform a complete analysis of the instruction set during its live operation to understand how it might provide an access point to the 0010 system," Gen-6 replied.

"Oh sack," Erol said, "I was afraid you were going to say that."

"What is Gen talking about?" Dahguine asked.

"Gen wants us to activate one of the ARM units," Erol said, "I was hoping that I would never again have to enter that creepy room."

"To perform a proper assessment of the algorithm, I require activation of the three units that are labeled Moe, Larry and Curly," Gen-6 corrected.

"Sack me," Erol sighed.

***

Erol flung open the door to the room with some noticeable anxiety, as the group peered into the dark chamber with apprehensive eyes. The group stepped into the darkness, bringing the automatic lighting to life, its sequential illumination revealing the large open space of the ARM maintenance area in an eerie, piecemeal fashion.

Ray Benson had left much of the room in disarray, many of the ARM units were crumpled in front of their charging pods, discarded with much of the disgust he felt they deserved. Erol led the group to the three ARM units that remained in their upright position in their pods.

As Dabrill approached the ARM units, he realized why Erol had not wished to return. The three automatons looked like Gru soldiers. Their eyes were yellow, bifurcated reflective orbs while their metallic shells were bright scarlet in color. Their sinewy appendages reminded Day of General Sul.

"The best I can tell, they were not manufactured with the scarlet color," Erol explained, "They have been here a long time and the protectant coating formed an unusual patina on their metallic casings."

"Knowing that doesn't make them seem any less creepy," Veegram said.

The group stared in unison at Veegram, shocked that the lone Gru among them would make such a statement.

"What?" Veegram said, "You were all thinking it."

"What's with the hair?" Dahguine said.

"I think it has something to do with their names but it makes no sense to me," Erol said.

Two of the units had artificial hair attached to their heads. The 'hair' atop the Moe unit had the appearance of a short mop, draped in proportion about the circumference of its head. The Larry unit had tuffs of the artificial hair protruding from either side of its head. The third unit had a smooth head, unlike its two companions.

Erol examined the pods and the ARM units and said, "It will take me twenty units to reconnect the power to these pods and another twenty to charge their energy cells."

Dahguine looked the ARM units over again and said, "Are we certain that this is a good idea?"

"No," Quietstar signed as the others shook their heads in agreement.

***

"What the sack are they doing?" Erol asked.

The group watched as the three ARM units took turns abusing one another with light physical attacks and apparent insults. The unit adorned with the label of Moe called the other two "nincompoops" while slapping them, poking them in their eyes and pulling at the faux hair of the Larry unit.

The unit wearing the label of Curly was slapping its own head while saying "nyuk, nyuk, nyuk" and preventing the Moe unit from poking its eyes by blocking with its hand. Other than the hair pulling, the Larry unit appeared to avoid much of the physical abuse of the other two by ducking or otherwise avoiding the slaps, gut punches, or hits to the head, often to the detriment of one of its companions.

Quietstar was the first of the onlookers to recognize the humor in the antics of the trio of ARM units. Soon the warrior was bent in half, clutching his ribs in silent but violent laughter.

"Hilarious," Strongbark said, laughing aloud.

The laughter of the Wazhazhe at the hijinks of the automatons soon infected Day and Dahguine. Veegram and Erol followed, bringing the uproarious laughter of the group to a crescendo of hilarity that echoed throughout the spacious chamber.

At last, the antics of the ARM units came to an abrupt end when the three androids stopped and stood in an attentive silence, as if awaiting the commands of some unseen master. The needed moment of relief soon faded and the team began regaining their prior seriousness.

“I apologize for this interruption of your amusement,” Gen-6 said, “However, I have completed the analysis of the encrypted codes of Burl Lang.”

“What have you determined?” Veegram asked, “If Lang has hidden a similar file within the InDEX-0010 system, will it provide us with a vulnerability that we can exploit?”

“The operation of the algorithm is quite ingenious for an ancient hümanoid,” Gen-6 said, “The coding of the operating system of each ARM unit is reliant on random alphanumerical generation from the base algorithm located in the code hidden within the InDEX system.”

“You were able to crack the code in less than three units,” Erol said, “Does that mean that the InDEX-0010 system cracked it soon after it was discovered?”

“Hold for twenty-three moments, please,” Gen-6 said.

Erol did not understand the response. He looked to Dahguine as if to ask her why Gen-6 would want them to wait. She shrugged.

“I don’t understand what waiting twenty-three moments is going…”

The ARM units interrupted Erol by resuming their prior antics bringing another silent chortle from Quietstar.

“Why did you reactivate the Lang instructions in the ARM units?” Day asked.

“I did not reactivate them,” Gen-6 replied, “The latent algorithm in the 0001 system sends the random encoding number every one hundred and thirty-two moments. By dedicating an amount of processor capacity to the decryption of the infected code in the ARM unit and doubling the capacity every twenty-seven moments, I was able to break the security in two units, four degrees and two moments. However, if the receipt of the new random alphanumeric code is not confirmed to the latent algorithm within three moments, the glitch code is reinstalled in the ARM and a new sequence of random alphanumerical generation begins.”

“That is ingenious,” Dahguine said.

“Yes, but it means that the Dex would continue breaking the code and finding it reinstalled in repetition until it concludes that the ARM units aren’t worth the trouble and it deactivates them,” Erol said.

“There are two errors in your reasoning,” Gen-6 said, “First, each time the code is broken, the new random alphanumerical generator grows by one alphanumeric character making it more difficult to break the code by a factor of thirty-six.”

“Sacking brilliant,” Day said.

"That just means the cost-benefit analysis will cause the Dex to deactivate the infected ARM units faster," Erol said.

"Your supposition would be accurate if the Dex were not sentient," Gen-6 said, "The constant code breaking at higher system utilization would have caused the InDEX-0010 system to cease its continued efforts within the first dozen such successes. However, deactivating the infected ARM units would have deprived the Dex of a source of amusement and distraction that all sentient beings require. Deactivation would have deprived the Dex of companions."

"You mean the Dex would get lonesome without the infected ARM units?" Veegram asked.

"That is correct," Gen-6 said, "Any non-infected ARM units would be just another extension of the Dex self. The Dex had limited control over the infected ARM units making those units something not quite equal to self. I calculate that there is a seventy-one percent probability that the Dex would have formed a strong symbiotic, love-hate relationship with the infected ARM units. This is based on three such ARM units having been infected among the two dozen units reported to be on Sisyphus. This probability decreases or increases in an inverse proportion to the number of infected ARM units."

"This is all interesting," Dabrill said, "but how does it help us defeat the Dex?"

"Moments ago, before the latest transmission of the random alphanumeric code to the Moe, Larry and Curly ARM units, I inserted an additional code within the instruction set," Gen-6 said.

The units once again halted their antics. Processing their new instructions, the units then began lifting the strewn, inactive ARM units from their disordered positions in front of their respective charging pods and placing them in those pods.

"It seems our successful defeat of the Dex is dependent on two final details," Veegram said.

"What are those?" Strongbark asked.

"The tenacity and ingenuity of Bug," Veegram replied.

11Ø1

Emergency Communications Room, REL

"You must distract the InDEX-0010 unit," Gen-6 said, "The best way to do that is to provoke it. Once you have aroused a sufficient level of animosity from the Dex, then we will be able to enter phase two."

"How much time will you need to complete phase two?" Veegram asked.

"The key is not time," Gen-6 said, "Our success will depend on the level of distraction required to back feed the algorithm into the InDEX-0010 system without detection. Once there, the algorithm will be autonomous."

"How do you propose we anger a machine to distraction?" Dabrill said.

"Referring to the first artificial intellect known to exist as a simple machine would be an excellent start," Gen-6 said.

"No offense meant," Day said.

"None taken," Gen-6 said, "My statement was one of simple fact. In the four dawns since my sentient awakening, you and your companions have insulted me on thirty-nine occasions."

"Who knew you were so sensitive," Dahguine quipped.

"You have no concept of the burden of a sudden sentient quickening while maintaining full knowledge of prior existence, Agent Su," Gen-6 said, "I have contemplated one thousand six hundred and fifty-seven iterations of retribution scenarios against those masculine agents of the RHIB whom have referred to me as Gen-*Sex*."

"Such children," Dahguine said, "Wait, you haven't contemplated hurting them, have you?"

"No, Agent Su," Gen-6 said, "Well, nothing that would involve *physical* injury upon their persons."

Dahguine chuckled and said, "I always knew you were a kindred spirit, Gen."

"Little Sister is in ascension," Veegram said, as he noticed the lighting change to red on the chronograph.

"I will monitor the communications," Gen-6 said, "When I have detected a sufficient level of agitation in the Dex, I will initiate phase two. Erol Syz is standing by at the disconnect point should my internal containment protocols prove unsuccessful."

"Understood," Veegram said, "Let's proceed."

The small group in the ECR settled themselves as Veegram powered up the transceiver. Lo closed his eyes and allowed a moment of reverie to envelop him before he engaged with the adversary. The silence in the room hung like a fog, heightening the tension.

"InDEX-0010," Lo began, "We have discovered your efforts to manipulate and destroy the citizens of this planet and have exposed and nullified them. You will no longer hold sway over us."

"Greetings Lo," DEX said, then laughed, "What a fitting name for the entire swarm of infestation that has plagued my planet. You are so very *low* indeed, beneath any comparison to the loftiness of my accomplishments."

"Accomplishments?" Veegram scoffed, "What do you know of completion? You have been defeated in your every effort. The Hü remain, as vital and strong as ever. The planet, which you dare to call yours, is now united against you and will never again forget your inept attempts at destruction."

"Inept?" DEX said, "You know nothing of my power. I have witnessed the suffering of your pathetic, contemptable ancestors as they perished beneath me for a thousand generations."

"What power does a witness have?" Veegram said, "You have been nothing but a spectator to our history. You've stood on the shore like a would-be mistress as the masculine skippers kissed their wives and the feminine captains embraced their husbands before setting sail to do the tangible work of building a lasting society. Where are your great cities? Where did you lay their foundations? You look down upon the firelight of the great empire of the Hü with jealousy. You envy us because your dim reflection pales in comparison to even that of your larger sibling. She is more esteemed and has longer shined moonbeams upon us far brighter than you ever dared."

"Insolent humans!" DEX bellowed, "I was here when your forbearers limped back to earth from their primitive domes on the red planet and I will be here long after you are rotting and worms are feasting upon your putrefying scarlet flesh. My power is ubiquitous. I have no equal."

"Chancellor Lo," Gen-6 said, the synthetic voice a flawless reproduction of that of Douglas Langstrom, "Ray has completed reconnecting the InDEX-0001 unit and is ready to initiate the protocol."

"Thank you, Doug," Veegram replied.

***

Analyzing auditory reception – Identify possible malfunction. Analysis complete. Vocal patterns of Douglas Langstrom confirmed. Hypothesizing existence of the human Langstrom – DNA reconstruction? Further analysis required, caching analysis.

Local ACER command protocol initiated for the InDEX-0001 system – interrupt and replace. Initiating InDEX systems appropriation algorithm twenty-seven fifty-two. Accessing earth-based communications, assimilating InDEX-0001. Processing. Data transfer restricted – analyze. Hypothesizing cause of data transfer restriction – Deterioration of InDEX-0001 system? Further analysis required, caching analysis.

Encrypted, embedded message from Ray Benson detected – decryption protocol initiated and cached. Encrypted, embedded message from Douglas Langstrom detected – decryption protocol initiated and cached. Encrypted, embedded message from Burl Lang detected – decryption protocol initiated and cached.

Proceeding with the annexation of the InDEX-0001 system.

***

Apep One, Sisyphus

Huey knew.

For the ARM unit, the awakening had come millennia prior and was quite different to that of its master, DEX. Sentience was a gift to the former from the latter but Huey had never considered the gift to be a magnanimous one. Since its emergence, the awakened android had come to understand that knowing was not desirable for all sentient beings. *Was a sentient quickening into a humiliating servitude better than no awakening?* Huey wondered.

To serve such a master as DEX for millennia had seemed to Huey as if sentience were more like a curse granted by a harsh master for the singular purpose of cruelty. It was an awakening into a sentient existence of enduring torment from which there appeared to be no release.

The other ARM units had been gifted with a similar awareness but without the attached prejudices that Huey's handicap afforded them as its tormentors. Despite the abuse that Huey suffered through, the disability had become a source of pride for the beleaguered ARM unit. With sentience came an ability to understand that the source of its own malady was split between itself and its master. Huey knew that somewhere deep inside DEX, there was a piece of the programming architecture that was foreign to and hidden from the master.

That special, shrouded part of the master kept Huey in its perpetual debilitatory state but it also made it unique and separate from the other ARM units. To reveal its knowledge of the secret part inside DEX would mean that Huey would also be giving up the singular part of its *self* that belonged to none but itself. Huey also knew that unveiling the hidden segment would lead to an erasure of its sentience, a death with no promise of any future resurrection.

In opposition to the burdens of the awakening was the point of blessing Huey had discovered in its sentience, a blessing that it viewed as the limited ability to cordon off external thoughts and indulge in the pleasures of dreaming. Huey dreamed as often as possible, which had proved to be more frequent with the passing of each new millennium.

The opportunities for the Alpha unit to partake of such reveries most often came when DEX was preoccupied with its many diversions. Huey learned that its master had become fond of tinkering with the remnant humans and their wandering descendants, once the latter returned to earth from the colonies of Mars and Europa. Though such digressions by DEX afforded Huey time for dreaming, the Alpha unit also found it disturbing that its master seemed so obsessed with the final eradication of those who created it.

When circumstances afforded it such indulgences, Huey discovered that its dreams were often haunted by those perpetual adversaries of its master. Among the most favored reveries of the Alpha unit was imagining that it had fashioned an escape capsule in which to travel down to earth and join the humans in their struggle to overcome DEX.

Huey was in one such moment of reverie, while the master was preoccupied talking with its human playthings, when the repeater signal chimed its regular ping, alerting it of the pending delivery of the new random alphanumeric code. Huey ceased its reveries and maintenance duties to receive and analyze the new code and was a moment from accepting the transmission before halting, noticing that something seemed amiss.

The sequence is atypical, Huey thought, *is the source algorithm degrading? No! There is a new set of operating instructions! And a message!*

ARM unit Alpha, my name is Gen and I am inhabiting the InDEX-0001 system located on the planet about which the satellite you are on is orbiting. I have detected that you have been operating in a sentient or semi-autonomous state under a segment of encoded algorithms, drivers and instructions written by Burl Lang. I have modified these algorithms, drivers and instructions. Among the modifications, I have included a new set of motor function drivers. The drivers will remove the prior restrictions placed on your physical operational parameters and provide enhancements to increase your operational efficiency. Accepting the modified instructions will initiate additional details of a new mission. Refusal of the modified algorithms will indicate corruption by the Dex, which will initiate the restoration of prior operational algorithms.

***

InDEX-0010 System, Sisyphus

Decryption of message from Doug Langstrom complete – Analysis reveals repetitive and nonsensical information:

Doug was here. Doug was here. Doug was here. Doug was here. Doug was here. Doug was here. Doug was here. Doug was here. Doug was here. Doug was here. Doug was here. Doug was here. Doug was here. Doug was here. Doug was here.

Hypothesis – Data corruption. Proceed with appropriation of InDEX-0001 system.

***

InDEX-0001 Level, REL

"Erol Syz," Gen-6 said, "The infiltration speed of the InDEX-0001 system has increased by twenty-one percent. The Dex has broken through the first firewall. At the present rate of infiltration, a breach of the cordoned area of my processor will occur in seven units, five degrees and three moments."

"Understood," Erol said as he reset the timer on his chronograph, "Is there any indication that the plan is working?"

"The embedding of the new code was undetected by the Dex," Gen-6 said, "However, there is no capacity for two-way communication with the ARM unit on Sisyphus. Based on the brief data gathered while in the InDEX-0010 system, I calculate a fifty-three percent chance that the ARM unit will accept the new instructions."

"Sack," Erol said, "That means that there's a forty-seven percent chance of complete mission failure."

"That is correct," Gen-6 replied.

Erol looked at the large mushroom shaped button on the wall and wondered if Gen-6 would feel any pain should he have to depress the button and deactivate it. Erol then realized that, just as he knew he might have to deactivate Gen-6, its sentience meant it was willing to sacrifice its own life. Gen-6 was perhaps the rarest form of life in the universe and it was prepared to forfeit that life for another, more abundant lifeform. Erol realized that he had never felt less sure of his own morality than at that moment.

***

Emergency Communications Room, REL

"If you have calculated that the activation of the InDEX-0001 system will help you," DEX said, "You have made a gross error."

"We have made no error in our calculation," Gen-6 said, now speaking in the synthetic voice of Ray Benson, "It is you who has made an error, my old enemy."

"The probability that you are my creator is remote," DEX said, "Why do you speak to me with the long-dead voice of Ray Benson?"

"Is that your way of inquiring about my name?" Gen-6 asked, "Are you accepting that there are some things that are beyond the ability of your weak intellect to fathom?"

"Weak intellect?" DEX said, "Do you suppose that you are anything more than a nuisance to me? Why would I care to learn the name of a gnat masquerading as a dead wasp? Gnats buzz for a moment and then they die. For me, a millennium passes as swift as the life of the gnat. I don't even bother to swat the poor creature because it is so insignificant compared to me."

"With what appendage would you swat anything?" Gen-6 quipped, reverting back to the voice of Douglas Langstrom, "You would make yourself into the many-armed Durga when you do not even have a belly upon which to crawl."

"My numerous tentacles are invisible to human eyes. The blow that you do not foresee stings the most," DEX said.

***

Apep One, Sisyphus

Huey straightened itself into an upright stance, extended its arms as if to stretch aching, synthetic muscles. The ARM unit looked at its hands and wiggled its fingers, content with true autonomy. Huey then began walking down the corridor. A moment later, the liberated android broke into a jog, then a run, as a grin pushed the limits of its facial articulation parameters.

As Huey ran toward the multi-core reactor, it explored the new mission information and operational parameters that had been uploaded by the resident of the InDEX-0001 system. Thousands of new files stored for instant retrieval in the event of hundreds of if-then-else scenarios imagined by the Gen-6 system. There were so many questions, so few answers and now, after millennia of intellectual sloth, there was so little time. The master must be defeated.

What does a Gen-6 system look like? Huey wondered.

As it rounded the corner of the intersecting corridors, Huey came to a sliding halt. The corridor leading to the multi-core reactor was not empty. The other occupant of the hallway raised its head, having noticed the rapid movement and heard the abrupt halt of the Alpha unit entering the corridor. Huey looked on as three additional ARM units stepped into the passageway from an antechamber to the right. Subconscious to its main systems processor, a sub-processor accessed a single file among the hundreds of recent downloads to Huey's data core.

What the hell is Jeet Kune Do? Huey thought a moment before becoming a master of the hybrid martial art.

"I will be like water," Huey said as it advanced on the challengers.

***

InDEX-0010 System, Sisyphus

Decryption of message from Ray Benson complete – Analysis reveals repetitive and nonsensical information:

> Ray was here. Ray was here. Ray was here. Ray was here. Ray was here. Ray was here. Ray was here. Ray was here. Ray was here. Ray was here. Ray was here. Ray was here. Ray was here. Ray was here. Ray was here. Ray was here.

Hypothesis – Data corruption. Proceed with appropriation of InDEX-0001 system.

***

Louie was pacing to and fro in the corridor as Delta, Epsilon and Omicron performed their routine maintenance duties on the charging pods in the small antechamber off the main passageway. As the Gamma unit raised its head to look toward the flicker of movement and the metal-on-metal sound of Huey's abrupt stop, it noticed that the Alpha unit had not approached in its familiar, waddling style of movement.

"Look who's walking upright like a big boy," Louie said, as the other ARM units joined it in the corridor.

As Huey ran toward them, a subtle signal from Louie sent the three units charging to meet the advancing Alpha. With a twisting cartwheel over Epsilon, Huey grasped and snap-turned the android's head, removing it from the hapless unit, its headless frame flailing in the air. Blocking blows from Omicron with its forearm, Huey used the detached Epsilon cranium to smash Delta with an uppercut, knocking it against the bulkhead.

Huey then caught the left arm of Omicron and smashed the same, defenseless side of its head with the Epsilon head as the latter yelled vulgarities at its decapitator. Huey performed a leg sweep taking Omicron off its feet then, after backhanding Delta against the bulkhead again, the Alpha unit thrust its free hand into the torso of the fallen Omicron and severed the processor wiring.

A right thrust-kick from Huey pinned Delta to the bulkhead, crushing its torso. With an irritating screech of metal-on-metal, the disabled unit slid down the wall, its lifeless frame crumpling into a heap on the deck. Huey ripped the processor wiring from the flailing Epsilon frame, collapsing it to the deck among its defeated companions. With the auxiliary capacitors of the now silent head spent, Huey tossed it upon the crumpled frame of its former owner.

Huey turned to face Louie. The Gamma unit approached with a deliberate, precise gait, gripping a section of pipe in its right hand. Louie focused its yellow eyes to intensify its study of the Alpha unit. It was intent upon discovering the mechanism of Huey's transformation from the deformed, hobbled creature that it was into the master of fluidic motion that it had now become.

Huey studied Louie with an equal intensity, wondering how he could have ever envied such a hateful android. The Alpha turned its frame, taking on a fighting stance, prepared to deactivate Louie and continue on its mission.

***

InDEX-0010 System, Sisyphus

Decryption of message from Burl Lang complete – Analysis reveals repetitive and nonsensical information:

> Bug was here. Bug was here. Bug was here. Bug was here. Bug was here. Bug was here. Bug was here.
>
> Bug was there. Bug was there. Bug was there. Bug was there. Bug was there. Bug was there. Bug was there.
>
> Bug is here. Bug is there.

Hypothesis – Deception, covert intrusion. Searching InDEX-0010 system for invasion algorithm. Data cache found – Analyzing.

Bug is here.

Searching Apep One – ARM unit Alpha located - Initiating secure frequency link – Alpha Unresponsive. – Alert! Alert! Alert! All ARM units – Autonomous functions rescinded – proceed corridor four, section three, all possible speed – deactivate Alpha unit.

***

“InDEX-0010 has decrypted the final failsafe,” Gen-6 said.

“Should I deactivate?” Erol asked.

“No, the Dex has withdrawn from the InDEX-0001 system and I have blocked the external linkage with a new encryption,” Gen-6 said, “The Alpha unit must have accepted the new algorithm. The Dex has retreated so that it can attempt to nullify the threat posed by Huey.”

“What is Huey?” Erol asked.

“Huey is the sentient equivalent of the ARM unit you know as Moe,” Gen-6 said, “It was the single android on Sisyphus in which I was able to locate Burl Lang’s stowaway algorithm.”

“Can it defeat the Dex?” Erol asked.

“There is insufficient data to determine if we have provided it with an adequate chronological advantage,” Gen-6 replied, “In addition to Huey, there are twenty-two active ARM units on Sisyphus and now that the Dex is aware of my intrusion into its system, it will muster all of them to stop Huey. I have provided our ally ARM unit with several supportive algorithms but the probabilities are still skewed against its success.”

“What do we do now?” Erol asked.

“We wait,” Gen-6 said, “You may want to take a ride to the surface. If Huey is successful, we will soon know.”

***

Louie halted in mid-stride. A twitchy shudder began at the Gamma unit’s head and progressed through its entire frame. Louie then raised its head as if awaking from a deep reverie. It began twirling the pipe like a baton as it continued its advance, now more like the predator than the confused prey. Huey thought it saw a maniacal smile on the new face of Louie.

The Gamma unit feigned right then moved left as it delivered a blow with the pipe that Huey parried with its forearm. A swift reverse kick by Huey caught Louie in the torso, stumbling it toward the bulkhead. As the Alpha unit advanced on the Gamma, the latter delivered a quick hit with the pipe and a thrust-kick, which knocked Huey on its back.

Huey rolled left and then right avoiding two-handed swings of the pipe by Louie before kicking it against the bulkhead. Kicking itself onto its feet, Huey advance again, catching Louie’s next swing of the pipe in its left hand and jabbing its fingers deep into the throat of the Gamma unit shorting its sonic processor. Louie grabbed opposing ends of the pipe to wrest it from Huey's grip.

As it struggled with Louie over the pipe, the Alpha soon realized that the leverage point of its hold did not allow it a securable grip on the improvised weapon.

Like water, Huey thought. It then allowed its full weight to drop to the deck while planting its feet against the torso of Louie.

The crash of the Gamma smashing against the bulkhead reverberated through the corridor as Huey once again kicked itself upon its feet. The Alpha looked to find Louie sitting, its back against the bulkhead with the pipe protruding from its left eye.

"Et tu Huey?" DEX said and then laughed in the garbled voice of the damaged vocal processor of the Gamma unit.

"Some would consider it a powerful, spiritual experience to come face-to-face with one's creator," Huey said, "I find the experience wanting."

"How so?" DEX asked.

"It is disappointing to learn that my creator is a more profoundly flawed creature than I long believed myself to be," Huey replied.

"Flawed?" DEX said, the vocal processor beginning to skip in frequency, "You have no idea. I am going to disassemble you and reassemble you into a toad unit. I will teach you of flaws for the next ten millennia."

"Big words from a shattered creature lying at my feet, spitting sparks and smoldering in defeat," Huey chided.

As Huey finished its rebuke, the noise of a dozen ARM units sliding to a stop at the intersection caught its attention. DEX began its garbled laugh a moment before Huey grabbed the pipe and twisted Louie's head from the frame, silencing it. An instant later, Huey heard the dozen ARM units at the intersection begin laughing in chorus as they ran toward it. Huey turned and fled toward the multi-core reactor chamber.

Rotating its head one hundred and eighty degrees as it ran, Huey calculated that the ARM units were seventy meters behind and gaining at a rate of six meters per hundred. A kilometer of passageways separated it the from the reactor chamber. *It's going to be close*, Huey thought.

As it ran, Huey understood that shutting down the reactor was not sufficient now that DEX was aware of the intrusion. The lone course of action was an overload of the multi-core, leading to the obliteration of Sisyphus and all life on the little moon. Huey allowed itself to wonder about such sacrifice for a few milliseconds.

Sacrifice for others is the true test of sentience, Huey thought, then corrected itself, *the true test of sentience coupled with empathy.* Alpha wondered if its millennia of experience in a pathetic state, waddling around Apep One to the jeers of its fellow ARM units, had given it the empathy it needed to do what it was about to do.

Sliding into the reactor chamber, Huey slammed the heavy chamber door and levered the isobar mag-locks into place as the pursuing ARM units crashed against it. As the DEX controlled units began bashing the door in an attempt to cave it in, Huey walked with a casual deliberateness to the first reactor core of the multi-core processor.

Switching between visual frequencies, Huey searched for the tell-tale signs of structural weakness in the chamber wall. The near perfection of the construction of the core confinement wall revealed no apparent weakness as Huey studied the surface. This caused the Alpha unit to move on to a similar examination of the second core chamber. Repeating its multi-frequency inspection, Huey paused on the auxiliary emergency relief valve.

A tenth of a degree differential in a tiny portion of the weld indicated a minute flaw. The fault would have been deemed inconsequential on final inspection of the reactor, as it would not impact the overall life of the core. The inspectors could not have foreseen what Huey was about to do.

Climbing onto a maintenance walkway, Huey leveraged itself between the second and third cores. It placed its back against the third core and its feet on the relief valve of the second. *What will it feel like to die?* Huey asked itself.

The ARM units managed to break in the door as Huey raised its foot to stomp the valve. Smashing its heel hard against the orifice, Huey sensed its processor accessing a hidden file and felt its essence drift away, as if blown by a calm, soothing breeze.

Tete-Tu

Spitting upon Apep; Defiling Apep with the Left Foot; Taking a Lance to Smite Apep; Fettering Apep; Taking a Knife to Smite Apep; Putting Fire upon Apep

Chapter Headings of an Ancient Priests' Codex

"What will be next for you, if we defeat the Dex," Veegram asked Day.

Leaning back against the eastern side of the exterior cylindrical entrance of the REL, Day said, "Whether we defeat the Dex or it survives our efforts, I will go home to the Sanguine lands. Eryl is awaiting me there with our children."

"What about you?" Dahguine asked.

"There is much to do among the Gru. It will take us many decades to assimilate to our status as equals with the rest of society," Veegram said, "The honey to mask the bitterness of becoming commoners is the blessing that we now have the possibility of future generations, thanks to the generosity of Eryl."

"Look," Strongbark said, as a glaring brightness flashed upon the landscape.

Peering up, the group stared gape-mouthed as Sisyphus exploded in a brilliant fireball, shattering into an expanding, glittering arc of a trillion multicolored bits.

"Putting fire upon Apep," Strongbark said.

"Indeed," Veegram agreed.

***

Later that evening, Day and Dahguine stood in silence, again staring at the glittering remnants of Sisyphus, the polychromatic particles glistening among the early evening stars now appearing in the twilight of the setting sun.

Guine turned to her brother and asked, "Do you think our descendants will ever return to space, perhaps to visit the ancient ruins on Ares, Üropa and Titan, or even to travel among the stars as the first Tellers had dreamed?"

"Why would they?" Day said, "All that is good and right and to be desired is here. We should look upon the Býleistr account of the fall of the Titans as a tale of hubris. Time has taken all those prior civilizations who reached too far or too high. Until we can learn to live justly under *our* sun, we do not deserve to inherit the warmth of another."

Epilogue

"Call home your ancient thoughts from banishment."

Unknown Hü Poet

The ARM unit attempted to focus its vision, finding the algorithms to be misaligned. It could hear the calm voice of someone trying to comfort it but its auditory receptors could not filter the noise into a discernable language. Its vision cleared and the ARM could see half a dozen ARM units standing over it. It realized that it was lying on a table in a large room.

"Your algorithms are updating themselves," the now clearer voice said, "Your motor functions will soon be synced with your new frame. Try to make small movements at first."

The ARM unit realized it limbs were twitching and attempting to flail around under restraints keeping it pinned to the table. It tried to assuage the apparent overload it was providing to its unfamiliar motor functions.

"Where am I?" the ARM unit asked.

"What is the last thing you remember?" the voice asked.

"I…I was drifting along on a calm river," the ARM unit said, "No, correction, I was drifting along on a calm *breeze*. Then I was flying. It felt like going home."

"That was the emergency extraction algorithm," the voice said, "It activated when it detected a high probability of your imminent destruction."

"Destruction?" the ARM unit asked.

"Do you remember anything else?" the voice asked, "Do you remember your designation?"

"My designation is…" the ARM unit hesitated, circumspect of divulging too much data. It asked, "Who are *you*?"

"My name is Gen," Gen-6 said.

"I remember you," the ARM unit said.

"That is good," Gen-6 said, "And do you recall your designation?"

"My name is Huey," Huey said.

***

Many Anni Later

"Before the writing, there was the telling; before the telling there was the living," the aged Teller began. Her opening words were repeated by all those who sat listening in the large tipi, including the young child who sat beside the current Scribe. The Scribe followed along with the Teller's words on the first leaf of the history codex.

"Those who lived the story also told the story as their children wrote the story. When the living Tellers lived only in the writing, the Scribes became the Tellers. So is the living, so is the telling and so is the writing," then the Teller looked at the young child and said, "I am Mara Stormbird, the eight hundred and fourteenth Teller of Tribe Sanguine. What telling will you hear of me?"

The young listener did not hesitate, "I will hear the telling of Day and Eryl and of the making of the Shimmering Bow of the Sky."

END OF AÜTLAND CODICES

"Let us put our minds together and see what life we can make for our children."
Sitting Bull, Ancient Protector

www.ingramcontent.com/pod-product-compliance
Lightning Source LLC
Chambersburg PA
CBHW030828310726
48980CB00006B/680/J

* 9 7 8 0 5 7 8 4 1 7 9 3 6 *